Camithon looked thoughtful, then turned to Drumold. "My lord, will you seek truce between the Romans, and alliance?"

Drumold looked thoughtful. "Alliance with Rome. 'Tis a strange thought. Strange indeed. And yet—I will not oppose it. Aye. The Lord Rick is convincing. There is danger in a strong Rome, but there is more in a divided Rome during these times."

There were murmurs of approval.

It doesn't look like anyone saw it was a setup, Rick thought. Which is just as well. Machine politics, medieval style...

"Then let it be done," Camithon said.

"Go with the blessings of Yatar Skyfather," Yanulf said. "Go swiftly, before The Time comes on us and we all perish..."

JANISSARIES
CLAN AND CROWN

JERRY POURNELLE
and
ROLAND GREEN

ILLUSTRATED BY
JOSEP M. MARTIN SAURI

ACE BOOKS, NEW YORK

This Ace Book contains the complete
text of the original trade edition.
It has been completely reset in a typeface
designed for easy reading, and was printed
from new film.

JANISSARIES: CLAN AND CROWN

An Ace Book / published by arrangement with
the authors

PRINTING HISTORY
Ace trade edition / November 1982
Ace mass market edition / November 1983

ISBN: 0-441-38298-3

Ace Books are published by The Berkley Publishing Group,
200 Madison Avenue, New York, New York 10016.
The name "ACE" and the "A" logo
are trademarks belonging to
Charter Communications, Inc.

CONTENTS

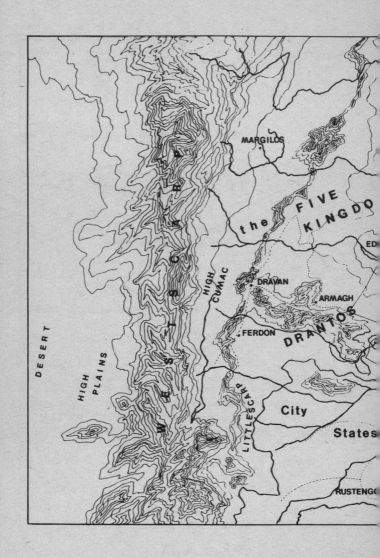

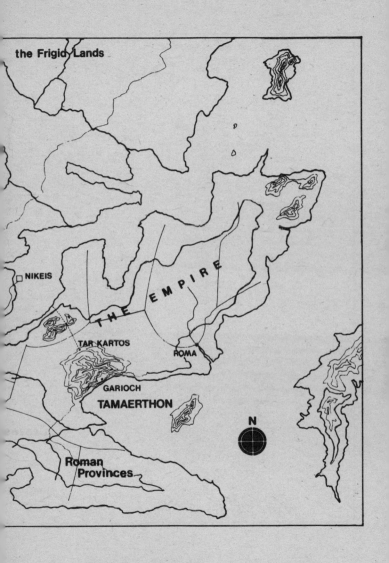

The Battle
with the Westmen

SIVHAUS

MASON

GANTOK

change

WESTMEN

N

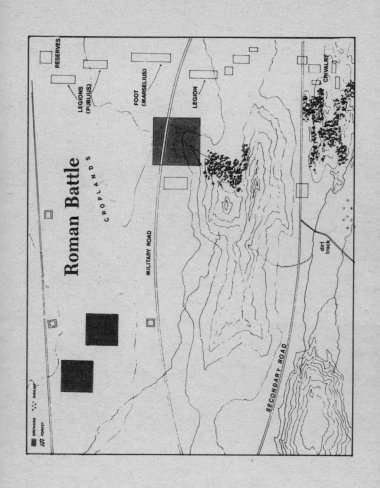

Roman Battle

CROPLANDS

RESERVES

LEGIONS (PUBLIUS)

FOOT (MARSELIUS)

LEGION

CHIVALRY

MILITARY ROAD

SECONDARY ROAD

dirt track

ORCHARD SWAMP

LEFT FOREST

JANISSARIES

CLAN AND CROWN

PART ONE

Thrones
and
Dominions

1

The rocket sputtered for a moment, then rose swiftly above the worn cobblestone courtyard of the old fortress. It hissed upwards in a column of fire, trailing golden sparks and a faint smell of brimstone as it climbed until, without warning, it burst loudly into a shower of silver. The crowd gasped in wonder.

High above the courtyard, two richly dressed boys about fifteen Earth years in age clapped their hands in wonder. They huddled together in a window cut in the wall of the keep thirty meters above the gawking populace. One of the boys shouted aloud when the rocket burst above Castle Edron.

"Quiet! The Protector will hear us," the other boy said. "He'll make us join the others."

"He is nowhere about, Majesty."

"Ah." Nothing like those rockets had ever been seen on the whole planet of Tran. Even kings should be able to gawk at them without losing status.

But, Ganton thought, kings must think first of their dignity, and for the opinions of the nobility. No monarch ever needed his lords' good opinions more than I do. Another rocket arced across the darkening sky. This one trailed blue sparks. "Oh—look!" he cried. The True Sun had long set, but the Firestealer was high enough to cast baleful shadows and light the summer sky above the fortress capital of Drantos.

Ganton shouted again as yet another rocket burst. Ganton son of Loron, Wanax of Drantos, he might be; but he was also nine years old, fifteen according to the reckoning of the starman Lord Rick; and the rockets were fun to watch. "Perhaps we could make weapons from those," Ganton said. "Do you think so?"

"The Lord Rick says he will," Morrone answered.

He speaks in those tones, Ganton thought. They all do, when they speak of Lord Rick. They never sound that way when the talk is about me. They rebelled against my father. The wonder is that I lived this long. It is no time to be Wanax, but I have no choice of times.

More rockets flashed upward from the palace courtyard. Each sent down silver and gold showers. One burst with a loud sound.

"Was it like that?" Morrone asked.

"Louder," Ganton answered. "Much louder." He had no need to ask what Morrone meant. "It was just a year ago."

"A whole army," Morrone said. "All killed in an instant—"

"No. Only their leaders were killed. We yet had a battle to win. Not that it was difficult, with the Wanax Sarakos dead, and all the starmen kneeling to Lord Rick. But the armies of Sarakos were defeated by good Drantos warriors, not star weapons."

Morrone nodded, but Ganton thought his companion didn't really believe it. Sarakos had conquered nearly the whole of the Kingdom of Drantos. Until the great battle, Sarakos held the entire County of Chelm and most lands of the other great lords. His writ ran everywhere except into the hills where Ganton had hidden with the Lord Protector and the remnants of the loyalist forces. Sarakos had defeated the best Ganton had, had killed the first Lord Protector. Then the starman Lord Rick had come with the wild clansmen who obeyed his wife's father, and in one day, one grand battle—

More rockets flashed upward. "You spend firepowder with both hands," Morrone said.

Ganton shrugged. "It is no small thing, the birth of the Lady Isobel as heiress to the greatest lord of Drantos. Besides, the firepowder was given to me by Lord Rick himself. Come, can't I show my pleasure at the honor he does me, to have his child born in my capital?" And without my leave, although I would have given it cheerfully—

He felt Morrone draw away, and wondered if his friend were angry. Ganton had few enough friends, and almost none his own age; soon, he supposed, Morrone too would treat him as Wanax rather than friend. All too soon. And that would be right and proper, but it would be lonely as well—

"There," Morrone said. He pointed toward the horizon to the south. "I can just see it. The Demon Sun."

Ganton shuddered slightly and hoped that Morrone wouldn't notice. Only a star, the starmen had said. A star that wandered close to Tran every six hundred years. Not a demon at all, only a star.

"It might as well be a demon," Morrone said, as if reading his thoughts. "The Demon Sun comes, and we live in The Time . . ." His voice lost its banter, and took on the singsong notes of a priest. "The Time draws near, when oceans will rise. Storms shall rage, and gods will come from the skies to offer gifts. Woe to those who trade with gods, for after the gods depart there shall be smoke and fire and destruction—" Morrone broke off as suddenly as he had begun. "There's someone coming." He pointed. "On the south road. "There, just below the Demon Sun."

Ganton stared into the dusky light. One of the Earthmen had told him that the Firestealer was as bright as a hundred full Moons, but the words meant little to Ganton. He was willing to believe that a place called Earth was the home of humanity, but the thought held little impact for him. Tran was home enough.

The light of the Firestealer was more than bright enough to see by, but it made for tricky light, and cast strange shadows. But—yes, there was a large party riding up to the south gate of the town. "Merchants, I'd say," Ganton muttered.

"Doubtless. From the southern cities, by their clothes. What would they be doing here?"

"Come to make obeisance to me," Ganton said. He chuckled.

"It may be," Morrone said. He sounded very serious.

Ganton laughed aloud. "The southern cities would sooner give up their gods than their councils and assemblies and meeting halls. What could they possibly gain?"

"Lord Rick's protection," Morrone said.

And once again that tone, Ganton thought.

"Caravan ho!" The guard's challenge faintly reached their high perch.

"They're too late," Morrone said. "The gates are locked for the night. But surely they know that . . ."

Someone in the caravan shouted to the sentries. Ganton couldn't hear what was said, but it seemed to cause a stir. "Officer of the day!" the sentry shouted.

Ganton frowned in puzzlement and looked at his friend. "What do you see?" he asked. "Who could cause such excitement?"

Morrone shook his head. "I can't make it out."

"The starmen have tools to see with," Ganton said. "They call them—*binoculars.*" He said the unfamiliar word gingerly. "Binoculars."

"You should have them," Morrone said.

Ganton shrugged. "Whose? They are the personal equipment of the starmen, and there are no more than a dozen of those—*binoculars*—in all this world of Tran. How should I have them?"

"You are Wanax!" Morrone said. "These starmen are not great lords. The Lord Rick himself is no more than Eqeta of Chelm. Aye, and that only through his wife's first husband. Ach. The Eqetassa Tylara no more deserves that title than I do. Less, for I was cousin to the last Eqeta, and she no more than his unbedded wife."

Ganton stared in amazement. He had heard complaints before, but none so open. "Yet when you speak of the Lord Rick," Ganton said. "Your voice. You speak of him as you would of—of Yatar."

"Your pardon, Majesty. I spoke in haste—"

"You will not do this to me!" Ganton shouted. "Finish what you have begun. What is this you say? If you have complaints against the Lord Rick, say them now. Speak to me as friend—"

"I say no more than do hundreds of your loyal nobility,"

Morrone said. "We respect the Lord Rick, and we would follow him—but we fear his upstart family. We fear they will bring their kilted barbarians to Drantos by scores—"

"I would they would bring tens of scores of their archers," Ganton said.

"Perhaps. But when they loose their gullfeathered arrows—who will wear the grey Tamaerthan plumage? Your enemies or your friends?" His voice fell. "Majesty. Ganton, my friend. I know it must be hard—"

"Hard," Ganton said. "Hard indeed. Even the Protector fears the Lord Rick and the star weapons. As he should. You were not there, but I was there, when the other starman, Parsons, the renegade, made common cause with Sarakos, and turned those weapons on my armies. Men, horses, all destroyed, and the sounds of thunder everywhere. No one safe. My Captain-General died at my side, and we five furlongs from the battle!

"But it will change," Ganton said. "I will not be in leading strings forever. Listen."

There were more shouts below. Then a rumble. "The gates," Morrone said. "They open the gates, even at this late hour! Who?"

"We must go see," Ganton said. "Race you—" He leaped from the window seat and was down half a flight of steps before Morrone could follow.

They raced down the stairs, shouting and laughing.

The Lord Protector was waiting for them at the second landing. His scarred, weatherbeaten face and the plain broadsword hung on his belt contrasted sharply with the rich blue and scarlet court attire and jeweled chain of office. He was obviously far more at home in the saddle than the throne room.

Ganton caught himself in mid-stride and drew himself to full height, trying to walk carefully and correctly, hoping that Camithon hadn't seen him running—

"Sire," Camithon began.

By Yatar, I'm for it now, Ganton thought.

"Sire, you should not have absented yourself for so long," the Protector said. "You do little honor to the lord and lady of Chelm, after they have so honored your house by bringing forth their first child here."

Once more, Ganton thought. Tell me once more how honored I am, and I will scream curses on your ancestors—"My house is honored indeed. But perhaps there were practical reasons as well? If the Lady Tylara bore her child in Chelm, her clansmen in Tamaerthon would be slighted—and if in Tamaerthon, would not the knights and bheromen of Chelm know insult? My house was a convenience to them. And to the realm, of course. To the realm."

Camithon frowned, and the great scar across his face grew dark. For a moment Ganton was afraid. The old warrior was perfectly capable of bending his sovereign over his knee—although, Ganton reassured himself, never in public.

"It's true enough," Ganton insisted.

Camithon nodded. "Aye. Yatar's own truth. But there is such a thing as the right words at the wrong time."

"I heard a disturbance," Ganton said. "I came to see—"

"Aye. A starman. Come to see Lord Rick. With a gift."

"Oh."

Camithon didn't have to explain the significance of that.

The walls were thick stone crowned with battlements. The gates were set in massive porticos, and made of heavy wood studded with large iron knobs. The small mounted party was barely through when the gates crashed shut, and they heard the locking bar, a log nearly as big around as a telephone pole, fall into place. Ben Murphy rode on in silence for a moment, then turned to his companion. "Guess it's too late for second thoughts now," he said in English.

In contrast to Murphy, the other man was mounted on a centaur. It didn't look much like the classical centaurs; the upper torso was more apelike than human, while the body itself resembled a moose as much as it did a horse. Its rider looked around through half-closed eyes. "I reckon we could get out of here," he said. He reached forward to stroke the centaur's back. "Dobbin and me've been through a bit on this stupid planet. Don't reckon we'd let these city types stop us."

"Naw," Murphy said. "We'd never make it."

"Hell we couldn't." Lafe Reznick patted the H&K battle rifle slung over his shoulder. "Say the word, Ben, and I'll hold 'em off while you break out the one-oh-six."

Murphy snorted. "And what'll you bet they don't have cross-

hairs on us right now?" He pointed up to the high tower of the castle that dominated the town. A skyrocket rose from the tower's base as he pointed.

"You really think the captain would do that?" Reznick demanded.

Murphy shrugged. "Maybe not. But what about Mason? Or Elliot?"

"Yeah. I forgot about Sergeant Major Elliot," Reznick said. "Guess they all went over when Captain Galloway shot Colonel Parsons. And Elliot's just the man to see we don't get away." He squinted up toward the castle. "Up there—or hell, maybe right over in one of those doorways with a submachine gun."

"He wouldn't even need that," Murphy said. "With those goddam Tamaerthan archers of his, Christ, they could have us stuck over with gullfeathers 'fore you could unsling that H&K."

"You do think of the cheerfullest things."

"You say what?" One of the riders drew level with Murphy and threw back her hood. She was quite pretty, and much younger than the two soldiers. "You have afraid?" she asked.

"Naw, I'm not afraid," Reznick said. "'Course not, Honey. I wouldn't bring you here if I was afraid."

"I hear afraid," she said. "The mounts know we afraid."

"Just nervous in the service," Murphy said. "To your place, if you please, Lady . . ."

The girl started to say something, but checked herself. She halted to let Murphy and Reznick draw ahead and the three other women catch up to her. Then she began to chatter to them, speaking the native language far too swiftly for Murphy to understand her words.

Murphy and Reznick rode on in silence until they reached the castle gates, which seemed at least as massive as the town portals had been. As they approached, the gates swung open.

"Expectin' us," Murphy said. "Well, here we go." He stood in his stirrups and turned to the group behind him. "No weapons," he said, grinning to himself. I don't speak this local stuff too bad, he thought. Better'n Honeypie speaks English. "No matter what happens, keep your hands off your weapons. You have seen our star weapons. These gentry will be watching us, and their captain has weapons to overpower any you have seen us use."

The women nodded solemnly. The five merchant adventurers behind them looked around uneasily.

"They could get us bloody well killed," Murphy said. "Tell them wives of yours I mean it."

"I already did," Reznick said. "Christ, Ben, there's times I can't believe any of this."

"I know what you mean." He shook his head wryly. "Fightin' in Africa, 'bout to be finished by the Cubans and we get picked up by a goddamn flyin' saucer. And even then it don't make sense. This whole planet, none of it makes sense."

"Except to Captain Galloway."

"Yeah. I guess."

"Hell, Ben, it was you said we ought to come here . . ."

"You agreed," Murphy reminded him. "I didn't twist your arm." He grinned. "Anyway, I still think it was best. That paper the Cap'n sent us, it said he really did understand things here. He knows why there's people here, and what those saucer critters want, and—"

"And you can believe as much of it as you want to," Reznick said. He paused a moment, then matched Murphy's grin. "And we both sure as hell want to believe a lot of it."

"Yeah. Let's go." He led the way through the open gates.

The courtyard behind the gates smelled of burned gunpowder. It was packed with people. Archers in kilts held them back to make a lane that Murphy's party could ride through. "Like MP's," Murphy said.

"Big deal." Reznick squinted upwards. "Don't look now, but there's a sniper up in the tower over the gate."

"Yeah, I spotted him. Don't matter. There's a dozen of those archer types on the wall up there, too. There's sure as hell only one way to play this now."

The wall ahead of them was taller than the first, and the gateway through it was so narrow they had to go single file. The gate itself was a long maze-like corridor, with two twists barely wide enough for their mounts. Then they came out into an inner court, empty except for half a dozen richly dressed courtiers.

"Welcome," one called. "In the name of Wanax Ganton, welcome to Castle Edron. I am Parilios, Chamberlain to Wanax Ganton and servant to the Lord Protector, in whose name I bid you welcome yet again."

"Sounds good so far," Murphy said. "Uh—we have come at the invitation of the Lord Rick, Eqeta of Chelm, Great Captain General of the Forces of Drantos, Colonel of Mercenaries . . ." He gave the last title in English. "We are Benjamin Murphy do Dirstval and Lafferty Reznick do Bathis, Merchant Traders of the Sun Lands."

"The Lord Rick is here and awaits you eagerly," the chamberlain said. "He has been foretold of your coming. He bade me say that his food will be no more than filling for his belly, and his drink no more than moisture for the tongue, until he has spoken with you at last."

"Fat chance the captain ever said that," Murphy said *sotto voce*. "Bid the Wanax, and the Lord Protector, and Lord Rick a thousand thanks in our names, and tell him that we came in haste to his summons."

There was more ceremony before they were invited to dismount. Eventually they were led into an antechamber. A cheerful fire blazed at one end of the room, and there was a table laid out with wine and food. Washbasins stood on a sideboard. "I will leave you to refresh yourselves," their escort said. He turned a pair of identical sand glasses, and took one with him. "I will return when this is done." The chamberlain bowed and left them.

The women began to chatter, but Murphy made a sharp gesture, and they fell quiet. He eyed the glass. "About twenty minutes. We going to take the women in with us?"

"Why not?" Reznick demanded.

Murphy shrugged. "This is royalist country," he said. "Not like the south where we were. And the girls aren't exactly out of the nobility—"

"Dirdre and Marva are now," Reznick said. "Married me, didn't they? That makes them as good as anybody."

"Okay if you say so. Wonder where the bloody plumbing is?"

"Through there, I'd say," Reznick said. He walked over to a small curtained doorway and looked inside. "Yep. Looks to me like it hangs out over the town. Shall we go relieve ourselves on the commoners?"

"Cap'n?"

Rick Galloway turned from the window as one of the sky-rockets burst in crimson. "Yes?"

"Two things," Art Mason said. "Lady Tylara says you're supposed to be downstairs enjoying the fireworks—"

"Hell, I know that," Rick said. He lifted a crystal goblet and tossed off the full cup of wine it held. "Three days we've been on display. Tylara likes all the fuss." He grinned slightly. "Isobel really is a beautiful little thing. I guess Tylara's earned all this glory. But why she wants it is beyond me." He poured another drink.

Mason shrugged. "I never claimed to understand women."

"What was the other thing?"

"Murphy's here."

"Murphy?"

"Private Ben Murphy," Mason said. "Along with Lafe Reznick. Two of the troops that ran away south with Warner and Gengrich. They just showed up at the gate, dressed up like rich southern merchants and attended by some women and bullyboys. Murphy told the officer of the guard that he's got a present for the Eqeta of Chelm, the great Captain General of the Host of Drantos—"

"Humph."

"Hell, he's layin' it on thicker'n glue, Cap'n. But I think you'll like the present. It's all wrapped up in silk and gold cloth, but it's about yay long and maybe this big around—"

"The recoilless!"

"Could be," Mason said. "It just could be. Anyway, he's downstairs in the entry hall. I checked with Elliot and we had the chamberlain give him wine and some chow, and I figured I'd better get you before that Camithon gets at him."

"Yes. Good thinking. I'll come." He started toward the door.

"Not without we dress you proper," Mason protested. "Wait, Cap'n. I'll help you into your armor."

"I do not need armor."

"Hell you don't," Mason said. "Cap'n, now dammit I mean it, don't you go down there without your mail shirt. Here, take the pistol off. That's it. Now duck—" Despite Rick's protests, Mason eased him into a shirt woven of tiny metal rings.

"Damn thing's too heavy," Rick said.

"Wasn't heavy it wouldn't do much good," Mason said. "Here, lift your arm—" Deftly he buckled Rick's pistol and combat knife under his captain's left arm. "Now you look proper."

"And feel like an idiot."

"No, sir." Mason was emphatic.. "You gotta be practical."

I've been practical all my life, Rick thought. I do the sensible, practical thing, and I feel like a coward half the time.

Mason saw Rick's expression. "Cap'n, you don't know what Murphy wants. I grant you, he probably didn't come to make trouble. Not coming inside the gates like that. But Christ, Cap'n, this whole place is about to explode. Ambassadors from both Roman outfits. That diplomat from the Five Kingdoms, he's nothing more than a spy—hell, they're still technically at war with us! Not to mention our own nobles. Wasn't an hour ago I had to disarm two of those barons, Dragomer and Kilantis—"

"Who?"

"Couple of the barons who went over to Sarakos," Mason said. "Took advantage of the amnesty after we beat Sarakos. They come from the north central hills."

"Yeah. I remember," Rick said. "Hard to blame them for going over, being that close to the Five Kingdoms and all. Why disarm them?"

"Fighting over something. I didn't bother to find out what. Just got their dirks."

"They drew steel in the palace?"

"Yeah."

"Where was Wanax Ganton?"

"Up watching the fireworks," Mason said. "Hell, Cap'n, if they'd drawn weapons while the kid or the old geezer was there I'd've done a lot more than disarm them, you know that."

"Yeah. Sorry. All right, let's go." He led the way to the thick nail-studded door and pulled. It opened slowly. It ought to, Rick thought. The damn thing must weigh five hundred pounds in this gravity. One heavy mother. There were men outside the door. Rick nodded to Jamiy, his orderly, and the brace of Guardsmen. Then he turned to the fourth man who stood stiffly aloof from the others. "Captain Caradoc."

"My lord." Caradoc was dressed in bright-colored kilts. He wore a jewel-handled dirk at his waist. A bow and quiver hung over his shoulder. He was no older than Rick. Caradoc bowed deeply, and waited until Rick returned the greeting before straightening.

"It's good to see you again," Rick said. "How went your journey?"

"Well enough, my lord. I had fast horses and Yatar's favor."

"I'm pleased to hear it." Rick put as much warmth in his voice as he could. More than once Caradoc had saved Rick— and his family. Caradoc was really Tylara's man, henchman of her father, son of one of her father's subchiefs. Loyal men high in the Tamaerthan clan system were rare ...

"We'll go down to audience hall," Mason said. One of the guards went ahead at a trot. The second walked ahead of Rick. Mason walked alongside Rick, with Jamiy and Caradoc following.

All this rigmarole just to go downstairs, Rick thought. Places of honor and all. And yet there really *are* damned few I can trust to walk behind me with weapons.

They went down a narrow stone stairway to a broad hall hung with tapestries, then along that to an arched entry into a much larger chamber.

Rick had just gotten inside when he heard a gravelly voice call, "Make way. Make way for the Wanax of Drantos." A party came through another entrance. First two men-at-arms. Then the King's Companion, Morrone, a lordling Rick found a bit pretentious. Next came Camithon, the scar-faced Lord Protector.

"Who ranks who?" Mason asked in English.

"I'll have to think," Rick said. It was a hell of a complex question. As Protector, Camithon ranked everyone except the king. On the other hand, before he became Lord Protector he'd been Tylara's general, and he held most of his lands as a mere bheroman in her service. If that wasn't complex enough, Rick and Tylara were technically host and hostess here, since Wanax Ganton had generously offered his palace to Tylara during her confinement and delivery. Which made Camithon guardian to Rick's honored guest—

"My lord," Camithon growled. He bowed slightly. Rick bowed in return, then bowed even deeper to Ganton as the boy came in.

"Majesty," Rick said. "I trust you have enjoyed the celebrations."

"We have," Ganton said. He looked around at the minor nobility and others who had come into the hall.

The boy's all right, Rick thought. Got a pretty level head. And he listens to Tylara. Then there's the rest of these. Half of 'em want to make me a god, and the other half want to put a knife in my ribs. "Majesty, I would ask a favor," Rick said. "The use of your hall to receive these starmen."

"This is your house," Ganton said ritually. "I wear no crowns while you and your lady are here. I would ask that you allow me the pleasure of watching you receive your friends."

"Certainly, sire. And my thanks."

One end of the room was dominated by a throne on a high dais. Below that was a lower dais with less elaborate chairs. Yanulf, chief priest of Yatar Day father, was already there. So was Sigrim, high priest of Vothan One-eye, Chooser of the Slain. They did not rise when Rick came to the dais. As he took his seat on the lower platform there was a stir at the door. Tylara had arrived.

She looks pale, Rick thought. She's still so damn beautiful it almost hurts to look at her, though. Her raven black hair shone as always, and her eyes were startlingly blue. There wasn't much to show that she'd been through a difficult labor, forty hours in the House of Yatar. Rick shuddered at the memory. If he'd lost her—

He couldn't follow that thought. "Sweetheart," he said in English. Then more formally for the court, "My lady. Will you join me?"

"Thank you." Her voice was like ice, and there was winter in her smile as she sat beside Rick.

Christ. I didn't send for her, Rick thought. I should have, but I just forgot. But—"I am pleased that you were able to join us. When you did not come I worried." And that ought to make her wonder. "Chamberlain, summon our guests if you please."

"You sent for me?" Tylara demanded.

"Benjamin Murphy do Dirstval and Lafe Reznick do Bathis, Star Lords and Merchant Traders of the Sun Lands," the chamberlain announced.

"Ah," Rick said to himself as Murphy came in. I remember him now. Belfast Irishman. Made a bundle playing poker until most of the others wouldn't play with him. Nobody thought he was cheating. Just good. Good man with the light machine gun, too.

He couldn't recall very much about Reznick, except that he always teamed with Murphy.

Murphy and Reznick came to the dais, followed by two women and four men, obviously armed servants. The men carried something heavy and bulky wrapped in silk and cloth of gold. They reached the dais and looked at Rick in mild confusion. Then Murphy stamped to attention and saluted.

Automatically Rick returned the salute. Then he laughed. "You're supposed to bow or kneel or something," he said in English. He heard a strangled grunt from Tylara as she suppressed a laugh. "Welcome to my house." Rick changed to the local dialect and raised his voice. "It is good that we meet again. Your other friends among the starmen will welcome you also."

"Yeah, well, I'm happy to be signing up with you again, Captain," Murphy said. "And I've brought you something—"

"Yes. I'm damned glad to get the recoilless back. That is the one-oh-six, isn't it?"

"Sure is." Murphy turned and gestured. His companions unwrapped the tube. Another took the cover off the tripod stand, and clapped the barrel onto it.

"You've trained them to use it?" Rick asked.

"Not really, sir," Reznick said. "But they *have* seen us use the thing."

"Yes. We'll continue this in private," Rick said. "Meanwhile, there's a ceremony. We'll coach you." He motioned to Murphy to kneel, and said in the local language, "We will accept you to our service. Do you offer me service, of your free will, according to the customs and uses of this land?"

"We do," Murphy and Reznick said in unison.

"Then your enemies shall be my enemies, and who wrongs you wrongs me," Rick said. He held out his hands. "Place your hands between mine. There. Now repeat after the chamberlain . . ."

"Thank Ghu that's over," Rick said.

"Who is Ghu?" Tylara asked seriously.

"Uh—a local deity back on Earth. Probably no jurisdiction here." He watched Murphy and Reznick leave the audience hall, and felt an overpowering urge to go with them. Fat chance, he thought. Now that the fireworks are over we have to go show Isobel off to every goddam bheroman and knight in the joint, and get the king's blessing and—"You needn't smirk about it," Rick said.

"Your desire is obvious," Tylara said. "It will do you no harm to be patient. Tonight you must be with me."

"Yeah." It *was* important. Tonight's ceremonies were supposed to be fun, but they would also mark his formal acknowledgment of Isobel's paternity. Until he did that, she was officially no more than a little bastard.

And Isobel was the most beautiful little thing he'd ever seen, and he certainly wanted everyone to know she was his—which still seemed like a miracle—but Lord, Lord, those lords were dull. . . .

2

"What now?" Reznick asked.

"The first thing I want is a drink," Ben Murphy said. They were led through corridors, then up stairs, then down a flight. "And I think I'm lost. Ho, guide there, where are our companions?"

"Your ladies have been shown to their chambers. You are wanted in the Orderly Room." The trooper who led them obviously spoke no English; but they had no difficulty recognizing the last two words.

Reznick laughed. "Just like the real army." They followed their guides until eventually they were led to a stone doorway guarded by two kilted archers. Murphy nudged his companion. "More of those MP's. Okay, let's go in..."

"Hats off in the orderly room," a voice said in English.

"Bat puckey," Murphy muttered, but he took off his hat.

He stared at the heavily bearded man who'd spoken. The man stared back, grim-faced. "Who—Warner? Larry Warner?"

"Sure is." Warner grinned broadly. "Here to welcome the geeks bearing gifts. How are you, Ben? Lafe? You're looking good. New beards and everything."

"Warner, for God's sake, we thought the locals took you off to sell you."

"They did. Sold me to Lord Rick."

"You look pretty rich," Reznick said. "For a slave."

"I'm no slave," Warner said. "Fact is, I've got the softest duty there is. Here, have a drink." He poured generous dollops into silver cups. "Go on, drink up."

"Yeah—" Murphy drank. "Holy Mother, Larry, what is that stuff?"

"Potent, eh? You bet your arse it's potent. That's McCleve's work. Can you imagine him doing without a still?"

"No. What's the old lush doing now?"

"He's Professor of Medicine at the University of Tran."

"The which at what?"

"Professor of Medicine. At the University. Of Tran."

"Tran's the name of the whole goddam planet," Reznick protested.

"Right on," Warner said. "And now it's got a university. Come Murphy, surely you've been hearin' of the University?"

"Oh, crap," Reznick said.

"Yeah," Murphy agreed. "One of the best things about staying down south was not having to listen to your crazy accents— Hey, what are you doing?" Warner had gone to the door and was gesturing to the guards outside.

"Sending for the MP's," Warner said. "You man, get the Corporal of the Guard."

"What for, because we didn't like your stupid accent?"

"No, you'll see, it's nothing to worry about. A detail somebody forgot to attend to. Anyway, about the University. About half teaching and half research. McCleve teaches the acolytes of Yatar about sanitation and cleanliness. I teach math. Campbell does engineering. Even the Captain takes a stint at teaching. But mostly we've got teams of students and acolytes doing research. Soap. Substitutes for penicillin. Grinding microscope lenses. Figuring out how to make nitric acid. All kinds of stuff. And history, too."

"Professor," Murphy said. "We used to call you 'Professor' back in Africa."

"Now it's for real," Warner said.

"So just where do you fit in?" Reznick demanded.

"Think of me as a kind of warrant officer," Warner said. "That'll be close enough. Ah. Here're the guards. Corporal, these star lords have not had their weapons peace bonded."

"Yes, sir." The guardsman gestured, and two of his troopers used thick line to tie Murphy's sword into its scabbard. They finished with an elaborate knot. Then the corporal took out a thin copper dish of red wax. He melted the wax over the lamp on the orderly room table and sealed the knot with a flat lens-shaped stone. Then they began working on Reznick's weapon.

"What the hell's this for?" Reznick demanded.

"Orders," Warner said. "Here, have another drink, and I'll tell you things." He waited until the locals had finished their business and left. "Officially, this whole palace is under the king's peace," Warner said. "No challenges can be issued here. In fact, though, there's lots of nobles with the hereditary right to fight their enemies even on palace grounds. But they can't challenge one of you to immediate combat since you've got your weapons bonded." Warner shrugged. "Protects you and the locals both . . ."

"What about—" Murphy cut himself off.

"Pistols?" Warner asked. "You'll turn those in here and now. Uh—I got to search you, too."

"You and which army?" Murphy demanded.

Warner shrugged. "Thought you'd rather have me do it than Mason," he said. "But if you'd rather deal with Mason. Or Sergeant Major Elliot—"

"No way," Murphy said. "I'll sit still for it. Here." He took out a .45 Colt Mark IV automatic and laid it on the desk. "My combat knife too?"

"No, you keep that for your own protection. I expect you'll get your pistol back in a couple of days, too, after you've learned a little about life here." He eyed Reznick suspiciously. "Lafe, I expect you've got a hideout gun somewhere. Let me give you some good advice. Be damned careful whom you kill, self-defense or not. The clan system is really strong here. You kill one guy and you got a hundred relatives after your blood. Not to mention the Captain if you knocked off one of the people he needs." Warner wrote out a receipt for the firearm. "Now you, Lafe."

"Yeah, yeah," Reznick said. He laid his .45 on the table. "Okay, what now?"

"Now I take you to the party," Warner said. "And try to brief you on all the stuff that's going on. Not that you'll understand it. I don't understand it myself, and I've been around a year." He paused. "Why'd you come in, anyway?"

"Seemed like a good idea," Murphy said. "It's getting messy down south. Sea raiders. Big wagon trains coming north, lots of weapons and bringing their whole families and damned well going to find a place to live. Looks like things are *really* bad a thousand miles south of us. Famine, war, plague—you name it."

Warner nodded. "We'd heard some of it. 'The Time approaches, when the seas shall rise.'"

"They have, too," Reznick said. "About half of Rustengo's docks are awash, and the harbor area is salt swamp."

"It'll get worse," Warner promised. "Still, you guys had a good setup. Got titles and everything." He chuckled. "I don't remember Dirstval giving out city knighthoods to mercenaries."

Ben Murphy chuckled. "Yeah, but I like the ring of it. 'Benjamin Murphy do Dirstval' sounds better'n Private Murphy, CIA . . ."

"So why'd you give up all that?"

"Did we? You told that MP we were 'star lords.' I heard you."

"Well, it's a little complicated," Warner said. "Far as the locals are concerned, you're important merchant traders from the south. That's near enough to noble, up here. But I'd act real respectful to Sergeant Major, was I you. And Art Mason's an officer now."

"Suits us," Reznick said. "We want to get along here."

Murphy nodded agreement. "Yeah. It's pretty bad down south, Larry. Damn all, it's getting worse, and nobody down there is going to watch our backs. We had each other, and Lafe's wives, and nothing." He stopped for a second, then went on. "Used to be, I had a wife. Nomads killed her. Lafe and I hunted the bastards for a ten-day. Hell with that. Anyway, one day the pistols will run dry. Or somebody'll catch us and torture us for our secrets. You heard the fables, about what they do to the Little People here?"

Warner nodded. "Grim fairy tales indeed."

"So when we heard Colonel Parsons had bought it, and the rest of the troops was doing all right and there wasn't even any war to fight—well, I figure Cap'n Galloway will take care of us. He always tried when we was back home."

They stood on the balcony behind the musicians and looked down at the grand hall with its kaleidoscope of colors. The granite walls had been hung with tapestries and rich colors, but the place still had a fortress-like look to it. Nearly everything on Tran did.

The musicians seemed in good form. Someone had brought up wineskins, and clay goblets were going around freely. Every few minutes someone raised a toast to the Infanta Isobel, and everyone had another drink. The music seemed mostly strings and drums, with little of the thin reedy wails that Murphy had become used to in the south. Most of the music was incomprehensible, but sometimes they struck up tunes Murphy recognized. "The Girl I Left Behind Me," the drinking song from *Student Prince*, "Garry Owens"...

Murphy estimated three hundred people were crammed into a hall built for half that many, and all were wearing their best clothes, which meant the most colorful.

"There's a hell of a lot of those MP's out there," Reznick said. "Who are they?"

"Well, technically they're Guardsmen to Mac Clallan Muir," Warner said.

"Mac which?"

"Mac Clallan Muir. Look, Captain Galloway—there he is, recognize him?—Captain Galloway married the Lady Tylara do Tamaerthon, widow and dowager countess—well the local title is Eqetassa, but that's pretty well countess—of Chelm. That made the Captain Eqeta. Lady Tylara's father is an old clan chief named Drumold. Tamaerthon has a goofy system of titles that *nobody* understands, but Mac Clallan Muir is Drumold's most important one. He made his son-in-law his war chief."

"War chief," Reznick said. "Of what?"

"In theory, of all of Tamaerthon," Warner said. "In practice,

Captain Galloway's war leader of all the clans that'll take orders from Drumold. That's most of 'em, but not all. There. That's Drumold over there." He pointed to a man in bright kilts studded with silver pins. He wore a dozen gold bracelets, and several gaudy necklaces. Warner noticed Murphy's grin. "Yeah, I think so too, but you better never say nothin' he can hear. Old bastard'll split your liver in a second, and don't think the Captain would do much about it, either.

"Anyway, back to the MP's. As war chief of the clans, Captain Galloway was entitled to a bodyguard. What he did was have Art Mason recruit a whole mess of 'em, lots more than anybody expected, and use 'em for military police. Not just young nobles, either. Kids from different clans. Even clanless ones, and freed slaves—"

"So now the only clan they've got is Captain Galloway," Murphy said.

"Yeah. Exactly," Warner said. "Smart of you."

"Just like us," Reznick said. "But where do we fit in?"

"Sort of like a headquarters company," Warner said. "First thing is you'll probably be posted back to the University and told to write down everything you remember. *Everything*. Then there's the travelling schools. You'll learn about them. Main thing to remember is that Captain Galloway's *our* boss and we're all right if we don't forget it."

"But these MP types. Excuse me, but this is Drantos. Tamaerthon isn't even a part of this kingdom, is it?"

"No. But remember they're supposed to be Captain Galloway's bodyguards, and he's the host this ten-day. Outside the palace Art's MP's wouldn't have any jurisdiction 'cause we're not in Tamaerthon, but Lord Rick—that's what they call the captain here—theoretically put them under the command of the Lord Protector. That one."

He pointed to a big scar-faced man with a perpetual scowl. "So they're keeping order in the kingdom as well as in this palace," Warner finished.

"And Corporal Mason takes orders from that Protector guy?"

"Major Mason. Sure he does," Warner said. "Sure."

"Christ, this is worse than the south," Reznick muttered.

Warner laughed. "Just getting started, Lafe. See those two? There, and on the other side of the room—"

"Yeah?"

"Romans. The one on the right is ambassador of the Emperor Flaminius—"

"And the other one from Marselius," Murphy finished. "Yeah. We've got a lot to tell the Captain about that situation."

"Oh? Like what?"

Murphy looked thoughtful. "Larry, not that we don't trust you, but the only thing we got left to deal is information. How about I tell the Captain, and he tells you?"

Warner chuckled. "You're learning, Ben. You're learning. Shall we go downstairs and join the party? Your ladies and friends will be along in a minute. Try to stay sober, and for God's sake don't insult anybody."

3

Rick's head was bursting. Hangover remedies didn't work any better on Tran than on Earth. Not as well. There was precious little aspirin on Tran, and a lot more fusel oils in the liquor.

"Two hours and I'm for the Grand Council," Rick said. "Holy Yatar, my head is killing me—"

"You earned it," Tylara said. "I thought you had determined to drink all the wine in Edros."

Close to right, Rick thought. I don't do that too often, but last night—Oh, well. What's really irritating her is that I was too drunk to pay attention to her after the party. "You will come to Grand Council, of course."

"Of course," she said. "Shall I accompany you now?"

"I think no," Rick said. "I think I'll get more information if I talk to them in English."

"As you will."

"Dammit, I'm not keeping secrets from you." He went to put his hands on her shoulders, but she seemed to draw away from him. "All right. I'll see you in Council." He left the bedroom hoping that she would call him back, but she said nothing.

He went downstairs to the stone chamber he'd had fitted out as a situation room, a copy of his offices in Tamaerthon. There were maps painted on three walls; the fourth was blank white, with charcoal nearby to write with. A big wooden slab table filled the room's center. Benches surrounded it; benches weren't comfortable, and that made for short meetings. In contrast, Rick's chair at the head of the table had been specially carved for him, with padded seat and thick arm rests. If need be he could out-sit those who argued with him in this room—

"Ten-shun!" Elliot commanded as Rick came in. The troopers around the table stamped to their feet. Murphy and Reznick seemed a bit surprised, but they didn't object. Rick said nothing until he had taken his place at the table's head and sat down. Then he nodded. "At ease," Elliot said.

"Thought we left that crap behind with Parsons," Murphy muttered.

"That'll do," Sergeant Major Elliot said sharply. He didn't like people who talked back to officers. Elliot's idea of perfection was an officer who knew his place commanding troopers who knew theirs. Of course the Sergeant Major was indispensable under any such scheme . . .

"Two reasons for this meeting," Rick said. "To find out what you know about the southern situation, and to bring you up to speed about the mission here. I'll start off."

Only where? he wondered. There's so damned much they don't know. So damned much *I* don't know. Humpty Dumpty told Alice to begin at the beginning and go through to the end. Then stop. But if I do that I'll be here all day.

"First, the basic mission hasn't changed," Rick said. "We're here to grow crops for the *Shalnuksis*, and if we don't grow their damned *surinomaz* they won't trade with us, meaning no more modern conveniences. So we've no choices there."

"Captain, are you sure those—those saucer things are coming back?" Murphy asked.

"Not entirely," Rick said. "But they told us they were, and they left communications gear. The pilot told Gwen Tremaine that the *surinomaz* crop was important, both to him and the *Shalnuksis*." And he left *her* a transceiver. Left her pregnant, too. So now she's got a year-old kid with no father within light years.

"The trouble is," Rick said, "that *surinomaz* isn't easy to grow. The locals call it 'madweed' and they hate the stuff."

"Uh—"

"Yes, Warner?"

"Captain, just 'fore I left the University, we got reports about witch women and shamans who used madweed for a useful drug."

"We'll want to check that out. Bring it up in the Science Council meeting." Another meeting, after the Grand Council. All I do the whole day through is sit in meetings—

"Yes, sir."

"Anyway. We need a lot of the stuff, and people don't want to grow it. Land's limited. With that rogue star coming close the growing seasons will be longer, and we can get more food out of each acre—but somebody's got to feed the people who grow madweed for us. For years. We'll want at least four years of bumper crops of the junk.

"So that's one problem. We need peace, only that rogue star is playing merry Hobb with the whole planet. I saw your reports, Murphy. Migrations. Wandering tribes in the south. I'm not surprised—fact is, it's going to get worse. What's the chances of holding off the migrations at the borders of the city-states?"

"Not much, sir," Murphy said. "If we could have done it, I would have, rather than come up here."

Rick nodded. It's like a ball of snakes, he thought. "What if I sent a big force? Twenty mercs and a couple of thousand local warriors?"

Murphy shrugged. "I don't think that would work very well," he said. "First thing, the city-states might not let your troops through without a fight. But even if you made some kind of alliance with them, there's not much for a defensible border down there."

"That was my impression," Rick said. He pointed to one of the maps on the wall. "But it also looks as if eventually there'll be impassable swamps to the south, after the Demon Star melts enough ice to get the seas up forty or fifty feet. Until then we'll just have to do the best we can. Now what do you hear of the Roman situation?"

"Stand-off," Murphy said. He turned to Reznick and got a nod of confirmation. "At first Marselius was winning. Had new tactics that I reckon he learned from you. But now old Flaminius has recruited some new legions and called out his reserves, and he's holding his own."

"Okay. I'll want all you know about that. Order of battle, force levels, anything you've got." Rick glanced at his watch. "You've got about an hour. Tell me."

Drumold drew himself to his full height, resplendent in bright kilts and golden bracelets. There was no doubt that he spoke not as Rick's father-in-law, but as Mac Clallan Muir, Grand Chief of the Clans of Tamaerthon.

His words echoed through the council chamber. "Man, are ye altogether daft?"

Rick tried to smile. It wasn't easy. The echoing voice hurt his head. For a moment he wondered just how many wars had begun because some king or general had come hung over to an important council meeting. Tylara's father had his rituals, and this was one of them; but there were plenty in the Grand Council who didn't know Drumold. For that matter there were plenty who did, and who might make political capital out of even the appearance of a quarrel between Rick and Drumold. "No more so than yesterday, I think. And today I am better informed."

"Och, perhaps I spoke in haste," Drumold said.

Lord, do I sound that grim? Rick wondered. He looked to Tylara, but her look was no help this time. Often she could interpret the impact Rick was making; despite her youth she'd had a lot more experience leading these hotheaded people than Rick had, and she'd presided over her own Councils before Rick ever met her.

"Yet," Drumold was saying, "let us think clearly what we want, and how best to get it. So long as Marselius and Flaminius make war, they can not send one legionary against us. Let them make peace—or let one side win—and where are we? Rome has long claimed the whole of Tamaerthon. Och, aye, there was a time when they claimed Drantos, indeed all this world of Tran. And will Marselius be such a friend and ally once he is undoubted Caesar and has no need of us?

"My Lord Rick, you propose to make an end to this war, even spend our blood and treasure to do it! I say you have not been well advised, and I understand it not."

There were loud murmurs, but no more than Rick had expected, given the number of people packed into the room: so many that the table, the largest in all of Drantos, could not hold them, so that many of the lesser nobility, as well as commoners, sat in chairs set in rows stretching all the way to the far wall.

The table itself held too many for a sensible meeting. The young Wanax Ganton, nominally in charge but delegating that to Rick; the Lord Protector Camithon, scarred face glaring at anyone who opposed him or forgot the least courtesy due the king; three of the five great counts of Drantos, four counting Rick and Tylara. Like William-and-Mary, Rick thought. Rick-and-Tylara, a two-headed monster to rule Chelm. Some of the wealthier bheromen and knights. Guildmasters. All to represent the Kingdom of Drantos.

Then the priesthoods. Old Yanulf, splendid in blue robes, scowling because the Council bickered instead of getting on with preparations for the Time. Sigrim, high priest of Vothan One-eye, Chooser of the Slain, a warrior god everyone feared and few loved. Florali, the elderly lady—Rick thought of her as a vestal virgin although she was a widow—to represent Hestia, the Good Goddess of grain.

The composition of the Council came from long tradition. Men had died contesting the right to sit in Council. Reducing its size was nearly impossible. King, lords, commons, and priestly orders together made up the Great Council of Drantos, an unwieldy structure at best; but there were lots more at today's meeting. Drantos was allied with Tamaerthon. Some of the Tamaerthan clansmen put it more bluntly. Tamaerthan warriors, led by Lord Rick, had only the year before saved Drantos from occupation by Sarakos, Heir Apparent of the Five Kingdoms, and despite the relative sizes of the two lands many clansmen thought Tamaerthon was and ought to be the senior partner. Certainly Tamaerthan chiefs and warriors must sit in the Grand Council. Consequently, one side of the table was filled by kilted hill tribesmen, scarcely thought more than barbarians by the great ones of Drantos—but they kept those thoughts to themselves.

Usually.

" 'Tis far to our interest to end these wars." The voice rose shrilly from Rick's left. Morron, father of the King's Companion and Eqeta of the south-central region of Drantos. "Our trade is ruined by this war," Morron said. "Each side takes its tolls, and all profit is lost to finance their wars. The sooner the issue is settled, the better for Drantos."

"Hah!" Drumold shouted. "So we have the truth of it. Tamaerthon is to be sold for the benefit of Drantos."

"Enough!" Rick shouted. He pounded the table again. "Enough, I say!" His hand went to his pistol. The babble ceased. Once, weeks before, Rick had fired a round into the ceiling as a means of shutting off debate. "Drumold, my old friend, you wrong me."

The old chieftan looked hurt, then thoughtful. "Aye," he said reluctantly. "I spoke in haste. Yet I cannot retract this much: it is not in our interest that the Romans make peace among themselves."

"Do not be so certain. True, while Roman fights Roman they cannot attack us—but they cannot defend themselves, either. Of the eleven legions in Rome before the civil war began, scarcely six remain in condition to fight."

"Och, and who will invade Rome?" This came from Dughuilas, Chief of Clan Calder. "Unless we do, divided as they are . . ."

"The High Rexja, for one," Tylara said.

Dughuilas and Drumold stared at her. Women did not speak at Council in Tamaerthon.

"He will want to avenge his son Sarakos," Tylara continued. "If we fight the Romans, the Five Kingdoms will be in Drantos within five ten-days. If we do not—will not Rexja Toris eye the Roman lands with greed? He has bheromen and knights, even sons of Wanaxxae who hoped for lands in Drantos. How shall they be rewarded, now that the Five hold no sway here?"

"Such a one as Sarakos deserves no revenge," Drumold muttered. Balquhain, his oldest son, pounded the table in agreement.

"Do you think you know that better than I?" Tylara demanded.

The room fell silent. Everyone had heard that Tylara had been tortured—some even whispered *raped*—by Sarakos, but no one expected her to mention it.

Rick took advantage of the silence. "We cannot fight Rome, for if we march east then Toris will lead the armies of the Five Kingdoms into Drantos."

"Then strike the Five," someone said. "Now, before they prepare."

"Leaving a divided Rome behind us?" Rick asked. "When we can't be certain of the friendship of *either* faction?"

"We have aided Marselius," Tylara said. "He sends us gifts."

"Aye. We sent him aid after we bested him in battle," Drumold said. "He is a proud man and his legionaries are prouder. They will not forget how the clans stood against them— and won."

"Another good reason for alliance," Rick said. "And how sure are you that Flaminius will not win while we flounder about in the north? It is certain enough that Flaminius bears nought but malice toward Tamaerthon. Let Flaminius win, and we will be as grain between the upper and nether millstones."

And about now, Rick thought, is when someone's going to think of the master stroke of dissolving the alliance and letting Tamaerthon float off on its own. There, Dragomer is about to speak—

"This is madness." The voice thundered from immediately to Rick's left. Yanulf, Archpriest of Yatar, stood defiantly, his arms thrown out wide. "The Time approaches. And in the Time of Burning, then shall the seas smoke and the lands melt as wax. The waters of ocean shall lap the mountains. Woe to those who have not prepared. Woe to the unbelievers.

"And how have we prepared?" he demanded. "The starmen have come, exactly as prophecy foretold; they themselves tell us of The Time. We bicker among ourselves and make talk of petty wars, when the ice caves are empty of stores. I say it is time we fill the caves with grain and meat against The Time, and cease this talk of 'interests.' There are no interests more important than preparation for The Time."

"Well said," someone shouted. The guildsmen stamped their feet in approval.

"Well said indeed," Rick agreed. "And another thing is certain: as the Demon Star comes closer, the lands to the south will be hurt first. Their people will stream north looking for places of refuge. That has already begun. The city-states of the south can scarce defend themselves; they will not seek to halt these migrations."

"We can hold the borders to the south," Dughuilas said.

"Perhaps," Rick agreed. "But what of the southeast? What of the river valleys there?"

"Roman land," Drumold muttered. "Under Roman truce from time out of mind—"

"Roman until city-state mercenaries take it," Tylara said. "Aye, take it and open the roads for those coming from the south. They will want soon enough to have the wanderers leave their lands."

There was silence again while the council members studied the great map Rick had caused to be drawn on one wall of the chamber. The Drantos contingent saw it first. The river valley with its roads pointed like a dagger at the heart of Drantos— but it equally threatened the western border of Tamaerthon.

"It could be," Dragomer said. "The cities have produced good soldiers."

"Mercenaries," Dughuilas said. His voice was filled with scorn. "No match for the chivalry of Tamaerthon."

"They have been a match for better cavalry than yours," Dragomer said.

Not the wisest thing he could have said, Rick thought. Dughuilas was chief of a large clan, and led a powerful faction of the Tamaerthan upper classes; and Dragomer was one of the Drantos lords who'd invited city-states mercenaries into Drantos in their revolt against young Ganton's father.

"I remind you of the King's Peace," Camithon said. "Answer gently, Eqeta Dragomer."

"I need not answer at all," Dragomer said. "Were the cities to find one leader—"

"They have not done so in memory." A new voice. Corgarff, a subchief. "Nor do I fear they will do now. Not so much as to send my sons to die in a Roman fight, to save lands for Rome. Unless—" He paused for a long moment, until he had everyone's attention. "Unless this Star Lord Gengrich, who leads the starmen lords in the south may yet come to lead all the cities? Perhaps the Lord Rick can tell us more of this man who once followed him."

I'll have his blood, Rick thought. I'll—

"Careful," Tylara said. She kept her voice low. "He is Dughuilas's man, and Dughuilas has good reason to wish you ill."

"That is not well said." Camithon was very much Lord

Protector when he spoke. "The Lord Parsons rebelled against the Lord Rick. The Lord Gengrich deserted the cause of the Lord Parsons, and by both our laws and the laws of the starmen remains in rebellion. How is the Lord Rick guilty of blood shed by rebels against his rule?"

But I am, Rick thought. I brought them here, and I let them get away from me. And now they're like wolves among sheep.

"They are rebels, but the Lord Rick has done little to capture them," Corgarff said. He didn't sound comfortable.

He's only following orders, Rick thought. Dughuilas's orders. Fairly crude way to embarrass me.

"He has done more than you," Yanulf said. "And by Yatar's blessing, the Lord Rick prevailed against the Lord Parsons." He glanced at Sigrim. "And the next day Vothan One-eye was pleased to smile upon our armies.

"But enough of this. Our talk does nothing. My lords, the Demon Star rises even as we speak! The ice forms thick in the caves. Yatar sends us the means of life, but we must grasp them. We must make sacrifice. We *must*."

"Indeed," Rick said.

"The stories of previous Times are clear," Yanulf continued. "Those whose castles stand on bare rock will learn their folly, and seek the caves of Yatar. There will be wars enough then.

"And then shall the gods come from the skies to trade; and from that trade shall come good and evil. And fire shall fall from the skies, and men shall smoke and burn as faggots, and their sores shall not heal. The only safety is the caves of Yatar and his Preserver."

"How can we grow the grains we need while our young men stand in arms?" Camithon demanded.

"Let the Star Lords protect us," shouted a guildsman. "They have power. Let them use it."

"Aye, we hold great power," Rick said. "Enough to turn the tide of battle, once, twice, several times. But I think not enough for the troubles that come."

There was a long pause, as everyone considered what Rick had said. "If the starmen cannot defend us, and we cannot defend ourselves—" "March north." "No, march east." "Plant crops and trust to Yatar ..." The babble rose in pitch.

"Your advice, Lord Rick?" Ganton spoke carefully and clearly, his boyish voice penetrating the noise. The room fell silent. "We would welcome your advice."

"Majesty. I would send an embassy to Marselius. A strong Rome has ever been important for the safety of Drantos. It is doubly important now. The Roman civil war must end, and Marselius owes us much already; while Flaminius owes us nought but hate.

"To see that Tamaerthon does not suffer from this, I say send Mac Clallan Muir himself as ambassador. Assisted by the Eqeta Morron and the Lady Gwen, and such others as I and the Lord Camithon shall agree to."

Camithon looked thoughtful, then turned to Drumold. "My lord. Will you seek truce between the Romans, and alliance?"

Drumold looked thoughtful. "Alliance with Rome. 'Tis a strange thought. Strange indeed. And yet—I will not oppose it. Aye. The Lord Rick is convincing. There is danger in a strong Rome, but there is more in a divided Rome during these times."

There were murmurs of approval.

It doesn't look like anyone saw it was a setup, Rick thought. Which is just as well. Machine politics, medieval style . . .

"Then let it be done," Camithon said.

"Go with the blessings of Yatar Skyfather," Yanulf said. "Go swiftly, before The Time comes on us and we all perish."

4

"How is your head?"

"Better," Rick said. "I wasn't sure you were speaking to me."

"You are my husband. How can I not speak to you?"

"Come off it," Rick said wearily. "What's wrong, anyway?"

"Nothing is wrong."

Sure. I can believe as much of that as I want. "I love you—"

"And I you."

"Do you?"

"Certainly." She seemed about to say something else, but instead she turned away. "The meeting begins soon, and I must see to Isobel. I will be there when you begin."

"Look, Gwen means nothing to me! But I have to see her. She's the only one who might know what the *Shalnuksis* are going to do. And she asked to see me alone. Don't you understand? We need her. The whole country needs her."

"Certainly I understand," Tylara said. "You told her that her child would have the stars."

"It was a way of speaking," Rick said. "Our children will have no less opportunity."

Her smile was wintry.

"For the stars, or here on Tran," Rick insisted. "You need have no jealousy of Gwen Tremaine!"

"I have none."

"You damned well don't act that way! And now you're angry, and I'm sorry."

"Have I reason to be angry?"

"Tylara, please. I don't need this," Rick said. "And I must speak to Gwen."

"I understand perfectly." She strode from the room.

Women, Rick thought. Is she determined to drive me away from her?

He brooded all the way down the stone corridors to the guest suite. He paused at the door, then knocked.

"Enter."

Gwen Tremaine was standing at the window. Yellow light streamed through light brown hair, showed up green eyes. She was very short; "five-foot-two," the song said, and that was about right. She wore a spectacular blue gown, cut in a style more Parisian than anything fashionable on Tran. It was made of some kind of blue silk that shone in the evening sunlight. She continued to stare out into the gathering dusk as Rick came in.

"A penny for your thoughts," he said in English.

She laughed. "There aren't any pennies here. But I'll tell you anyway. I was trying to decide which made me sadder, that Earth is out there somewhere, or that my baby's father is there—"

"You do miss him, then?"

She shook her head slowly. "Rick, I don't know. Sometimes I want him so bad I could die. And sometimes I just want to kill him." She turned away from the window. "I was in love with him, you know. I could say I was kidnapped, but I wasn't, I got on that damned flying saucer of my own free will because the man I loved asked me to."

"And left you here when you got pregnant."

"Yes." She went over to the small table and sat down in one of the wooden chairs. "Wine? Yes, let's both have some."

"The real question is did Les mean it when he said he'd come back?"

"Yes. That's the real question." She drank the full glass of wine and poured another. "He said he'd come back—but Rick, have you ever thought that maybe he intended all along to dump me here? That he never did tell me the truth about anything? Sure, I got pregnant and wouldn't let his damn machine do an abortion, but maybe that was just a good excuse to get rid of me. Maybe he was tired of me anyway."

"You didn't think that last time we talked." Rick took the chair across from her and lifted his own wine glass. "Cheers."

"Cheers. No. Last time we talked I was sure he loved me. Next time maybe I will be, too. But just now—just now I'm not sure."

"Okay. But he did give you the transceiver. And he told you about the rebellion among the human troops of the Confederation—"

"It's not a rebellion," Gwen said. "More a—a dissent. And— Rick, have you told anyone about this? Anyone at all?"

"No."

"Not even Tylara?"

"Not even Tylara. I won't tell any locals. Or any of the troops, either. Not unless I have to—if you and I are both killed, someone here has to know. Warner, maybe."

"Yes, I've thought of that too. But don't tell him yet."

"I won't. Next subject. You know more than me about what the *Shalnuksis* will do. Had any more thoughts?"

"Some. Over there—that wooden chest. It has maps, areas I think might be best for raising *surinomaz*. One good area would be along the western border of the Roman Empire."

"Which we don't own. Oh—have you heard about the Council this morning? I'd like you to be on the delegation to Rome."

She nodded. "Another journey. More time away from my son."

"Take him with you—"

"Into a civil war? Don't be silly. But you're right, I have to go. I can inspect the potential cropland on the way. Meanwhile, we want to begin growing madweed on our side of the border. We won't get a full crop this year, but we ought to start experimental plots now. Get some experience with the stuff. It's tricky, Rick. The ecology is all bound up with some little mammals that are something like rats. They swarm into the fields and die, and when they rot they fertilize the plants. They also stink to the throne of God."

"Not to mention necrotic products—"

She nodded agreement. "I'd think those fields get pretty unhealthy. Which is one reason the peasants don't want to grow madweed. You've got your work cut out to make them do it."

"Convicts. Criminals—"

"I suppose. And when you're done with them, when the madweed fields have killed most of them, the *Shalnuksis* will finish the job for you."

"When?"

She shrugged. "I don't know. Certainly they'll want to trade with us as long as we have *surinomaz*, but after that—you have as much evidence as I do. I think they'll try to find out which is our center of culture, and destroy it."

Rick nodded thoughtfully. Certainly there was plenty of evidence. Every six hundred years, when *surinomaz* grew well under the influence of the Demon Star, the *Shalnuksis* came to Tran with a fresh crop of Earth mercenaries. Roman legionaries, Celtish warriors, Franks. And every time, when the aliens had got all they wanted, they tried to exterminate their agents. The legends told over and over of *skyfire,* and everyone knew where there were fields of glass . . .

"So we'll want to be sure we don't build anything modern-looking."

"That may not be good enough. Rick, there were Tran languages in the computer on Les's ship. They talk to locals. They'll ask questions, and I think our University will be the first target."

"I thought of that too," Rick agreed. "Which is why I'm not putting much into brick and mortar. By the time your boyfriend starts dropping atom bombs on us, all the important people will be long gone to the caves. Meanwhile the travelling teams go teaching science to every villager in Drantos. And— Gwen, this is all crazy! A galactic civil war over Earth—"

"I told you, it's not a civil war. Just a disagreement among the leaders of the Confederate Council," Gwen said. "And I think it's crazy too, but—" She pointed out the window.

"Yeah." Crazy or not, they are here, on Tran. It wasn't Earth. Given that one undoubted fact, what couldn't they believe? "Look, your friend Les is the best chance we'll ever have for getting off of this planet. And he told you he'd come for you—"

"If he could. Yes."

"And you believe him."

"I remember I did when he told me," she said. "I don't know about now. What difference does it make? He *is* our only chance."

"And what about the rest of us?"

"Rick, I don't know."

"Yeah." But it wasn't likely that Les would give a damn about the mercenaries. He might care for Gwen and their child. That might even be likely. But there was no reason at all for him to worry about a bunch of mercs. "Gwen, why did you want to see me alone?"

"Your wife doesn't like me. I don't much care for her, either."

"She's jealous. She thinks I'm your baby's father. Or that I could have been, anyway. Your wanting to see me alone didn't help the situation."

"It didn't hurt it, either."

"No, I expect you're right. Not much would."

"And I just wanted the chance to speak English and talk without having to worry about what I say. Rick, it gets pretty bad up there in Tamaerthon. Always on guard so that I don't give away something—"

"And you're not on guard with me. You're not keeping any more secrets?"

"No, of course not."

You sure as hell did, Rick thought. For damned near too long. So how can I trust you now? "So. How are things at the University? Any trouble?"

"No. And of course I have the pistol you gave me—"

Another point of contention with Tylara. She thought she should have had Andre Parson's .45 Colt. But Tylara had plenty of experience protecting herself on Tran, and Gwen had none—

"Do you like my dress?" she asked.

"Yes. I was just admiring it."

"It's called *garta* cloth. Larry Warner got it. Rick, it's a *very* close weave."

"So?"

"So we could make a hot-air balloon from it."

"You're kidding. Hot damn, of course! Observation balloons! They used them in the Civil War, and the Franco-Prussian War, and—can you really sew the seams tight enough?"

"Yes. We've tested a small model, and Larry made glue from horses' hooves. It will really work. The only problem is the cloth. It comes from the south. We don't have enough, because the trade routes are in a mess. It's very expensive—"

"Sure looks it. Warner got that lot?"

She nodded.

"And gave some to you?"

"He had the dress made for me," Gwen said.

"Why?"

"None of your business—"

"The devil it's not," Rick said.

"Captain Galloway, I have not asked you to be my protector. I don't ask now."

"Sure, Gwen. I thought Caradoc was sweet on you."

"He likes me—"

"Seems to me you encouraged him, back when you were pregnant."

"I might have—"

"And now Warner. Gwen, I need both of them. You play them off against each other, and you'll get one killed sure as hell!"

"No, that won't happen."

And there's not a lot I can do anyway. Keep them apart? Nonsense. Warner and Gwen are needed at the University, and Caradoc goes there to see her whenever he gets the chance, and how do I stop him?

"There's more news," she said.

"All right. What?"

"I know of a village where they make drugs out of *surinomaz*."

"Somebody else mentioned that. Warner?"

"Probably. Anyway, there is such a place. One of the travelling medicine-show teams came in with the news."

"Which one?"

"Doesn't matter. The merc with the outfit was Beazeley, but it was an acolyte, Salanos, who had wits enough to come tell me."

"That could be important. If there's some local use for the stuff it might be easier to get people to grow it."

"Yes. I'll check that out, shall I?"

"Please. And the balloon—that's a great idea. It could be decisive in the Roman civil war. Observation of the enemy, command and control of our own forces, artillery spotting—Gwen, it could really be the winning factor."

"Thank you."

"You don't look too happy—"

"Should I be? More battles—"

"They'll be fought anyway," Rick said. "And people will starve no matter what we do, too. But at least we can save some of them, this time, and we can get civilization spread so far across this planet that the *Shalnuksis* and their goddam *skyfire* can't root it out—"

"We can try," Gwen said.

5

Tylara stared at the roughly whitewashed door of the farmhouse. The one-eyed image of Vothan stared back. She waited until she heard a faint click and saw movement behind the one eye.

"Who seeks entry to the House of the Wolf?" a voice demanded.

"Tylara do Tamaerthon, Eqetassa of Chelm."

"Enter, lady," said a rough voice, followed by the sound of a lock turning.

Tylara stepped into the house, stamped the mud off her riding boots, then glared at the man who'd let her in. "What are your orders about tending the door, Bartolf?"

The man turned the color of a winter sunset. He swallowed. "To recognize all who come, and let them enter with hands open and empty."

"Did you ask me to open my hands?"

"No, but—"

"But *nothing*. I might have been a spy disguised as the Lady Tylara. If I had been—" Her right hand darted into the full left sleeve of her riding tunic. Then she raised it. As the sleeve fell back, it exposed her husband's Gerber Mark II combat knife. She'd borrowed it for just this sort of demonstration.

"You'd have been dead from that mistake, Bartolf."

"Perhaps, Lady Tylara," he said. "But an enemy in your place wouldn't have lived enough longer to do hurt or learn much." He raised his voice. "Bennok! The berries are ripe."

The tapestry on the opposite wall of the antechamber rippled, then rose as a dark-haired, pimple-faced youth slipped through a waist-high opening it had concealed. He held a small crossbow, the sort noblewomen used for shooting birds and rabbits. Not enough, thought Tylara, then saw that the thin point of the quarrel was barbed and glistening with something green and sticky.

"Poison?" she asked. "And the point has been made small enough to enter ringmail."

Bartolf nodded. "That was Monira's idea. The rest was all his." He reached down to tousle the boy's hair. The boy carefully sidestepped out of reach.

"That was a very good idea, Bennok," said Tylara. "Are there others who keep watch?"

"Oh yes, lady. With the poison on the quarrel, any of us can do the work. So we all take turns."

"Very good." She reached into her purse and pulled out a silver piece. "This is for your good work."

Bennok didn't reach for the silver. "Will there be one for all the others, lady? I can't take it unless there is."

Tylara tried not to sound as confused as she felt. "I think there will be silver for all of you."

"Oh thank you, lady. Now maybe we can buy those longbows ourselves if Bartolf goes on saying he won't give them to us." He darted back under the tapestry and vanished.

Bartolf was red-faced again. "I'm sorry, Lady Tylara. I should have told you. They've all eleven of them sworn an oath to be as brothers and sisters and have all their wealth in common. The only things they'll call their own are weapons and clothing."

"And Monira was the leader in this, I'll wager?" said Tylara, smiling to show that she wasn't offended.

Bartolf returned her smile uncertainly. "She spoke for them all when they told us. I don't know if that was her idea, though."

"And you don't think you ever will?"

"No. They are good at keeping even the secrets we don't want them to keep."

Someday that might make trouble. Now it proved to Tylara that her idea was succeeding beyond anything she'd expected.

Thoughts sometimes took on a life of their own. This one was born in bitter sleeplessness during the early days of pregnancy. She lay awake, unable to sleep, unable to stop torturing herself with restless thoughts—

She was certain that Rick had not fathered Gwen's child, but her mind would not let go of the matter. Let her think of stars and star weapons, and it would end with that question. That night it began simply enough, when Rick musingly told her that the star-folk would come and it might be useful to capture one of their ships.

Tylara could scarcely conceive of a starship. She never expected to see one. Yet certainly something had brought Rick and the others to Tran. All the priesthoods agreed that mankind had not been created here. If humanity came from another world, then there must be ships to travel between the worlds.

And Rick wanted one. He wanted one badly.

If he had a ship, would he leave her?

Or would he first teach everyone on Tran the secrets of star weapons and starships, as he said he would do? It scarcely mattered. There was no way to capture a starship. Rick had laughed at his own idea. His star weapons would be useless.

And Tylara lay pondering stars and starships and weapons and children— There were no dangerous weapons. Only dangerous men—and women, and children. If the starmen were all like Rick, reluctant to kill, sentimental, fastidious to the point of squeamishness . . .

How *would* you take a ship of the sky-folk? You would certainly need to surprise them, so they would not be able to use their fire weapons.

But suppose, suppose half a dozen children could get aboard such a ship. Not ordinary children. Children well trained, dedicated, fanatic followers devoted to service . . . Then at a signal they pulled out knives and fell on the crew. That would be surprise indeed. No one thinks that an eight-year-old girl can be dangerous, unless he is a trained warrior, and maybe not even then. The *Shalnuksis*, according to both Rick and Gwen, would not be sending trained warriors. They would send merchants, easily surprised and once surprised easily killed.

But you would need to have the children trained and ready long before the sky-folk came. And they would have to be kept a secret from *everyone* until then. There were those on Tran who might warn the sky-folk if they could. Lady Gwen could be one of those. And Rick surely would not approve of this. Why should he know?

So began the Houses of the Children of Vothan, for boys and girls up to the age of ten who'd been orphaned in the wars. There were plenty of those, enough to fill many more than the seven Houses everyone knew about.

In those seven Houses orphans were fed, clothed, sheltered, and taught trades. Some learned to be midwives, seamstresses, carpenters, shepherds, smiths. Some learned new skills, such as wire-making or distilling. In one House the boys were destined to become acolytes of Yatar, the girls to serve the hearth goddess Hestia. There was a House near Rick's precious University.

And there was an eighth House. Six boys and five girls, from six to nine, picked for quick wits, strong muscles, and keen eyes and ears, brought here to learn one thing and one thing only—how to kill. Some of them had good reasons to learn, others just had talent. All had been doing well at their lessons, the last time she visited them, six ten-days before her confinement.

Bartolf led her through the door from the antechamber into the main room of the house. As she stepped into the room she heard a thump, a squeal like a piglet's, and the rasp of a knife blade.

"Aiiii, lass!" shouted a wheezing male voice. "Have ye learned nothing about holding a knife? That one—it'ud stick between his ribs, even the rope round his neck canna save ye then! Fast in, faster out, that's the way it must be."

Tylara stepped out into the room. In one corner a man-sized dummy lay on the floor. One boy lay under its head and upper body, gripping a rope drawn tightly around its neck. On top of it lay the girl Monira, her knife thrust up to the hilt in its chest. As Tylara approached, Monira sprang up, bowed quickly, then helped her companion crawl out from under the dummy.

"Are you hurt, Haddo?"

"No, Monira. Only my breath knocked out." He also bowed to Tylara, then walked off with Monira as if both Tylara and their teachers had become invisible.

"My regrets, lady," said the teacher with a shrug. "Sometimes she gets taken so that she forgets everything. Mostly, though, she's a joy to watch. Ah, if I'd had a girl like her when I—" He broke off abruptly as he remembered to whom he was talking.

The teacher's name was Chai, and he had reason to be cautious in talking about his past. He was a former thief who'd taken advantage of the wars to practice his skills, and in due time came before the Eqetassa's justice. Unlike most common thieves, he had real skills. He could even read and write. And he'd once been a priest of Yatar. A spoiled priest, but admitted to the mysteries...

That was the morning that Tylara decided to establish the Houses; and Chai, his name and appearance changed, became one of the Masters...

Tylara watched Monira and Haddo sit down cross-legged in a corner and wipe each other's faces with damp clothes. Monira was beginning to have a woman's body, but she would never be beautiful even with her thick fair hair. A troop of Sarakos's cavalry had taken care of that. At least nothing showed when she was dressed, except her broken nose and the scars on her chin and one ear.

Tylara had been through a similar ordeal, at Sarakos's own hands, and she also would bear scars both inside and out for the rest of her life. Compared with what Monira had survived, though, Tylara knew her own experience was a child's game. No great wonder that Monira sometimes saw one of those men instead of the training dummy.

In another corner of the room stood the third teacher, Rathiemay, wearing a knight's armor. He was showing three of the Children how to attack an armored man.

"—get him to bow his head, if he's wearing a helmet like this. That will leave a patch exposed at the back of the neck. Yes, that's it," he added, as one of the Children prodded it with a blunted dagger. "A good hard thrust right there. If he's not dead at once he's easy to finish off." He saw Tylara and straightened up. "Good day, my lady."

"Good day, Lord Rathiemay. How are they doing?"

"No one could wish for better pupils, my lady. They seem

to have been born with steel in their hands." His face was bright with his smile, reminding Tylara oddly of her husband's expression when he spoke of the University or some other great scheme for bringing hope and life to Tran. She remembered how he'd looked the first time she came, sour and grumbling over being a knight sent to teach commoner children how to strike down his brothers in arms. To be sure, he was grateful that the Eqetassa had given him this chance to restore his fortunes, but still . . . Now he looked almost like a father teaching the children of his own body the family trade.

"Where are the other Children?"

"Out in the woods, learning tree-climbing," said Chai.

"Without a teacher?"

"Na, na, lady. They're learning from Alanis. His father was a woodsman, there's no sort of tree he can't climb. It's a mizzling gray sort of day, so no one's likely to be seeing them."

Tylara pulled eleven silver coins out of her purse and handed them to Bartolf. "For the Children. I hear they want some new bows."

"Aye, but they've also spoken about some sandfish buskins for the tree-climbing. We'll have to let them decide."

"You let *them*—choose what they'll buy?"

"Oh, not everything, lady. Only the things likely to be life or death for them. Why not? Does a carpenter let a butcher choose his mallets for him?"

Tylara thanked the man, drew the hood of her cloak over her head, and was outside in the rain without remembering quite how she got there. What had she done? The Children of Vothan were no weapon to lie quietly in a scabbard until she choose to draw it. They were a sword with a life and a will of its own, which might choose its own moment to be drawn and drink blood.

Whose?

A dangerous experiment. Was it best ended now, while she had control? Or—

Or might there be uses for this weapon? Used well, used now, before the sky folk came . . .

Tylara grew more hopeful as she walked back to her horse. By the time she was in the saddle and returning to where she'd left her escort, she knew the Children of Vothan would not be a weapon only for a single battle. The sky-folk were not the only enemies to her and her house.

PART TWO

If
This
Be
Treason...

6

Corgarff knew that he was out of favor with Dughuilas when his clan chief did not invite him to sit or offer him a drink. He stood in front of the table facing Dughuilas and another man he didn't know, until he felt like a small boy waiting to be whipped by his father. The only light in the cellar came from two candles on the table, throwing strange twisted shadows on the cobweb-shrouded brick of the walls.

"That was not well done, what you said at the Grand Council," said Dughuilas.

"I thought it the best thing to say at the time. And indeed, is it not possible that the Lord of Chelm thinks too much of his countrymen still?"

"Whether he does or not is no concern of yours," said Dughuilas. "You thought poorly, and spoke worse. If you wish to sit longer on the Council with me, you will need to think better or speak less."

"I will do neither unless I know why you are so tender toward the Lord Rick so suddenly," said Corgarff. "Was it not he who spoke harshly to you and did all but smite you with the open hand the day we fought the Romans? Was it not he who made fighting men out of plowboys and swineherds? Is it not he—?"

"He has done all this and more," said the second man. He wore a hooded cloak, and kept the hood drawn over his head so that his face stayed shadowed.

But his accent was not that of the Tamaerthan upper classes. Nor yet that of the Drantos nobility. Who, then? Corgarff thought it would be dangerous to ask—and probably death to know.

"And speak more softly," the man continued. "We cannot trust the tavern keeper if he thinks he has anything worth selling." Dughuilas put a hand on his dagger but the other shook his head. "In time, perhaps, but not now on the mere chance that he might have heard something useful. If we kill too many rats, the wolves will escape."

"If the Lord Rick is a wolf, what harm to oppose him in Council?" Corgarff demanded. "And he will send our sons to die in Roman wars for Roman causes. Rome, whose slave-masters have tormented us these centuries—"

Dughuilas held up his hands to gesture for silence. "Spare me. I can make the speech better than you."

"The Lord Rick will be strong as long as he and the Lady Tylara keep their wits," said the second man. "We can do nothing to change this. Indeed, we should not. Your friend who thinks so well of the Lady Tylara would not have any injury done to her or her blood. Without your friend, much we hope can not be done."

"You should not have said that," said Dughuilas sourly. "You have given this rattle-jaw knowledge I had not intended he should have."

"If you have plans for Corgarff which you are not telling me, expect little from me," said the second man. His voice was so even it was impossible to tell if he was angry or not. "I think you need my friendship as much as we both need— our friend's."

Who could he be, that he could speak to the chieftain in that manner? But if he was not angry, Corgarff was. He almost forgot to lower his voice. "Lord Dughuilas. I have perhaps spoken unwisely. Yet you speak as though I were a traitor. Were you not my sworn chief, I would have your blood for this."

"I did not wish to call you traitor, for indeed you are no such," said Dughuilas smoothly. "Forgive me those words, and I will forgive you for yours."

Corgarff took his hand from the knife hilt.

"Sit. Sit and join us." Dughuilas poured wine and lifted his own glass in salute. "Drink, clansman."

"Aye. Thank you, my chieftain." Two mysteries here. This man, this conspirator; and beyond him a mysterious ally. Hah! thought Corgarff. That one I can guess. Probably the Lady Tylara's brother, Balquhain. A hothead, the darling of old Drumold's age, bound to become Mac Clallan Muir in time ... Certainly no other noble of Tamaerthon was as likely to wish to uphold the old rights of the warriors without injuring the Lady Tylara.

"The Lord Rick has brought victories," Dughuilas's companion said. "Victory over Rome—"

"A mockery," Dughuilas said. "What matters victory at the price of all we hold dear? Lord Rick makes knights of crofters and peasants. They obey their chiefs not at all."

"It will become worse," the second man said. "It is this 'University' that spawns your troubles. It is from there that these dangerous ideas come. This place is important to Lord Rick. Harm that, and he will know of the anger of the knights."

"If we wish to injure the University, I can give some aid," said Corgarff. "A smith's boy from my land works there. I have heard that his father has not long to live, and he fears his mother and sister will want. Only a little gold could buy him, I think."

"Is he fit for any work we might give him?"

"As fit as anyone of such blood can be."

"The Lord Rick would not have said that," said the second man.

"Hang the Lord Rick!" snarled Dughuilas.

"As Yatar wills," said the second man quietly. "But I think he is more likely to hang us, if we cannot use whatever tools come our way."

Dughuilas nodded sourly. "Och, aye. But a man of the old blood must keep watch on this peasant lad. You, Corgarff."

"Aye, Chieftain." He paused a moment. "Perhaps there is

a way. One hears that the University prepares a new machine. They say it will fly through the air! That men may fly as gulls!"

"Och!" Dughuilas stared in wonder. "Can this be true? Then woe to our enemies, when warriors can fly—"

"And when they do, your order is finished. What need of knights then?" Dughuilas's companion asked.

"Och. Aye, it is so," Dughuilas said. "The Lord Rick will raise up peasants, while the men of blood fall. This must not be."

Corgarff nodded grimly. "I had not thought—but it is true enough. Already the University is guarded by the sons of crofters. Even freedmen. Freedmen with arms! But hear. In the past, when a new machine is prepared, the University is open to all who wish to come and watch. The Lord Rick does not seem to care who learns his secrets."

"He is a fool," said Dughuilas.

"One wonders," said the second man. "Perhaps he plays a game too deep for our understanding. Surely we *would* be fools if we did not reckon on that."

"Fools we are not," Dughuilas said. "And our cause is just. Lord Rick would destroy all we ever lived for. It is our right to oppose him. Let us destroy this University, and all its arts, forever and aye. Swear it!"

The three stood. "We swear," they said in unison. Then they raised their glasses, drained them, and dashed them to the floor.

The University was located in a town at the northwestern border of Tamaerthon. The place had been noted for its medicinal springs, and had long boasted a small temple of Yatar where acolytes came for training; a natural place for a center of learning, but open and vulnerable.

Rick had the town's defenses repaired, and now a proper city wall was under construction. There were also a mortar and a light machine gun. It wasn't likely that the University would fall to an enemy.

Larry Warner locked the armory door and returned the salutes of the archers who stood outside it. He was going to his quarters when he heard a call for the proctor on duty. Warner immediately changed his plans and headed for the gate area. He arrived to see a small caravan ride up.

"Who comes?" a local guardsman called.

"Sergeant Major Elliot."

Holy shit, that's who it was all right. With a pretty big crew, too. Damn, Warner thought. With Gwen Tremaine gone off on embassy duty, Warner had been senior man present. He rather liked being in charge. Now here was Elliot. Crap.

"Let the Sergeant Major in," Warner commanded. Maybe I ought to keep him out—that's too silly to think about. What do I do, set up as some kind of king here? Stupid. "And ask him to join me in my quarters after he has been shown to the Visiting Officers' Quarters."

"Ho, Sarge, what brings you here?"

"Cap'n sent me down south," Elliot said. "Buyin' some of that *garta* cloth you like. Brought you a whole mess of it."

"Hey. That's all right." Rick Galloway had been pleased with the balloon idea when Warner described it back at Castle Edron. The problem had been the cloth, which could only come from the south, and Warner had been afraid he would be sent there to buy some. Instead, Rick sent Warner and the two new troopers back to the University, where for two ten-days Warner had enjoyed being in charge... "Have to get to work on the balloon, then."

Elliot nodded in agreement. "I brought orders on that. Cap'n wants a test model in a ten-day."

"Can't do it."

"You can try!"

"Sarge, I'll do my goddam best, but nobody is going to sew up that thing in a ten-day! You got any idea how *big* that sucker is?"

"No—"

"It's *big*. Take that from me. Uh—Sarge, why are you here?"

"Captain's orders. I'm the new Provost for the university."

"You?"

"Yeah. Show you the written orders tomorrow."

"Shit. And where do I fit in?"

"Hell, Professor, I treat you like a civilian. You're my boss—so long as it's not a military situation. Comes a military situation, you're back in uniform. Like a weekend warrior. It's all in the orders."

"Oh." That's not bad. Not bad at all. Makes good sense. Elliot was Parsons's man. Killed a lot of Drantos soldiers while he was working for Parsons. Must be a ton of nobles who'd like to even the score for their relatives. Blood-feuds and all that. Makes sense to get Sergeant Major Elliot out of Drantos, and God knows the University's important enough.

"I'm also supposed to help you with the bookkeeping," Elliot said. "For the travellin' medicine shows." He frowned heavily. "Do those things do any good, Professor?"

"Sure. Look, we send out a merc and a couple of local warriors and some junior priests of Yatar. They go out and make maps and get a resource survey. That's worth it all alone— Sarge, the maps here are really something else! Most of 'em have their own country bigger'n the Roman Empire, for chrissake!

"But there's more to it. They go to the towns and teach hygiene. Germ theory of disease. Antiseptic practices."

"Does it work?"

"Yeah, sometimes," Warner said. "And sometimes not, I guess. Sometimes we get the old 'what was good enough for Granny' routine—"

"So you convert Granny," Elliot said.

"Right-o. Or we try to." He drank another glass of wine. "Sarge, I had a thought. The Captain likes you around him. Is he going to base his Roman expedition out of here?"

"He may have to."

"Crap."

"You don't like that?"

"Don't like this place mixed up with war," Warner said. "Yeah, I know how that sounds, coming from me, but it's true."

"Funny, I agree with you," Elliot said. "More to the point, I think the Captain does too. But what else has he got? Anyplace else is controlled by the local lords—Larry, why do the lords hate Captain Galloway so much?"

"I would too," Warner said. "Lord Rick comes in and makes his pikemen and archers more effective than the knights, pretty soon the troops are going to wonder what it is the heavy cavalrymen do that makes them so important. It's a good question, too."

"How bad is it?"

"Bad enough that Captain Galloway had better wear armor any time he's got Tamaerthan lords around," Warner said. "Bad enough that you and I ought to keep lookin' over our shoulders, too."

"Yeah. All right, I'll do just that. Hey, have you got a drink? It's hot work, riding up these hill paths."

"Sure." Warner clapped his hands and a girl about eighteen years old came in. "Sara. Cold beer, please. Thank you—"

"She's a looker."

"Want to borrow her?"

"Hooker?"

"Naw, slave," Warner said. "Yeah, I know, the Captain doesn't approve of slavery. I liberated her, Sarge, but she won't leave. Where would she go? One day a freedman will marry her, I expect, but meanwhile she works here and she likes working for starmen—"

"Well, Larry, I don't have anybody to clean up for me—"

"I'll send her over to help until you get something permanent set up. One thing, be polite to her. I always am—ah. Thank you, Sara."

She set down two large tankards and curtsied. They drank. "Good beer," Elliot said. "Soft duty up here."

"You wouldn't say that if you'd seen me today," Warner said. "Working on fuels for the balloon. Hot air's all right, but I think I can figure a way to make hydrogen for the next one. If I can make a good sizing for the cloth to seal it so it'll hold hydrogen."

"Hydrogen. What's the matter, Professor, afraid you'll run out of hot air after the first one?"

"Ho-ho. Anyway, now that the cloth's here I can really get to work. Have any trouble?"

"I don't ever have trouble, Professor."

"Yeah." Actually, Warner thought, that must have been a hell of an expedition. Mercs, locals, Tamaerthan archers, pack animals for the trade goods, more pack animals for the fodder— taking a zoo like that over muddy roads and through the hills couldn't have been much of a picnic.

"Usual market for this stuff is Rome," Elliot said. "So we got it at a good price."

"Where? Rustengo?"

"Found a whole warehouse full about a hundred klicks north of there. With the roads to Rome closed off they were grateful for the chance to sell."

"Hmm. And the Romans really like the stuff—"

"That's what I hear."

"Maybe a good bargaining point for Miss Gwen. I think we'll send a messenger tomorrow to tell her."

"All right by me. I got a few other items of interest."

"Good. Seriously, did you run into any trouble?"

Elliot grinned. "Nothing I can't handle, Professor. Some bandits in the hills outside Viys. About two hundred."

"That's damned near an army, around here."

"We unlimbered the H&K's," Elliot said. "No sweat." He seemed pleased at the memory. "Didn't have to use too many rounds, either. After that, nobody wanted to give us any gas. Word spread pretty fast."

"Yeah. No sign of Gengrich?"

"No. He could have been trouble."

Larry Warner nodded. "I hear he's set up as a pirate king. One of these days we may have to deal with him. More beer?"

"Sure. And don't forget to tell that girl I want to borrow her. You're right about Gengrich, they're scared of him down there. But they're scared of everything. The whole south's talking about the Roman situation. Half of 'em want the Romans to keep on fighting each other. Long as that war goes, the Roman frontier posts aren't manned, and the southerners have a place to send the refugees that keep streaming in.

"Then there's the others, who mutter about the lost trade, and how things are going to hell. And all the priests of Yatar are out soapboxin' about The Time, and how they better store up food against the years of famine—"

"They're right there," Warner said. "One reason for this University. We're as much an agricultural research station as anything else. And there's our travelling road shows—"

"Right. Captain said I was to help you get those organized." Elliot stretched elaborately. "Larry, things look pretty good, considerin' where the Cubans had us."

"Sure," Warner said.

"Relax. Captain Galloway knows what he's doing."

"I hope so," Warner said. "Damn, I hope so."

Rick put down the report from Sergeant Elliot and nodded in satisfaction. Tylara came and took it from the table. She puzzled over each word.

"I'll read it to you if you like," Rick said.

"I'll ask you to do so. Later," she said. She went on reading.

"Your English is getting very good," Rick said. "I'm proud of you."

"Thank you." She went on poring over the parchment, her finger resting at each word. Finally she looked up. "You have promised mediation in the Roman Wars," she said. "You had Elliot make that promise in our names."

"Yes."

"You did not consult me about this, yet the promise is as Eqeta of Chelm—"

"Dammit, I don't have to consult you! I am the Eqeta of Chelm!"

"So much for your fine promises," she said. "We rule as equals. But you are perhaps more equal than I."

"I am also Captain-General of Drantos, War Chief of Tamaerthon, and Colonel of Mercenaries," Rick said. "Posts I had *before* I married you. Do you tell me everything you do?"

"The important things. Must we quarrel?"

"That's what I was going to ask."

"Then let us not. I was going to say that I approve of your strategem in the south. It brought us the cloth at a lower price, and there is no way for them to know if you keep the promise. Soon no one on Tran will be teaching you anything about bargaining."

In spite of Tylara's heart-stopping smile, Rick wasn't entirely sure those words were a compliment. He frowned. "I intend to keep the promise and try to negotiate a peace, if we can't give Marselius a victory."

She stared at him. "That is impossible. How can there be peace in Rome after three seasons of war?"

"Not easily, I admit," said Rick. "But if Marselius issues the proclamation I'm about to suggest, the chances will be better. He should announce that he will punish no man for any act done in obedience to a proclaimed Caesar. I've already proposed to the ambassador that Flaminius do the same. A mutual pardon for everything done during the war." They did that during the Wars of the Roses, when the English Parliament formally legislated that no man could commit treason by obeying a crowned king. If they hadn't, there wouldn't have been a Yorkist or Lancastrian left.

"Marselius might agree. He might even keep such an agreement. Not Flaminius. The man is a fool. Otherwise he wouldn't have pushed Marselius into rebellion at all."

"Perhaps Flaminius wouldn't agree, by himself. But can he go against all of his commanders? They're losing soldiers, sons, estates. Some of them must be wiser than he is about what needs to be done to prepare for The Time. If they no longer need fear for their lives, who knows what advice they might give? I don't."

"It is still a pardon for treason. Do we want anyone to make the lot of the rebel so much easier?"

"There are different kinds of rebels, it seems to me. Marselius with his legions is not the same as a mountain bandit with a dozen ragged followers."

"Not in your eyes, at least. I hope that this does not mean that all starmen take their oaths as lightly as Colonel Parsons did."

Rick sighed. When she got this sharp-tongued, he could either change the subject or be sure of a fight. It wasn't worth having a fight now. He would have to lead her gradually if at all toward his own position on how to treat rebels. There were going to be many of them, as The Time approached. The Time itself would kill enough people on Tran. If being generous with pardons could reduce the toll of life and property from the rebellions, wasn't it at least worth trying?

It wouldn't be Tylara's way, of course. For her or any other Tran dynast, the rule for rebels had been, whenever possible, "Hang first and ask questions afterward." One more thing to be changed. If possible.

The charts on his office wall grew more detailed, and he collected chests of papers.

Item. It had been the warmest spring in living memory. Some farmers, heeding the priests of Yatar, planted early, and found their crops growing high. Others waited. All chanced heavy rains and hail. The entire pattern of Tran agriculture was changing.

Rick's survey teams went through the land, teaching and gathering data.

According to the reports, they did more data gathering than teaching; but they had accomplished the first agricultural survey in Tran history. What crops here? What last year? Are you using the new plows introduced by the University? What fertilizers?

Those using the new plows were able to get their seeds in so fast they were heard to talk of being able to get a second crop before winter. Those who'd used the new plows the year before talked even louder. With more fodder during the winter, their draft animals were stronger than usual.

Rick gathered all the information and reduced it to statistics. The raw data sheets went up to the University. Slowly his data base grew.

He also dictated letters. One went to Gwen; that one he wrote himself. Except for Tylara no Tran native could read English, so that for sending messages to Gwen and the mercs it was better than code. That was worth the inconvenience of writing for yourself.

Find out if Marselius can send us a dozen or so trained clerks and scribes who can write well and teach things like basic filing procedures. It may be, of course, that the Roman civil service of the time of Septimius Severus has vanished, but I rather think something very like it must have survived. Else how could they have kept even this much of an Empire together for so long? And I am told the Roman "scribes" are said to know magic. Probably simple scientific training. Whatever it is, we can use it.

Which would set Gwen hunting bureaucrats among the Roman rebels. The priesthood of Yatar would be another problem. If Rick could forge a Roman alliance, would the priests cooperate? The Romans were Christians who persecuted Yatar and Vothan One-eye as pagan gods. Lord, Rick thought. What must I do? I *need* the hierarchy of Yatar, to spread science through the land. And will the Christians cooperate?

The priests of Yatar were the key to survival. They must have a strong organization, or the temples couldn't have survived the Rogue Star and the nuclear bombardments, not once but at least three times. With the cooperation of Yanulf and the priesthood much could be accomplished; without it, Rick was in trouble.

It was ironic, his going to all this trouble to re-invent bureau-cracy. However, the whole idea looked different here on Tran, where information that could save thousands of lives might be lost because there *wasn't* a policy of writing up three copies of everything.

Rick put down the pen and held his head in his hands. More than ever he felt the pressure. "Every time I want to do anything, I first have to do two other things, one of which is impossible," he shouted. "Tiger by the tail, hell! I've got two tigers, and I've got to get them together so I can ride them. One foot on each!"

There was no one to hear him but the walls of his office, and they made no answer. Rick sighed and lifted his pen again. He had to write Warner at the University . . .

7

The chair creaked under the weight of Caius Marius Marselius, onetime Prefect of the Western Marches, now Caesar by right of conquest and proclamation of the legions. It was not a title he had sought, but once the proclamation was made it was one he had to win—or be killed for. Not just him. His son as well. All his house. Flaminius would leave none alive.

And when Marselius marched in triumph to Rome? What of the house of Flaminius? Time to think of that when it happened.

Outside they were lighting the street lamps. Marselius could see them go on, one by one, down at the base of the hill where his villa stood. Benevenutum was a large city, third largest in the empire, and in many ways as pleasant as Rome; but it wasn't Rome, and an Emperor who did not hold Rome was only a rebel.

Marselius bent forward to squint at the parchment he held.

The late-afternoon light was fast failing. His freedman Lucius wrote with a firm hand, but it seemed harder to read lately.

Well, neither of them was getting any younger. His own eyes were not what they used to be. He summoned a servant to bring lamps, then he waited until the man went out before spreading the letter again. Not that he did not trust his servants, but this was too important. The confidential report on the embassy coming to him from the Lord and Lady of Chelm and the Kingdom of Drantos, written by the one man he trusted entirely . . .

—Drumold, father to the Eqetassa Tylara, would seem a typical barbarian chieftain. However, he is very intelligent and entirely trusted by the Lord Rick. He has made enemies among the clan chiefs of his own land in his loyalty to the Eqeta, which hints of a kind of courage most uncommon among barbarians. They are often brave in battle, but seldom understand and still more seldom show the higher civic virtues.

Lucius, Lucius, my old friend, thought Marselius. You spent too long as tutor to my son Publius. Now you *will* lecture, whether it is needed or not. Or perhaps you are rambling as old men often do. Well, before the snow comes again we shall both be so high in the world that everyone will listen to us for as long as we want, or else we shall be forever silent.

The Lady Gwen Tremaine is of the star-folk, but knows much history and reads Latin well. She is said to be very intelligent but is certainly young for the place she holds in the embassy. It is said that she owes this to having been Lord Rick's mistress, after the death of her husband.

The Guardsmen of Chelm—

Marselius skimmed the description of the embassy's escort until he found mention of star weapons. Good. They were bringing one which used the firepowder. Too many of his officers were skeptical about the star weapons and badly needed a demonstration, his own son among them. He himself would not mind learning more about these new war machines, so that if the alliance came about he would be able to plan the battles properly.

Certainly he would not need that many more ordinary soldiers. He had two full good legions of his own and a third which was neither so full or so good, plus enough cohorts of foot archers and pikemen to make up two more legions if that honorable title could ever again be allowed to foot soldiers. Then there were the light horse and foot scouts recruited locally. No lack of men.

Except—if Lord Rick did send a strong force as well as star weapons, it would release more of his own men for local defense. The reservists in the legions whose homes were close to the boundary between the two Caesars would fight better if they knew their own homes were safe. More militiamen would come forward. And there were the borders to the south to be held. He could use what Rick might send—and it was never good to let a man know that he could buy your friendship cheaply. No, Lord Rick would have to be ready to send an army to Rome if he ever wanted an army from Rome.

Marselius got up to pace back and forth in front of the great map on the wall. Mentally he shifted a cohort here, sent a tribune to raise more militia there. Everything would of course be discussed at length in the council of war he must hold before the embassy came, but he wanted his own ideas fully prepared before then. The older he grew, the more necessary it was to appear infallible and the harder it was to do so.

Gwen Tremaine stretched luxuriously and let herself slide down into the hot water until only her face was above the surface. The tiled tank wasn't *quite* large enough for a swimming pool, but otherwise it was living up to everything the name "Roman bath" implied. It was the first really adequate bath she'd had since Les dumped her on Tran.

It had surprised her, how much more important the little things of civilization seemed when you didn't have them. Sometimes they loomed larger than the big ones. She knew that if she got a cavity the tooth would have to come out, with no anaesthetic except ethanol. She knew that if she had another baby and needed a Caesarian, she would probably die, and the baby hadn't a much better chance. She could accept these dangers, at least intellectually.

Hot baths were another matter. You missed them every

© Josep W. Martin Sauri

morning and every night and every time you got sweaty or dirty. It was the same way with Vivaldi concertos, cold beer, Chicken Kiev, pantyhose—

"Lady Gwen?" said a small voice from right above her head.

Gwen controlled a foolish impulse to plunge out of sight. Instead she sat up, crossing her arms over her breasts. "Yes?"

"My name is Octavia. I've been sent to help you with your bath."

Which was no surprise. She'd rather expected someone waiting for her when she went in to take her bath. If Marselius was going to do her the courtesy of letting her bathe alone, he would certainly not leave out things like servants, towels, and scented oil.

"Thank you, Octavia." Gwen ducked under to get the last of the soap out of her hair, then climbed out of the bath. Octavia clapped her hands, and two older girls came in with deliciously warmed towels. When they wrapped her in a robe of fine wool, Gwen felt she had found civilization at last. Eventually the others were dismissed, and Gwen was alone with Octavia.

Who was she? While the others had dried her body and combed her hair, Gwen examined the girl minutely. Octavia looked to be about twelve or thirteen, and was already at least two inches taller than Gwen. With her big bones she'd grow even more. She was red-haired, but apart from that her strong, rather plain features had a lot in common with Marselius's.

And although her manners were impeccable, she spoke to the servants in a voice which made her requests orders to be obeyed. Gwen looked down at the hem of the girl's robe. It was embroidered with an elaborate pattern done in gold thread and what looked like pieces of blue enamel or seashells.

When the others had left, Gwen said, "You're kin to Marselius Caesar, aren't you?"

The girl dropped the towel and blushed as red as her hair. She didn't seem to know which way to look, other than not at Gwen. Finally she said, with an admirable effort to control her voice, "Are you a witch?"

"No. You just look like Marselius, and your gown doesn't look like a servant's clothing."

Octavia looked down at the hem but couldn't blush any brighter. "Grandfather will be angry with me for not changing my gown. It's the sort of thing he never forgets himself. I suppose you learned to notice it too, when you were a soldier."

"I'm not a real soldier," said Gwen. "My husband was. After he was killed they needed someone to read all sorts of books for information about our enemies. I was going to have a baby, so they wanted to help me and gave me the job." Gwen had told that story so often that she almost believed it herself. She smiled. "Don't imagine me in armor and a plumed helmet, waving a sword at the head of my troops."

"If we had your kind of soldier in Rome, I could be one too," said Octavia. "I like to read. In fact, my father says I spend too much time with the books."

Impulsively Gwen hugged the girl. She stiffened but didn't draw away. "I'm sorry. It's just that you sound like me when I was your age. My father said the same thing about me."

Fortunately she'd been able to do other things besides read, and get straight A's, like sell stale bread to chicken farmers and other things which made money. Also, she'd never been short of boyfriends, although none of them stayed around for more than three dates after they realized how much brighter she was. Octavia wasn't going to be able to do much except read her books until she was old enough to be married off. That wouldn't be long. Caesar's family must marry, and quickly, to cement alliances...

"Are you a spy?" Gwen asked.

Octavia giggled. "Yes, but it's not what you think." She paused, then said impulsively, "Lady Gwen, if you promise not to tell anybody what I say, I'll tell you why I'm here."

What an offer! Gwen didn't hesitate a moment. "By Yatar Skyfather and Hestia I swear I will never tell anybody what you say except the Lord Rick, and then only if he needs to know. I can't break my oath to him, you see. Is there anything else I should swear by?"

"No." Octavia looked thoughtful. "You must tell me some-time of Yatar, and I'll tell you about Christ." Then she really smiled for the first time. "You see, my father Publius wants to sleep with you. So my grandfather asked me to be in your company a lot. That way my father will be unable to get you alone. He would be ashamed to ask you to go to bed with him while I was around."

"I should hope so!" said Gwen indignantly. Then she laughed. The idea of this likable twelve-year-old girl as a chaperone to Gwen Tremaine was impossible to take with a straight face. If Octavia only knew how Gwen had lived—

Except—if it really did save her from having to either refuse Publius or submit to him, there was nothing funny about it. She hadn't heard that Publius was a Don Juan, but she had heard that he was arrogant and hot-tempered. That sort of man often disliked being turned down, enough to make trouble for the woman. Refusing him could be trouble.

And some day Publius would be Caesar, if Rick's plans worked, and they probably would.

Actually, the offer was flattering. Caesar's heir must have his choice of women. And there were advantages to being Caesar's lover . . . but not on a planet with no contraception except the rhythm method and very little obstetrical knowledge! If she'd wanted a man in her bed, she could have had Caradoc for a husband a year ago. Or Larry Warner, who was kind and gentle and intelligent and a very good partner in managing the University. Or—

"How does your father know he would find me attractive?" Gwen asked.

"He saw your arrival. When your party was greeted by my grandfather's officers, my father was among the guardsmen. He often does that."

"I see." So. Intelligent, if devious. At least Publius knew the value of information. "I'm flattered," she said. "But I'm still really in mourning for my husband. Sometimes it's hard to believe he's dead. You know they never found his body?" Another story she'd told so many times that she had to fight not to believe it herself.

"That must make it worse, doesn't it?"

"Yes." Something could be made of this girl. Caesar's granddaughter. "Have you brothers?" Gwen asked, although she was certain she'd heard—

"No. I'm my father's only child. To his great disappointment." She lowered her voice. "He doesn't even have illegitimate children. Not since he was ill—"

Mumps, probably, Gwen thought. "That makes you an important girl." It also removes one chief reason for refusing an offer by Publius. We'll play that one as it lies—

"They say I will be. If Grandfather can capture Rome, then some day my husband will be Caesar." Octavia looked very serious. "I don't think I'll have much to say about who that is, either. Did you choose your husband?"

"Yes. Where I'm from women always choose their own."

And it doesn't seem to work any better than arranged marriages, either. "Octavia, you must swear an oath to me, one like I swore to you. You must not talk about anything I tell you, except with your grandfather and your father. Then we can be friends."

"Do I have to tell my father? Grandfather doesn't tell him a lot of things he thinks he should know. I've heard Father cursing about that."

So Marselius did not entirely trust his own son and presumptive heir. That was information worth a good deal—so much so that Gwen almost felt guilty about making friends with the girl. She was so obviously lonely, desperate for intelligent company where she didn't have to hide her talents, that—

The next moment Octavia made matters worse. "I'm glad we're going to be friends, Lady Gwen. It will be a lot easier to keep my father away from you, if you know what I'm doing. I told my grandfather that, but he didn't seem to understand what I was talking about."

"He has a lot on his mind," said Gwen absently. And even when he didn't, Marselius Caesar didn't seem like the sort of man to listen to his granddaughter's complaints.

She needs a friend, Gwen thought. And I can be that to her. Our cause is her cause, and she may some day come to see that. And she needs a teacher, someone to tell her of the changes coming to Tran. If—*when* her grandfather becomes undisputed Caesar, Octavia will hold power enough. Power during The Time, power for two generations after. In Rome, the best organized nation on Tran. I will deceive her as little as I can, but I have no real choice. This opportunity—

"By Saints Matthew, Mark, Luke, and John, and by Holy Mary, I swear that I shall say nothing of what the Lady Gwen tells me, except to my grandfather Marselius Caesar," said Octavia. "And him only if he asks me."

"Good," said Gwen, in a normal tone. She was tired of whispering. She dropped her robe on the couch and started pulling on her clothes. "And you can tell me of Christ," she said.

After all, Gwen thought, I was raised Christian. If I have a religion, that's it. If I let the Romans convert me—I'll have to ask Rick about that. It might be useful.

Marselius Caesar's chair creaked not quite in rhythm with his pen. This letter to Lucius could not be trusted to any scribe. If he could have sent it by a bird of the air or a starman's flying machine he would have done so.

—would have seen their way clear to aiding us anyway, certainly the utter folly of Flaminius the Dotard hastened matters. He not only refused to permit the embassy to enter his claimed land, he even refused to offer them safe conduct. When the Lord Drumold heard this last, his anger was frightful.

In fact, the clan chief had nearly provoked a fight with Flaminius's patrol by the language he used about their Caesar, his habits, and all his ancestors back to the founding of Rome.

So we will have the aid of the Lord Rick, in whatever amount we may need. I still hope we will not need any. Flaminius may not be his own master; that evil message may have come from Senators and officers who fear to lose everything if he submits himself to me. It is to be hoped that these men will listen to reason after we issue a proclamation of a general pardon. I do not think the Senate will delay long in issuing it, although there is some opposition.

He started to add, "including Publius," then decided against it. Lucius had known Publius since the boy was six; he could fill in that sort of detail for himself.

Much honor is also due to the Lady Gwen. She has done good work, particularly in choosing the scribes and clerks we are sending to Drantos under the treaty. The Westerner's asking for them helped convince many of the Senate that we were not dealing with barbarians, much as the firepowder weapons helped convince the army. The Lady Gwen showed so much knowledge of scribes' work that one wonders how a woman of equestrian rank came by it.

She has also become a good friend to the Lady Octavia. This I welcome. Except for yourself, none of Octavia's teachers have been worthy of her. As she will be of an age for betrothal within no more than a year and a half, this has caused some concern.

Another sign of age—worrying about your grandchildren's fitness for marriage.
Back to what he knew best.

What we can ask for from the Westerners, is likely to be more than we need. However, we can ask for two legions of foot, one of pikes and one of archers. There will also be a force of horsemen equal to another legion, including mounted archers. We will have firepowder weapons, and the starmen will bring all of their star weapons which are fit for a long campaign.

I hope there will be no need of a long campaign. With such strength, we can stand up to Flaminius in a pitched battle with a good hope of winning it. One such victory would be enough to give us Rome, before men and wealth which will be needed for The Time is destroyed.

Let us pray for the favor of Christ and the aid of St. Michael.

> To Lucius, Freedman of this house,
> Friend to Caesar,
> Honor and Farewell.

Caius Marius Marselius Caesar.

8

Larry Warner looked up at the balloon swaying overhead and decided that it was about as inflated as it would ever be. He nodded to the man standing beside him.

"Okay, Murphy."

Ben Murphy raised both hands. "Let go the top rope! Second crew, heave away!"

Five men at the foot of one fifty-foot pole let go the first line and stepped back. At the foot of the second pole on the opposite side of the hot-air balloon, five more men started pulling. The rope slipped through a ring at the top of the first pole, then a loop at the top of the balloon, sixty feet above the ground. Finally it slipped through the ring at the top of the last pole and fell on top of the men pulling it. From the way they were laughing and cursing, Warner didn't think anyone was hurt.

He folded his arms on his chest, hoping for Murphy to give

the next order on his own. Ben would be taking the First Balloon Squadron (one balloon and about forty men) on campaign against Flaminius Caesar in another three or four ten-days. It would have been simpler for Warner to go himself, but Captain Rick's orders were strict: nobody from the University faculty into combat. Murphy and Reznick tossed for it, and Reznick won. Or had Murphy? Warner knew better than to ask.

It didn't matter much anyway. Larry Warner was happy not to be shot at. Besides, he'd been first up, the first aeronaut anywhere on Tran! That had impressed everyone, including all the girls and even Gwen Tremaine. There were rewards to be gained from heroism—

But all in all, the life of a university professor was better. Especially in this University, where the faculty was in full control.

The balloon swayed a little more with the overhead rope gone, but the men on the ground lines had it firmly under control. The overhead rope strung between the poles had held it up while the hot air from the fire under the launching platform flowed up the inflation tube underneath and filled the balloon. Warner had figured that one out himself, and was quite proud of his invention.

"Draw the neck rope!" shouted Murphy. A team of men pulled on the rope which tightened the neck of the tube hanging down from the balloon. Now the balloon looked like a gigantic mushroom, with a large misshapen head and a very short stem. Warner checked his gear and walked toward the platform. Murphy could finish the job on his own now, except for the last order to "Let go."

"Cover the fire!" The men who'd tightened the tube pulled a brass plate over the hole in the platform. Warner climbed up onto the platform as the men wrestled the observation basket on to the brass plate. When the balloon rose, it had to lift the observation basket and crew straight up. Dragging was a real danger at launch and landing times, which was why the balloon needed such a large ground crew.

But the benefits! "Your turn next, Ben," Warner called.

"Right. Sure you don't want me this time?"

"No, I'd better check things out." Not that Murphy couldn't do it, but that would be bad for Warner's image. And there was the new telegraph system, a thin wire stretching from the balloon along the tether; the only Morse operators in the University were Larry Warner and two of his crewmen, and they didn't speak English...

Warner checked the observation basket and its gear even more carefully than he'd checked his own. Today was supposed to be an endurance test, to see how long the balloon could stay up with extra ballast and fuel in place of a second man. There were extra bricks of the resin-coated straw they used for fuel when aloft tied to the netting above the basket. If sparks from the brass firepot in the floor of the basket reached them, they could be cut loose before they set the reed basket itself afire. Around the rim of the basket were hung sandbags for ballast and two skins of drinking water.

All improvised, all Warner's inventions. Well, with a little help from the others, but not much. And he'd got it all done before Gwen came back from Benevenutum.

Everything seemed to be all right. Some of the men in the Squadron believed that Warner was a wizard and the balloon was his familiar spirit, which would tell him of any negligence on their part in preparing it for the flight. He was supposed to discourage superstitions, and he would—eventually. Just now it was handy for them to think that. It was a long way down if anything went wrong.

Warner climbed into the basket and braced himself, legs spread wide and the fingers of one hand twined in the netting. The men on the ropes slacked off a little and the balloon lifted a few inches clear of the platform. Warner grinned. He had a lot of excuses for taking this flight, but one he didn't admit was simple enough. He liked it. The nearest thing to flying...

Except for the length, this flight should be almost routine. It looked like there might to too much wind up high, but here in the lee of Ben Hakon he should be safe enough. Idly he wondered who the hill had been named for.

The men who'd moved the basket and handled the overhead ropes now took their places on the handles of the winch. If Campbell had been allowed to make gears for the winch, it wouldn't have needed twelve or fifteen men. However, that was another of Captain Rick's orders—"I don't want it perfect, I want it Thursday!" So the winch needed a dozen men on the handles when the balloon was full, and the balloon itself had no rip cord or top vent. It rose or fell with the air inside it and the sheer strength of the men on the winch.

That, though, was the Mark I, and his crews were already

at work on Mark II. They might have it finished by the time Murphy took it to battle.

He made one last check. "Looking good," he called. "Let it play out some." Murphy nodded. The balloon rose about three feet above the platform, before the winch crew caught it. It *was* crude, but as long as it was the only balloon on the planet, who cared?

Warner took a deep breath and began to sing as the winch crew let the balloon rise. He'd sung on the first ascent, to keep his teeth from chattering from sheer blue funk. Some of his crew thought it was a hymn to Yatar Skyfather, and now they expected him to sing every time the balloon went up. He wondered what Murphy would do. Oh, well.

> Off we go, into the wild blue yonder,
> Flying high, into the sun....

As the platform dropped away below him, he saw Gwen standing by one of the poles, trying not to laugh. Was it the song, or his singing?

Therrit had planned to do his work while the balloon was still rising. Lord Corgarff had said this would do the most damage. However, Lord Corgarff didn't know how many men were around the winch while the balloon was going up. Therrit did not trust Lord Corgarff to pay the promised gold to his family if he was caught before he could even do the work.

So Therrit stood well back, until the balloon looked no larger than his fist held out in front of his nose. Then the men on the winch pushed a long wooden rod in under the drum, to stop its turning. The rod could be put in place and then pulled out again quickly, without anyone having to reach in under the drum and risk getting their hands broken.

More than half the drum was still covered with rope when the balloon stopped rising. Therrit realized that if he could pull out the rod, the balloon would probably start rising again, just as Lord Corgarff wanted. It would be harder to make pulling the rod out look like an accident, but if there was enough smoke no one would see him, and they would never know. The crewmen thought the balloon could talk, but Therrit knew better. Warner had told him many times.

It was too bad that Professor Warner had to die. He was a gentle master, considerate of his servants. But Warner had no gold to keep Therrit's sisters from starving. They could enter Warner's service, but the Star Lords had no understanding of what was fit for the daughters of yeoman and what work was fit only for slaves or freedwomen. He might—he might loan Therrit's sister to the Lord Elliot, as he did with his own Sara!

No. The only safety for his family was the protection of his clan. Lord Corgarff would not order this without the consent of Chief Dughuilas, and Dughuilas could protect anyone!

Therrit waited a little longer, until he saw the Lady Gwen walking back to her tent. Corgarff did not seem to care if the lady was hurt or not, but Therrit did not want to make war on women, particularly this one. She treated the sons and daughters of yeomen as if they were the children of knights.

Therrit waited so long that he became aware that Corgarff was looking at him, rather than up at the balloon like everyone else. The lord's patience must be running out. Therrit walked cautiously toward the platform, pulling a brick of *sky fire* out of his pouch. It looked like any other brick from the outside, but it was only a thin layer of straw and resin pasted over a leather lining. The leather was filled with firepowder and other things to make smoke. Therrit walked until he was within easy range of the banked-up fire under the platform. Then he tossed the brick underhanded on to the coals.

The firepowder made all the smoke he'd expected, also a noise like the time when lightning struck his father's barn and a smell like the hot spring behind the University. Everybody except Therrit was caught by surprise. All those near the platform scrambled up, and a few ran. Therrit threw in a second brick, there was more noise and smoke, and it looked like everyone was running.

He couldn't wait to see better. He ran up to the platform, drawing his knife as he did so. Having gone this far, he had to be ready to cut the rope if everything else failed.

The locking rod came out at the second pull. He saw the winch handles begin to move and jumped aside. The winch rattled, the handles whirled fast enough to break a careless man's bones, and the rope on the drum shrank. Therrit pulled away the bronze lid over the firehole, cursing as it scorched his fingers, and tossed in the last two bricks. The noises made the platform shake and the winch creak, and the smoke came up so thickly that Therrit could barely see or breathe. Choking and holding the rod out in front of him like a blind man's stick, he groped his way to the edge of the platform and jumped down to the ground.

Warner knew something was wrong when he saw the smoke swallow the platform and winch and heard the explosions. He didn't know what until the balloon suddenly started rising. Even then he was more interested than frightened. The winch getting out of control was something he'd lived through before, for a couple of minutes at least. The Balloon Squadron was a pretty good outfit, considering that he was the only man in it who'd ever heard of balloons six ten-days ago.

Then he saw the men scattering from around the winch, and more smoke billowing up. He hoped whatever was wrong didn't wreck the winch completely.

The balloon jerked sideways, like a mouse batted by a playful cat. Warner shouted heartfelt obscenities. Then he had to cling to the basket and the netting with both hands and both feet, wishing he was a monkey with a tail he could use as well.

He'd risen out of the lee of Ben Hakon into the wind. From the way the grass on the hilltop was moving, the wind must be blowing half a gale. He swore again. He should have sent somebody up to the hilltop to test the wind, or carried more ballast so that the balloon wouldn't rise—

The balloon jerked again. Now Warner felt more like a fish being played by a fisherman. A cold spray drenched him as one of the water bags burst. That would make the balloon even lighter, which right now was the last thing he needed. More jerks and Warner heard the frame of the basket creak and ropes part in the netting. If this went on much longer, the basket would rack itself apart and leave him—

Suddenly the balloon was rising again. Warner froze in the netting until it stopped for a moment, then peered over the edge. The rope was loose and someone was clinging to the free end. As Warner watched, the man dropped to the ground and lay there. The balloon shot up again. The basket still

swayed ominously, but with the rope loose the strain on it was less. Warner slipped down inside the basket and wished he could sing. Right now, Yatar Skyfather really needed propitiating! His mouth was so dry that he couldn't have sung a note with a gun pointed at him.

Therrit was slipping away from the platform when the rope came loose. His heart was pounding like a drum and he was sure that everyone was looking at him and fingering their swords.

He still stopped to watch Murphy's frantic chase after the loose end of the rope. He cheered when the star lord caught it, and groaned when he lost his grip and fell.

Murphy lay like the dead.

"You did it!" screamed a voice almost in Therrit's ear. "I saw you! Traitor!"

Therrit whirled, to see Lord Corgarff coming at him with a drawn sword. He looked wildly around, his universe crumbling. His laird, his chief, accusing him! "No, lord! Lord, you owe me protection!"

"I am chief to no traitors!" Corgarff screamed.

Therrit cursed. There was no place to run. Even so he hesitated to raise weapons against his lord—but it was that or die here. And who then to watch over his sisters?

He'd sheathed his dagger and Corgarff attacked so fast there was no time to draw it. He was still holding the locking rod from the winch. He swung frantically and the heavy rod smashed into Corgarff's sword arm. He howled and his weapon went flying.

Therrit didn't bother to pick it up. Men had heard Corgarff and were running toward him. It would be hopeless to fight. Yet—where could he run?

Was there no one to protect him? Warner might, but the Professor was high in the balloon, a dead man. Murphy? The star lord lay on the grass. He would be no help. Then who?

The Lady Gwen might protect him. Run, then, run to her and clasp her knees to beg for mercy for his family. He was a lost man, but the Lady Gwen might spare his sisters—

Gwen ran to the entrance of her tent when she heard the explosions. She was in time to see the balloon shoot up and break loose and Murphy's heroic try at catching it. She sent one of the Guardsmen off to bring Sergeant McCleve for the injured man and another to get Sergeant Elliot. He was going to be needed, if only to make her feel that she knew what she was doing until she really did. Then she turned back into the tent, to dismiss her scribe and pull on her cloak.

Thus there was only one Guardsman on duty outside the tent when Therrit ran up and threw himself at Gwen's feet. The Guardsman tried to pull him away but he clutched her knees. "Lady, lady, save me! Lord Corgarff wants my blood, but I only followed him for gold. My family will starve if they do not—"

"Wait!" said Gwen: His babbling was making it impossible for her to think. "Lord Corgarff paid you to let the balloon go?"

"Yes."

"Now he wants to kill you, to keep from talking?"

"Yes. If you save me, I will tell—"

"There's that damned dung-spawned traitor now!" came from outside the tent. Gwen jumped back and nearly fell as the man clutched her skirt.

"Let go, you fool!"

"Lord Corgarff, the Lady Gwen has—" began the Guardsman.

"The Lady Gwen will not protect a traitor, unless the High Rexja's bought her too!"

"You cannot pass, Lord—ahhhggghhh!" and the sound of steel into flesh and against bone.

The Guardsman's fidelity to his oath bought the fugitive the time to crawl under the table, the scribe the time to crawl out of the tent, and Gwen the time to pull out her pistol. She could barely hold the .45 with two hands, but she had it aimed at the door when Corgarff charged through.

The sight of a star weapon in a woman's hands stopped him for a moment. "Lady Gwen, put that away. You have drawn it in the cause of an evil—"

"I heard what you think, Corgarff," she said. After she was sure both her hands and her voice would stay steady, she went on, "I will protect this man until he has told me everything—"

Corgarff's cry was an animal's. Fortunately his first slash

was wild. His sword hacked into the tent pole. He was raising it for a cut at Gwen's head when Elliot's voice came from outside.

"Freeze, you son of a bitch!"

In desperation Corgarff whirled to slash at Elliot. Sergeant Major Elliot laughed as he jumped back out of range.

"Don't kill him!" Gwen shouted.

"No problem." Elliot's Colt blasted twice and Corgarff screamed as the slugs ploughed into his thigh and leg. He took a step forward, then started to fall. Elliot slammed the pistol alongside his head to make sure he went down all the way.

"Is it over?" Gwen asked.

"So far," Elliot said. "'Cept we might lose this one." He raised his voice. "Send for the corpsmen!"

Gwen held the tent pole to keep from falling. Elliot caught her before she brought the tent down on top of them, then led her to a chair and checked her pistol. "Miss Tremaine, you really ought to practice more with that. You had the safety on. He'd have run you through before you could fire a shot."

"Really?" Gwen started to laugh at the silliness of her own remark, then caught herself before she lost control. "Get McCleve and more Guardsmen. Make sure nobody we don't know gets near these two until we've talked to them. I mean *nobody*, Sergeant Major."

Elliot automatically snapped to attention. He knew when an officer was speaking. "Yes, Ma'am."

"Thank you. And we'll want messengers to go to the Garioch and Drantos." She swallowed. "Is there anything I've left out?"

"Not that I know of, Ma'am." He bent over Corgarff. "But this one's going to need first aid, or he'll bleed to death before McCleve gets here. Those forty-fives tear a man up some."

"All right. You stand guard. No one comes in, Sergeant. I'll try to help him."

What lay under Corgarff's bloody clothing was as bad as Gwen expected. Somehow she managed to go to work on it. After a while she found it was no harder than cutting up onions and green peppers for a homemade pizza. Maybe she was finally adapting to living in the Middle Ages. She'd have to, or spend half her time in her room and the other half being sick to her stomach.

9

This is it, Larry Warner thought. Jesus Christ. Come all the way here on a mucking flying saucer, and get killed in a hot-air balloon. Jesus H. Christ.

The balloon continued to rise. The air inside was cooling, so that it had lost part of its lift, but the balloon's slightly flattened shape gave additional lift from the updrafts. Warner huddled in the bottom of the basket while he worked this out. Eventually he got up the nerve to look over the edge at the ground below.

It was hard to judge his ground speed. He tried to estimate distances between farms as he passed over them, timing his passage with his watch as he swept across the valley below. It was difficult because there were few roads, and nothing was square. Tran was a planet of horse—and centaur—carts, not automobiles.

After several attempts he got the same result twice. He was

probably doing about thirty-five miles an hour, much faster than the best any rescue party could do. If he stayed up no more than an hour, he'd be nearly a day's ride from the University. The only hope he had for quick rescue was to come down on top of someone friendly—which wasn't very likely, because he had no control over altitude.

He could rise—a little—by dropping ballast, but as for bringing the balloon down before the hot air cooled and it lost lift—well, that was what rip panels were for, in balloons back on Earth. In theory, he could climb up the netting and slash at the cloth with a knife, to let out some of the hot air. One look at all the empty air between him and the ground cured him of the notion. He wasn't that desperate yet.

The best course looked to be letting the balloon cool naturally. He could slow its fall if necessary by dropping ballast, rather than by lighting up the fire. Meanwhile he would pull up the rope and make a big loop in the end. He hoped he remembered enough of his Boy Scout knot-tying to make one which would hold. That would give people on the ground a better hold on the rope.

Then—wait until he passed low enough over a village for the rope to reach the ground. Throw the rope out, shout to the people, and hope they would understand what he was saying. It would still take luck, but not as much as bringing the balloon down by himself. It was going to take luck to live through this. He'd have to be *very* lucky to save the balloon for the campaign.

Moving cautiously, with one hand always gripping the rigging, Warner made a complete scan around the balloon. When he looked to the north–northwest, he let out a yell which would have scared any seagulls within a half a mile. Then he took the names of most of Tran's gods in vain.

He'd completely forgotten about the Labyrinth Range, a tangle of jagged peaks and dense thickets at the head of the Saronic Gulf. They got their name because few who tried finding a path through them ever got out the other side. Sensible people preferred to go around either end of the range.

Warner wouldn't have any choice. The range was a good seventy miles from end to end, and there was no way at all to steer a free balloon. He would have to go over.

How high? One task of the University was mapping Tran; they were the only geodetic survey the planet had. He'd sent a team of locals out with a crude transit to measure mountain heights—

And if he remembered right, the Labyrinth Range was three thousand meters high.

Nine thousand feet. More than that. A lot higher than he was just now. Twice as high, maybe.

Would it be better to try to land? No. Not in this wind. Neither he nor the balloon would live through the experience. I'll just have to go over, he thought. Be still, my heart—

Tain't funny, another part of him said, but he ignored that. Better to laugh, and not think about it.

He looked down once more to be sure, and decided. The ground was already rising into the foothills of the Labyrinths. He'd have to get up to ten thousand feet and stay there for at least an hour. The Labyrinths were thirty miles across at their widest point. If he came down anywhere inside them, he'd freeze or starve to death before they found him, if anyone could be persuaded to go looking, and assuming he was lucky enough to survive landing on a glacier...

Get the rope up first. Can't dump that. Need it. Have to come down on the other side.

Which is the Pirate Lands, more or less claimed by Rome but in practice abandoned to anyone who wanted to live there. They weren't worth the troops it would take to garrison them. And beyond there are salt marshes, far too wide to cross. It's the Pirate Lands or nothing...

So. First things first. Get a fire going, then pull up the rope. He took three fire bricks from the rigging and stuffed them into the fire pot. His Zippo was filled with naptha, and hard to light, but eventually it burned, and once he had flame the bricks caught nicely. The resin in the fire bricks was extracted from something the natives called volcano-bush. It grew in patches in the forests to the south. People said that in late summer, when the bushes were full of resin, lightning striking a patch could make it go up like a bomb, acres at a time. In winter and spring the bush wasn't as resin-loaded, but there was still plenty to provide fuel for the balloon's firepot.

He had to lay on six more bricks before the balloon was rising fast enough to suit him. He was sure he'd overdone it. There was undoubtedly a long lag between making heat and getting lift. But the mountains were coming closer and closer, and it was better to be too high than too low . . .

The fire blazed hotter and hotter. Soon he had to flatten himself against the side of the basket to keep from being scorched. He hoped the firepot wouldn't crack or the basket catch fire.

At least there seemed to be plenty of wind over the Labyrinths. He saw a plume of snow trailing from one peak in his path. Unfortunately that peak was also still above him. He threw on another brick, then counted what was left of his fuel supply. About half gone. Better try dumping ballast for a change. There was also the second water bag, but everything he'd been taught said that drinking water is the *last* thing to go.

He dropped two sandbags, then the mountains were on him.

The balloon came closer to the range; then, suddenly, it began to rise, plummeting higher and swifter than Warner had ever seen.

"Updrafts!" he shouted. Of course there'd be an updraft on the windward side of the mountains. It lifted him so fast that his nose began to bleed, and his ears hurt dreadfully until he could make them pop. Even the fillings in his teeth hurt.

By noon he'd left the Labyrinths behind him, after crossing them with several thousand feet to spare. Now the problem was cold. He'd been dressed for a summer day in Tamaerthon, and the temperature up here was well below freezing. The thinner air of Tran meant the temperature dropped off faster with height. It also meant that his present altitude was the equivalent of the tops of the Alps or Rockies on Earth, high enough to make breathing hard.

"Hoo-hah," he shouted. "Mucking bastards. Join the army and see the world, they said. Hell, they said *the* world. Didn't say dogmeat about any *other* worlds. Recruiting officers. They *always* lie to you—"

There was a terrible temptation to *do something*, but he was just rational enough to know he was suffering from oxygen starvation. Better to sit still and rage at the world. Presently he began to sing "The Friggin' Falcon."

When the balloon descended to a lower altitude, Warner could think again. This time he had few choices. His fire bricks were nearly gone, and if he didn't come down here, he'd be into the salt marshes.

The cold dry air at high altitude had left him thirsty. He pulled the plug on the water bag and drank until he was clear-headed and hungry. He munched a piece of dried meat from his ration pouch and composed a mental memo, suggesting that the next *Shalnuksi* ship be asked to bring a few parachutes for the Balloon Squadron.

Now that his fingers were thawed out, he could tie a large bowline in the end of the rope. He was just in time. The balloon sank so rapidly that he knew that something would break if he hit the ground this hard. The last brick went into the fire and the last of the ballast went overboard. Then he threw the loop over the side. The ground below was forested now. If he could lasso a treetop he could pull himself down, and have something to tell Elliot besides. The sergeant could use a lariat as well as an assault rifle! He'd even roped a centaur on a bet.

Warner wasn't Elliot, but then the treetops weren't centaurs. They stayed put, and eventually Warner got lucky. The loop caught a branch and went tight. By now the balloon had lost so much lift that Warner's muscles were enough to pull it down into the trees. The minute the basket was at the level of a good stout branch, Warner grabbed it with both hands and swung himself into the tree.

The branch promptly bent under his weight, letting him dangle until he lost his grip and dropped to the branch below. It bounced him like a ping-pong ball on to the next branch, and that one let him slide down on to the ground, a drop of ten feet onto leaves and needles. Warner hit with a paratrooper's five-point roll.

The first thing he did when he got his breath back was kneel and kiss the solid ground. The second thing he did was look up.

Four bearded men looked back at him. They wore homespun breeches and leather shirts. Two carried crossbows, one a spear, and one an ax. None of them looked ready to use the weapons, but none of them looked particularly friendly either.

Warner knelt and kissed the ground again, then stood up, holding his hands out to show he bore no weapons. After a moment the man with the bushiest beard laid down his crossbow, knelt, and also kissed the ground. The others followed him. Then they all stood up. The leader pointed upward at the balloon now draped over the treetops, then at Warner. Warner nodded. The leader made what Warner recognized as one of the signs

against evil spirits, then raised his crossbow.

Warner shook his head sharply. They probably thought the balloon was a monster which had carried him off. "No," he said aloud. "Do not hurt it." He hoped they'd understand him. Most of Tran spoke dialects of the same language, but some of the dialects were pretty far apart.

"It—is yours?" asked the leader.

So he wouldn't have to conduct the discussion in sign language. "Yes. It is my sky-beast. A wizard who is my enemy cast an evil spell on it, so that it fell from the sky. I must stay with you for some days, until I can call other wizards to my aid. They will come, take off the evil spell, and reward you well if you help me."

He looked sternly at them. "They will also punish you if you do not treat me well. The beast will see everything which happens among you, and tell the other wizards."

"You have nothing to fear," said the leader. "We are of Two Springs village, we live by law." He fumbled in his pouch and brought out a cake of what looked like ground-up nuts. Warner ate half of it. There were nut shells as well as meats in the cake, but that didn't matter. They had fed him, and that made him their guest. More than unknown wizards would punish them now if they harmed him.

He turned back to the balloon, raised his arms, and recited a few Army regulations in English. Then he smiled at the men. "The beast has seen what you did, and is glad. Now let us go to your village."

"Your beast will be safe?" said one of the men.

"It will be now that it is on the ground," said Warner. Right now the last thing he wanted to do was straw-boss a gang of Pirate Land villagers into lowering his balloon from the top of a fifty-foot tree. He wanted a drink, a meal, and a girl, and not to have to think about balloons for a while.

10

"You're wearing a new perfume?" said Warner, toying with his glass. Gwen smiled and picked up the wine jug to refill it.

"Yes. Marselius Caesar sent it. He said it was a gift from the Lady Octavia."

"How is she?"

"She is well, but unhappy that I won't be coming with the army."

"I'm glad you're not going."

"I'm not," she said tartly. Warner covered himself by taking a sip from his glass and mopping his plate with a piece of bread.

It was frustrating. She'd obviously laid on this dinner and put on the blue gown to welcome him. She looked good, she smelled good, and he was damned sure she'd feel good if he got close enough. So far though, that blue gown might have been armor plate.

Then she giggled.

"Yes?" he prompted.

"I was thinking about that girl, the one on the second night."

Warner was puzzled for a moment. "Oh. You mean the one who was afraid the sky-beast could see us."

"Yes. Did she really think it would tell tales to the other wizards?"

"I don't think it was the other wizards she was worried about. I think she was afraid the Great Balloon God was going to tell her husband."

"Oh." She giggled again.

He wondered what had gotten into Gwen, other than more wine than usual. She was curious about everything he'd done in Two Springs village, including the girls he'd bedded. You'd have thought she'd be jealous of that.

"You know, I think I should have seen this before," she said. "The people really think a balloon is magical. Even some of the people around the University, who can see that it's a machine. Out in the villages, if someone comes in a balloon, they'll think he's a wizard. They'll listen to what he says! We can start teaching them all the things they won't learn otherwise!"

Warner stared. It made a weird kind of sense. If the teaching squads went out with a balloon, they'd get a lot more attention. People wouldn't sit around waiting for Old MacDonald or the village granny to try the star knowledge. It might not even have to be a man-carrying balloon, either. That would save a lot of cloth and—

"The *surinomaz* processing!" Gwen looked ready to jump out of her chair. "We can start in that village where the mid-wives know how to make *surinomaz* into a medicine. If they'll teach the wizards what they know, we can prove that the *surinomaz* is useful. People will start *wanting* to grow it. Larry, you may have just saved a whole planet!"

Warner got up and went around the table. "Gwen, you're as smart as you are beautiful. You thought of what to do with the balloons. I just went along for the ride, so to speak."

She stood up and kissed him on the cheek. "Larry, you're a lot braver than you think you are."

Warner put his arms around her and bent to kiss her lips. For a moment he thought she would turn away. Then her face came up and their lips met. Hers trembled, then opened. He tightened his grip. Small fireworks started to go off in various parts of his body.

He held her closely, then let his hands wander downwards.

"Don't."

"Don't what?"

She sighed. "Maybe I mean 'do.' It's been a long time. But just for the moment, I'd like to be held, and not have to think about what happens next."

"Suits me." He held her, and they stood that way for a while.

This could be damn serious, Warner thought. She's one hell of a girl. Nobody like her. And we've done pretty well, running this place. Is it time Larry Warner settled down?

To what? Fidelity? She'd want that. More'n the local girls would. Monogamy, too. And she knows I'm no damned wizard. But it wouldn't be so bad, and besides, it don't have to be decided now. Nobody's said anything about forever, just tonight . . .

He bent to kiss her again.

Crash! Wood slammed against stone and metal rang.

"Dog!"

An angry voice made more echoes in the room. Something struck Larry Warner's head. A hard blow, that left a ringing in his ears. Gwen screamed.

Warner fell to the floor as if unconscious. The instant he was down he snap-rolled under the table, then rolled again to get behind it. As he stood he drew his Walther .380 automatic, wishing it were the .45 hanging by the door with his jacket. The Walther would just have to do. By the time he was back on his feet he had spread his legs and was holding the piece in both hands, his eye sighting down the barrel at the kilted figure in the room—

"Larry! No!" Gwen shouted. "No!" She dashed across the room and into Warner's line of fire.

He'd almost squeezed off the round! He jerked the piece upwards to point at the ceiling, and from pure rage and frustration he fired. The shot sounded very loud in the enclosed room.

"Larry!" Gwen screamed again. Then she saw where the pistol was pointed.

"Move!" Warner commanded. "No son of a bitch comes bustin' in on me! I'll blow the bastard away—" He stopped shouting as he realized who the intruder was. "Caradoc?"

The archer captain had been in command of the search party that found Warner. He'd stayed behind to see that the balloon was safely loaded on the pack animals. And, Warner realized, he'd not only finished that task in record time, he must have ridden like hell to get here. Why? To see Gwen. And maybe jealous of Warner, too.

Now he stood there defiantly. "If you have honor, you will allow me a weapon," Caradoc said. "You may have your star weapons, and I my bow..."

Warner laughed. *"You* talk about honor, Boy Scout. Not me. I fight for pay. And you're dead."

"Larry, you can't." Gwen wasn't shouting any longer.

"Why not?"

"Captain Galloway will have you shot, that's why."

"I need no woman to argue for my life!" Caradoc shouted.

"You need something you haven't got," Warner said. "You also need to explain how you got in here."

"Miss Tremaine!" The shout came from the hall.

"Jesus, that's Elliot," Warner said. He raised his voice. "In here, Sergeant Major."

Elliot came in. His .45 was cocked and ready. He looked at Warner, then at Caradoc. "Okay, Professor, what's happening?"

"Nothing," Gwen said. "It's nothing at all. Please leave."

"Not friggin' likely."

"It's okay, Sarge," Warner said. "We were showin' Captain Caradoc a couple of moves, and maybe it got out of hand. I let a round go into the ceiling."

Elliot looked suspiciously at them. "Sure that's all?"

"Yeah."

"It's all right," Gwen said.

"Okay, if you say so." He snapped on the safety and holstered his pistol. "If you say so."

Warner waited until Elliot was gone before he spoke again. "I'm still waiting to know how you got in here, Captain," he said finally. "Past the guards. My guards. They weren't supposed to let anyone in here, not anyone at all. But I guess I know, don't I? You had them betray their trust. You being their commander and all, you could do that. So now you just tell me why I shouldn't have them and you both up on charges?"

For the first time Caradoc looked worried. "There is no reason," he said finally. "You are correct. But the men are not at fault."

"Larry—"

"Yes, my lady?"

"Larry, don't do that. He—had a right to think he could come here."

"I see."

"I have said it already," Caradoc said. "I will not listen more to—"

He's going to try it, Warner thought. He'll come for me. He's one of those, one of the berserker types and he'll dive for the gun. When he does, it'll be chancy. A .380 just isn't that much slug. No fancy shooting, just empty the damn piece into him and take my chances after that. Should work.

But damn all, I don't really want to kill him—

Abruptly Warner put the pistol in his pocket.

"What are you doing?" Caradoc demanded. "Have you discovered honor, or—"

"Main thing is, I'm unarmed," Warner said. "And you, my friend, aren't going to try unarmed combat with me. You've seen me practicing."

Caradoc fingered his sword. "Get a weapon. Any weapon," he said. "It may be said that Caradoc son of Cadaric is a fool. It will never be said that he slew an unarmed man."

"Nobody's going to be slain," Warner said. "Gwen, would you please leave us?" He changed to English. "I got some talking to do with Muscles here."

"You're sure it's all right?"

"Yeah, no problems now."

"I want promises from both of you. That you won't fight," she said. She looked thoroughly miserable.

"Sure," Warner said.

"I swear I will not draw weapons against this man except on a field of honor with all due ceremony," Caradoc said.

"Good enough for me," Warner said. He eyed Caradoc thoughtfully. I didn't promise I wouldn't draw weapons if he gets physical. "Gwen?"

"Oh, all right." She paused in the door. "I—I'm really sorry."

"Have a seat," Warner said. He indicated the table. "There's wine and glasses. Have some."

"You make free with the lady's table. As if—as if it is *your* table."

"No," Warner said. "That is not the way of it. But understand that the Lady Gwen and I are from the same lands. I have known her for many years. I know she would wish us to make ourselves comfortable."

Caradoc went to the table and sat. He waited until Warner had poured for both of them, then drained his glass in one gulp. "It is not finished," he said finally.

"Maybe it is," Warner said.

"You have sometimes acted as a friend," Caradoc said. He stared moodily into his empty wine glass. "And I think I have been a fool."

"We all are, sometimes," Warner said.

Caradoc took in a deep breath. "Lord Warner," he said formally. "What is the Lady Gwen to you?"

"Why is that your business?"

"Perhaps it is not. And yet—If she has been more than a friend, without you promising a lawful marriage, I will have your blood. No, hear me out," he said, raising a hand as Warner opened his mouth to reply.

"I know that if I kill you, the Lord Eqeta Rick will have my head. You are worth ten of me, in his plans for facing The Time. Perhaps he is even right to value you so highly.

"I do know this, however. No lord can ask me to stand by like a capon, while you play the cock with Gwen. I love her. If she does not love me, then let her say so and she can be free to bed any man she wishes. Until she speaks her mind, beware of my sword."

Warner nodded. Nobly said, he thought. Corny, but noble. Larry me lad, you didn't think it through. Old Musclebound here isn't just a rival for a quick roll in the hay. He wants to marry the girl.

Come to that, you were thinking about it too—

That was when she was right here, and we were about to go in there.

He means it all. He'll challenge me if he thinks I've wronged her. And what the hell, I might not win. He's good with a sword, and better with that bow. Warner shuddered at the thought of a belly wound. And suppose I win? Captain Galloway would have my hide. And Caradoc's got relatives and they'll all want my blood. He's sure as hell got more relatives than I have rounds. Sooner or later one of them will get me. Unless Captain Rick buys off Caradoc's family. He might do that, and then lock me in some castle tower and let me have a girl once in a while if I'm a good little wizard...

What was it Samuel Johnson said about sex? "The expense is damnable, the position is ridiculous, and the pleasure is fleeting." Yep. Just now I can sympathize.

"You've no horns from me," Warner said. "My word on it."

The look of relief on Caradoc's face made Warner glad he'd said it. Hell, Gwen was all right, but there were other girls, and Jesus, the archer seems like he's really in love with her.

Warner poured more wine for both of them. "Caradoc, I like Gwen. I like her a lot. She's smart and pretty and I can talk about a lot of things with her I can't talk about with anyone else. I don't love her. She doesn't love me. If there is anyone she loves besides her dead husband, it's you." He hoped that wasn't laying it on too thick.

"Nothing has happened between us that you need to worry

about. Nothing will, either. If you get her to marry you, I'll dance at the wedding and take your kids up in my balloon."

Caradoc's face twisted. He was trying to talk, but nothing happened.

"You mean that—" Caradoc said finally.

"Sure do."

"But—" Caradoc sighed. "And yet it is too late."

"Why in the name of Yatar's pissoir is it too late?"

"I have betrayed my trust—"

"Not by me," Warner said. "If anybody has you on charges for that, it'll be the lady." He laughed. "Go to her, you Yatar-damned idiot!"

Gwen sat in the chair by her bed, her face buried in her hands. She felt frightened, ashamed, and guilty all at once, and she wasn't sure which was the worst.

She'd done wrong by her own standards, never mind those of Tran. She'd as good as played the tease with Larry Warner, and that was something she always tried not to do. Usually she succeeded too, particularly when she liked the man as much as she did Larry. She'd hurt Caradoc even worse, and more stupidly. She'd *never* played off one man against another. Nobody deserved that, not even some of the real turkeys she'd met the summer she worked as a secretary. Certainly Caradoc didn't.

So much for her own standards. She'd done an even worse job by the standards of Tran, and right now they were what really counted. A woman was a wife, daughter, or mother of some man on this planet. She could also be a widow for a while, but her time for that was running out. Even if it wasn't, being a widow didn't give her the right to play around after a respectable man had made an offer of honorable marriage. Noblewomen here had more rights than she'd expected, but this wasn't one of them.

If she went on this way, she would soon be considered to have lost her rank. She would no longer have a chance for an honorable marriage. Instead, she'd be getting one proposition after another, none of them honorable. If she accepted, she'd be hardly better than a common prostitute. If she refused, she'd need Rick's protection from the angry man, and Tylara might not let him give it.

I could retreat. Be something like an abbess of the University.

The thought almost made her laugh. She wasn't likely to take any vows of celibacy, or even pretend to have. And without that, the University might be wrecked and her own life would certainly be miserable.

So would Caradoc, the man who loved her.

Well, ducks, said the voice in her mind. It's like this. You can't be your own woman here.

Tell me something I don't know.

All right, but if you can't be your own woman, what about being the woman of the best man around?

Can I get him?

There was a knock on her door.

Maybe you've got him, she thought. She knew what she'd say if that were him—

Caradoc came in, kicked the door shut, and promptly knelt. Everything she'd planned to say went right out of her mind. For a man to kneel to a woman was to place himself totally at her mercy. He would listen to any insult from her, carry out any command, abandon kin or honor or life itself at her word. He was giving her absolute power over him, trusting that she would not abuse it.

He started to talk when she wound her fingers into his hair. She didn't remember most of what he said, because she was trying too hard not to cry. All she remembered was a phrase about "my kin are beginning to wonder where my wits have gone."

"Caradoc," she said, and repeated it until he looked up.

"Yes, my lady."

"No lady. Just Gwen." She took a deep breath. "Caradoc, you know they never found my husband's body, after the battle where he was killed."

"Yes."

"That is why I have not felt free to take another husband. I have not been sure that he was dead."

"But—more than a year?"

"Caradoc, he was—so full of life. Like you. If you died

but no one found your body, how long would your kin go on wondering about you?"

He smiled for the first time. "Quite a while, I think. Particularly my aunt, who is sure I am doomed for hanging."

"It is the same for my husband. I have not until now been ready to think of another man."

The smile faded. "But—now?"

"I am ready."

Then she did cry. Fortunately Caradoc was there, with his

arms around her and a shoulder for her to cry on, even if it was clothed in muddy sweat-fouled wool. Being in his arms felt so comfortable that before long she knew that if he led her to the bed she would go happily.

"No."

"No what?"

"No, I shall not ask for my betrothal rights tonight, or until I return from the war."

"But—you might not return."

"All the more reason for us to sleep apart until we know my fate. You are the mother of one child who will never see his father. Do you want to be the mother of a second?"

He was right, of course. But—"The priests of Yatar are said to know—"

"I will let no priest tell me when I may bed my wife!" He kissed her. "It will be enough to ride against Flaminius as your betrothed husband. My kin will swear to guard you if I do not return, or I will know why!"

Ah. This alliance made sense, more than any other. There was no man on Tran to whom Tylara owed more. While Gwen was unmarried Tylara could object to Rick working at the University; but Tylara do Tamaerthon wouldn't risk offending the man who'd rescued her from Sarakos.

Even if Caradoc were killed—no. I won't think of that.

And Les? Your baby's father?

But Les was a long way off, and Caradoc was here; and Gwen had been lonely a long time. Too long. She drew in a deep breath. "Very well. I accept it as you wish."

"Good. Now you can help me take a bath. Either that, or put me in the cellar so that my stink will kill the rats!"

11

Dughuilas dropped a handful of coins on the table without counting them, drew his cloak over his shoulders, and stepped out into the second-floor hallway. He did not look back. The girl was hardly worth it, and certainly not worth more than a fraction of the price the mistress of the house asked.

There must be something to be said for her, of course. Otherwise she wouldn't have been whoring long enough to have a maid of her own. The maid was a little blonde who would have been lovely but for her broken nose. Probably a war orphan, and Dughuilas suspected she'd have been more interesting than her mistress. However, old Echenia wouldn't let such things go on in her house, and that was an end to it.

Dughuilas tasted sour bile. The war would begin in less than a ten-day, and it was wrong. Far wiser to let the Romans tear each other like hungry stoats in a cage. Why couldn't

Drumold understand that? Fascinated by that warlock son-in-law, the upstart.

And I must follow him! A coward, who has never proved himself in battle. Even in the Roman battle—yes, yes a great victory for the Lord Rick—even there he avoided combat. He raced for the pikemen rather than falling upon the Romans like a man!

Dughuilas shuddered at that memory. The Lord Rick shamed him before a whole army, firing his star weapon to startle Dughuilas and nearly bringing him off his horse. He'd felt fear—real fear—and of Rick, a man whose blood would turn to water if he ever got within sword's reach of a proper battle. He ruled from Tylara's bed, not from the saddle, and what sort of chief was that for a man to follow?

At least they'd had a scare at the University over the sky-machine! Whatever Corgarff might have said under torture, it shouldn't be enough to allow a trial of Dughuilas before the other clan chiefs. At worst, he could demand right of trial by combat against his accuser, and since that would be Lord Rick or perhaps Drumold, neither of them his match—

Something struck Dughuilas hard in the side of the neck. It hurt like a rat bite, and when he put his hand up to the pain he felt blood trickling and the tip of a dart. Some child's prank with a crossbow. Curse Madam Echenia, she couldn't keep order in her own house! She'd get no more custom from him or his clansmen.

He took another downward step, but unaccountably his foot came down on empty air. He fell forward, swallowing a shout and throwing his arms out to break his fall. He didn't want anyone to see his clumsiness.

Pain shot up his arms and he didn't quite protect his head. He tasted blood where a broken tooth had gashed his tongue, but somehow it didn't hurt as much as he'd expected. In fact, nothing felt quite normal any more. His tongue seemed thick and swollen, filling his mouth. Now he tried to shout, but only a croak came out.

Poison.

Poison on the dart.

The High Rexja's men, a plot to ruin Tamaerthon! He had to live, to warn Drumold before it was too late—or could it be—

He couldn't finish the thought. He rolled over to draw his

dagger, but fell heavily on his back, his arms unwilling to obey. Above him the light from the candle on the stair landing shone on blonde hair. Another shape bent over him, and hands fumbled at his purse and sword. Dimly, as if from the bottom of a well, he heard leather tear and thongs snap.

Then a small hand in a glove clamped down over his mouth. He tried to bite, got a mouthful of leather, felt his stomach heave. Something cold struck him in the eye and he floated away on the pain until it and everything else ended.

"The dagger in the eye went straight into Dughuilas's brain," said Tylara. "Instant death. His killers took his purse, sword, and boots. They must have been well away before anyone found the body."

"Is it known who did it?" asked Rick, as his head popped out from the fur chamber robe. The messenger with the news of Dughuilas's death had arrived as he and Tylara were getting ready for bed.

"The maid to one of the women of the house has disappeared," said Tylara. "She may have been working with the killers, or she may have been slain as well. She was only a half-grown girl, so she could hardly have done the work herself.

"Beyond that, who knows? We know that both the High Rexja and Flaminius have spies among us. Dughuilas was a champion and clan leader, a bannerman. But more like, it was some enemy. He had enough, and all knew how he spent his nights before going to war."

She says the right words, but she does not seem upset, Rick thought. One of our officers dead . . . a man I never liked. "He was an important leader, and his clan will demand blood," Rick said. "A proven captain in war—"

Tylara stared. "A proven captain in the kind of war we used to fight! The kind of war which would have destroyed us a year ago. For the kind of war you have taught us, the fewer like Dughuilas we have, the better."

"Perhaps, up to a point. But I cannot be everywhere at once—"

"The more reason for not having Dughuilas in any of the places where you are not."

"Are you then glad that he is dead?" Rick demanded.

"I am not as unhappy as you seem to be. Why, I cannot understand. He was no friend to you or your cause."

Ah, but you do understand, my love. Don't you? "He was yet a brave man. A proven leader, a man of courage . . . and if we seem to care little for finding the killers, people may wonder why. You say Dughuilas had enemies. This is true. He also had fellow clansmen, who will be at my back on campaign."

"The Guardsmen can keep watch."

"How many of Clan Calder can we afford to kill?"

"None. But I doubt we must kill any. Dughuilas's killers will be found."

"And if they are not?" Rick asked.

She shrugged. "It is in the hands of Yatar." She wriggled into the bed and pulled the covers about her. The bed was large, so that there remained a little distance between her and Rick. "Vothan One-eye has done us no ill turn by this."

"Exactly what everyone will be saying. He was our enemy, and he is dead. It is not much of a secret that Dughuilas is suspected of planning the balloon accident."

"It is also not much of a secret that Dughuilas has been the leader in half of what the knights and bheromen have done against you. Do you care so little for your plans that you will fret over the death of one of their worst enemies?"

"I do not. But there are honorable and dishonorable ways—"

She looked ready to spit on the floor, or even in his face. "You are not the only judge of honor here. I also have to judge what honor demands, for us and for our plans and for our children. Have you forgotten that? Or was André Parsons perhaps right? Are you too soft toward enemies to live long among us?"

"Enough!" Rick leaped from the bed. "I will go to my rooms. I have never laid hands on you, but by Christ—" He stalked toward the door, then stopped and turned. "I've lived longer here than Parsons," he said. "But then perhaps this is because I'm a coward. Go on, you can say that. Everyone else has."

He fumbled with the bolts of the heavy door. Can't even make a decent exit, he thought. Crap.

"My love." She stood next to him, and her face held grief. "My love. Forgive me." He gently gathered her into his arms and held her while she cried into the fur of his robe. Her hair had its old silky springiness back, now that she'd completely recovered from Isobel's birth.

"Forgive me, my love," she said finally. "Nor I, nor anyone doubts your courage or your honor. Only you. You have doubts enough for all of us, foolish doubts, for you are the bravest man I have ever known."

"Not likely—"

"Enough for me, then. Now come to bed. How can we let a man like Dughuilas ruin our last nights together? Come to bed, my love . . ."

Later, after they had made love, he woke and lay sleepless. In a few days he would lead an army to war. Vothan One-eye would be loose in the land again. And how many soldiers have told themselves that what they do is right? All of them?

Now I've got to fight, and if I'm killed, will any of my plans be carried out? I think I'm indispensable. Necessary. Have to stay alive or no one will. Easy thing to talk yourself into. Easiest thing in the world.

Reasonable. Makes sense. Hah! The man who wondered if he was a coward because he'd gone out for track instead of football in college still lurked inside the Eqeta of Chelm. Not very far inside, at times like these.

I can change what they think. I can prove myself. If I don't—

Dundee. John Graham of Claverhouse, Viscount Dundee, the only man since the Bruce to unite the Highlanders; the man who might have kept Scotland independent of England and the Stuarts on its throne. He'd known he was indispensable. So had the chiefs.

But at Killiecrankie, Dundee personally led the army. "Once," he promised his allies. "Once only. But until they know I am worthy to lead them, I cannot lead them where we must go."

And he'd fallen at Killiecrankie, ending the Highlander cause . . .

I have to win their respect. How, I don't know. But I have to do something . . . with Dughuilas dead by assassins it's even more necessary. Reasons of state. And I have to live with myself as well.

She stirred slightly, and he covered her bare arm, resisting an impulse to waken her and lose himself in her. Then he stared at the ceiling again.

PART THREE

Angels
and
Ministers
of
Grace

12

"Pass in review!"

Drums thundered and pipes skirled as the massed forces of Rick's army marched across the parade ground.

"Eyes—RIGHT!"

The First Pike Regiment marched past, their pikes held aslant, the regimental banner dipped in homage to Rick and the others on the reviewing stand. The banner held three battle streamers; one, Sentinius, might be an embarrassment under the circumstances, but most of Rick's units had been there and were proud of it.

He glanced to his right where Publius stood at attention, but gained no clue as to what the Roman was thinking. Publius was an enigma; his manners were perfect when in public with Rick, but spies said he was given to cursing the barbarians whenever there was the slightest reason. He was also interested in women, and his success as a Don Juan impressed even the lustiest of Tamaerthan lords.

And what, Rick wondered, must Bishop Arrhenius think of his Emperor-to-be? The Roman Christian Church seemed considerably less preoccupied with chastity than did its counterpart on Earth, but even so there *was* the Sixth Commandment . . . More to the point, though, what did His Lordship think of all these pagan allies? Whatever he thought, he said nothing. He stood next to Publius, splendid in his cope and mitre; and if he longed to go make converts among Rick's army, he showed no signs of it.

Second Pikes marched past, then Third and Fourth. They kept their lines straight enough, although they were not expert at parade ground formations. Rick wondered again what impression he was making on the Roman officers. His army was hardly uniform; it seemed that no two men wore the same equipment. Some had breastplates, some mail byrnies. Some had Roman helmets, others had modified captured Roman equipment until it was hardly recognizable; some men wore leather jerkins and no armor at all. None had a lot; the pikes were supposed to be lightly armed, able to march hard and fast, then fight for a long time. Rich knew their value; but would these haughty Roman officers understand?

"Present—Arms! Eyes—RIGHT!" Battalion guide—on banners rose high, then snapped downward to the salute. There was another thunder of drums, then fifty pipers; and finally the archers.

Rick saw Publius nod sagely as they went by. They were impressive enough even to look at, their long bows held at high port, and over their backs quivers filled with grey gull-feathered arrows a clothyard long, tipped with a deadly bodkin point that would penetrate armor at short ranges, and kill a horse at two hundred paces and more. There were never enough archers; it took years to train them, years spent at the archery butts when you might be doing something more lucrative. Many wealthy enough to become archers would not; they considered themselves part of the chivalry of Tamaerthon, and learned to ride and fight with lance, usually neglecting the art of the bow. Most of the archers were sons of yeomen and freeholders, the closest thing to a middle class Tamaerthon had.

The archers wore kilts of bright colors, and colored shirts, and many had jewelry, particularly bracelets. They'd fared well in Rick's previous battles, and being lightly armed and mobile they'd been able to get extra loot despite Rick's orders about sharing the booty.

Even the Romans appreciated their value; although Rick suspected that Publius did not understand the value of combined arms, cavalry, pikes, and archers fighting together as a unit, each covering the others' weaknesses.

Behind the archers came Tamaerthon's knights. They were impressive enough in their haughty ways, but they were not as well mounted as Drantos knights and bheromen—certainly not as well as the Roman heavy cavalry, the splendid cataphracti who'd once dominated most of this continent. Their armor wasn't as good, either; the chivalry of Tamaerthon couldn't really take its place in the main battle line. With training they could make good scouts. He'd organized about three hundred of them into a Hussar Regiment. The rest had too much pride for that.

"You have brought mostly Tamaerthan troops," Publius said. "I see few enough of the chivalry of Drantos."

"True, my lord," Rick said. "I saw little need for more heavy cavalry. Your legions should suffice for that. Instead, the Lord Protector chose to send auxiliary troops. Light infantry and cavalry. And foragers, and wagons, and siege engineers. We will have trouble enough feeding this army as it is; why add to that trouble?"

Publius frowned. "It is the cataphracti who decide battles," he said. "Others can be useful, but the art of war consists of having heavy cavalry in the right place and using them well."

So far it does, Rick thought. I hope to change that . . . "Aye, my lord. But the chivalry of Drantos can hardly match your legionaries. It would seem a worthless exercise to bring them when we have more need of wagons and transport."

And I can just hear Drumold grinding his teeth at that one, Rick thought. He knows his cavalrymen are no match for Romans, not even one-on-one— certainly not in unit engagements.

"You honor us," Publius said. "But—I see few enough soldiers here—"

Fewer than these defeated one of your legions, Rick thought. And did it in their first battle. Now they've got pride, and they *know* they can stand up to a Roman charge . . .

The Tamaerthan Hussars trotted by. Their nominal colonel-

in-chief was Tylara; today they were led by Teuthras, one of her cousins. Tylara, after many protests, had seen the necessity of having someone completely trustworthy to hold Castle Dravan, their home. Rick sent her with most of the mercenaries, their ammunition, and weapons; the weapons were under guard of Tamaerthan Mounted Archers, and there were equal numbers of loyal Drantos and Tamaerthan troops with her. Rick had no real doubts that the dozen mercs he sent with her would remain loyal—but there was no point in tempting them.

Behind the light cavalry came engineers with siege engines, including portable ballistae and catapulta—and wagonloads of their ammunition, clay pots filled with gunpowder and potshard shrapnel.

And finally the mercs: Sergeant Major Elliot, Corporal Bisso, and a dozen troopers in camouflage coveralls and web belts, carrying rifles and grenades.

"We have brought enough, I think," Rick told Publius. "Those men alone can win any battle we might fight. Each holds a thousand men's lives in his hand."

"That is still not all of Flaminius's army."

"If you saw a thousand of your men die, suddenly and violently, for no reason you could see, while the enemy was yet a mile away, would that not be decisive?" Rick asked gently.

Publius shuddered. "Indeed."

And you're wondering how much of that to believe, aren't you? Well, you'll find out soon enough.

They were five days march into territory claimed by Flaminius. There had been no battles; only an endless series of minor crises, decisions to be made, looters to be punished—

"We come as liberators and allies, not as thieves and enemies!" Rick had thundered to his army; but if the military police weren't watching, the soldiers would take anything they could carry. Chickens, pigs, sheep, cattle; it didn't matter, if it were edible they'd soon have it.

At least they weren't setting fire to things; and after Rick hanged two men, the rapes stopped. Of course there were the ambiguous cases, where the girl's relatives claimed rape while the trooper claimed seduction; those had to be settled as they came up, generally in favor of the trooper if he had half a story. "Nobody ever got raped in an upper bunk," Rick remembered as a judgment of an American military court; if the girl didn't appear abused, the same principles applied here.

They rode on. Toward evening, Corporal Mason came in, followed by a score of his Mounted-Archer MP's. "More trouble, Captain," he said in English.

"How?" Rick asked wearily.

"Clan Calder types. They're still talking."

Dughuilas's clan. Rick could guess what they were saying. That the forces of Tamaerthon were led by a coward, a man who'd struck their clan chief in battle, but had never faced an enemy man to man.

"Anyone in particular?" Rick asked.

"No sir. I kept an eye on Dwyfyd, but it don't seem to be him."

Dwyfyd was Dughuilas's eldest son; now he had the name Dughuilas as well, although not everyone used it yet. They would, eventually; for the moment there was talk about this twenty-year-old who'd inherited the leadership of one of the largest clans. He was a good friend to Tylara's brother Balquhain, which might help, and then again might not.

"No suggestions as to who killed Chief Dughuilas?" Rick asked.

Mason shook his head. "Most reckon that a man who goes to whorehouses often enough is eventually gonna get something he didn't want."

"Too right."

"Here come the Hussars," Mason said. "I'll go—"

"No, stick around for the report."

"Okay, if you say so."

The light cavalry officers rode in. Today the force had been headed by Balquhain, Teuthras, and Drumold himself.

"Hail, Mac Clallan Muir," Rick said formally.

"Hail, son-in-law."

"Any sign of Marselius?"

"None. Nothing but enemies. Enough of those. Skirmishers, raiders, light cavalrymen—"

"We drove them off easily enough," Balquhain said.

"At the cost of seven troopers," Drumold said. "That was no' well done, boy."

"I am no boy," Balquhain protested. "And since what hour has Mac Clallan Muir counseled retreat when we have not yet fought? We drove them away, and we killed nearly a score. A small victory—but it was victory."

"Headstrong, headstrong," Drumold said. "Lad, lad, do you not yet realize, the important thing is to win the battle. Not these tiny fights that are no more than tournaments! They do us nae good at all. Is this not so, Lord Rick?"

"We need all the light cavalrymen we have," Rick said slowly. "And we need information more than small victories . . ."

"It is no surprise that *you* would say that," a young officer said.

"Tethryn!" Drumold said sharply.

Tethryn. Dwyfyd's youngest brother, another young lordling of Clan Calder.

"That was not well said," Balquhain said. "The Lord Rick has strange ways, but he wins victories . . ."

"Men who fight *win* victories," Tethryn said. "Wizards have other ways." He wheeled and rode away.

Rick rode with Drumold back to his camp after they had supper with Publius. They rode in silence for a while through a light drizzle. Drumold had sent their guards a few lengths away so they could talk without being overheard, but then he said nothing for a long time.

Finally he drew closer. "Did my daughter put some new worm in your guts, Rick? Or is it the old one eating at you?"

"The old one. They're all certain I'm a coward. I have to show them. But how?"

"You've no need, lad. We know—"

"You, perhaps." And perhaps not. "Not the others. I've got to do something. But I can't get within twenty stadia of the fighting!"

"You'll no' be so far from battle when we meet Flaminius."

"By then it could be too late."

The older man flicked something invisible from his horse's mane. "I think it is eating you more than usual," he said. "Doubtless the affair of Dughuilas has provoked more talk than usual, and you hear it. Or—has my daughter been at you? If so, thrash her. I'll no' say a word against you or let one be said."

Rick sighed. "And how long before Tylara repaid me with usury? It is no light thing, to lay hands on your daughter."

"Aye. I have cause to know," Drumold said pensively. "Lad, you are concerned about more than this."

"Yes. We received word from Marselius today. He marches from the north—on the east side of the River Pydnae. We have yet to reach that river. If Flaminius can cut us off—"

"Perhaps it will be that Marselius will come upon him first."

"That, too, concerns me. Mostly, though, we're getting deeper and deeper into the Empire—I'd not want to face the whole of Flaminius's strength unaided."

"Nor I. Even with your star weapons."

"They might be enough. They might not be." Rick sighed. "Converging columns is a tricky enough war plan when you have good communications. It can be disaster without. We're inviting defeat in detail—"

"A phrase I know not," Drumold said.

"Military strategic term. If you can divide your enemy into small forces and fight them one at a time—"

"Ah."

"And that's what we invite," Rick said.

"Do you think Marselius has played us false?" Drumold demanded.

"No. He has no reason to. And we have his son hostage, too." Rick laughed. "Actually, nothing has gone wrong, my old friend. We are well within the time limits we set."

"And yet you fash yourself—"

"Yes."

"I see." Drumold rode in silence for a few moments. "You wish to find Flaminius's army, and Marselius. And you wish to force a crossing of this river." Drumold looked thoughtful, then grinned. "I think I shall wake up with a fever tomorrow morning."

"A fever?"

"Aye. A light fever, of the sort which keeps me from riding with the scouts. I shall stay back with the main body, to do what you have done here. *You* can lead the scouts in my place, and no one will spend a moment wondering why."

With any luck at all, there'd be at least one good fight with Flaminius's patrols. The Emperor couldn't simply go on giving ground forever. There might be a stiff fight at the river . . .

I'll be at the head of the army, Rick thought. For a few

days, anyway. Lead from in front. Yeah.

Idiot. You'll get yourself killed, and there's no one able to extract your forces out of this trap. Nobody but you. And without this army, Tamaerthon is finished. The imperial slave masters will be in the Garioch. Your friends, relatives, sold into slavery because you had to prove yourself. You're brave enough, now stop trying to—

Shut up! You talked me into track because it was sensible. All my life I do what's sensible. This time I'm going to lead my troops to battle, and that's that!

Only—there's Tylara to think of. She'll find out, and ask why I've risked myself when I didn't have to.

"And if my daughter says aye about it, send her to me," Drumold said. "She may now be so great a lady that she will say aught to her husband—but let us see what she says to her father, who remembers her a naked babe making puddles in his lap."

13

Rain fell lightly all through the day. The cavalry troopers didn't want to ride out in that. After all, the Roman cavalry wouldn't be out either.

Their reluctance was mostly for show, Rick found. And they were flattered that Lord Rick, the Commander-in-Chief, was riding with them. But the rain continued, so that he could hardly see the men to either side of him, and they made no contact with the enemy.

And the next day, messengers arrived at dawn. Marselius was indeed across the River Pydnae, marching south through the low hills to the east of the river. Directly ahead of Rick lay more hills and thin forests, good territory for battle. North and east, though, were swamps; if the two armies were to link up, they'd have to do so east of the river.

Where was Flaminius? His generals could read maps as well as Rick . . .

"Mount up!" Rick ordered. "We ride hard for the bridge. I want a mixed force of pikes and archers across that river before nightfall."

The sky was grey with low-hanging clouds. The horses picked their way cautiously over muddy patches as the scouts rode out across fields to either side of the hard-packed dirt road. Rick led two hundred Hussars, plus Caradoc with twenty Guardsmen and Elliot with two other mercs.

They'd covered about seven kilometers when a Guardsman from the point squad rode back.

"Fresh dung, my lord. Horses, with a few centaurs."

"Hmm. How shod?"

"Iron shod," the scout reported.

That meant cavalry. Roman farmers didn't usually bother. Time to mark up a map. One thing about this campaign, he had decent maps, done by Roman scribes. The enemy might surprise him, but the terrain wouldn't—at least not too much. The scale of the maps did leave something to be desired: the little clearing ahead wasn't marked. Not far beyond was the river, with its convenient bridge. Not far to go at all—

Rick rode to the center of the clearing, then reined in and held up his hand for a halt. The well-used dirt road ran across the clearing and into the woods on the other side.

He'd just got out the map—

"Ho! Look out, godammit!" someone shouted from behind him. There were three pistol shots, close together, then the shouts of his troops mingled with Roman battle cries.

Rick stuffed the map hurriedly into his saddle bag and stood in his stirrups to look back along the dirt track they'd followed. Men in Roman helmets darkened with mud were darting out of the trees, their swords flashing among the scouts. One of the mercs was down, and two more were firing from horseback, wasting ammunition.

The Roman troopers slashed at the horses with their swords, while archers farther back in the woods let fly at the riders. There were more shots from the mercs, but the Romans were mixed well with Rick's troops and there weren't clear targets.

"Cease fire!" he shouted in English. "Elliot! Get out here in the clear! Dismount and set up weapons. Prepare to receive cavalry! They're sure to be coming."

Switch languages again. "Caradoc! You and your Guardsmen, stay with Elliot! Guard their weapons!" Now for his Tamaerthan scouts. "Hussars move out this way! Follow me!" He rode toward the other edge of the clearing.

I've got to get my people disengaged, get some kind of order into this, get them out of the tangle with the ambushers. Elliot can take care of them after that. Dammit, those Romans were good!

They'd almost reached the other edge of the clearing when the woods on both sides of the pathway sprouted archers and the air came alive with arrows.

Too damn late, Rick thought. We're tangled up with them again. We've got to buy Elliot and the Guards enough time to set up. "Charge!" he ordered. "Forward!" He spurred toward the enemy.

Arrows whistled in. Rick's armor turned the two which hit him, but a third hit his horse in the shoulder. It jumped and squealed, but the arrow wasn't in deep enough to be a major wound. Rick raised his M-16 and squeezed off five rounds. He thought he hit three men. Then he was at the clearing's edge.

He slung the rifle across his saddle horn and drew his saber. In among the trees the sword was as good a weapon as a firearm. He slashed at one man, striking him at the shoulder, then he was past and into the woods.

He had time to notice that the woods stank. Most of the trees were lower and bushier than Earth trees would be; but mixed in with them were what could only be European scrub oak.

He bore to the right. The road would be there, and more of his scouts were forcing their way along the track. Behind him a trumpeter sounded; the high pitch of a Tamaerthan horn, not the low rumble of Roman signals. Someone had ordered recall of the point group. Who? It was the right move. Rick should have given the order himself, but he was separated from his staff. He heard men behind him. His, he hoped.

There were crashing sounds, and someone rode up behind and to his left. Rick turned, sword raised.

"Hold, my lord!"

It was Jamiy, his orderly, holding his round target to protect Rick. Just then they burst through to a second clearing; the patch of woods between this clearing and the one where they'd been attacked couldn't be more than fifty yards thick.

Shouts and screams erupted ahead. The Guardsmen of the point squad came pounding back down the path into the clearing. Hard on their heels was a mass of mounted Romans. As Rick and Jamiy rode into the clearing, the point troopers rallied to them, while from behind another dozen men who'd been following Jamiy came into clear territory.

The Romans ahead weren't the splendid legionary cataphracti; these were more lightly armored, with round shields, looking more like traditional Roman cavalry of the older days. They were scattered from chasing the point men; and Rick's troopers were lining up in a passable formation—

An organized charge will always carry against disorganized force. Which dry lecturer had he heard say that, light years away and a lifetime ago? But it was probably true. And there was Rick's trumpeter—

"Make ready to charge!" he ordered. He unslung his rifle and began a slow deliberate aimed fire, chopping down anyone in the Roman group who looked like an officer. He hit five men. The rest were still coming. Lord, what soldiers!

"Sound the charge!" Rick ordered. "Forward!"

His light cavalry moved ahead in a passable line, sweeping toward the more numerous but scattered Romans. Rick held the rifle uncertainly. It would be better if he halted and fired but that wouldn't do at all, not now with his troops at his back. Better to sling it again and use saber and pistol.

They struck the Romans, cut down more leaders, and were swept into the thick of the action. More and more of Rick's troops were coming from behind him, while extra supplies of Romans kept bursting into the clearing. Rick quickly lost track of what was happening to anyone except himself. This wasn't a battle; it was a series of small-unit actions, two- and three-man engagements moving as rapidly as horses and centaurs could carry them.

And it was getting out of hand. There'd be no point to fighting his way to the river unless he had enough troops to force a passage. "Rally back to the first clearing!" Rick ordered. "We must see to the star weapons! Sound 'Follow me'!" He turned to ride back toward the woods, followed by what was left of his troops—how many? He had no idea at all. More than a hundred, he thought. The trumpet sang behind him as he rode.

They reached the edge of the clearing just as a fresh wave of Romans burst through from the other side. Rick had no chance to count them, but it looked like a lot, enough to spread all across the clearing and still have depth to the formation. Enough to be a serious threat to Rick's whole command—

And behind that first wave of light cavalry the orange light of the True Sun glinted on silver links! Cataphracti, regular legionaries. Except for star weapons there wasn't a thing in Rick's cavalry command that could stand up to them.

Well, I've found Flaminius's army, he thought. Now all I have to do is live to get back and report it. Run like hell!

They reached the first clearing. Elliot had that situation under control; he'd set up a fire base in the clearing's center, and was shepherding wounded and stragglers into its protection. There were still archers in the woods, and Elliot's position was within extreme bowshot; but an engagement between a scope-sighted rifle fired by a man lying prone, and a bow used by a man who had to expose himself to shoot, wasn't really a contest. The Romans would soon run out of archers.

"More troops coming!" Rick announced. "Heavies. We'll want to blunt their charge and get the hell out of here!"

"Yes, sir!" Elliot answered. "Better get down—"

Too late for that, Rick thought. The rest of his Hussars were entering the clearing in headlong retreat. There were more of them than Rick had expected, at least a hundred. They'd come part way across when the Romans came through the trees.

"Caradoc!" Rick shouted. "Send four men back to Drumold! Have him bring up the rest of the cavalry on the double. We've found the enemy's main army." Caradoc said something that might be an acknowledgment.

Rick fired six rounds into the advancing Romans. Three riders went down and a fourth was thrown as his horse stumbled over one of the bodies. Rick wished he had the H&K instead of an M-16. The lighter bullet would punch through armor just as well if it hit squarely, but could more easily be deflected if it didn't.

Then the retreating Hussars swept past and the Romans were nearly on him. Rick spurred forward; better to be moving than a standing target. A Roman soldier came at him with lance, but Rick swerved, firing at him as they closed; he missed, but the noise startled the trooper so that he raised the lance point. Then a Roman with an officer's breastplate was straight ahead, lance lowered and ready to skewer Rick in the saddle. Rick flattened himself on the horse's neck. The lance dipped, too far. The point drove into the side of Rick's horse a moment before the two mounts crashed together. Rick's horse started to topple. He hurled himself out of the saddle, trying to leap clear of the falling horse.

The thrashing animal missed him by a yard. Rick fell heavily on the M-16. He rolled off it to find the action hopelessly jammed with mud. He scrabbled at his pistol; his hand was numb from the fall, and his thumb swollen so that he had to use both hands to get the safety off. He shot the Roman officer at point blank range, letting the heavy .45 slug batter through the man's armor. Another Roman mounted on a centaur was charging toward him; there was no clear shot at the man. Rick aimed at the center of the centaur's body and fired twice.

The animal screamed, a nearly human sound, its stumpy arms and badly formed hands tearing at the wound. The Roman screamed also, in rage and something more, horror and sorrow. He jumped to the ground and charged at Rick, his sword held high. Rick fired, once, twice, before the Roman staggered; the force of his charge carried him to Rick, and the sword swept down. It never hit. Suddenly there was a round shield held in front of Rick; Jamiy stood left flank rear, his sword bloodied from some previous action.

"Thanks," Rick grunted.

His orderly didn't answer.

The Romans charged once more, to be cut down by fire from Elliot and his mercs. Even Roman discipline wasn't good enough to get them to charge again, and they withdrew toward the woods.

Rick's charge had carried him almost to the clearing edge; a Roman horseman swept past, and Rick shot him out of the saddle. The horse stopped in its tracks, within easy reach. Rick quickly holstered his pistol and gripped the reins, ready to mount. He got one foot in the stirrup before the horse had time to react.

Then more shouts. The Guardsmen had swept forward to

rescue their leader. Rick's new mount panicked and reared, throwing Rick forward. He landed sprawled across the saddle like a bag of grain, and the horse bolted forward into the woods.

He was among the Romans. One of their troopers slashed at his head. The sword glanced off his helmet. Rick struggled to get back into the saddle and draw his pistol, but he knew he would be too late. There'd be no Jamiy to take this blow. His orderly was back there, down, maybe dead, maybe not, but Rick was alone except for two Guardsmen and a Tamaerthan officer who lay in a tangled pile just ahead.

The Roman moved in for the kill. Stupid, Rick thought. This is what you get, trying to lead the goddam army yourself. You get dead, and who leads now?

Then the Tamaerthan clan officer who lay at his feet lurched upward, barely able to stand. He staggered between the two horses, and his rising shoulder caught the Roman's second downcut. The clansman stabbed at the Roman's horse.

"Tethryn!" Rick shouted.

The Roman's horse jumped as Tethryn's knife entered his belly. The Roman trooper had to grab for the reins, and his next sword cut was spoiled. Rick managed to get astride his mount and get out his .45. There was one shot left in the magazine. Rick held the pistol to within a foot of the Roman's chest and fired. The man screamed and fell backward, and Rick's horse bolted again. This time it plunged out of the woods into the clearing, galloping across and up the narrow road toward the second clearing, as Rick tried frantically to secure his pistol before he dropped it.

The second clearing was empty except for dead and wounded. Rick's runaway mount carried him across at a slowing gallop; by the time they were to the other side, Rick had managed to holster his pistol and get the reins in both hands. The horse was tiring fast; it shouldn't be long before he could control it—

Except that he was being carried into unknown territory toward the Roman army.

14

The forest beyond the second clearing was only a thin screen of trees along the bank of the narrow, swift-flowing River Pydnae. Rick's horse was tiring fast before he reached the river. When they reached the bank, the animal was more or less under control.

A dozen Guardsmen, led by Caradoc, trotted up behind. "Are you well, my lord?" Caradoc called.

"Well enough now," Rick said. "Except for them." He pointed.

Not quite three hundred meters off to his left was a bridge, wooden roadway on stone piers. Between him and the bridge stood more than two hundred mounted Roman cataphracti. Their officer, easily recognized by his scarlet cape, was pointing at Rick, but the troops were not moving. Possibly afraid of star weapons?

Nonsense. Their mission was to control the bridge. But there weren't any troops visible on the other side, which meant—

"Caradoc, get your fastest messengers riding back to the main army. I want the whole Tamaerthan army here as soon as possible. They're to keep in formations, but I need them fast."

"Pikes too?" Caradoc asked.

"Especially the Pikes. Have another messenger go to Publius and ask him for as many *alae* of heavy cavalry as he can send. Tell him the main bridge over the Pydnae is intact, if we can just get enough troops across to hold it."

Caradoc turned to ride back and find messengers.

Rick and the Roman officer faced each other at three hundred yards. The Roman still did nothing.

Trying to make up his mind, Rick thought. Wonder how old he is? His ambush worked perfectly, but his outfit was shattered by weapons he can't understand. He ought to be terrified, but there he is, defending that bridge, trying to decide whether his best move is to stay there or attack me. He can't know who won back there in the clearing, or how many troops are left on either side. But he does know where his main army is—

Suddenly the Roman officer made his decision. About half the Romans formed up and came toward Rick at the trot. A hundred of them, against his dozen; impossible odds, even with a new magazine in his pistol. "Let's get out of here," Rick called. He pointed back toward the trees.

The Guardsmen wheeled, and they rode back the way they'd come. About half the Romans took out bows and let fly; the rest came on at a fast trot, lances lowered; and now Rick's horse was under control, but exhausted, impossible to get moving at anything more than a fast walk. Rick swore and dug in his spurs. He wasn't going to make it to the woods in time. He drew his Colt, cursing as he worked the safety with his swollen thumb.

A flight of arrows whizzed past, then another. He felt wasp-sting pains as a couple of points just got through his armor, and felt his horse shudder. This time he got out of the saddle before the horse started to go down, but still he landed clumsily. A worse pain than the arrows shot through one ankle. He lurched to his feet and tried to sight on the Roman commander. Good luck, Tylara—

Elliot rode out of the woods at a canter, leading a spare horse. At the same time arrows and bullets flew from behind several trees. Four Romans went down, but others kept on coming. Elliot unslung his H&K and emptied a magazine at full automatic. This time the effect was obvious. The Roman point was scattered, with a dozen horses wounded. They plunged and reared, leaving the Roman force in disarray. The officer shouted something, and they wheeled to fall back to the bridge.

Elliot rode up with the spare mount. "Need a lift, Captain?"

"Damn straight." Rick mounted and rode into the trees. Finally he had time to stop and survey the situation. Nothing broken. Maybe. His ankle hurt like hell, and his thumb throbbed like fury, but he didn't have time for them just now. "Thanks, Sarge."

"Nothing to it," Elliot said.

"Yeah. Sarge, have you got that one-oh-six with you?"

"Yes, sir." He pointed; Bisso was about fifty yards away with the weapon. "Want me to drop the bridge?"

"Christ, no! We need that bridge. No, what I have in mind is blowing open a path for some of our troops to get across. Do that and we've got the Romans trapped."

"Yeah. Why don't they retreat?"

"I don't know. But I can guess. They don't want to go tell Flaminius Caesar that they retreated from a bunch of barbarians. They're probably supposed to hold this side of the bridge so Flaminius can get his army across."

"You think his army is near?" Elliot asked.

"Looks like it. Why else would there be both scouts and legionaries? I think we've run into their vanguard, and that officer there knows it. So he's waiting for reinforcements he's pretty sure to get."

Elliot looked thoughtful. "Be hard to hold too many more with just the troops we have here."

"I know. I've sent for the whole army. First thing, I'll need to borrow your H&K. Fine. Now, let's see if we can get across that bridge."

Elliot dismounted and shouted orders. Bisso and his companion moved to the edge of the woods and set up the 106 on its tripod. The Romans, meanwhile, did nothing.

"What the hell?" Bisso asked.

"Still don't want to retreat," Rick said. "Not from barbarians. But that last clip spooked 'em enough they don't want to charge, either—set up the light machine gun over here."

Elliot fussed with the machine gun sights, then bent over the 106 recoilless rifle. "Clear everyone from behind," he said. "All of you—get! Move, dammit. Okay, Captain, ready when you are."

Rick faced his dismounted Guardsmen. "Stand easy. When that gun goes off, it will be damned noisy. The mounts won't like it, so hold them. When you hear the charge, ride like hell for the bridge. We'll go right over. Don't stop to fight. Just get over that bridge. Okay, Sergeant Major, stay ready. We'll wait as long as we can. I'd like to have some reinforcements."

"Sir."

Only we can't wait too long, Rick thought. The rest of Flaminius's army will be coming up too. Or that detachment will decide to retreat across the bridge and we'll really be for it. I ought to go now—

Yeah. Now, before you lose your bloody nerve and won't be able to do it. Who the hell do you think you are, Napoleon at the Bridge of Lodi?

While Elliot was making sure of his sights, a dozen Guards archers came up on foot, with a fresh supply of arrows and a message from Caradoc. The ambush in the rear was defeated, and new troops had come in from the main force. There were a lot of Romans scattered in among the forests, but they'd ceased to exist as an organized force.

The main army was coming, but it would be an hour or more before any infantry could arrive. Drumold and the Tamaerthan heavies ought to be along sooner. There was as yet no reply from the Romans.

And Rick thought he could see dust rising far down the road across the river. Flaminius? Or imagination? Whatever, it was time.

"Guardsmen, mount up! Elliot, stand ready to fire!"

"Sir." He bent over the sights.

"Mind your mounts!" Rick called. "Shoot!"

"Fire in the hole!" Elliot shouted. The recoilless blasted leaves off trees in a triangle behind it. Horses reared.

The shell exploded among the Romans just at the bridge. Horses reared and plunged, and one whole section of Roman cavalry bolted away. A number of Romans were down.

"Got the range first shot," Elliot said proudly.

The Roman troops milled in disorganization. Their officer shouted at them.

"Fire!" Eliot shouted.

This time the round struck near the Roman officer. More of their cavalry went down.

"Ride!" Rick ordered. "Sound the charge."

Trumpets blared, and they were riding forward at the gallop. There was no time to shoot at anyone, and nothing to shoot at either. Rick had drawn his saber; he held it point forward as he rode hunkered down to the horse's neck. He hoped someone was behind him.

He galloped onto the bridge, then across it. Some of the bridge planking was missing; his horse barely jumped across one gap. Then he was at the other side. He turned to the right and brought the horse up sharply.

Twenty Guardsmen had followed and were on the bridge. Jamiy, his sword arm bound to his chest, was in their lead, mounted on the centaur he favored. He shouted at the beast and it turned to stand next to Rick.

"Dismount!" Rick commanded. "Dismount and hold the bridge!"

The Roman officer saw his danger now, and was trying to rally his troops to charge across. A score made for the bridge approach, then fell as Elliot's light machine gun stuttered. Rick unslung the H&K and waited; two Romans made it onto the bridge. He shot them off it, feeling ashamed as he did.

The Roman officer rallied his troops and drew up in column formation fifty yards from the bridge. There was more rifle fire from the woods, and some Romans dropped. By now Rick's Guardsmen were also dismounted and had unlimbered their bows.

"You haven't a chance!" Rick shouted. "Surrender in honor!"

The Roman officer stood in his stirrups and waved forward. The Roman line charged. Lances dipped in unison as they thundered toward the bridge—

Elliot's machine gun stuttered again. Rick added to the fire with his H&K. He found he had trouble seeing. There was a mist in his eyes. Lord God, what troops! He aimed low, at the mounts, hoping not to kill any more of the Romans.

The charge was broken, but still a half dozen Roman troopers managed to get to the bridge. They rode on, and now there was nothing for it but to shoot them down in a hail of arrows and bullets.

The other Romans withdrew. Their officer was down, lying half under his mount.

A dozen Tamaerthan heavy cavalry burst from the woods. Drumold's banner led the way. More of the chivalry of Tamaerthon followed. They charged toward the Romans.

"No!" Rick screamed. He struggled to get onto his mount. "You! Ischerald! You're in charge. Hold on here. Jamiy, follow me!" Rick spurred back across the bridge.

They reached the other side. "See to their officer," Rick shouted to Jamiy. "Get an acolyte of Yatar. Instantly, damn you! He's too good a man to die like that!"

He rode slantwise until he was between Drumold and the Romans. Then he led the Tamaerthan troopers forward. The Romans rode away until their remnant was brought to bay, the river bank at their backs. A few stripped off armor and dove in. They vanished in the swift, muddy water, and Rick couldn't see what happened to them.

Probably doomed, he thought. One of the more unpleasant life forms on Tran was the hydra, a fresh-water squid-like mollusk that could grow to twenty feet in length. The big hydras preferred clear, slow-moving water, but there were smaller forms in nearly all deep streams. One forded Tran rivers with care.

The remaining Romans sat their horses defiantly. There were no more than fifty left, and now they faced fifty Tamaerthan heavies and twice that many Guardsmen. Still they stood proudly.

Rick reined up a hundred yards from the Romans.

Drumold rode up. "I came as soon as possible."

"Thank you. We must get reinforcements over the bridge. We've got to hold the other side."

"That may no' be so easy," Drumold said. "As I topped the rise yonder I saw the flash of armor. Perhaps twenty stadia away. Legionaries, I think."

"All the more reason to hold the bridge," Rick said. He thought for a moment. "We'll need to ride out and show ourselves to the Romans, before they get close enough to see how few we have across the river. That should stop them for the day. Can you get your chaps to let themselves be seen and then retreat back here?"

"Aye, although they will not be pleased to do so. But they

will do it—Rick, we have already been told of your charge for the bridge. And earlier, in the clearing. No man will call you coward now."

Yeah. I knew that. And I've killed a lot of good men to make it happen. Ah, hell.

"And what do we do here?" Drumold asked. He pointed at the Romans.

"I go to speak with them."

"And if they shoot you down?"

"Then you're in command." Rick rode forward alone, his hands spread out empty. When he was fifty yards from the Roman line he held his hand up, palm forward. "Hail, soldiers of Rome."

There was a long pause. Finally a Roman soldier rode forward. "Hail, barbarian."

"Lay down your arms," Rick shouted. "You have fought honorably, against star weapons and great odds. Now accept honor and take quarter."

"From whose hand?" the Roman demanded.

"In the name of Marselius Caesar," Rick replied. "You will have heard of his amnesty for all who follow an enthroned Caesar. This I too swear. I am Rick Galloway, Colonel of Mercenaries, Eqeta of Chelm, War Leader of Tamaerthon, War Lord of Drantos, Ally and Friend to Marselius Caesar."

The Roman seemed to think that one over.

"Archers!" Drumold shouted from behind him. "Prepare the gulls."

A group of guardsmen dismounted. They drew their long bows from bowcases.

"You know what Tamaerthan archers can do," Rick shouted. "You will die to no purpose. How can it serve Rome to have her finest soldiers slaughtered? Lay down your arms."

"Way! Way there!" someone called from behind.

A group of guardsmen and acolytes of Yatar came out toward Rick. They carried the Roman officer in a blanket.

"Your tribune lives," Rick shouted. "We tend his wounds. He bids you lay down your arms."

The Roman decurion looked back at his companions. Then slowly he rode forward. A few yards away he halted, drew his sword, and dismounted. Silently he came forward and presented it hilt first. Then he knelt in submission.

Drumold led the Tamaerthan heavy cavalry across the bridge

and down the road, as guardsmen collected the Roman weapons. Half an hour later, the first blocks of pikemen arrived. Rick sent them across the bridge to secure their foothold on the other side.

And now there was nothing to do but wait. And hurt. His clothes were stuck to him with blood from the arrow wounds, his ankle was starting to swell, and his thumb and whole right hand were already swollen. He'd forgotten to take off his ring; they would have to cut that off, and soon, too, or he'd lose the finger. There were other bumps and bruises he felt now that the adrenalin was no longer flowing.

But we won, he thought. "'Twas a famous victory..."

Caradoc rode up with the rest of the Guard.

"You'll be personally responsible for the Roman prisoners," Rick said. "I have promised them safety. They keep all their property except weapons, and they're to be well treated. All of them. And guarded by enough troops that they won't *try* to escape. I don't want one single one of them harmed. Is this understood?"

"Yes, lord," Caradoc said.

And there aren't a hell of a lot of people I can give that order to and be sure it will be carried out.

"Can you come now?" Caradoc asked. "There is a man you must see."

Rick sighed wearily. "It is urgent?"

"Very urgent, lord. It is Tethryn."

"He lives?"

"For the moment. The priests did not think he should be moved, but he was determined to speak to you, and has come." Caradoc paused for a moment. "I think it makes little difference whether we move him or not."

"I'll come," Rick said. "I owe him my life."

Tethryn lay on a horse litter at the edge of the clearing. His brother Dwyfyd bent over him. They look so much alike, Rick thought. Alike, and young and—Dwyfyd's eyes were wet with tears.

"Lord Rick." The dying boy's voice was almost inaudible.

"Hail, my friend and companion—"

"Thank you."

"You must rest."

"There is no time, lord. Vothan One-eye has chosen me to guest in his hall this day. But I hope—you will not believe you see only enemies—in Clan Calder now. Some—some of the lesser chiefs. . . ."

"Some of them would rather I did, so they can continue to plot against me?"

The boy was silent so long that Rick thought he'd fainted or died. Then he nodded. "Aye. Couldn't let you die—to make them happy. Not—when—they lied. My father was wrong. You are—no coward."

Tethryn's eyes closed, and Rick moved away to leave Dwyfyd alone with his brother.

Damn. Hell and damn. The kid wasn't eighteen yet.

"It is done?" Rick asked.

Dwyfyd nodded silently.

"He was a brave companion," Rick said. "He will have no minor place in Vothan's hall."

"Lord—"

"Yes?"

"May—may I ask a boon in Tethryn's name?"

"Yes."

Dwyfyd didn't hesitate. "Corgarff's life, lord."

"Why?"

"He is my clansman. And—there are reasons."

Aha. So you know that your father was involved in the plot against the balloon. Probably ordered Corgarff's part in it. And you want to make that up.

"You do him no great service," Rick said. "He will be a cripple—"

"None the less, I owe him. And his family."

And you've probably paid off that crofter's family, too. "Clan Calder has a worthy chief," Rick said. "Caradoc, have messengers ride swiftly. Carry my orders to Lady Gwen that Corgarff is to be pardoned. Tell her that a writ will come soon. She is to stay the headsman's ax."

"Aye," Caradoc said.

And you don't approve. But you'll send the fastest man

anyway, won't you? There's real loyalty. If there's time to save Corgarff, you'll save him, though you'd rather watch him die.

Pity we don't have working radios. A couple of sets would make a lot of difference. Semaphore? Heliograph? Telegraph towers? We could put those up. Have to think about it. Certainly we could link key points to share messages within a few hours . . .

And there were a thousand other details, and meetings to hold tonight, now that he'd located the edges of at least one legion. Battles to plan and kingdoms to govern and he hadn't even planted the first stick of *surinomaz* and Lord how every joint and muscle ached!

But some problems were solved. They held the bridge. There would be no difficulty in linking up with Marselius— indeed, Flaminius might be caught between them. He'd have to fight.

And there were political victories. Clan Calder an ally. Or at least its chief is. The Romans I killed today haven't died to no purpose. There'll be fewer knives aimed at my back, and the longer I live the more I can do on this world—

How many get the chance to change the destiny of a whole world? I've been given that chance. Every man who died today will save hundreds over the next few years.

He told himself this as he swung up into the saddle. He would go on telling himself this, until perhaps someday he would believe it. And through it all, he could still hear the small voice in his mind which said, "Rick Galloway, are you *sure* you're not a coward?"

15

The monontonous beat of the kettledrums ceased. Second Pike Regiment spread forward to stand guard, while Third Pikes began construction of a temporary camp. Roman engineers supervised as the pikemen, assisted by archers, drove stakes and dug ditches.

"Bloody waste of effort," someone muttered behind Rick. One of the Tamaerthan knights.

"It will not be *your* effort wasted," said another knight. Dwyfyd, Rick thought. Better, though, to pretend he hadn't heard at all.

At least none of the knights was arguing that they ought to dismount and take their ease while the foot soldiers built their camp.

"Aye. We hae learned from the Romans to sleep well at night, knowing we will no be surprised. And that, my lords, is no small thing."

Drumold, of course, Rick thought. But the voice seemed to come from a very long way away. Suddenly he swayed in the saddle—

"My lord."

Rick didn't want to open his eyes. There was a hot smell. Lamp oil. Why would they be burning lamps in the afternoon? He opened one eye. Yellow light. Brown walls. He tried to sit up.

"Stay easy, my lord."

His eyes focussed at last. A young acolyte of Yatar. And Rick was on a cot, in his own tent. It was late enough that lamps were lit.

"Is he awake?" Drumold's voice came from outside.

"Yes, lord. I will go for the priest."

"Do that." Drumold came in to sit next to Rick. "Are ye well, lad?"

"Certainly." He tried to sit up, but his head felt light. "I don't understand what happened—"

"Hah. You're battered and torn, lost blood from three wounds. Your thumb's the size of a gull's head and your ankle larger than his body. Withall, you sit a horse all day and you wonder you faint? Rest, lad."

"Can't," Rick said. "Where is Publius?"

"Camped nearby. All is well, Rick."

"Is there word from Marselius?"

Drumold hesitated.

"There is, then."

"Aye. But—"

"Drumold, we have a battle to plan!"

"It will wait a day."

It won't, Rick wanted to say; but instead he let his head fall back on the pillow.

He awakened the next morning to the sounds of trumpets and shouting men. He tried to leap from his cot, but his ankle wouldn't hold him. Then Mason was there to help him back to bed.

"What—"

"It's nothin' to be worried about, Cap'n. Some bigwig from Marselius's army, with a legion for escort."

"A legion? That's Marselius himself!"

"Likely it is," Mason said.

"I have to go meet him—"

"How?" Mason asked. "You can't hardly stand long enough to dress yourself."

"Damn it, I can't greet Caesar from my bed! Get my robes!"

"Robes, hell," Mason said. "You go out, you wear armor. And you eat some hot soup first."

Soup. That sounded good. But armor? Yes. Not for the reason Mason thought. Not assassination; but it would be fitting to greet Marselius Caesar in armor. Marselius would be wearing his best, no question about that. "All right, help me get on my mail. The shiny set."

"How about this?" Mason asked. "Arrived an hour ago."

It was a new set of armor, featuring the breastplate fancied by Roman officers. Bronze oak leaves—no, by God, those were gold!—were soldered to the shoulders. There was a shirt with mail sleeves to go under it. The links were silvered, and the finest Rick had ever seen.

"Fancy enough," Mason said.

"A king's ransom," Rick said. "From Marselius?"

"No, sir. From Publius. In honor of your taking the bridge."

"I will be dipped in—" Publius? That ass?

The armor fit perfectly. Which of Rick's people had Publius got his measurements from? It hardly mattered. And certainly this was the right thing to wear . . .

"Hail, Caesar," Rick said.

"Hail, friend and ally." Marselius smiled and came closer to clasp Rick's hand and shoulder. It was a genuine embrace, making Rick wince. "Your pardon—"

"It's nothing." But he was glad for the armor.

Both armies stood in ranks in the bright light of the True Sun, watching their commanders greet each other. Wine was poured, and Rick and Marselius drank, then exchanged goblets and drank again. "Silly ritual," Marselius said. "But I suppose necessary—shall we go inside, while Publius and Drumold carry on?"

"Yes." He followed the Roman into the command tent. Maps were already spread on the table.

There was a man seated by the table. Two of Marselius's personal guards stood next to him.

"I think you did not meet Aulus Sempronius," Marselius

JOSEF M. HERTLE SOUKE 1912

said. "He was the tribune commanding Flaminius's troops at the bridge."

"Hail," Rick said. "I am pleased to see that you live."

"I understand that was your doing. Thank you."

"You will recover, then?"

He didn't look good. His left leg was stretched stiffly before him. It was bound in leather splints. His left arm was also bound to his chest.

"I do not know," Sempronius said. "Your—" He struggled with the word. Finally he said it. "—priests say I will. Our healers are less certain. Your rituals are strange but they seem efficient—"

Marselius looked worried. "My Lord Bishop will arrive in a moment," he warned. "Does it go well, son of my oldest friend?"

"You call him friend even now?"

"Certainly. Because your father sees his duty to serve Flaminius makes his friendship no less valuable. More."

"Ah." Aulus Sempronius was silent for a moment. "I do not think your son shares this view. Left to him, I would be in the hands of the *quaestionairii.*"

"Never," Rick said. "You surrendered to me. Who harms you answers to me!"

"By what right do you speak thus to Caesar?"

Publius had come in. Rick turned slowly. *What I'd like to say, you pompous little bastard, is by right of the magazine in this Colt. But that won't work too well—*

"By the right that any honorable man holds. By the rights of honor," Marselius said. "Hail, Publius."

"Hail, father. Hail, Lord Rick."

"Have you no more to say to our ally?" Marselius demanded.

Publius nodded, his lips pressed tightly together. Then, in a rush, he said, "I ask pardon. I should not have spoken as I did."

"Why hasn't he attacked?" Publius demanded. He turned to Aulus Sempronius. "Why?"

"I cannot answer—"

"Aulus," Marselius said. "Aulus, I have granted full pardon and amnesty to all who will accept. There were no conditions, and there will be none. But—will you not submit to me as Caesar? Will you not aid me in ending this war? How can it harm Rome, that this war end?"

Aulus frowned. "And yet— Ah. How can it matter? He has no need of battle," Aulus said. "As you must know."

Rick nodded. "I thought that bridge too lightly guarded. We were intended to cross."

"Your spies have served you well," Aulus said bitterly.

"No. It should have been obvious there were too few troops to hold it long," Rick said. "Only you fought so well I did not understand until now. And when we march for Rome—"

"He will let you go forward. Then we retake the bridges, and hold you to this side of the river until you starve. May I have wine? Thank you. It deadens the pain."

"It is not good for you," Rick said.

"More witchcraft of Yatar?" Deliberately he poured another goblet of wine and drank it off. "Soon you will lose your army to desertion." Aulus laughed sharply. "If we do not lose ours first."

"You have many deserters?" Rick asked.

"As must you."

"We've seen few enough of yours," Rick said. He looked to Publius. "Have they come to you?"

"They do not go to Marselius Caesar," Aulus said. "They go home, to protect their families from bandits and slave revolts, and the legends of—of—"

"Of The Time," Rick said softly. "So you know of that also."

Aulus nodded, and drank again, his third large cup. "Our bishops say that God will punish this world."

That's one way to look at it. I wonder how many deserters Publius has had? None we caught, but we weren't really looking for them.

"So Flaminius will not attack," Marselius said.

"Caesar, he will not," Aulus Sempronius said. "But say not Flaminius, who is not here."

"Who commands?"

"Titus Licinius Frugi."

"Gah," Publius said.

"I feared as much," Marselius said. "My best legate. He was with me at Sentinius."

At Sentinius. "Then he will find my pikes and archers no surprise," Rick said.

"None," Aulus said.

And he knows my secret. The secret of any hedgehog formation. If you don't attack it—how can we take the battle to cavalry? We can't even *catch* their cavalry. And if they wait until we're in line of march and sweep in—

"Then we march on Rome," Marselius said. "If he refuses battle, so do we."

"Except that the further we go—"

"The more recruits we will have," Publius said. "We come closer to our home estates. And to lands which know Flaminius the Dotard all too well."

"He will burn the crops," Rick said.

"How can he?" Marselius demanded. "His own troops won't let him. Nor will Flaminius. Nor will the Church. He *can't* burn himself out. No. We march on, and when he attacks, we've got him."

Or he's got us, Rick thought, but there was no point in saying that. How did it go?

> On foot shuld all Scottis weire,
> By hyll and mosse themselffs to reare.
> Let wood for walls be bow and spear,
> That enemies do them na dare.
> In strait places gar keep all store,
> And byrnen ye planeland them before,
> Then shall they pass away in haist,
> What that they find na thing but waist.
> With wiles and waykings in the night,
> And meikill noyse maid on hyte,
> Them shall ye turnen with great affrai,
> As they were chassit with sword away.
> This is the counsel and intent
> Of gud King Robert's testiment.

But Flaminius couldn't possibly have heard of Robert the Bruce. Or could he?

Two days march were two days of agony for Rick. His ankle remained swollen, so that he could not stand in the stirrups. He recalled the ancient joke, a cavalry manual: *Forty*

Miles in the Saddle, by Major Assburns. It took on new meaning with each mile.

But I can't lead from a wagon, he thought. Though I'm going to have to, if this keeps up.

They marched onward into Flaminius's territory; and the deeper they went, the hungrier they were. Despite Marselius's certainties, the land *had* been laid waste; there was little or nothing to eat. All food and stores had been carried away, and the fields burned.

They grew weaker in other ways, too. For every recruit they collected, they had to leave two men behind as garrison. They had, when they began, three legions of cataphracti, two veteran and one militia, and two cohorts of Roman pikemen, nowhere near the standards of Rick's veterans. Now one of the legions was under strength, and there was only one cohort of Roman pikes.

They had also begun with three cohorts of *cohortes equitatae*, a mixed force of two light-armed infantrymen for each light cavalryman. The infantrymen ran alongside the cavalry, supporting themselves by holding the horse's mane so that they could keep up. An excellent idea in theory; Rick wondered how well trained they were. However good, there were only two cohorts of those now; the third was left to guard the crossing of the River Pydnae.

The whole Roman army wasn't much larger than Rick's force; while Flaminius was said to have five legions, three of them veterans, as well as numerous militia and auxiliaries.

"My lord."

Rick looked up to see one of his cavalry officers. "Yes?"

"Five stadia ahead, lord. There is a villa. It will not open its gates to us."

Rick frowned. "Yes?"

"My lord, Balquhain wished to batter down the gates, but Lord Drumold sent me to find you. Lord, the villa is defended only by women and loyal slaves. Balquhain told them to surrender or they would be given to the soldiers. They slammed the gates in his face. Then Lords Drumold and Caradoc came."

"I see. Go and tell Drumold I'll be there as soon as I can." He looked back down the road. Art Mason and Jamiy were close behind. Jamiy's arm was bound in a tight sling against his chest. Wearily Rick waved them forward and spurred his horse to a fast trot. The result was agony.

And I can't tell anyone what my problem is . . .

"Surrender in the name of Marselius Caesar," Rick shouted.

"My lady says that she will never open her gates to barbarians."

Was that an intentional pun? The double meaning was obvious, but it certainly wasn't intended to be humorous. And undoubtedly it expressed the deepest fears of the matron who guarded that villa.

"We need Tylara here," Rick said.

Drumold nodded. "Aye. You see now why I sent for you."

"Yes. There's little honor in victory over women. But a damn good chance of an incident worth more to Flaminius than a new legion."

"So I have told my son," Drumold muttered.

Balquhain bowed his head. "Aye. I see that now. I was a fool."

First damn sign of wisdom I've seen from you, Rick thought. But no time for that now. "Mason, bring up the one-oh-six."

"You have a plan?" Balquhain asked.

"Yes. You're part of it." Part of it now, anyway. "Listen . . ."

"Fire in the hole!" Reznick shouted. The 106 recoilless blasted in fire; the shell smashed against the stout gates of the villa.

The instant the larger weapon fired, Rick and Mason fired concussion grenades from the grenade launchers on their H&K rifles. The grenades went over the wall to explode inside the courtyard beyond.

At the same moment, Balquhain, Caradoc, and ten other picked Guardsmen rode to the gate. They flung themselves off their mounts. The gates sagged on their hinges; four men hit them at once, and the topmost hinge of one gave way. They scrambled into the villa.

Rick rode up behind them, and painfully climbed inside the ruined gate. "My ladies!" he shouted. "You see we have broached your defense. Yet only officers stand in your courtyard. My army stays outside. You will not be harmed. Come out, in the name of Marselius Caesar—"

Caradoc and two Guardsmen brought over prisoners from the outer wall; two young men, obviously slaves, and another, no more than ten. The boy struggled, but could not move in Caradoc's grip.

The villa door opened, and a woman about thirty-five ran out. "Rutilius!" she screamed.

Rick nodded in satisfaction. *That's one victory I can be proud of. Why can't they all be like that?*

It was late in the day, and Rick made camp at the villa. Only his officers were permitted inside; and before they entered, Rick asked formal permission from the mistress of the household.

"You will be paid for what we consume," Rick told her. "We are allies to a lawful Caesar, not conquerors."

She shrugged and gave a bitter laugh. "There's little enough to consume."

Her name was Aemelia, and her husband, Marcus Trebius, was an officer in Flaminius's army. She didn't know if he was alive or dead; but three days before, Titus Frugi's soldiers had stripped her villa of every able-bodied slave and freedman. They had also taken nearly all her food, and burned what was left.

"You seem to bear little love for Flaminius," Rick said.

"I have little."

"Then why did you not surrender to Marselius?"

"You are not Marselius," she said.

"Ah. My barbarians—"

She blushed. "We were told—told that it would be far better to fall into the hands of Publius than among the barbarians."

"Ah. Meaning—"

"That Publius asks," she said. "But I wronged you. I— thank you. For saving my son. For sparing my home." She came and stood near him. "Welcome, to my home and hearth . . ."

"Captain . . ."

What the hell? Aemelia moved next to him in the dark. She was tense with fear.

"Captain."

The voice was Mason's. Out in the hall. Quickly Rick rose and went through the connecting door to the other room. He pulled on a robe and opened the door. "Here. What is it?"

"Messenger, Captain. From Marselius. Said it was too important to wait until morning."

"I'll come—"

"Armor, Captain. I'll help you—"

"Give me five minutes," Rick said wearily. "Then come help." And just how close a friend to Tylara *are* you?

Lucius, Marselius's trusted freedman, stood in the library of the villa. Drumold, Elliot, Balquhain, Caradoc, and a dozen other officers waited with him.

"Hail, Lord Rick."

"Hail, Lucius. You bring a message from Caesar. It must be that you have found Flaminius's main army."

"Yes. No more than forty stadia. Some march toward us. Their light cavalry are everywhere—"

Rick bent over the maps. "Good territory for it. They'll be trying to circle past us, get some behind and some ahead. With more troops strung along this ridge above our line of march."

And worse than that. There were a number of parallel roads here, and Marselius's army was split into columns, divided into three main forces: Rick's on the left, Marselius himself in the center, and Publius on the right. With luck, Flaminius could hit one of the flanking columns and punish it before Marselius could come to its rescue. Or circle behind them and harass from the rear. Or—

"It is clear that we must know what Flaminius is doing," Rick said. He turned to his officers. "Send out the Hussars. But in a body, to patrol and return. Not to fight. They're our eyes, and we'll need them."

"I'll go myself," Drumold said. "Now?"

"Yes," Rick said. "Elliot, get the troops on alert, but keep them in camp. Until we know what Flaminius is doing it's silly to do anything—"

"And yet we have no choice but to continue," Lucius said quietly. "Or soon we will have no grain for the horses."

"Yeah," Rick said. He tasted sour bile. Horses eat a *lot*. Cavalry horses eat more than that. Stay here a week, and they'd have no striking force at all.

"Caesar demands that we march tomorrow," Lucius said. "I have brought his plan of battle."

The battle plan was no plan at all. March ahead and trust to God. Not that Rick knew of anything better.

"There is one more message," Lucius said. "I have waited until we are alone to give it."

Rick poured two goblets of wine. "Yes?"

"Your officer, Tethryn, shall have the Untipped Spear."

"Ah." So the Romans of Tran had preserved that ancient Imperial honor. "Dwyfyd will be pleased to add that to his brother's tomb carvings."

"Publius wanted instead to give money."

"He had a reason?"

"Ah. He said to his father, 'If I were as close to the purple as you, I would not waste Roman honors on dead barbarians.'" Lucius smiled. "Caesar replied, 'If I did not honor my friends, I would not be as close to the purple as I am.'"

"And what happens if Caesar falls in battle?"

Lucius shrugged. "Publius is not evil, Lord. He is a strange lad. Well educated. Perhaps I was too strict. I do not know. But—well, we can pray to the saints that Marselius lives to be enthroned. I am unlikely to outlive him. And Publius may yet grow to a stature worthy of Rome."

The cavalry returned an hour past full light.

"We found nothing," Drumold said. He pointed to the map spread on Rick's field desk. "So far as I can tell, we went to this spur of the ridge."

"A good ten stadia past where you should have been ambushed."

"Aye—"

"Meaning there will be an ambush there when the full army marches up that road," Rick said. "You can be sure of it."

"So what shall we do?" Balquhain demanded.

"What would you do?" Rick asked.

Balquhain spread his hands. "I know not, truly. Time was, and no so long ago, I would ride that road thinking myself safe. Now—now I see the danger, but I know little what to do about it."

Nor I, Rick thought. He was about to say that—

"My lord!" Jamiy burst in. "Lord, the Captain of the Guard sends word. New forces coming from the west."

"New forces?"

"Drantos soldiers, Lord. Royal Guardsmen."

"What the de'il?" Drumold demanded. "Why? Could aught be—no, no, I will not think such things."

Nor I, Rick thought. Lord God. And last night I betrayed her. Could this be Tylara coming? Or has something happened to her? Or—I'm a damned fool.

Camithon stood at the door. His head was bowed, and the old soldier actually stammered. "Lord—lord, I knew not how to prevent him. Aye, our young Wanax has grown—"

"And so you came with him."

"Aye," Camithon said. "What was my duty? I am a soldier. I know well enough that I am 'Protector' of young Ganton, not of the Realm, which I know not how to govern. And as our Wanax conceived this mad notion while the Lady Tylara was no more than a day's ride from the capital, I sent messengers to inform her that she should remain as Justiciar of Drantos, while I escort the Wanax. What else could I do, lord? For he *would* come. To prevent him I must lay violent hands upon him—and I cannot believe his nobility and Guardsmen would allow that. Must I then begin civil war?"

"No. Where is the king?"

"Ah—the servants are erecting his tent, and he is at his ablutions—in truth he hides until I bring him word of how you receive his visit. I think he fears you somewhat."

"He cannot overly fear me, or he would not be here. What forces have you brought?"

"A hundred lances, lord."

Three hundred heavy cavalrymen. Probably more; each lance was led by a knight, and many of them would have brought squires as well as men at arms. Picked men, no doubt. Man for man as good as Romans. Possibly better. But not disciplined; a hundred Roman cataphracti would be more than a match for these three hundred.

But they were heavy cavalry, trained to fight in ranks three deep and cover a three-meter front. They could hold a third of a kilometer, at least for a while.

"And servants, and fifty porters leading a hundred pack animals," Camithon continued.

"Rations? How long can you live without forage?"

Camithon shrugged. "A day? There was little enough forage in the wake of this army!"

Rick nodded. Well, that was another four hundred mouths to feed. Plus horses, who'd need grain and hay. There'd be no centaurs among picked Drantos troops.

One more damn thing to worry about.

"This is primarily a Tamaerthan expedition," Rick said. "And it is my command. This is understood?"

"Aye, lord. By me and by His Majesty."

"Good. Then have the courtesy to inform the Wanax that when His Majesty is finished with his ablutions, the Commander-in-Chief would like to see him."

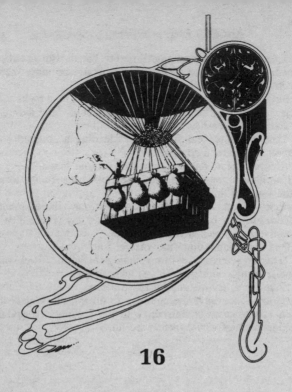

16

Titus Licinius Frugi reined in his horse and resisted the impulse to stand in the stirrups. His officers were watching; they should not see him appear uneasy.

They were among a thin wood at the top of a long ridge that lay parallel to his enemy's line of march. They could see most of Marselius's force from here: the center, with Marselius himself, lay on Frugi's left, ready to march up the military road to Rome.

On that side Frugi had four legions to face Marselius. More than enough to sweep Marselius from the field—but that would be wasteful of men. Frontal assaults always were.

But if he could bring a legion around the ridge to take Marselius from behind—

Marselius had entrusted his left wing to barbarians. To Frugi's right, at the bottom of the ridge, was a secondary road in a thin strip of cleared level ground perfect for his heavy cavalry. The barbarians, separated from Marselius by the ridge, would march into that.

He pointed to the road. "How far up it did they come?" he asked.

"There." One of his staff officers pointed down the slope.

"That far. Excellent." If the barbarians had scouted that distance last night, they would surely do so again now that they were marching . . .

First would come the barbarian light cavalry. They'd be no match for cataphracti; drive them back, back upon their own marching columns—and charge on, using the fleeing enemy as a screen.

And if the enemy came on without sending scouts ahead? Even better. The road ran between the forest and a stream. The barbarians would have to march close to the trees; close enough that their archers would have little time for their deadly volleys as his hidden troops burst out. Let his legionaries get among the archers, and the barbarian army was his. Kill the archers! The pikemen were not of themselves dangerous. Horse archers could shoot them down—provided that they were not in turn shot down by those bright-kilted fiends with their long, gull-feathered arrows that could outrange his best by half again.

He shuddered at the memory of the disaster at Sentinius. Not again! Never again would he send cataphracti charging at the pikes while the grey gulls flew in thick flights . . .

From his ridge he could see all the way back to the river. Most of it was fertile farmland, but there were scattered orchards, patches of forest, and low rolling hills to block his view.

A horseman rode up behind him. "It is a splendid view. A pity to spoil it with the ugliness of war."

"Yes, my Lord Bishop." And how much of that did my Lord Bishop Polycarp believe? Possibly all of it. To the best of Frugi's knowledge, Polycarp was a good man—despite having the favor of Flaminius.

Marselius, my old friend. Were you right to revolt? Has Flaminius the Scholar brought us to that? But civil war is always the worst of disasters, the worst of evils. Better a dozen bad emperors than an endless series of wars for the purple. Once, Rome ruled from the sea to the West Escarpment, to the borders of the Five Kingdoms. Aye, even the High Rexja sent gifts to

Caesar. Then came a year when three Caesars claimed the throne at once.

"But will not the trees and hills there prove troublesome?" the bishop asked. "They will hide your enemy."

"They serve to block Marselius's view as well, Your Grace."

"And that is important?"

"All important, Your Grace. If we but knew where *all* of Marselius's forces were, we would have them. We could win a bloodless—well, nearly bloodless—victory."

"How is this?"

Have I better things to do than give lessons in tactics to a servant of the Prince of Peace? No. Not for an hour. Perhaps longer. "If we know where each is, we can concentrate all our force against a small part of theirs. Break through their line, sweep about their flanks, come from behind. Their soldiers like this war no more than we. Given the chance, they will come to us rather than die for Marselius."

"Will you give them quarter, then?"

"Yes."

"Yet Caesar has ordered—"

"I know what Caesar has ordered, Your Grace. And I know what I must do. I will send the remnants of Marselius's force to the frontier posts." If there are any remnants. I have six legions. Two that Marselius doesn't know about. Enough force to roll right over, smash my way—"I will give them quarter if I can."

"And you are certain of winning?"

"I am, Your Grace. We have six legions plus the foot. Even counting the barbarians as a legion, Marselius has but four."

"So you have half again his strength."

"More, Your Grace. With forces matched this evenly, it is as the square of the two. Say thirty-six to sixteen. As if we had double his force. But that would be for a frontal assault. I think we can do better when Marselius advances. He always was a rash leader."

Polycarp looked at him sharply. "Be certain of victory. Then go with God. For Rome can little enough afford the loss of her knights, when the barbarians pound at our gates, and the star our ancestors called Beelzebub hangs higher each day. But—will not Marselius simply remain where he is? Why should he place his head in your snare?"

"He has little choice, Your Grace. There is very nearly

nothing to eat where he is encamped." Flaminius Caesar had rightly forbidden him to strip *all* of the lands along Marselius's line of march; but he had allowed him this valley. A raven crossing that land would need to carry rations.

Marselius and the barbarians carried rations, of course. Grain and fodder for the horses, too. But never enough, not for that army. Marselius would have to fight, on ground chosen by Frugi. And Marselius would lose.

An hour passed. Trumpets sounded from the west. Marselius was on the march. But the barbarians were deploying as if for battle. They hadn't moved up the road. Not even their light cavalry.

Then there were shouts from his troops. A staff officer rode up jabbering.

"What? Speak up, man!"

The officer pointed.

Two miles away, a brightly colored object trailing black smoke rose in the sky. A wind carried it toward him. When he strained his eyes, he thought he could see a thin line connecting it to the ground. Smoke rose from the place it was tethered.

"What?" Frugi asked. "Surely it is nothing to fear." But he felt fear, all the same. Fear and terror of the unknown. Star weapons . . .

Star weapons are only weapons, he told himself. Like bows, with long-ranging arrows. Like ballistae that shoot far. But as bows need arrows, the star weapons need—need something I don't have a word for. But something. And their supplies are limited.

Another staff officer rode up. A *frumentarius*. Why was he so excited?

"*Balloon,*" the intelligence officer stammered.

Titus Frugi frowned in puzzlement.

"We heard of them from the Pirate Lands, Proconsul," the officer said. "But we paid no heed. Until now."

"What are you jabbering about?"

"*Balloon,*" he said. "See, it drifts toward us on the wind. And it is higher than we can shoot. Look closely, Proconsul."

Titus Frugi looked, and saw disaster. There were men in the basket hanging below the balloon. They were pointing at the troops hidden in ambush.

The semaphore flags waved. An acolyte of Yatar stared at the basket beneath the balloon and called out letters. Another wrote the message.

"S-T-A-F-F BREAK O-N BREAK Y-O-N-D-E-R BREAK R-I-D-G-E BREAK STOP."

"We have found the enemy's staff officers, Lord," the scribe said.

Rick hid a thin smile of amusement. These lads were so proud of being among the very few who could read that they forgot that anyone else could. "Thank you." He turned to Mason. "Think it's worth dropping a couple on the ridge?"

Mason shrugged. "Sure."

"We'll wait a bit more, though," Rick said. "Ah. Murphy's located an ambush force. Just about where I'd figured from the map. But it's nice to have it confirmed. Dismounted. They'll be out of action for a while—"

Gradually he gathered details as the semaphore flags wagged and waved. Two legions poised here. Another there, masked by an orchard. Two more in reserve. Hah. Titus Frugi had more force than Marselius had suspected. Must have drained everything, every trooper he could raise—

"Caradoc!" Rick shouted. "Get me messengers to ride to Marselius. Win this battle and by Yatar we've won the whole bloody war!"

"It was you who said it would be disaster," Bishop Polycarp reminded him.

And it damned well is, too, Titus Frugi thought. But how can I avoid a battle? I can't even disengage! By now Marselius knows every formation I have, how many, where they are—

Is he wise enough to divine which troops I can trust and which I can't? Which I can allow to wander through the trees, and which must stay under the eyes of their centurions? (And one legion whose centurions weren't trustworthy; that whole legion had to be watched by another.)

"What would you have me do, Your Grace?"

Polycarp shook his head slowly. "Avoid slaughter. If you must fight—fight barbarians. Do not let Roman armies kill each other while the heathens remain!"

Good advise, old man. But I've fought those barbarians. You haven't. Still, I suppose there's nothing for it.

It had looked so simple. Until that thing rose in the sky. And now—now everything he did would be reported to Marselius. While he had no information at all on where his enemies marched.

Disaster. Strange how small a thing can bring disaster. And how little you expect it.

Presently the enemy strategy was clear. Marselius's right wing advanced, slowly, through the croplands and orchards, while the barbarian left wing stayed behind. With his army split by the ridge, Frugi couldn't simply sweep Marselius from the field; and how could he break past the barbarians and fall on Marselius from behind now that his ambush was discovered?

"They are only foot soldiers," one of the legates said. "Barbarians at that. How can they withstand a charge of legionary horse?"

"I have described Sentinius to you," Frugi said wearily. "And then they had no *balloon*." The evil thing hung in the sky directly to the west. It must somehow communicate with the ground, because Marselius deployed against the legion Frugi had hidden in the orchards; and when the legion withdrew, Marselius closed his ranks again.

"It is held to the ground by that rope," the *frumentarius* said. "Cut the rope and it must drift free. This has happened before."

"How do you know this?"

"We heard this from spies," the intelligence officer said. "But we did not believe them."

"So." Frugi pointed to where the end of the balloon's tether lay. "We need go only there—"

"Where there are few barbarians," the legate said.

That was true enough. There were no more than a hundred to guard the balloon's tether. But— "Few indeed," Frugi said.

"Now consider this. Their whole formation is like a funnel, with only emptiness at the bottom. With nothing where they keep their *balloon*. As if they cannot believe we know it to be vulnerable. Or that we do not know its value. Tell me, Legate: would Caius Marius Marselius know the value of a *balloon?*"

"He would, Proconsul."

"Then can we not assume that the barbarians who possess it must know?"

"We can—"

"Then we must assume they will protect it. With their star weapons, perhaps. With *something*. No. I will not send a legion down those lanes to chase a lure." Frugi studied the battle ground again. "But—perhaps—"

"Yes, Proconsul?"

"Their left flank. Spearmen. Supported by archers, but the archers are further in. There is a gap between their spearmen and the woods. I would suppose their horse waits there, just beyond where we can see, hidden by those woods. But—their horse is no match for a legion; and we have horse archers in plenty. These barbarians have never seen *our* archery. Perhaps, Valerius, it is time they learned."

"It will be my pleasure to teach them," the legate said.

"Do so. Recall the Eleventh from hiding in the trees and remount them. Take them and the Eighth. Deploy the Eighth against the barbarian cavalry which will surely be hidden on your right. Bring the Eleventh to archery range and shoot down those spearmen. Shoot enough and they will run. When you have broken through their line, ride behind the enemy. Ignore the *balloon* and whatever protects it. Sweep behind the barbarian force and fall upon Marselius in the center. As you do, I will send the other legions in a general charge. We will crush Marselius."

His enthusiasm was infectious, and the legate was caught up with it. "Hail, Titus Frugi!" he shouted as he rode away. When he was gone, Frugi's smile vanished. Go with God, Valerius, Frugi thought. As for me, I am afraid.

"I still think it's stupid," Art Mason said. "Hell, Cap'n, let *me* go—"

"No. You and Elliot are needed here. Just see that Frugi doesn't break through anywhere. And look out for the king."

"Ye're daft," Drumold said. "But I hae long ceased to vex myself wi' thoughts of controlling you. Still, what will you accomplish?"

"Possibly nothing," Rick said. "But you exaggerate the danger. There is none to me, and little to anyone else. You do not have the game 'chess' here, do you?"

"Not by that name," Drumold said.

"No matter. It is a war game. There are many ways to win, but only one way to win quickly without great slaughter. Let's go." Rick waved his group forward: Reznick, Bisso, and two other mercs, plus a half dozen Guardsmen. The mercenaries wore kilts and bright tabards, and their battle rifles were wrapped in cloth bowcases. From a distance they looked like any Tamaerthan light cavalry.

They rode southeast, toward Marselius's legions. When they were close to the base of the ridge, they dismounted and turned the horses over to two Guardsmen. Rick led the others into the thin scrub that covered the ridge.

"Okay," he said. "This is as good a place as any."

The mercenaries shed their kilts and pulled on camouflage coveralls. The Guardsmen also abandoned bright colors and put on drab kilts and leather helmets. When they were dressed, Rick led them up the ridge.

Halfway up they paused in a wooded draw. Rick took out his binoculars, while Reznick shook out signal flags and waved them. Rick focussed in on the balloon, "Okay, they've seen us," he said. He watched the flag man. "'L-E-G-I-O-N-S A-T-T-A-C-K-I-N-G L-E-F-T W-I-N-G.' Get the rest of that signal and acknowledge. I want a look over that way."

He couldn't see. The brush was too thick and the draw too deep. Then he heard distant thunder. The recoilless, and possibly grenades.

"Murphy says First Pikes are holding," Reznick reported. "No change otherwise."

"Nobody above us on the slopes?"

"Not until we reach the top."

"Okay. Let's move." They climbed up the draw.

When they were nearly at the top of the ridge, they took more signals from Murphy in the balloon. Rick nodded and waved Reznick forward.

Reznick screwed the sound suppressor on his 9mm Ingram submachine gun. He moved carefully up the draw, guided by Murphy's directions, until he was near a small thicket. The Ingram made no more noise than the loud tearing of cloth as he fired an entire clip into the bushes. Then he reloaded and went to inspect his work.

After a few moments Rick heard a low whistle. He waved the others forward.

Twice more Reznick took the silenced Ingram forward. Then they were at the top of the ridge.

"Move!" Rick ordered. "Up. Go like hell!"

They dashed over onto the level ground on top. Rick was panting, and his legs felt like lead. My arse aches, too, he thought. Hell, a man with piles didn't ought to be doing this! A Roman trooper stood just in front of him. Rick fired twice with his .45 and the Roman went down. Then there were two more Roman soldiers. One held his shield forward and raised his sword—

Rick shot through the shield. Reznick fired from behind him and three more Romans went down. There were a dozen more dismounted Roman troopers. Reznick and Bisso fired at full automatic, short bursts, slow, methodical fire; the Romans collapsed in heaps. Then they faced five mounted Roman officers.

"Surrender!" Rick shouted. When one of the Romans wheeled, Rick shot his horse. The animal screamed in pain. "Kill the horses!" Rick shouted.

Bisso's battle rifle thundered. Then it was joined by two more. As the horses began to buck and plunge, a Roman in a scarlet cape leaped free and drew his sword.

"Hail, Titus Frugi!" Rick called. "Why throw your life away to no purpose? I have come to speak with you."

Frugi licked his lips and looked around. One of his officers was struggling to free himself from a fallen horse. Bishop Polycarp's animal had not yet been killed; His Grace sat with his hands raised as if in blessing. His other three officers were taken, struck down and seized by these grim men; and his bodyguards lay in heaps.

"Set up over there," Rick shouted. Bisso and the other two mercs laid out their battle rifles. "Anything comes over that lip, kill it." He turned to the Roman commander. "Now, Proconsul, let us talk."

"Who are you, barbarian?"

Hah, Rick thought. The way he asks that, it's a good thing I came myself. "Rick Galloway, Colonel of Mercenaries, War Lord of Tamaerthon—and friend to Marselius Caesar, who sends you greetings. Only two days ago I heard Marselius himself praise your courage and honor. And your good sense— however, you must not run away, Proconsul. And while I permit you to hold that sword for the moment, you must eventually put it down."

"While I hold it—"

"While you hold it you can kill yourself," Rick said.

"That, Titus Frugi, is forbidden," Bishop Polycarp warned.

"My Lord Bishop," Rick said. "I had hoped to include Your Grace in our meeting. Can you not prevail upon the Proconsul to lay down that sword?"

Titus Frugi looked around helplessly. His officers were taken or dead. The strangers looked perfectly capable of dealing with any rescue attempt—not that there was any sizable force nearby anyway. He stood shaking with rage and frustration, then threw down the weapon with a curse. "Speak, barbarian," he said. "I have little choice but to listen."

17

"Here they come." Art Mason raised his rifle.

The two legions of cataphracti moved in formation, certain of themselves, riding proudly. The lead formation deployed, ready to ride through the chivalry of Tamaerthon to Drumold's banner lifted high above them.

The Roman trumpets sounded. Lances came down in unison. The Romans moved forward. At a walk. A trot—

"Now," Mason said.

The light machine gun opened up in sharp, staccato bursts. Then the recoilless. The center of the Roman line went down; the troopers behind crashed into them, and the orderly line dissolved into confusion. The rear ranks crowded against each other.

"Fire in the hole!" Elliot shouted. The recoilless blasted again. More Romans fell. Their charge was broken before it had ever begun.

Tamaerthan and Drantos horse alike surged forward into the confusion. The Roman forces were bunched together, so that only the outer troops could use their weapons. The Allied cavalry, heavy and light alike, could dart in, strike, and dash back to charge again.

The other Roman legion reined in about a hundred yards from the pikemen and took out their bows.

Mason turned to his trumpeter and nodded. Shrill notes sounded, and two hundred Tamaerthan longbowmen ran out of the trees where they'd hidden.

"Let the grey gulls fly!" Caradoc ordered. The first flight of arrows fell upon the Romans from behind.

The trumpets sounded again, followed by the thutter of drums and the squeal of pipes. First Pike Regiment surged forward at double time. They flowed across the ground toward the Romans.

Mason dismounted and opened the bipod of his H&K battle rifle. He lay on the ground and fired randomly into the Roman formation until the pikemen closed. The Romans found themselves in a desperate engagement.

"I had not known," Titus Frugi said. He raised Rick's *binoculars* again and stared at the scene below, then cursed. "Who ever saw foot soldiers attack cavalry?" It was an event totally outside his experience; the surprise was as complete as if the pikemen had risen into the air.

First the star weapons. The Eighth Legion's charge was thoroughly broken before they ever engaged the enemy. Now they were trapped, forced back against the Eleventh which was in desperate straits, archers behind it and those spear men in front. Could Valerius withdraw? Would he? He searched for a sign of his subordinate, hardly able to hold the binoculars still. What other marvels did these starmen have?

"You see," Rick said gently. "Two legions could not break my pikes. Not when they have the aid of star weapons. As you must know." He waved to indicate the dead and dying heaped around them. "Your bodyguards fared no better. What use is this slaughter? How will Rome survive if all her soldiers are dead?"

"And you?" Polycarp asked. "What do you gain from this?"

"I am a friend of Marselius Caesar," Rick said. "When Rome's borders are safely held by my friends, Tamaerthon and Drantos are safe. These are perilous times, Your Grace. More perilous than even you can know. We all need friends."

"Indeed."

"Even Rome," Rick said. "Perhaps Rome most of all."

On the field below the slaughter continued. Now the Romans were trying to withdraw, as the deadly Tamaerthan gulls flew again and again.

"Two legions," Bishop Polycarp said. "Two legions destroyed, and you have not yet met Marselius."

Not destroyed. Not yet. Disorganized, useless as fighting instruments until reformed. Doomed, unless they withdrew. But not yet destroyed . . . "What would you have me do, Your Grace?" Titus Frugi asked.

"You yourself said it was disaster," Polycarp said. He pointed to the balloon. "Will it not continue? Today your forces retreat with what Valerius can save. Tomorrow the barbarians advance. With *that*, watching, always watching. Wherever we go, it follows." He shuddered. "And I say nothing of the fire and thunder weapons."

"I ask again. What would you have me do, Your Grace?"

"End this madness."

"How?"

"One of your trumpeters survives," Rick said. "Sound the retreat."

"So that your cavalry can pursue."

"What of that?" Rick asked. "Will any be saved if they stand and fight? Where will Valerius take those legions?"

"Along the road, to hold the ford."

"Then send one of these," Rick said. He indicated the captured officers. "Have Valerius take his legions to the next crossroad and make camp. You and I will meanwhile go to speak with Marselius Caesar." Suddenly Rick's calm detachment snapped. "For God's sake, stop this slaughter," he shouted. "Haven't we had enough?"

"More than enough," Polycarp said. "More than enough."

Titus Frugi ground his teeth together. Then, grimly, grudging every word, he spoke to his trumpeter. "Sound the general retreat," he ordered.

"Forward, lads!" Drumold shouted. "Up the road! Forward!"

"For Drantos! Forward!"

The young king was right alongside the Tamaerthan leader. No way to stop them, Mason thought. It even makes sense. If we can get any sizable force around the ridge and behind the Roman main body, we've won the day. The same plan Titus Frugi had, only he couldn't carry it off. As long as there's no ambush.

Not sure we can do it. The Tamaerthan cavalry aren't that good, and there aren't that many of them, even with those Drantos troops. Either way, best send a couple of mercs to look out for Ganton—

"Sir!" The young rider was nearly as out of breath as his horse. An acolyte of Yatar.

"Yes, lad?"

"Orders from the *balloon*. Halt at the ford. The Romans are going to surrender."

So, Mason thought. Captain's done it again. Now all I have to do is convince Drumold and the kid. He spurred his horse forward.

Drumold paced around and around the table in the largest room of the villa. "Och," he said. "I canna say I care for the situation. The Romans have their forces intact. All their forces, and all Flaminius's forces. While we are here, in their midst, without rations—"

"Which they're sending—"

Drumold cut off Rick's protest. "Which they *say* they are sending. But we have none yet. And I do not think they will let *their* troops—nor their horses!—starve to feed us."

"Your fears are groundless," Rick said. "They will send food. And why do you fear the Romans?"

"Iron," Camithon said.

"Iron?" Drumold asked.

"Iron," the Protector repeated. "Iron makes Rome what she is. They have much, we have little."

"That's a pretty sharp observation, Cap'n," Elliot said. "Like those mills I've seen. They've got millponds behind dams, and overshot wheels with gear trains. They can run on less water than any mill I saw in Drantos."

Or in Tamaerthon, Rick thought. Which means they can run during more of the year. "Iron mines and good mills—I suppose they use them to drive bellows?"

Elliot nodded. "Saw just that about five klicks from here. Regular foundry."

"Which means when the Romans discover gunpowder— and they will—they'll have the means to make guns. Lots of them," Rick mused. One more headache. Add gunpowder and guns to Roman discipline and record-keeping and they'll own this end of Tran.

Which might be no bad thing—although Drumold and Tylara weren't likely to see it that way.

"If Tamaerthon is threatened, how long before Drantos falls?" Ganton asked.

Smart lad, Rich thought. Ganton seemed more sure of himself, now that he'd led troops in a battle. It hadn't been much of a battle, nor had Ganton played a large part in it, but he'd been at the head of his Guards, right alongside Drumold and Balquhain.

"What should we do, then?" Rick demanded.

"What we should have done before," Drumold said. "Take hostages. Think, lad. They have here the whole strength of Tamaerthon, and Wanax Ganton to boot. Surely Publius has thought of this. And 'tis Publius who will remain, while Marselius marches on to Rome."

"Without us," Camithon added. "Without us."

"You yourself refused his offer to take us to Rome," Rick protested.

"And what of that?" Drumold demanded. "Should we put our heads deeper in a noose? Protector Camithon did well to refuse such a dangerous offer."

"And you genuinely fear for our lives?"

Drumold shrugged. "Perhaps not now. But later—when Publius realizes that he holds all the strength of Rome? What will happen to Tamaerthon then? Aye, and to Drantos as well.

You ask it yourself, lad—what happens when the Romans have star weapons for themselves? We can no conquer Rome. We can no destroy the Romans. We can take hostages. Take them, lad. Now. While we yet can."

"Is that your advice also?" Rick asked Camithon.

"Aye."

"Elliot?"

Sergeant Major Elliot shrugged. "You know these people better than I do, sir. But I'd feel some better if we could be *sure* we'll get home—and after, who knows what they might do? How can it hurt?"

"Majesty?"

Ganton shrugged. "I must heed the advice of those wiser than I."

Rick sighed. "It's no substitute for a policy," he said. "Even if it is traditional. But I dine tonight with Marselius, and I'll see what I can do."

There were only Rick, Marselius, and Lucius at the dinner; Publius had to see to the ordering of the troops and the final surrender of Frugi's camp.

Rick waited until the dinner was finished and they had both had wine. "Some of my officers are concerned," he said.

Marselius frowned. "About what?" he demanded.

"Loot, for one thing."

"Ah. There was little fighting, thus few fallen enemies to despoil." Marselius shrugged. "I will see to it. There should be ample gold in Titus Frugi's camp. I will arrange a donative to our gallant allies."

"Thank you. There is another concern."

Marselius looked puzzled. "Of what? The victory could not be more complete. With few casualties on either side. A brilliant stroke—"

"Which increased the size of your army," Rick said. "But leaves us in desolate territory, dependent on rations we do not have."

"Food is coming," Marselius protested. "Wagonloads of grain. The first arrive tomorrow." He drained a goblet of wine. "What are you saying?"

"That some of my soldiers are afraid they'll never leave Roman territory alive," Rick said. "And Drumold fears that the strength of Rome may be sent against Tamaerthon, now that Rome has no civil strife. My apologies, Caesar, for being so blunt."

"Better to be blunt," Lucius said. "Tell me, Caesar, would you not be, ah, concerned, also, were you in his situation?"

"I suppose I might," Marselius said. "And what do you suggest I do?"

"Drumold wants hostages," Rick said.

"And you?"

"I want only to return to my University. There is much more I must do before The Time—"

"But you do not protest. You prefer to take hostages."

Rick said nothing.

Marselius frowned. "Then you do not trust me—"

"Nonsense," Lucius said. "Caesar, are you under the illusion that you are immortal?"

Marselius looked thoughtful. "I think I see an answer," he

said at last. "My granddaughter has asked me to visit the Lady
Gwen. Now I shall let her. Lucius, ride to Benevenutum, and
inform Octavia that it is my desire that she continue her studies
in Tamaerthon. Choose suitable companions and servants to
join her—but she is to meet the Lord Rick's forces and accompany them on their return. It is fitting that she be escorted
by our allies." He turned to Rick. "Will that be satisfactory?"

"Certainly."

For a few moments the room seemed cold; then Lucius
smiled broadly. "It is a scheme that has merit. May I join her,
after we have taken Rome?" The old man sighed. "I have often
dreamed of retiring to some center of learning. I would appreciate the opportunity to see this place. And the Lady Octavia
will be very pleased."

"You will always be welcome," Rick said. "Caesar, this is
inspired. The Lady Octavia can learn much to aid Rome during
The Time; and not even the most suspicious will believe that
you or your son would endanger her."

And beyond that, Rick thought. Beyond that, she'll meet
young Ganton—and who knows what might come of that. It's
time Ganton got a systematic education. Golden years and all
that—he can't object to being a student prince for a while.
Where he'll be with Octavia. Gwen says she's intelligent and
attractive, and Ganton's young. . . .

"An excellent plan," Rick said again.

INTERLUDE

Luna

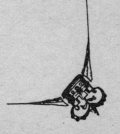

18

Earth, bluc and fragile and lovely, swirling storms and shining seas, filled one wall of the office. Les had seen half a hundred planets, and none were lovelier.

I suppose it could depend on your viewpoint, he thought. Humanity came from there. A lot longer ago than most of them suspect. But home is always the nicest place...

Stupid thought. I haven't got a home.

Les stood in the doorway a moment longer, then entered the office. The room was panelled in wood, with a Kashdan carpet and luxurious furniture; but Les noticed little of that. Despite the opulence, the office was dominated by the Earth.

The colors swirled gently. Earth wasn't really visible from that office, but a real-time holographic display was trivial among the honors and privileges earned by the man Rick Galloway had known as Inspector Agzaral.

Even so, neither Agzaral nor any other human had earned

the right to do what Agzaral did next. He opened his desk drawer and took out a small electronic device. After inspecting it carefully, he nodded to Les. "Hail, Slave," Agzaral said.

"I greet you, Important Slave," Les replied formally. He fell silent as Agzaral adjusted the electronic gear. After a moment, Les could hear faint voices: his and Agzaral's, speaking meaningless pleasantries in the official Confederation Standard tongue for civil servants.

Agzaral nodded in satisfaction and leaned back in his chair. "That should be sufficient," he said. "Sit down. Have some sherry. I regret that the shipment of Praither's Amontillado has been delayed, but Hawkers is a substitute I have found acceptable. Did you have a pleasant journey?"

Les waited as Agzaral poured sherry into a crystal glass, then solemnly tasted it. "Excellent," he said. He glanced at his hands. No tremble. Voice all right. Emotions nicely under control. It was difficult to deceive Agzaral, but not impossible. "Pleasant enough trip going," he said. "Dull coming back."

Agzaral smiled faintly. "Ah. You found it pleasant to learn that the woman was pregnant?"

"How the hell—?"

"Gently," Agzaral cautioned. "That goblet would be difficult to replace. There is no cause for alarm. Our employers do not know. Your efforts to deceive the recorders were entirely successful with regard to the *Shalnuksis*. But tell me, did you really expect to deceive *me?*"

"I'd hoped to."

"Unwise," Agzaral said. "Most unwise. You would do far better to trust me."

"Trust you? How the hell can I trust you when I don't even know what side you're on?"

Agzaral spread his hands wide and let them drop to his lap. "Side? You would seriously have me choose a faction? Now, when the alternatives are still forming? Try not to be too great an ass, my friend.

"And don't protest. When it comes to politics, you are an ass. I can admire your courage. Your skill with languages. Your prowess as a pilot, and— Yes. I envy your successes with women. You even seem to understand some of Earth's political quarrels. But when it comes to the important skills, the ability to know the High Commission and the Council—" He shrugged. "You're an ass."

"At least I take a stand. I'm not a damned trimmer like you—"

Agzaral laughed. "Some day one of your stands will be against a wall. As to being a trimmer, is it unwise to have every faction think I am its agent?"

"When they find out—"

"If," Agzaral said. "And think upon it, my fellow Slave. If *you* do not know which faction I truly favor, then *they* cannot know either." He chuckled again. "So. You have taken a stand. Tell me where."

"Well—"

"Come, come, a simple question. Which faction do you favor? Who is its leader? Which race champions your position?"

"All right, so I don't know," Les said. "But I know this. I'm for leaving Earth alone. And Tran, too. Leave them develop by themselves."

Agzaral nodded. "The position taken by many of the more powerful Ader'at'eel. Unfortunately not all of them. They are joined by the Enlightenment Party of the Finsit'tuvii. But I fear that coalition is not the most powerful faction."

"Is that true?" Les demanded. "The Ader'at'eel want Earth and Tran left alone?"

"Substantially. Of course they don't know that Tran exists. But four of the Five Families do indeed support that position."

"Then—?"

"But then there are the Fusttael," Agzaral continued smoothly. "Their opposition is formidable. They hold no overpowering advantage, but they have the most strength at the moment."

"And what do they want?" Les demanded.

"They want to destroy Earth . . ."

"Destroy the Earth!"

"More or less."

More or less. He looked at the holograph again. A beautiful planet, filled with humans. Wild humans, not slaves of the millennia-old Confederation. Humans who would soon burst into space, find their way to the stars—who were about to come uninvited into Confederate territory.

More or less meant more. Bomb Earth civilization back to the stone age, and trust there'd be enough humans left for breeding stock. They only needed enough wild genes to temper the corps of Slave soldiers. Enough to improve the breed of Janissaries . . .

"What does the Navy think of this?" Les demanded. "Or your service?"

"The opinions of Slaves do not matter—"

"Come off it."

"But certainly the Navy has divided opinions," Agzaral said smoothly. "It is likely that some ships would refuse to take part in the necessary operations. But—enough would obey the orders."

"We can't let that happen!"

Agzaral spread his hands. "How do we prevent it? But I agree, it would be regrettable. And there is the third alternative."

Sure, Les thought. Human membership in the Confederation. Forced membership, imposed now while Earth was helpless. A junior membership, with Earth controlled by the High Commission. Peace, unity, and—stagnation. A static society. Stasis for a thousand years. Still, it had to be preferable to bombardment and destruction . . .

"The balance of the Ader'at'eel would bring Earth into the Confederacy now," Agzaral said. "But enough of this. Your report. Will they be able to grow *surinomaz?*"

"Possibly," Les said. "Of course there will be the mutiny. It will be settled by now."

"Yes. With what outcome?"

"Either of the mercenary leaders should be competent with those weapons against that population."

"Ah. So the survey ship will not be wasted."

"I think not. And the soldiers will want resupply. Ammunition, soap, penicillin—"

"You understand their needs," Agzaral said. "I will send you to Earth to procure for them. I recall that you enjoy that work."

"I'll do it, but I want to pilot the ship that goes back to Tran."

"To what purpose?" Agzaral asked.

"Why do you ask? I'm a pilot. I know Tran exists. Not too many pilots do. I'd think you'd want me to."

"It's reasonable," Agzaral said. "You will not be able to take the first ship, however. One leaves immediately. Piloted by *Shalnuksis*. Tran is not too far off their course, and they want to see for themselves how Tran has revived since their last series of visits."

"Last time they went there, they bombed out half the civilization. What will they do this time?"

"On this journey, nothing—"

"That's not what I meant," Les said.

"I know. But I have no better answer."

Les nodded in submission. "Is their first ship carrying supplies?"

"A few. Whatever we had. The mercenary leader Galloway had made suggestions before they departed, you may recall. We used his list. Some of what they wanted was easily obtained. For the rest—your task, now."

"All right. Provided I get to go back myself."

"Why are you so anxious to go back?"

"Does it matter?"

"It might." Agzaral was silent, obviously waiting for Les to speak, but Les said nothing. "Very well. I took the trouble to look up your ancestry," Agzaral said finally. "Rather a lot of wild human strain." He paused. "They'll never allow the child to live if they learn of it."

"How will they learn?" Les demanded.

"Gently." Agzaral glanced at a timer on his desk. "We do not have much longer to speak freely. Let us not waste these minutes. They will not learn from me. But I must know what you intend." He pointed to the Earth. "You have lived long among wild humans. In some ways you act like them. Many wild humans mate for life. This seems unnatural to me, but I know they do it. Is this your intent?"

Les didn't answer.

"I must know."

"I don't know," Les said. "I've thought of it. Live on Tran, with Gwen and my children. Doesn't that tempt you?"

"Earth would tempt me more. But it is not so attractive that I would forsake what I have. Consider. The girl and the child may both be dead."

"You think that hasn't haunted me ever since I let her go planetside?"

"Yet she seemed competent enough," Agzaral mused. "I expect she has survived. She may, however, have found another mate."

"Yeah. I thought of that, too."

"What will you do in that case?"

"I don't know that, either."

Agzaral nodded in sympathy. "Certainly your interest in Tran would be much abated?"

"Yes. But I have to find out."

Agzaral looked at the hologram for long enough that Les saw movement in Earth's clouds. Then he spoke decisively. "You will have that chance," Agzaral said. "I hope the knowledge pleases you."

PART FOUR

Invaders

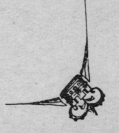

19

Autumn had come. Despite his charcoal brazier Apelles felt the chill damp of the stone chamber high in the tower of Castle Armagh. The Firestealer crept toward the True Sun, and now both were in the sky together; the days grew short. Evening came and lamps had to be lit, but still there was work to be done.

Armagh was three hundred stadia east of Castle Dravan, and nowhere near as comfortable; once again Apelles marvelled that Lord Rick would move so much of his household to this godless place. Truly there was no accounting for the ways of the starmen! Even so, Apelles was content, now that he was a consecrated priest of Yatar. The room's present discomforts were small compared to those he'd endured as an acolyte. He was more concerned about his pen, which was made of soft iron and had a blunt point that scratched the paper.

Despite the scratchy pen, Apelles worked steadily. He was

careful not to make a blot. A blotted sheet had to go back to the pulp vats, and there was never enough paper no matter how hard the acolytes labored. It took time to pound logs to pulp, shred rags, then soak and stir and matt the resulting brew until it yielded thick sheets to be rolled out on sieves. It took even more time for the paper to dry satisfactorily. Then it had to be coated with a wash of clay and dried again. Making paper was no easy work; Apelles knew, because it had not been long since he had done it—until he had learned to read and write.

He had learned his new work from Roman scribes, and he was proud of his knowledge. Work carefully, record everything; that was the way to control a nation. The power that he held was great, real power, power easily abused had he been so inclined; but he was a sworn priest of Yatar, a shepherd, not a wolf.

He wrote steadily, and finally his desk was clear. He leaned back in his chair and smiled in satisfaction at his files. Truly they held power! Here, the manpower lists; names and locations of officers of the Army of Drantos, those on active duty and on leave, fit for service and on the invalid list. Over there were duties and taxes owed and paid; equipment issued; every detail. Some day he'd have the entire Army in his files, and then let the bheromen try to shirk their sworn service to the crown!

He nodded soberly at that thought. Yatar save the Wanax! Some bheromen and knights resented young Ganton's stay at the University, but Apelles knew the value of education, which gave even young swineherds the power of writing...

In another file were the names of every field in the Cumac region of County Chelm. Who owned them. Who worked them, and whether villein or free, and for what service or rent. What was planted, and what seed, and what fertilizer for what yield. Endless rows of words and numbers, carefully arranged.

And in yet another file, the names of all the acolytes and deacons and priests and archpriests, those who would be promoted and those who would serve out their lives as laborers in Yatar's fields and caves and monasteries...

The caves were not in his files. Their locations, and what stores they held, and how thick the ice and ice plant; these were state secrets, and those files were kept by Archpriest Yanulf himself. Apelles had seen them, once; he'd have to be content with that.

And here—

The magic box made squawking noises. Apelles stared dumbfounded. One of his duties was to guard that box and listen for messages; but he'd had little regard for that task. Privately he would have expected Yatar himself to appear before a small box like that could speak to him.

But it *was* speaking. First in the local Tran dialect, but wretchedly. "Ait, are there anyone there?" it demanded.

Then in other languages Apelles didn't know, but always demanding, insistent.

When he shouted for a messenger there was real fear in his voice.

The voice on the transceiver was thick and sibilant with trillings and drawn-out vowels. Rick was certain he was speaking to one of the *Shalnuksis*. He had only seen the aliens on three brief occasions, all more than two Earth years in the past, but he had no trouble recalling them: humanoid, two arms and two legs, but with the wrong proportions. Shoulders too high, necks short or nonexistent. Short torso but long arms and legs. Three fingers and two opposed thumbs, thin lips surrounding a mouth too high in the face. Fleshy snout-slit instead of a true nose, almost like a vertical second mouth rising to eye level . . .

The alien spoke in bursts. They'd done that before, Rick recalled; although not always. When they'd made set speeches the words flowed smoothly; it was when they engaged in spontaneous conversation that they hesitated.

The transceiver was a simple device: a rectangular sealed box, with a grill on one face. Below the grill was a colored square. There were no other controls, not even an on/off button.

He touched the control square. "Galloway here," he said.

"Ah," the alien voice answered. "Captain Galloway."

"Is this Karreeel?" Rick asked. The name Karreeel translated to 'Goldsmith,' Inspector Agzaral had said. Karreeel had seemed to be in command of the *Shalnuksi* who'd hired him. At least he'd done most of the talking.

"Karreeel is not here," the voice said. "I am Paarirre. Captain Galloway, are you in control of your men?"

"Yes."

"And where is Mr. Parsons?"

"Dead," Rick said.

"Ah. And you have—gained political mastery of a—suitable region?"

"Yes. We hold the area around this castle, and we are preparing to plant it all in *surinomaz*."

There was a period of silence while the aliens digested this information. Then: "Excellent. We have brought goods for you. Where do you prefer that we land them?"

"North and east of this castle there is a high plateau," Rick said.

"We see it."

Aha, Rick thought. They know where we are. He nodded significantly to Mason, who solemnly responded. "It is a large plateau. You may leave the goods at the southern edge."

"We will choose our own place on the—plateau."

"As you will. I prefer that you land at night, so that you are seen by as few inhabitants as possible. They have frightening legends about sky gods."

"We may—discuss—this later. For now, tell us: how large a territory do you control?"

"How should I describe it?"

"We understand all your—common units of measure. Use those."

Rick looked at Mason and shrugged. Best be somewhat truthful, he thought. Enough to show good faith. But don't give them enough information to help pick targets for *Shalnuksi* bombs. "I hold the land for a hundred kilometers around this castle," he said. "And I have an agreement with the neighboring kingdoms."

There was another pause. "*Surinomaz* requires much cultivation. Those who work its fields must be fed."

"I know. I can trade for food. But I must have more ammunition before I can take a larger territory. How did your troops do this in the past? You must have helped them directly."

There was another pause. "That is not your concern. Can you secure sufficient territory?" the alien voice demanded.

"Certainly. I have that now."

"Very well. This night, when it is fully dark, will be—convenient to us. Come to the—plateau."

"I can't get there that quickly," Rick said. And since you know where I am, you must know I can't get there by tonight.

"You need not come at all."

"I have three kilos of partially refined *surinomaz* sap," Rick said. "If you care to have it."

There was another pause. "The crop this—year—will not be of high—quality. Still, it may be worth taking. When you come to collect the goods we have brought, bring the *surinomaz* and the transceiver. Do not bring heavy weapons. We will be watching as you approach. Farewell."

"Tells us one thing," Art Mason said. He followed Rick out of the chamber, enclosing the transceiver, and shut the door, just in case the push-to-talk switch wasn't the only way the device could operate.

"What's that?" Rick asked.

"They're scared of our heavy weapons. We can hurt their ships."

"Seems reasonable," Rick agreed. Les, the human pilot of the ship that had brought them to Tran, had acted the same way, insisting that the ammunition and the recoilless and mortars be kept separate when they unloaded. "I wonder what they've brought us? Whatever it is, we'd better get ready to ride."

The escort was saddled and waiting. Beazeley and Davis, with Art Mason. Six Royal Drantos Guardsmen, and a dozen Tamaerthan mounted archers with Caradoc. A string of pack mules.

Tylara nodded in satisfaction. "It says much for our rule. You go to bring as great a treasure as this kingdom has ever known, yet you feel safe with no more than a dozen lances."

Never thought of it that way, but I guess she's right. "We should return in two days," he said. "Sure you don't want me to leave Caradoc with you?"

"There is no need. The lands are quiet. I have more fear for you."

"Nothing will happen." Not this time, anyway. He held her close for a moment.

The trail was wide enough for two abreast, and presently Rick found himself beside his captain of archers. Caradoc was singing. The words were in the Old Speech, but the tune seemed familiar to Rick. After a moment, Caradoc turned to Rick and grinned. "An air from our wedding dances," he said proudly.

"Ah," Rick said. And aha. A song from the Top Fifty a

couple of years ago. Gwen must have put new words to it.

"With your consent, I would return to the University for the winter, Lord," Caradoc said.

"Certainly. I'd intended for you to be with your wife."

"I thank you." Caradoc grinned again. "It is doubly important now."

"Aha?"

"Yes. As I left, my lady told me she believes that we have been blessed by Hestia."

"Congratulations." And I really ought to cheer, Rick thought. This should make life with Tylara a bit easier...

There were a dozen cartons of cigarettes; a case of penicillin; ten bottles of Bufferin and four of vitamins; some needles and thread and sewing supplies including an ancient foot-powered sewing machine; baling wire and pliers, which Mason eagerly seized; a carton of paperback mysteries; and a box of random supplies with items as disparate as nutcrackers and soap. The rest was ammunition: cartridges for both the H&K and M-16 battle rifles, .45's and 9mm for the pistols and the submachine guns, grenades, mortar bombs, and fifty rounds for the recoilless.

Tylara looked at the supplies with satisfaction. "Now they have come. Are they likely to come again this season?"

"They said not," Rick answered. "They won't be here for a long time, possibly a full Tran year. They'll probably come next fall, when we have a full crop of *surinomaz*."

"Then I wish to return to Castle Dravan."

"Need we go there?" Rick asked. "There is little to attack us from the west."

"I hear tales of Westmen in the High Cumac," Tylara said. "More have been seen this fall than in the previous twenty years."

The Westmen were nomads who generally stayed on the high desert above the enormous fault known as the Westscarp. "If more come, Margilos should warn us," Rick said.

Tylara snorted contempt. In times long past, Margilos had paid tribute to the Five Kingdoms. Now it was in theory an independent city state famous for breeding centaurs. "I doubt they would," Tylara said. "They're half nomad themselves. Unless one believes the old tales."

Rick looked helpless. Tylara giggled. "It is said the men of Margilos have centaur blood, and there is much debate whether the first was begotten by a man on a centaur mare, or did a lady of Drantos enjoy the favor of a centaur stallion." They laughed, then she said urgently, "It is not a joke one makes when men of Margilos are present. They are quick to anger, and when enraged they feel no pain. Like the centaurs they breed."

"I'll remember. But surely you're not worried about Westmen?"

"No."

"Then it might be better to stay here. We can't be *sure* the *Shalnuksis* won't come again until next year—and I don't want them to know we value Castle Dravan. They may find out, of course. But why help choose targets for their *skyfire?*"

"I do not disagree," Tylara said. "Yet the risk is worthwhile. Armagh is no comfortable place to winter. I would be in Dravan

before the thaws, and travel in winter is difficult."

Something in her voice made him turn to look at her. She smiled and patted her belly.

"You too?" Rick demanded.

She frowned.

"Gwen is also pregnant. Caradoc just told me."

"Ah." Tylara laughed. "That is one child of Gwen's who will cost me no sleep." Then she came into his arms. "This time it will be a boy. I know it. And our son should be born in his own castle."

20

A hot wind blew down from the high escarpment. The day was already a scorcher, although it was only spring here in the foothill country. There ought still to have been a nip in the air. The hot air provided less lift for the balloon, too.

"She looks ready to me, Murph," said Corporal Walinski. "What about you?"

Ben Murphy looked at the twelve-foot balloon. It was already straining at the ropes held by the two archers. He tossed one more fuel brick into the firebasket underneath it, then gripped the main rope in both large hands. For a moment he glanced back into the wagon bed where Lafe Reznick was napping, but Lafe was still asleep. Or pretending to be. "Ready to lift," Murphy reported.

"Let go on the hold-downs!" shouted Walinski. The two archers let go and stepped back, while the balloon rose freely into the afternoon air. Murphy let the rope run through the blocks mounted on the wagon until the hundred-foot mark passed, then snubbed it around the cleat by the driver's seat. The balloon was now high enough to be visible from the next village, but low enough to be controllable.

"Think she'll stay up long enough?" Walinski asked.

"Yeah, if we give the pitch fast," Murphy said. "We're getting good at the spiel. Sure is hot, though."

"Compressive heating," Walinski said.

"Which?" And where in hell did Ski learn words like that?

"They called it compressive heating back in Los Angeles," Walinski said. "A special wind, a Santa Ana. Hotter'n hell, even in winter. And dry. Real dry. That's what this is, I think. Comes down off those high deserts. As it comes down lower it compresses, just like the Santa Ana in L.A."

"Well, it sure makes it hot enough," Murphy said. Winter had been wet in Drantos. Lots of snow in the east, not so much in the west. And nowhere near as cold as the locals expected, meaning the whole damn planet was heating up right on schedule as the rogue star came closer.

Murphy pulled off his jacket and pulled his wizard's robe out from under the seat. "Hey Lafe, better wake up. Duty time."

Reznick sat up sleepily. "Anything special about this village, Ski?"

"Not that I've heard."

"Same here," Murphy said. "The standard routine." He could damned near do that in his sleep by now. Take the wagon in. Use the balloon to get everybody's attention, and show the wizards' mighty power, then bring it down. Demonstrate magic, and let the deacons and acolytes of Yatar show the local clergy about sanitation. Make holy water by literally boiling the hell out of it! Ask about madweed. Do the crop survey—what was planted and how it grew. Tell 'em about the new plows, and show the blacksmith how to make one. Have Lafe put on his weapons show, a demonstration of star weapons so they'd know what they'd face if they ever revolted against their rightful lord the Eqeta of Chelm. And—

"Some new orders come by messenger this morning while you both was still in the sack," Walinski said. "Find out about the Westmen."

* * *

"More been spotted?" Reznick asked.

"They didn't *tell* me nothing. Just orders."

Murphy sighed. If he'd been awake, he could have questioned the messenger. Fat chance Ski would ever think of doing that. Ski could fight, but he wasn't much for questions. Wasn't much for brains, for that matter. But he had seniority over Ben Murphy, because he'd stayed with Parsons and came over to Captain Galloway with Elliot. He hadn't gone south and set up on his own.

Can't win 'em all, Murphy thought. And Ski don't give me much trouble, 'cept when he's drunk, and at least he knows it when he is. I've had worse bosses.

He could remember better bosses, too. His luck had been strange, these past few years. Strange, but better than it used to be. There'd been a time when he had no luck at all. It was because of that time that he was on Tran, ten light years from home, calling himself Ben Murphy and playing wizard to the heathen, instead of following his father's trade under the name his father gave him. Now at least things weren't all running against him.

He pulled on his robe, then picked up his assault rifle and kept watch while Walinski and Reznick put on their wizard suits. Walinski's was by far the fanciest, since he was supposed to be the master wizard and Murphy and Reznick his journeymen, with the acolytes of Yatar to help them.

Walinski had just finished dressing when Agikon, the senior acolyte, shouted in alarm and pointed upward. The balloon was wobbling alarmingly on the end of the rope.

"Wind?" Murphy called.

"Wind, hell!" Ski shouted. "Look!"

A flight of arrows leaped out of the woods to the left of the road. Two hit, and the balloon wobbled again.

Walinski unslung his battle rifle.

"What's to shoot?" Murphy demanded. "Probably some local kids. I'm surprised nobody took a shot at it before."

"Maybe. That was good shootin'," Ski said.

"Uh." Come to that, it *was* good shooting. About as good as Tamerthan archers, and they were the best on Tran. "Ski, I don't like this. Let's laager the wagons out in the open field. Just in case."

"Well—"

Murphy didn't wait. He turned his wagon sharply and stood

up, bringing his hands together over his head. He repeated the
signal, then whipped up the horses. Lafe Reznick looked puzzled for a moment, then jumped down and ran back to the next
wagon to urge its driver along.

"Gonna feel stupid," Ski muttered. "But we hafta patch the
balloon anyway."

That was for sure. The balloon was losing altitude fast.
Murphy looked back. The other carts were following, closing
up as Ben sent his in a circular track. He was halfway into the
field, the laager not yet formed, when he hit a soft patch of
mud. The wagon stuck fast.

"Holy shit, that's all we needed," Ski said. "We'll have to
patch the balloon just to lift us out of the mud." He looked at
Murphy. What did you get us into now?

Murphy swore. He was about to jump down from the cart
when a flight of arrows fell around them. Walinski screamed
and reeled against the cart with an arrow sticking out of his
face. One of the acolytes fell with an arrow in his chest. The
horses were untouched.

There was another flight of arrows. The Drantos Guards
archers yelled and brought up their crossbows. Walinski was
screaming his head off, clawing at the arrow in his face. He'd
dropped his rifle. Murphy threw himself down into the wagon
box and peeked over the edge, his rifle ready.

"What the hell do we do?" Reznick shouted.

"How the hell should I know?" Ben answered. There weren't
any targets. Murphy squinted, estimating the distance to the
trees. Two hundred meters, near enough. He whistled. "That
was long bow shot!" he shouted. "Even for Tamaerthans!"

"Damn straight!" Reznick answered.

Murphy thought about the implications. One of Captain
Galloway's high cards were those Tamaerthan archers. Used
in connection with other troops they could be devastating, because they outranged everyone else. Drantos crossbows could
carry about as far as Tamaerthan longbows, but they were slow
to load, and nobody in Drantos really believed in long-range
archery. Tamaerthan archers loved long-distance shooting. But
those weren't Tamaerthan troopers out there, so who were they?

More arrows fell. By now everyone was behind a wagon
or under cover, and nobody else was hit. Curious, Murphy
thought. The horses and oxen pulling the carts hadn't been

touched. Not even Reznick's centaur. Dobbin was cowering behind Lafe's wagon, whimpering the way the animals did when something threatened them and they couldn't fight or run away.

About my own situation. Can't fight and can't run. Things were quiet now, but—"It's a horse raid," Ben called.

"Yeah, that's what I figure," Lafe answered. "Somebody wants them beasts alive."

Murphy strained to see into the forest, but there was nothing visible. "Hell, maybe we ought to let 'em have 'em."

"Not Dobbin, they don't."

"Probably don't want him. Just want the horses and oxen. Probably too smart to want a centaur," Murphy said.

"Now you lay off," Reznick said. "But we better do something here. Want me to look at Ski?"

"Yeah, in a minute. You stay down just now, first things first. Move them carts!" Murphy shouted. "Go around me! Laager those damn wagons!" Just because the lead wagon couldn't move didn't mean they couldn't make a wagon laager. Murphy nodded in satisfaction. Agikon had caught on, and was bringing up the other carts. At least they'd have some cover—

A dozen light cavalrymen burst from the woods. They rode crouched low against their mounts, most of their bodies invisible behind their horses. They didn't look like anyone Murphy had ever seen.

"Westmen!" one of the acolytes shouted.

Murphy snapped down the battle rifle's bipod and rested the legs on the wagon seat. Ski was still screaming, but Murphy put that out of his mind along with everything else except his sight picture. Aim for the rider, but low enough to hit the mount if you miss. Get a good sight picture. Squeeze off a round—

The first rider fell. Ben shifted targets. On the second shot both horse and rider went down. The rider leaped free, but Lafe Reznick's burst took him in the chest. Ben looked up long enough to wave thanks.

Shift aim again. Keep it smooth. Another down. Three shots for the fourth. *Don't rush it!* Concentrate. New sight picture—

The nearest enemy was no more than twenty meters away when Murphy shot him off his horse. Then, suddenly, the

Westmen were riding back toward the woods. Murphy picked off one more rider, and a last one seemed to fall out of the saddle in sheer surprise.

Then there weren't any more targets. One of the downed riders tried to get up, but a crossbowman took care of him. Two more Westmen rode from the woods and grabbed a loose horse while Murphy was changing magazines. Then things were still.

Not quite, though. Walinski was still yelling his head off. One of the acolytes was trying to hold him while another looked at the arrow piercing from near his left eye down across the cheek to come out at the neck. It was a bloody mess, but it hadn't hit a major artery or Ski wouldn't be able to yell.

"Lafe! Go look after Ski," Murphy yelled. "But be ready to cover me. Agikon!"

"My lord!"

"Take Lord Walinski's rifle. Keep watch on the trees."

"Aye, lord."

The acolyte handled the H&K with confidence. Captain Galloway didn't encourage training locals to use star weapons, but out here in the marches you needed all the help you could get.

"The rest of you stand guard! I won't be long." *I hope.* Going out in the open is probably stupid, Murphy thought. *But I'd best see what I'm up against, and maybe get some information the Captain can use.*

Murphy knelt by the six dead men while Agikon watched the forest. The closest man had a bronze sword, a thing he'd seen only in shrines to Vothan farther north and east. It was long enough to be used from horseback, and had gold wire wound around the hilt.

The rest of the men were armed with short spears or light lances, and long wicked hornbacked compound bows, almost too big to use from horseback, only they sure could. They also had knives. Most had no armor, but one was wearing a mail shirt obviously made in Drantos. They didn't have much clothing, breechcloths and a rough wool cloak, but just about every one of them had something of gold: an armlet, or a brooch, or just gold wire wound loosely around his neck.

They were all muscle and bone, and it looked as if they hadn't enough to eat for a long time.

So these were the Westmen. Not many ever saw them. They

lived in the unexplored high plains beyond the Westcarp, and few who'd entered their territory ever returned. Not that there was anything to go up there for.

The last man lay too near the trees, and he could just lie there. Ben Murphy wasn't about to get that close. But as Murphy turned away, the man leaped to his feet. He started to run toward him, but after a step he fell again. Ben whirled and leveled the rifle—

"Mercy, I beg you!" the man shouted. "I am not one of— one of the Horse People!"

"What the hell?"

"Mercy!" He stretched out on the ground, reaching toward Ben, crawling painfully toward him. "Mercy!" he screamed again.

Think fast, Ben. Maybe a trick. But— He went over to him. The man was bald, no better dressed than the Westmen— and he had no weapons at all.

"Who the hell are you?" Ben demanded.

"A priest of Vothan! Take me to your wagons, before the Horse People come to kill me!"

"Maybe. What were you doing with the Westmen?" Murphy demanded.

"I was priest of Vothan, at a shrine outside Margilos." The man spoke haltingly, with good grammar but hesitating sometimes. "A fool of a merchant from the—south wanted a guide, to lead him to the—the Westmen, that he might trade for gold. The chief priest thought that a good thing, and ordered me to go, for I had been to the top of the Scarp in my ordeal. But when we went again, the Horse People sacrificed the merchant to Pirin the Thunderer and made me a slave."

"So what the hell are you doing here?" Murphy demanded.

"The chief of the Red Rocks thought I brought him war luck, and now all the Horse People are coming down from the Westscarp. Above, all is heat and drying streams and death."

"Holy shit," Murphy said. "They're *all* coming down?"

"Those who can," the priest said. "So they brought me with them, slave and translator. I thought you evil wizards until I saw the blue robes of Yatar among you. Then I threw myself from the saddle and lay on the ground in hopes the Red Rocks would believe me dead. But I think my leg is broken."

A cool customer, Murphy thought. And a damned lucky find, a man who's been up there with them horse archers for

years. "Okay, Baldy, let's get you to the wagons." And away
from them trees, which give me the willies. "Here, get up,
lean on me. You'll have to hobble."

It was slow going. When they were halfway to the wagons,
Lafe Reznick came out to help. "What did you find?" he asked.

"Priest of Vothan the Westmen kept as a slave. Could be
valuable to the captain—"

Suddenly Agikon was shouting, and before Murphy could
see why, the acolyte fired five rounds, semi-automatic but so
fast it sounded like full rock and roll. A horse screamed. "Lords,
the Westmen!" Agikon shouted.

There were a dozen of the light cavalry coming across the
field at a gallop. Some had spears held low like lances. The
others carried short javelins ready to throw.

They seemed awfully close. People were yelling all around,
and it was hard to concentrate. Wish I had a grenade, Murphy
thought.

"Don't leave me!" the old priest shouted.

"Get him movin'," Reznick said. He unslung his rifle and
knelt. "Go on, Ben, go like hell."

Murphy helped the priest toward the wagons. It was like a
nightmare, the kind where no matter what happens you can't
move fast enough. He glanced back over his shoulder. More
Westmen, maybe twenty of them, riding like hell straight toward the laager. "Let's go, let's go," Murphy said. He pulled
the old man along, heedless of the priest's gasp of pain. As
they reached the laager he heard Reznick's H&K chatter at full
auto.

Murphy handed the priest to an acolyte. "Take care of him!"
He ran back into the field. Reznick was changing magazines.
He slammed the actuating lever home and fired again. The
Westmen were galloping toward him, getting too close.

"Run like hell, Lafe! I'll cover you!" Murphy shouted.

"Right!" Reznick turned and ran toward the wagons. Three
of the onrushing horsemen let fly with arrows. Lafe stumbled
and fell. He got up, not running as fast. The horsemen were
getting closer and closer to him. Murphy fired over his partner's
head, full automatic, but the horsemen kept coming. Reznick
stumbled again. "Ben, Ben, look after my wives—"

He tried to get to his feet, but there were two arrows in his
back. Murphy tried to ignore him, concentrate on shooting,
cut down the horsemen before they could reach Lafe, but they

kept coming, and one was getting closer and closer and his lance came down, and Murphy shot him four times but the lance came on anyway. Reznick turned in time to see it coming. He tried to dodge, but it hit him full in the chest.

"You mucking bastards!" Murphy slammed a new magazine into his rifle. Agikon came up behind him with three of the archers and they fired another volley. There were only three Westmen left, but they kept coming until Murphy shot them all down.

Lafe Reznick was already dead when Murphy knelt beside him. Ben looked up at the sky, then muttered prayers he hadn't remembered since he left home. He felt something snuffle against his neck and turned. It was Dobbin. The centaur must have broken his tether when he saw Reznick fall.

The centaur bent down and sniffed at the blood on Reznick's chest and face. His half-formed hands patted Lafe's clothing clumsily, as if trying to tidy it. Then he reared, threw back his head, and let out a long, wailing scream. It reminded Murphy chillingly of the legends of the banshee.

21

Ben Murphy screamed curses to the sky. Then he went back to the laager. Dobbin could do as much for Lafe now as anyone. Scratch one man who'd do to ride the river with. The hell with that.

Two archers were holding Walinski. Lafe had worked on getting the arrow out, but he hadn't finished the job. First things first, Murphy thought. Methodically he gave orders. Collect all the enemy's weapons and gear. Retrieve the balloon. Lighten the bogged-down wagon. And keep guard, there might be more out there. When the archers and acolytes started on all that, he had time to deal with Ski.

"It's going to hurt," Ben said. "I got to cut it out of there."

Walinski screamed something.

Ah, quit your bitching, Murphy thought. Why couldn't it have been you? No, that's not fair. Hell. He found a bottle of McCleve's best tucked into Lafe's gear, and brought it over to

210

Ski. "Drink it!" he shouted. "Take a good slug. Right. Another. Now I'll have one, gimme."

He took a drink from the bottle, then added a teaspoon of fine powder. It was made from madweed, and the old woman from the last village had sworn by it. Untested drug, Murphy thought. Probably the wrong thing to do, but what choices have I got? "Here, Ski, have another couple of slugs."

While Walinski drank, Murphy heated an iron rod in the wagon's balloon firepot. When it was red-hot he took it and went back to Ski. "Gimme the bottle—"

He handed the bottle to an acolyte and took a deep breath. Well, here goes— He used his combat knife to slice quickly down the shaft of the arrow, cutting open the tunnel it had made. Ski screamed again, and blood poured out. Too much blood. Murphy drew the heated iron rod along the wound. There was a smell of burning meat.

Probably the wrong thing, Ben thought. God knows I've made a hell of a scar. But it's got to be open. Too much risk of tetanus, and maybe the Westmen poison their arrows. Got to be open and cleaned out and got to stop the bleeding.

He used a Johnson & Johnson sterile dressing to cover the wound. There were a dozen in the first-aid kit, and when would there ever be more? And the bottle of peroxide was small, it would all be used treating Ski and the wounded archer.

Ben Murphy felt a long way from home.

The village was about a klick away, and nobody had come out to help them. Murphy gave Walinski the rest of the bottle, and supervised getting the wagon train going again. They'd have to go in without the balloon, one wizard dead and another wounded; if they were going to impress the locals at all, they'd need all their gear. And a story. And meanwhile, somebody had to get word back to Captain Galloway.

The hardest part was getting Lafe's body. Dobbin stood guard, ready to fight anyone approaching.

"We could kill it," Agikon said; but when he saw Ben's face, he shrank away in fear. "Forgive me, lord."

Murphy didn't answer. He tried talking to the centaur in soothing tones. "This is me. I've ridden you a dozen times. I'll take you back to Lafe's wives, but you got to let me have Lafe. Come on, Dobbin, it's all right—"

Eventually he whimpered and stood aside, letting Ben and

Agikon put Lafe's body in the wagon. Murphy covered his partner with wizard's robes.

The village was called Irakla, and like all high plains settlements it had a wall. This far west it wouldn't really be as much for defense against men as against a native beast called the gunkel, an omnivorous rodent the size of a dog, with an elongated body like a weasel, a scaly hairless tail, and armor plates something like an armadillo. It had sharp claws, big teeth, and a stink spray that wasn't as bad as a skunk but more than enough to keep humans away from it. Unfortunately, the gunkel was perpetually hungry, stupid, and fearless, and it thought humans built houses to store food for it to eat.

The wall had been supplemented by a hastily dug ditch. There was also a watch tower. The gates were shut, and there were no animals in the fields. The watch tower was manned, and through chinks in the wicker areas of the wall Murphy could see the glint of helmets and spear points.

Murphy had put the robed acolytes in the lead wagon, and the gates opened quickly when they came near. A squad of villagers carrying spears and scythes came out to cover their entrance. One elderly man came to Murphy. He pointed to the wizard robes. "Where is your sky-beast?" he demanded.

Aha, they've heard of our travelling magic show. "The Westmen slew the sky-beast with arrows," Murphy said. "And they have killed others, and wounded the master wizard."

"An evil day. I am Panar, chief of this village. You are welcome here, lords, but I fear the Westmen will destroy us all."

Murphy patted his battle rifle. "Though there are many Westmen, still we have our magic," he said. "The Westmen slew two of us and wounded my master, but we have killed all of the Westmen we have seen."

The caravan moved into the village. There was only one street, and the wagon train nearly filled it. The gates were hastily shut again.

Most of the population crowded around them. A couple of pretty girls caught Murphy's eye. Were they interested in having a child with sky-wizard blood? A lot of village girls were, which was one reason Murphy hadn't married again. Not like Lafe, who was happy enough with two wives, and what would they do now? They weren't noble, except that Lafe made the locals accept them, and—

The chief came back from seeing the gate closed. "Lord, Bheroman Harkon sent messages three days ago, warning us of Westmen in strong bands. He was leading his knights against them, and summoned the men of our village. Thus we have few fighting men, and could not come to your aid when we heard the battle nearby. Forgive us, lord."

Murphy waved his hands in a blessing sign he'd seen old Yanulf use. "No problem," he said in English. "You are forgiven, and indeed had you tried to aid us you would all have been killed. How many lances does Bheroman Harkon lead?"

"Lord, I do not know how far he proclaimed the ban," Panar said. "I would guess no more than fifty."

Murphy nodded. No point in scaring people, but he could guess what would happen if the average Drantos heavy cavalry leader ran into a sizable band of Westmen. Those hornbacked bows would be punching his men at arms out of their saddles before they knew there was an enemy near them. The next Drantos bheroman would probably face Westmen armored with the spoils from Harkon's army.

"Has anyone told the Lord Eqeta?" Murphy demanded.

"Lord, I do not know."

So it comes down to how smart Harkon is, and there's no way I'm going to find that out from this group.

"Lord, will you stay and protect us with your magic?" Panar asked. Some of the others crowded close to hear Murphy's answer.

The first levy of young men went to Harkon. There's me, and there's the secondary levy, not one whole hell of a lot to hold this place with if I've got to face any number of those Westmen. But what the hell, you knew the job was dangerous when you took it, Fred . . .

"I will stay," Murphy said. "But we must send messages to the Lord Eqeta. That is more important than our lives."

He'd expected opposition to that, but the village chief nodded sagely. "If the Lord Eqeta knows, we may yet be saved," he said. He looked thoughtful, started to turn away, and finally turned back. "There are two young men here who have won many races. Their horses are very good."

Obviously the right troops to take a message, but what was

Panar looking so nervous about? Hah. "I will not inform Lord Harkon that you did not send your best men," Murphy said. "It is well for us that you did not." He pointed to the wagon's shadows. "When there is but one shadow, have them come to me. We will send them when it is dark. Meantime I will write a message for Lord Rick."

"Ah."

He's impressed, Murphy thought. Because I know Lord Rick, or because I can write? Don't matter much. "Before then I must tend to the wounded, and all your women must watch, as must you and your village deacon." This place would be too small to have a real priest. "We will show them the healing magic revealed by Yatar to High Priest Yanulf. For now, have them boil water."

"Aye, lord." Panar left to give orders.

Murphy was alone with Lafe's body. Bloody hell, he thought. I'm not as young as I used to be. He looked over to the wagon where Ski lay in a drunken stupor, and envied him. There was a lot of the powdered extract of madweed in the medicine chest . . .

Batshit, Murphy thought. Not that again. I took that trip back on Earth.

Why not, though? You ain't going to live through this anyway, might as well go out happy—

That's not happy, that's dead already, and shut up, he told himself. Christ, Lafe, why you? You got me off the stuff. And into Africa. Damn this goddam planet, first Sindy and then Lafe—

You found Sindy here, and you had a good year. Do you wish you'd never married her?

No. But damn all, Ski looks happy. And it's sure going to be tough without Lafe. Nobody to watch my back. Nobody I trust now, except maybe the Captain. Sure nobody else. Don't trust Warner, Lafe said. And not Gengrich either. Lafe had been right about Gengrich. Maybe not the Professor, maybe Warner would do, but Lafe had been right, don't trust anybody you don't have to. They'd smuggled the 106 away from Parsons without letting anybody else know. "Keep a couple of aces," Lafe used to say. "Can't hurt." Hadn't hurt, either, and a fat friggin' lot of good that does Lafe now. Jesus, God, are you up there? He was a good man. Please, somebody, remember that.

An ugly column of smoke rose against the sky. One of the village women saw it and began to wail. Must be another village, Murphy thought. He called for Panar and pointed out the smoke to him.

"Aye, lord, Katos lies in that direction."

Christ, what do I do now? I'm too damned tired to think. "What other villages are there near here?"

"Four within one day's ride, lord. Five, counting Katos."

"Forget Katos. Send to the others. Do not send your best messengers. Have all the people come here. They should bring their flocks and beasts and everything they have, food and fodder, and come here quickly where I can defend them with sky weapons."

"There is not room inside the wall for half of them!"

"Well, we build a new wall, and a ditch." That would keep the cattle from straying and the Westmen from riding up to the walls. They weren't likely to be dangerous on foot. Except for those long-ranging arrows. But I've got three rifles, and maybe Ski'll be able to fight.

"Building a wall will take many hands from the crops," said the chief.

Jeez, the soul of a bureaucrat. "How many crops will you harvest if the Westmen burn you out and kill you all?"

Panar shrugged. "What matter, if Lord Harkon does the same?"

"The hell with Harkon. I speak with the voice of the Lord Eqeta."

The old chief spat into the dirt, then squinted into Murphy's face. He said nothing.

"Look, dammit!" Murphy said. He patted his rifle, then opened his wizard robe to reveal his pistol and combat webbing. "Watch!" He drew the pistol and fired at a gourd in a nearby market stall. Everyone turned to stare at the sound, so he blew another gourd away while they were watching. "There. That is small magic." He patted the rifle again. "And this is big magic."

The chief nodded. "I have heard. You are a sky god."

"Not a god, but I know the sky magic."

"You know the Lord Eqeta, who is a sky god," Panar said. "And that is enough. You will tell the Lord Harkon?"

"I will."

"The messengers will go now."

"Good."

The chief left, and Murphy sat down in the wagon. A couple of village kids looked shyly at him, then dodged back into their home behind the market stall. A girl about sixteen walked by, carefully not looking at him, but she'd changed into her best clothes.

My people, Murphy thought. He laughed at himself, but even as he did he thought of what he could teach the villagers about self-defense. Pikes and spears. Stand your ground against cavalry. Discipline and trust the man next to you, and you're as good as any cavalry.

He realized he was taking on a lot of responsibilities. The villagers would be grateful, but their lord wouldn't much care for his giving military training to the peasants. But if that kept Ben Murphy alive long enough to get a message back, that ought to square things with Captain Galloway.

What of Lady Tylara? What if the local lord didn't like his villagers taking matters into their own hands this way?

Ben laughed again. Too bad for Bheroman Harkon. The pike regiments had already taught peasants they could do things for themselves. Murphy wasn't doing anything new. Besides, he was the great-grandson of a man who'd been hanged for shooting a landlord's agent, and he wasn't inclined to be very tender about landlords' feelings.

PART FIVE

Principalities
and
Powers

22

Escorted by eight Royal Guardsmen on each side, the roasted stag marched up the aisle between the banqueting tables. Halfway to the high table, it stopped and bowed to Wanax Ganton. The two men under the draperies hanging from the platter were excellent puppeteers; the stag seemed alive, although, much to his host's surprise, Ganton had personally speared it in yesterday's hunt.

Lord Ajacias beamed when Ganton acknowledged the stag's obeisance. His daughter Lady Cara also saw that Ganton approved, and giggled. "Is that not marvelous, Majesty? Hakour our chef has been a good and faithful servant for many years, but he has never given us such a meal as this."

For the tenth time, Ganton wished that the Lady Cara seated beside him was instead the Lady Octavia Caesar. Octavia did not try to gain his favor. She did not always agree with him. Quite the contrary. She also did not giggle. And though her

219

ankles were not so slim as the Lady Cara's, Caesar's grand-daughter had far the best clothing on Tran, and wore her gowns and robes with a grace and dignity that suited—

His thoughts were shattered by the metallic click of a star weapon made ready to fire. "HALT! WHO IS THERE?" the Lord Mason thundered in a voice like Yatar passing judgment. He came forward from his place at the end of the table, his rifle leveled at the stag, the small knife—*bayonet*, that was the word—pointed at the animal's throat.

"The stag!" The response was given by Hanzar, Guards Officer of the Day. The other Guards, splendid in their new clothing—*uniforms*, Lord Rick called them—presented their weapons.

"What stag?" Mason demanded.

"Wanax Ganton's stag!"

"Then pass, friend!" Mason acknowledged. "Make way for Wanax Ganton's stag!"

Then from within the stag a loud voice shouted "Long live Wanax Ganton!" Lord Rick himself leaped from his place to repeat the cry, and all the banqueters, two hundred and more, stood and joined the cheering.

Ganton threw back his head to laugh with the others, but inwardly he could hear Lucius speaking in his ancient dry voice. "And in the midst of the triumph, at the time of a conqueror's greatest glory, there rides in his chariot the lowest-born slave of the Empire, who never ceases to say, 'Remember Caesar, thou art but a mortal man.' The cheers of a throng are easily gained. Honor is more elusive." He could hear the old man, and see Octavia nodding agreement—and also hear the Lady Cara giggle.

The stag was brought forward to the salutes of the starmen and the Guards. Their—*uniforms*—green shirts and trousers, green jackets, black boots and black belts with sheathed daggers, silver badges on their black berets, made them look remarkably like starmen in the dim light. Lord Ajacias had done his best with candles and torches, but a hall large enough for two hundred was far too large to be lighted properly.

Now the Guards, the starmen, and picked men from Lord Rick's Mounted Archers and Hussars all came forward, presented their weapons, and crashed them against the floor while the stag and its table passed between their lines on its way to the sand pit between the banqueting tables. The men who'd animated the stag came out from beneath the draperies, and they were also in the uniform of Royal Guards. All presented their weapons, then saluted in the starman's manner. "Permission to withdraw?" Hanzar shouted.

There was a long pause. Ganton realized that Lord Rick was staring at him. "Permission granted!" Ganton called, and guards and starmen and Tamaerthans all retired in a complex drill, halting in pairs and clashing weapons as others passed between them, twirling weapons as they knelt on one knee, then rising with more flourishes. They left the hall to the thunder of applause.

Morrone appeared from somewhere. He held a knife as long as an archer's sword. As King's Companion, it was his duty to carve and taste the first portion of all meat brought to the high table. Ganton had always thought his friend graceful, but now he looked just a bit awkward and unrehearsed after the performance of those soldiers.

But first Yanulf. The Archpriest rose from his place opposite Ganton, and spread his arms wide. "Yatar, Great Skyfather, we thy servants give thee praise and thanks . . ."

"Majesty?"

His host was trying to get his attention. Ganton acknowledged him with a nod.

"Majesty, the weapon carried by the starman who challenged the stag—was this the same weapon they showed this afternoon?" He shuddered. "Is it safe that such weapons be brought into my hall?"

"Star weapons are safe while starmen are loyal," Ganton said.

"And are they loyal, Majesty?"

"You saw," Ganton said.

"Aye, Majesty. I saw disciplined men perform well what they have learned."

"And—"

"I say no more—"

"I command you, speak what you think."

"I saw them loyal to the starman," Ajacias said. "I saw them cheer my Wanax. But I have not seen them obey the anointed of Yatar."

". . . and we thank Thee for the abundant rains of spring and the mildness of the winter," Yanulf was saying. "And we beg

Thy aid, that Thou might intercede with Hestia and all Thy great family, that our seed might not rot in the ground, but flourish and multiply, and our harvest be great that we may offer great sacrifice to Thee. And as The Time approaches, incline the hearts of our lawful rulers to know and do Thy will . . ."

"You demand a demonstration?" Ganton asked. "They have come with me—"

"Majesty, I demand nothing!" Ajacias protested. "I spoke only when commanded! Forgive me!"

"There is nothing to forgive—"

" . . . and let it be Thy will to aid us. Arise, lord, hasten to aid us, for our need is great . . ."

"—and perhaps you have been of more service than you know," Ganton said.

One good thing about Yanulf. Lady Cara was silenced. She wouldn't giggle while the Primate of Drantos invoked the blessings of Yatar. Indeed, she stared as if hypnotized—and yet she probably wouldn't be able to remember a word that Yanulf had said. While Octavia would have been eager to talk, to discuss Yanulf's sermon and compare Yatar to the Roman Jehovah and his son Jesus Christ, to ponder the vision of Bishop Polycarp that the Christ was in fact the Son of Yatar, that Yatar and Jehovah were One—

"—the Time of Testing cometh upon us. Woe to that man who fails to prepare. Woe to him, great lord or villein, who has not done the will of Yatar and laid by goods for The Time . . ."

"I am told that smiths to the south have learned to make star weapons of their own."

Ganton pretended not to have heard. Ajacias would learn of the new weapons in due season. For now there was not enough firepowder in the realm to stoke all the *guns* for more than a few blasts. There was a shortage of ingredients, especially saltpeter. Ganton had learned how to make firepowder, but not how to extract saltpeter from dungheaps. He wondered if he should not have paid more attention to that day's lecture. But a Wanax was no mechanic!

"And so we invoke Thy aid." Yanulf's prayer ended. Morrone attacked the stag as if it were his blood foe, then tasted the slice he carved and pronounced it good. And now, finally, the cooks' apprentices could come out and carve the beast and all could get down to the serious business of eating.

But Ganton couldn't forget the idea he'd had while Ajacias was questioning him. There was one way to show all that the starmen were loyal to the Crown. If only Lord Rick would agree! But for now, there was dinner, and the giggles of Lady Cara . . .

The Royal Guardsmen began a sword dance, complex beyond belief, with elements of Tamaerthan dancing mixed with something very like a polka. Their razor-sharp sabers flashed in the candlelight, earning the king's applause.

Rick Galloway watched with approval as young Ganton refused another cup of wine and asked for water instead. The king's request probably shocked the steward, but it meant Ganton would have a clear head. He was going to need it to fend off Ajacias's questions.

"Boy's learnin' the king business," Art Mason said as he took his place beside Rick. "And damn good thing you made 'em put these tables up."

They were seated behind and to the left of the high table, in a place near an entrance. Rick had insisted that every entrance to the hall be blocked by a table with mercs and Royal Guardsmen, and to hell with protocol. "Yeah?" Rick prompted.

"You been listenin' to that Ajacias?" Mason asked. "Every question, everything he says, he tries to stir up trouble. That business about making star weapons to use with firepowder, he's really trying to talk the kid into something. And when he's not stirring up trouble or fishing for classified information, he tells how it's time to make peace with the Five Kingdoms."

"You think he's a traitor?"

"Hell, Cap'n, you thought so or we wouldn't be here." Mason grinned. "I thought you was nuts, wanting to honor a guy that might be plotting against us, but I see it makes sense." He pointed to the candles at every pillar. "Candles and new livery for the servants. Just those must have cost him a fortune."

Rick returned the grin and poured wine. "We needed to come north anyway," Rick said. "We had to stay somewhere. Why not with Ajacias? Anyway, it seemed like a good idea at the time." A good idea, but not mine, he thought. But nobody

on Tran is going to know that. Except maybe Gwen. Who else ever read about Queen Elizabeth I, and her answer to plots?

Silly plots, like Babington's, she could leave to Walsingham and his secret police, who needed a spectacular success every now and then. More serious situations, involving persons of wealth and stature and importance, she took care of herself: her method was to visit them. As Parkinson, Rick's favorite historian, had put it, they could hardly plot while she was there, and they were financially ruined by the time she left. Her visit to Euston Hall in 1578 rendered the Rockwoods harmless for at least a decade . . .

And Lord Ajacias, a bheroman in the vital Sutmarg region bordering the Five Kingdoms, was far too important to accuse without evidence—or to be allowed to get away with treason.

"Anyway, we got him on trading with the enemy," Mason said.

Rick nodded. Mason's patrols had intercepted a pack train of hides and fine wine just as it reached the border. Not only did the hides have Ajacias's brand, but the idiot had written a letter to the Wanax of Ta-Meltemos inquiring about the last shipment and detailing what special payments were wanted. "Hang onto the smugglers," Rick said. "We might not want to accuse Ajacias. Not just yet, anyway—"

"Right." Mason waved expansively. "He's sure not going to hire many troopers this year. Not after two weeks of this."

"Yeah, but you know, he doesn't seem to mind. Really acts like he's being honored to have the Wanax here."

"Well, sure, he'd like his daughter to be Wannaxae."

"Fat chance," Rick said. "What else did your patrols turn up?"

"Confirmation," Mason said. "Just like you thought, they're raising armies in the Five Kingdoms. Just how big and what for I can't tell. Too many cavalry screens. But they're mobilizing. Funny thing, not so much cavalry as stores. Like they're expecting a siege."

Rick shrugged. "The Time—"

"Sure, but they're increasing the garrisons, too," Mason said. "Least I think so, but it's hard to find out anything for certain."

"One more problem," Rick said. He turned as his orderly came up behind him. "Yes, Jamiy?"

"A message, Lord. From the Lady Tylara."

"Ah. Give it to me. Wait, I'll move away from the table. Impolite to read while the Wanax is eating his dinner. Mason, if you don't mind I'd rather you stayed here to watch out for the Wanax." Rick got up from the hard bench with relief. The Guards started a new dance as Rick retreated to the corridor behind the banqueting hall.

He broke the wax seals and unfolded the letter, noting that it was paper, not parchment. Fairly good quality paper, too; the University's mills had got the knack of it now, so there were few ink runs mixed with her painstakingly written words. As he held the parchment close to the beeswax candles, he wondered how far the University's research into illuminating gas had gone.

> To the Lord Rick, Eqeta of Chelm, War Lord of Tamaerthon, Captain General of the Hosts of Drantos, Beloved of Yatar, from Lady Tylara, Eqetassa of Chelm and Justiciar of Drantos, Greetings!
> My beloved, your children and heirs are safe and well, and I trust this finds you the same. I am also well, though I miss you greatly and wish only for our reunion.

Rick nodded and smiled to himself. Leave it to Tylara to put things in that order. Titles. Health of the children. And only then the really important news, that she was all right.

> The feud with the Mac Naile has proven more troublesome than I like. It is well that I have come, for this may yet become a challenge to Mac Clallan Muir. Aye, and there is worse, for there is murmur among the lesser clans that much booty may be found at your University. Thus must I strengthen its defenses, yet do so from afar so that it will not seem that Mac Clallan Muir holds sway in this place which you insist must remain above all clans and crowns.

And you're doing the right thing even though you don't agree with me about the University, Rick thought. Thank God I met you, Tylara. I'd better come up there now. It makes sense, it's not just that I want to see you, my love—

> My father sends his greetings, and his thanks that you have sent Makail his first grandson to visit him. Though he has not said so, you may be certain that he is even more grateful for my escort.

Eight mercs, Caradoc with two hundred Mounted Archers, and a hundred lances of Chelm chivalry. Tylara had been sure they would be more than enough to persuade the recalcitrant Mac Naile.

And though that dispute is I think soon ended, there are rumors of others, and it seemed to me that there must be a source to this strife. Thus I spoke with Corgarff, reminding him of your generosity in sparing his life, and of the loyalty of his sons, and of the devotion his new chief holds to you. In this way I persuaded him to tell what he knows of the Dughuilas affair. What he told me has earned him a visit by the headsman—

Oh, Lord! Rick thought. What—

—but mindful of your wishes, I have given him a second pardon, which will assuredly be his last.

As you suspected, there was indeed a plot, with Dughuilas, and a highly placed henchman to Mac Clallan Muir, to the end that only the high-born would command, and all your work would be undone. Corgarff will not name my father's traitor henchman, but says again and again that he knows not the name, only that he was assured that none of the conspirators bore ill will toward my father or myself, nor indeed toward you, but only toward the changes you make. As you are fond of saying, you may believe as much of that as you will; for my part I do believe it, or rather that Corgarff believes it.

And there was yet one more conspirator, one that Corgarff actually met, but the man was hooded and the light dim, so that Corgarff would not know him, aye though he met him again. From his speech he seemed not of the Drantos nobles, yet certainly he was not of Tamaerthon, yet indeed he was a man of parts and gentle speech and ways. When I put it to Corgarff that the man was likely a priest, Corgarff seemed surprised, then agreed it was possible. You must speak with Yanulf and ask him to see to the loyalty of his archpriests, for there may be one who bears us ill will. The danger is small, now that his instruments are taken, but treason must never be allowed to pass unpunished.

If there be time I will enclose more, telling you of my love, and of our children, for Lady Isobel ceases not to ask for her father, and is quite put out that you do not place her in her bed each night as was your custom. And I would have you do the same with me, each night aye and each day as well. . . .

"My lord," Jamiy said. "If you have a moment."

"Eh?" Rick looked up from Tylara's letter. He'd been staring at it for a long time. His eyes felt the strain from the dim light, and he blinked several times. "What is it?"

"Carlga the smith and Fnor the master miller would speak with you."

"How much did they bribe you?"

"A silver each, lord."

"Ah." Quite a tidy sum. "Their business must be important. Bring them."

Jamiy grinned and pocketed the money. Sometimes Lord Rick demanded a share of the bribes paid to get his attention.

The miller and smith were in their finest clothing, with leather purses and jeweled peace-bonded daggers hanging from their belts. Men of substance, Rick thought.

They stammered a bit, but their manners were good, and they were obviously accustomed to speaking to the nobility. Rick learned that the smith employed five journeymen and a dozen apprentices, while the miller was a town Councillor. Even so, they had difficulty coming to the point.

"And the demonstration with the stag was indeed marvelous," Fnor was saying. "The Royal Guardsmen in particular. Is there aught they cannot do?"

"We have sons," Carlga said. "The miller and I both. They would gladly serve in the Guard."

"And our hearts would be gladdened to see them so honored," Fnor added.

Aha. The point at last. Rick said nothing, and the silence dragged on. Can't ask them direct what bribe they're offering, Rick thought. How long do I have to wait?

"Indeed, my heart would be so gladdened," Fnor said at last, "that I would build a new mill. Beside my present mill, for there is ample water, more than ample now with the greater rains. I would build a wheel of the sort that your clerks describe, of the kind that the Romans have. Carlga will bring his forge to that mill, so that the wheel might drive his bellows and work trip hammers in the new manner. All this at our expense, and a year's products of the mill and forge to the Guards."

Generous offer indeed, Rick thought. But year's products

be damned, what's needed is a real hammer mill here where transportation's hard to come by. There's coal, and iron ore, and this is a damned good place for a foundry. Long way from any likely targets, too. Not likely to be bombed out.

"Your forge is fired with wood?" Rick asked.

"Aye, lord. I have heard of using blackrock, but I have never seen a forge like that. We tried once, but without success."

"There will not be many years before burning wood to make metal and glass will be forbidden," Rick said. "As wood grows more scarce, you must learn to use blackrock."

"Where may we learn?" Carlga asked.

"The travelling clerks will know, but there is a better way. Have you a son to follow in your trade? Excellent. Send him a year to the University near Tar Kartos in Tamaerthon. There he will learn to use the blackrock, and much else."

"We would also learn the arts of making the—*guns*—which use firepowder," Fnor added. "Master smith Carlga makes strong iron."

"Not all strong iron is strong enough," Rick said. "The art of making *guns* is not so easily acquired." Especially not here in a border county ruled by a possible traitor. "Nor can I promise your sons, nor any man, a place in the Guards.

"Yet you need not look so downcast," Rick continued. "The Guards are sworn as brothers, and will accept among them none who have not earned their place, and who will not take the same oath to Vothan."

The men looked sobered at the mention of Vothan. Like his Earth counterpart, Old One-eye was more feared than loved. "But I can promise this," Rick added quickly. "Let them present themselves to Lord Mason before the Wanax departs, and if they please him, we will take them with us; and if they work hard—" Dammit, what I want to say is apply themselves, but that sounds stupid in the local language—"if they will work and give their attention to the task before them, I doubt not they can earn a place in the Guards." And take the first step toward ennobling their families . . .

"So. Since I cannot grant what you asked, I cannot accept what you offer. Yet I wish the mill and forge to be built, and to that end I will loan half the cost from the Captain-General's purse. You will repay the debt in iron, and the first fruits of the forge belong to the crown."

"Generous, lord," Fnor said. "You deserve your reputation. And we will send our sons to the Lord Mason in the morning. Thank you, lord."

Ganton sat cross-legged on the great bed, cradling a cup of wine in his lap and looking around the comfortable tapestry-hung room. It was, of course, Lord Ajacias's bedchamber. Idly Ganton wondered where Ajacias was sleeping, and who he had displaced, and who that one had caused to move.

Morrone was hovering at the foot of the bed, casting an occasional glance at the door. "Oh, go to whatever girl you've asked," Ganton said irritably. "I can undress myself."

Morrone grinned. "Thank you, sire. But it would be best if I did my duty first."

"Then do it. Lord Rick received a message tonight. They brought it during dinner, and he went out to read it. My guess is that it came from the Lady Tylara, else why would they not wait until morning, or at least until dinner was finished?"

"Yes, sire?"

"If from Tylara, then it may have come from the University," Ganton said. "I would know if it did."

"Aha. Majesty, had there been letters for you, they would have been brought by now."

"Perhaps."

"Surely."

"Then Octavia has chosen not to write to me."

"You cannot be certain. Indeed, you do not know the message was from Lady Tylara, and certainly you do not know that it was sent from the University. Can you doubt that the Lady Octavia would take any opportunity to write to you? I cannot."

"Ah. You believe then that she does not dislike me?"

Morrone shrugged. "What matter her likes and dislikes? I believe that she is intelligent. As to you—you brood too much. I am certain that my lady of the evening has a friend—"

"But are you certain your lady mother did not play the Eqeta false with a panderer from the stews of Rustengo?"

Morrone laughed again. As indeed, Ganton thought, he must, for if there were any hint that I was serious—I should watch my tongue, even alone with my only friend.

Then Morrone's laugh died, and his voice became very serious. "Are *you* certain that you are not getting yourself into more of a coil about the Lady Octavia than she deserves?"

"And why do you reckon her desserts?" There was a hint of danger in Ganton's voice.

"Majesty, it is my duty to advise you."

Yes. It is, Ganton thought. And indeed, you were one of the few who supported me when I thought to bring the Lady Octavia north on this tour. But I did not, through the advice of the Lord and Lady of Chelm, and Chancellor Yanulf, and Camithon—

"Advice! I hear nothing but advice, from my first visit to the jakes in the morning until you blow out the last candle at night! Only Yatar could listen to so much advice!"

"Yatar does not need advice," Morrone reminded him. "You do. Or you have said you do. You are of age now, and the time has passed when I could speak to you as once I did, but I will, once more. Ganton, my friend, if ever you wish my silence, you have only to say so, and I will remain your friend yet."

"Ach, not you also!" Ganton shouted. "They all say that! All, all, they threaten to withdraw their counsel, and though they do not always say so, it is in their minds, that my father lost his throne through failure to listen to his advisors. And yes, yes, that is true enough, but much of what I hear is senseless! Yet must I listen, and smile, lest someone with more power than wits be mortally offended! Surely there is more to being Wanax than this?"

Morrone made a wry face. "I offered one of the rewards of majesty, and you made free to insult my mother for reply." He grinned to show he wasn't offended. "And there is little chance that Lady Octavia would ever know, though why you remain so tender for the feelings of Lord Rick's hostage to the Roman alliance I will never know."

"Is she no more than that?"

"How can she be else?"

"If Lord Rick and Chancellor Yanulf think of nothing but hostages, why have they not gathered in the children of Publius' dead sister?"

Morrone shrugged again. "The discussion grows serious. Will you have more wine?"

"Yes."

Morrone poured and brought the goblets to the bed. "Caesar's other grandchildren are not important because they cannot be offered in marriage. Not when the eldest is five. While the Lady Octavia is ripe enough. Majesty, think you that I oppose your suit?"

"Of course not." Morrone had more than once been messenger when the University authorities tried to keep Ganton and Octavia apart.

"For indeed, were she queen, the way might lie open to more than ever we dream," Morrone said. "Rome itself." He stepped back and raised his hand in the Roman manner, and there was no mockery in his voice at all as he said, "Hail, Caesar."

"Only if—only if Lord Rick permits it," Ganton said.

Morrone nodded. "Aye, for the moment the starmen hold power over us. But they will not forever mock the anointed of Yatar!"

That phrase, and the way Morrone said it, reminded Ganton of something, someone else who'd said that in just that way, but the wine and the venison and the lateness of the hour overcame him before he could remember who it had been.

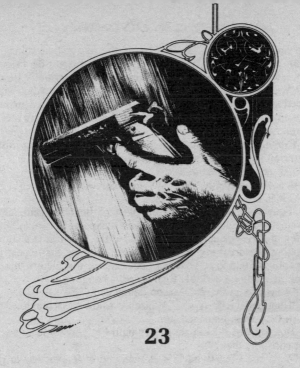

23

The morning ritual was the same here as at the palace. Rick dressed, put on armor, and with Mason beside him came out for his first appointments. His personal guards waited for him in the corridor. Today they were commanded by Padraic, the under-captain of the Mounted Archers. Four Guardsmen walked ahead, then Rick and Mason, followed by Jamiy and Padraic.

Mason hadn't much cared to have a new man armed and behind his captain, but he hadn't any choice. Caradoc went with Tylara to the Garioch, and somebody had to be Mason's second in command of the MP's. Padraic, son of a Drantos lord and a Tamaerthan mother, knew the customs of both lands, and had been loyal since the archers were formed. There wouldn't be anyone better... which didn't stop Art Mason from worrying.

Rick had no trouble reading his companion's mind. Mason worried a lot about loyalties. At least, Rick thought, he understands why we've got to expand the leadership, bring in locals and govern by Tran custom and law, not just be a flock of wolves here. Mason understands. And Gwen. I think Elliot and Warner. The rest—well, the rest of them saw what happened when Parsons tried taking over by force, but I'm not sure how well they learned the lesson. And how loyal are they? To me, to anyone?

They reached the chamber set aside for them by their host. Beazeley and four locals stood guard outside.

"All secure?" Mason asked.

Beazeley grinned. "Yes, sir, all secure *now*."

"Eh?"

"Found two different listening places," Beazeley said. "Alcove behind a tapestry, about like you'd expect. But something different." He opened the door and led the way inside a stone chamber about twenty-five feet square. "Behind that tapestry, there, by the window. That was one. And see that picture there? Back of that's a corridor. Real secret passage."

"Who was in there?" Mason demanded.

"Unarmed clerk types," Beazeley said. "Real anxious to prove they were unarmed, too."

Rick nodded. "I expect they would be. Have you secured that corridor, then?"

"Yes, sir. I put two MP's at each end of it. Nobody to go in without your permission. Rest of the room's clean, as far as I can tell." Beazeley laughed. "I didn't look too hard for electronics."

"No. Thank you," Rick said. "All right, we'll deal with Lord Ajacias later. Meanwhile, Art, go escort the king, please. And I expect we'll need wine, and a pot of that stuff that passes for tea. Morrone will have to see to that."

"Yes, sir," Mason said. "Okay, Jack, let's go."

Rick paced around the room. It held a carved slab table, two side tables, three comfortable chairs, some benches, and a solid-looking cabinet that probably unfolded into a writing desk. On a whim Rick went to it and opened it. There were no dwarves inside, but it did have goose quills, parchment, and ink.

"Make way," someone called outside. The door opened, and Mason stood aside to let Wanax Ganton enter. Lord Morrone followed him in.

"Welcome, Majesty," Rick said.

"Thank you."

Morrone gestured, and servants brought in wine and a silver service of the local equivalent of tea. It was bitter stuff, but it did have caffeine. If only the *Shalnuksis* would bring a few pounds of real coffee—

"Thank you," Ganton told Morrone. His voice held dismissal, and Morrone left Rick and Ganton alone in the room.

"Your Companion was not overly pleased to leave us," Rick said.

"Nor your soldiers."

"Shall we sit?" Rick asked.

"Thank you." Ganton took one of the chairs.

"Wine or tea?" Rick asked.

"Wine, but it is not right that you—"

"I have no fear for my dignity," Rick said. He poured a goblet of wine and a large mug of tea and brought them to the table. The boy's nervous, Rick thought.

"I think we have not been alone since I came of age," Ganton said. He smiled thinly. "Nor do my advisors approve now."

Why would they? Last thing any public official needs is to find out his sovereign is cutting deals the civil service doesn't know about. "It is good to see you. You look well."

"Thank you. As do you." He looked nervously around.

"The room is safe, Majesty," Rick said. "My soldiers personally removed the scribes Lord Ajacias had set to listen to us, and now they guard the passageway behind that picture."

"I see. Is that not a treason?"

"Only if you wish it to be."

"But the law—"

Ganton seemed very serious, and Rick suppressed a chuckle. "Majesty, law and justice may be served when there has been a crime that harms someone. Here there has been no harm, and thus the matter of treason may be left to expediency and advantage."

"Do you see advantage in accusing Ajacias?"

"Not at present," Rick said. "He seems popular with his knights and villeins. Who would replace him?"

"My question exactly," Ganton said. "Then that is settled."

There was a long awkward silence.

"Lord Rick," Ganton said. "The banquet last night was splendid. The guards, and the star warriors, all were magnificent—"

"But?" Rick prompted.

"But there were questions. Some asked—some asked if the starmen were truly loyal to me," Ganton said with a rush. "And though I assure them they are, though I assure them you are loyal, though I believe this with all my heart, still will there be doubts."

Rick frowned. Just what was eating the kid? "I will not remind you of the proofs we have already given," Rick said. "You must know them all."

"Aye," Ganton said. "And yet still are there doubts! But— it came to me at the banquet. There is a way. If you could— if you could give me a star weapon. A small magic, not the large. The weapon that Lady Tylara used to kill Lord Parsons. And binoculars," Ganton continued. "A different kind of magic. Together they would show—they would show that you do not fear to have your Wanax armed in your presence!"

"Um," Rick said. Oh, boy! The trouble is, it's not unreasonable. Not the way he looks at it, not the way his Council will see it.

"I can pay," Ganton said. "I would not expect you to take the personal equipment of one of your warriors, but perhaps one would sell for much gold?"

Hell's bells, there's half a dozen would sell every goddam thing they've got if Mason and Elliot didn't hold equipment checks every ten-day, Rick thought. And I'm not sure some of 'em haven't sold gear already. We never did have a complete inventory of personal weapons and equipment.

"This is no small request," Rick said.

"I know."

"By God, I think you do know," Rick said. "But let's be certain. You ask that I place my life—that of any of my soldiers—in your hands. Not just in law, but in plain fact. Wait— I would not interrupt lightly. I know that I have already done this, and deliberately. I do not keep a large bodyguard, I travel with the Court rather than stay in my stronghold of Dravan. But what I know may not be so plain to my soldiers. You ask that I show them that I trust you with their lives."

"Aye. A great favor to ask, yet one I think necessary, if I am truly to be Wanax of Drantos."

No question about that. Which means you've given me a decision to make. And you know that, too. Meanwhile, we're making changes everywhere. Triphammers and water mills. Paper and ink. Deep plows. Fertilizer.

"It is not a decision lightly to be made," Rick said. "I must take counsel."

"But you will consider the matter?"

"I will—"

"Captain!" Mason's voice came from beyond the door. What the hell? "With your permission, Majesty?"

"I confess as much curiosity as you, my lord."

"Come in, Mason."

Art Mason came in quickly. Morrone followed before anyone could stop him. "Messengers, Cap'n," Mason said in English. "From Murphy, up on the plateau. Peasant boys. They brought a parchment, but they've already told everybody in the castle. Horse archers from the high desert, Westmen. They attacked the wizard train. Killed Lafe Reznick and wounded Ski, chopped up a couple of villages, killed the local borderer baron. Everybody in the castle knows."

Mason spoke too fast in the star language, and Ganton could catch only a few words. Outside he could hear people shouting in the courtyard, and someone ran through the corridors.

"Lord Rick—"

Lord Rick didn't seem to hear. He took a parchment from Lord Mason and spread it out on the table. Ganton stood and moved closer to Rick. Neither Rick nor Mason objected, so he looked over Rick's shoulder, and made a firm vow to spend more time at his English lessons when he went back to the University. *If* he went back, and that seemed more and more an impossible thought.

Westmen. The word was a literal translation of the Tran term, and it leaped at him from the page. The Westmen had come to the southwest high plains. They'd come in strength, and had slain a bheroman and his knights, and—

Lord Rick looked up to see Ganton trying to read. For a moment he hesitated, then handed the letter to Mason. "Read it to us," he ordered. "Translate as you go."

"Uh, Cap'n—"

"Please."

"Yes, sir." Mason cleared his throat and began to read.

The news was worse than Ganton had imagined. Hundreds of Westmen, mounted archers, every bit as skilled as the dreaded Tamaerthan archers. There—there was nothing on Tran to match them! Nothing but star weapons. How many did the Westmen number? In the Tales of The Time there were stories of fierce monsters from the west, tens of thousands of demons mounted on horses that ate human flesh. Could they be Westmen?

—I regret to report that Private Lafferty Reznick was killed in action. I would put him up for the Legion of Merit if I could. He saved my ass, and more important he saved Baldy, this Priest of Vothan who lived with the Westmen for ten years and more, so I got good intelligence on the Westmen. If I get a chance before I have to send this off I'll put down some of what he told me, but the most important thing is, there's drought up there in their desert. They're all coming down. Not so many right now, not more than a few hundred, but they'll all come down sooner or later. God knows how many that is, but it's a lot.

Corporal Jerzy Walinski has been severely wounded, and is not yet returned to duty, but is expected to recover. Four knights, three esquires, and nine men-at-arms with full armor, plus twenty-five farm boys of the local militia, are all that have come back from Baron Harkon's force. I keep hoping there'll be more, but I don't think there will be. There's no sign of the baron.

A star lord dead, another wounded, and of a bheroman's forces not one of ten alive!

Ski can't travel, and I don't have enough troops to fight my way back to Castle Dravan. So I holed up here, and we're digging in. I hope to God this gets through, Captain, because if it don't, we've had it and no mistake. I can hold on for a while. This is no strategic hamlet, but I know a few tricks, and the villagers are willing to fight if somebody shows them how. Which is me, I guess, because there's nobody else to do it, and I just hope that ammo holds out.

So I hope you can send me some help before it's too late. I know you got troubles of your own, but you got to get here pretty quick if you want to see us alive. If you don't make it, I'll try to wreck the H&K's before they get me.

Yours very respectfully,
Benjamin Murphy do Dirstval,
Onetime Private, U.S.A.

Mason finished reading and handed the parchment to Rick. "We must send aid," Ganton said. "And quickly."

Lord Mason and Lord Rick were looking at each other. They didn't seem to hear.

Other parchments lay on the table. Maps, and a sketch of one of the Westmen. Ganton also noted the bow, longer and thicker than the horse bows of Drantos or the Five Kingdoms, or even of the Romans.

"Your Lord Murphy seems a wise captain," Ganton said. "I would honor him. With your permission. And a grant to the wives—" he could make himself say it now, although the idea had grated on him while Reznick was alive. "—to the wives of the Lord Reznick. Only upon your advice, my lord."

He had not forgotten. One of his first acts upon coming of age was a grant of land to Protector Camithon—which earned him the cold scorn of the Lady Tylara. Not that she objected to honors given Camithon, who was, after all, her general; but he was *her* general now that he was no longer Protector. Her advice and consent had not been asked, and that she was slow to forgive.

Lord Rick said nothing.

"Forgive us, Majesty," Mason said. "We can—we can talk about that later."

"Aye." Ganton went to the side table. Before Morrone could interfere, he poured three goblets of wine and brought them to the center table. "My lords," he said, and set the goblets down. "To the memory of Lord Reznick."

They drank, and Rick looked up woodenly. "He came a long way to die."

"Aye," Ganton said. "Yet the Chooser will find a man, however far he travels. But he will have an honored place in Vothan's Hall, I think."

"Yeah." Rick looked thoughtful. "Art, what can we send Murphy?"

"Not a hell of a lot. You know what's mobilized."

"You'll have to go. He needs some quick reinforcements. Ammunition, and a mobile force." Rick strode quickly to the door and opened it. "Jamiy!"

"Sir!"

"Alert Captain Padraic. The Mounted Archers will prepare to move out. Combat gear and rations."

"Sir!" Rick's orderly ran off down the corridor.

I wish I were obeyed as Lord Rick is, Ganton thought. And command as he does. He took no advice, no counsel. He needed none.

"Your pardon, Majesty," Rick said, as if suddenly realizing that Ganton was in the room. "It is best we act quickly. Have I your permission to alert your Guards? We should return to Armagh, and quickly."

"Armagh, my lord?" Ganton asked. "Not Dravan?" Lord Rick's Castle Dravan was certainly the proper place to organize the defense of the High Cumac. One of the castle's functions was to guard the passes up the Littlescarp.

"Aye, sire," Rick said. "But first there must be a Council of the Realm, and meetings with our allies of Tamaerthon and Rome. And I must see to the growing of *surinomaz* and other affairs at Armagh, which is as easy to reach from the University as your capital of Edron. Thus I suggest you send word to summon the council to Armagh."

"It is hardly convenient," Morrone said. "Nor comfortable—"

"Murphy's not very comfortable out there facin' those Westmen," Mason muttered.

"Let us hear no more of comfort!" Ganton said. "My Lord Morrone, it is my will that the Council of Drantos be summoned to Armagh, to meet within the ten-day. See to it."

Morrone was about to reply, but Ganton's look silenced him. "Aye, Majesty. Immediately."

Ganton wanted to leap and shout. He felt as he had the first time he had seen the sea, or bedded a woman. This was power, of the kind Lord Rick held, real power...

"So that is done," Ganton said. "Another thing, Lord Rick. Harkon's stronghold. Westrook. A strong place, I have heard. With Lord Harkon dead, someone must hold it. Perhaps Lord Murphy should go there."

"That makes sense," Mason said.

"We don't know the roads," Rick said. "Not enough information to make a decision."

"Yeah, but it stands to reason a castle's easier to hold than a village," Mason said. "When we get back to Dravan, we can send up some of those new bombards, and gunpowder. Who'll be in charge up there, now that the regular baron's had it?"

They speak to me as a companion, Ganton thought. Not as a boy, not as a king, but as a fellow warrior! They listen, and consider, and ask— "I believe Bheroman Harkon has a son not yet of age."

"Maybe Murph could take over that place," Mason said. "He's pretty sharp, Cap'n."

"We'll see," Rick said. "Time enough when we get him some ammo and find out what the score is." Someone had refilled his goblet. He drained it and set it down. "So now we have Westmen."

"Yeah," Mason said. "The Time's coming. Weather's gone crazy. Gotta raise madweed. Feuds in Tamaerthon. Clansmen eyeing the University's wealth. Riots and migrations in the south. The Five Kingdoms raising new armies, God knows what for. So we get to deal with Westmen. Why not?"

Rick joined Mason in laughter. Mason fetched the wine jug and poured the last into their three glasses. Ganton had never seen the starmen act this way before. This is what it is to be a man, he thought. To do what must be done, and know that you will, and that your companions will not fail you.

And I am here with them, but can I do what I must? Can I do what they expect of me?

Again they raised their glasses. "Why the hell not?" Rick said, and again they laughed, and Ganton drank with them, while inside he was afraid.

24

They rode hard through foothills covered with thorny scrub. Just before midday, the stark battlements of Castle Armagh loomed up ahead. Ganton spurred his horse and rode up alongside Rick. "Not the most comfortable of places, but yet a welcome sight," he said.

"Aye, Majesty." Forty miles in the saddle. Major Assburns. Not a joke to tell the king, but bloody hell my arse is sore!

"Your County is peaceful," Ganton said. "I had half thought so small a party might meet up with robbers."

"It could have been," Rick acknowledged. The party they'd taken to visit Lord Ajacias in the Sutmarg had been enormous: Guards, Mounted Archers, Yanulf's train of scribes and priests and acolytes, musicians, courtiers... The intention had been to eat up Ajacias's substance, and they'd done that. There were only ten in the group riding to Armagh. The others had been sent back to the capital, or up the Littlescarp to aid Murphy, or, like Yanulf, followed at a more leisurely pace.

"Perhaps messengers already await us at Armagh," Ganton suggested. "From the University."

"Possible," Rick conceded.

"By Yatar, I like this!" Ganton shouted. "To ride hard, all day and half the night! To eat venison roasted over a camp fire, and sleep in furs on the ground—hardships, but we do this as friends, without advisors, without endless ceremony. I have not felt so alive since—since I led men to battle!"

"It can be a good feeling." Until the battle's over, and you have to look at the butcher's bill.

"I wish we had gone with the Lord Mason," Ganton said.

Rick shifted uncomfortably in the saddle. "If the Lord Mason and the Guard cannot relieve the Lord Murphy, we two would be of little use."

Ganton nodded seriously. "Aye. We must needs send an army, and only you and I can arrange that, so we are needed here. I know this, but it galls me to send my friends where I cannot go."

"Me too, sire. But it's part of leadership, to learn to be sensible. The semaphore will tell us when Mason gets back to Castle Dravan and is on his way here. Meantime, we have plenty to do."

"Aye." Ganton stood in his stirrups and turned. "Hanzar!" he shouted. "Ride ahead and tell them the Wanax of Drantos comes to guest with the Eqeta of Chelm."

Rick shifted his weight again. At least one of his problems was about to solve itself. In an hour he'd get a hot bath, and there was still half a tube of Preparation H...

Sergeant Chester Walbrook came out of the low doorway followed by two Guardsmen. Their backs were bent under the load of heavy crates wrapped in mylar sheeting. Walbrook sent the Guards ahead with acolyte torchbearers, then ticked off entries in his notebook. Finally he nodded to Rick. "That's the lot of it, sir."

Rick turned to the blue robed priest. "You may seal the caves."

Apelles motioned to his acolytes.

Rick suppressed a grin. *Somebody's got to work. Who should it be, me? Not that I won't get my chance, with Mason coming in tomorrow. And the Grand Council of Drantos to meet in another ten-day. First things first, get this ammunition off to Castle Dravan. It'll be needed.*

The door was heavy wood with heavily greased thick iron-work, set firmly into carved stone lintels deep in the bowels of Castle Armagh. "This is fine work," Rick said. "I have not seen its like in Drantos."

Apelles nodded. "I too was impressed, lord, and wished to have another like it, but alas, when I inquired, I found that is not to be. The mason was from the southern Roman provinces, the lands south of Tamaerthon where Roman law is weak. He had got a Roman matron with child, but fled before he could be brought before the magistrates. How he came here I know not, but so I was told."

"And now?"

Apelles shook his head sadly. "He had learned nothing, for he bedded the daughter of the local village chief. Her father and brothers killed him."

Sergeant Walbrook chuckled. "It happens. Too bad, though. That's a good storage place for the ammunition." He eyed Apelles, then changed to English. "Captain, are you sure you want these locals to guard our ammo?"

"You have a better plan? Want to sit guard over it yourself?"

"No, sir—"

"It would be soft duty, but I can't spare troops for that," Rick said. "And the rest of this place is theirs anyway." He turned to Apelles. "We can go now."

Apelles motioned to the acolytes. Two carried torches and led the way uphill. The rest fell in behind Rick, Walbrook, and Apelles. *Mason would have a fit,* Rick thought.

The acolytes led the way up, then turned sharply left and down again. The smell of ammonia, always present in the caves, grew stronger. The trail narrowed. It was still a full yard wide, but seemed narrower because to their left was a sheer drop into black nothingness too deep for Rick's flashlight to illuminate.

Across the ten-yard gap was a rock wall covered with a bulbous slimy mass hung over with icicles and ammonia drop-lets. There was a slight wind through the cave, enough to bring in fresh air; otherwise they would not have been able to breathe because of the ammonia.

"Hard to believe that damn iceplant reaches all the way up to the surface," Walbrook said. "I reckon we're three hundred feet down."

"Yeah, the root system is amazing," Rick agreed. "I'm even more amazed at how it makes ice." The local name for the plant was "The Protector." It was sacred to Yatar; legend had it that the nearer the rogue star came to Tran, the more efficient the icemaking capabilities of the Protector. That was interesting enough that Rick had asked for weekly measurements, but so far the data were insufficient for any real conclusions.

The acolytes hurried them through this area. The entrance and main corridor of the cave were far too large to be kept secret, but somewhere nearby the cave branched into a labyrinth of ammonia-filled passages that only Yatar's servants could enter. Grain and meat were stored there in the ice, gifts to Yatar—gifts to be returned from Yatar to his people during the worst seasons of the Time.

"We have not guarded weapons before," Apelles said. He paused a moment as if making up his mind. "And I am told it would be more fitting that those consecrated to Vothan One-eye guard your weapons."

"I have heard this also," Rick said. Not least from the Vothan priesthood. "But the servants of Yatar have always held the Caves of the Protector, and have distributed the gifts of Yatar fairly and with honor. How should I change what has always served the people and the god alike?"

Apelles bowed to acknowledge the compliment.

Sharp lad, Rick thought. Get my opinion now, while nobody's listening. Next he'll try to get me to say it in public. He's learning his bureaucratic skills—and I can't even complain, since we brought in Roman scribes to *teach* them how to set up a bureaucracy.

Christ, I hate paperwork! But we can't live without it. It takes a quart of wheat every day to feed a man. A bushel of oats to feed a war horse. The food has to come from somewhere. Food, wagons, weapons, ammunition—all the details of keeping an army in the field, and then there's food for all the peasants growing madweed. We're getting very dependent on this bureaucracy, which means the priests of Yatar. So long as Yanulf is in charge of the Yatar cult in Drantos, that's all right. But he won't live forever...

As they reached the cave entrance, a junior acolyte ran up to them. "Master Apelles," he shouted. "Master, you are to tell the Lord Rick that the Lady Tylara has arrived."

Tylara was lovely. She ran toward him, but before she could reach him they were intercepted by a tiny dark-haired bombshell. "Daddy!" she screamed. Rick scooped Isobel up and held her high, while she laughed, and her hounds bared their canine teeth and growled that anyone, even the master, would so treat their charge.

"She's grown so," Rick said.

"They do, lord," Erinia the nursemaid said. She sniffed, her comment on men who let their children grow up without them.

"And the boy?" Rick asked.

"He sleeps, lord," Erinia said. "As well, after a ride like today's." She spoke with a thick Tamaerthan accent, and her manners were of the clans, not the households of Drantos. There would be no point in asking her to fetch the boy; she'd let him see his son when he woke, and not before.

There was no talking with Tylara, either, not while Isobel was there. She clutched at Rick and laughed, and when he put her down she held his legs.

So little time, Rick thought. So damned little time to spend with them, and so much to do.

"How could I not come?" Tylara said when they were alone at last. "Dravan is our home, and these Westmen menace it. Should I then stay in Tamaerthon?"

Rick laughed. "I hoped you would come." He went to her.

She returned his kisses, then pushed his hands firmly away. "Later. First we talk alone. Then with the Wanax. And then we bathe." She kissed him again. "It will no be so long . . ."

"Long enough." He went back to the writing table where her last letters lay. "The University," he said. "You say it may not be safe."

She shrugged. "The minor clans and lawless ones see much wealth and few soldiers in a town bordered by wild hills and lochs. They dream of more booty taken in hours than they will see in their lives. Can you blame them for those dreams?"

"Maybe not, but we can't let it happen. Is it safe there?"

"For the moment. Until Mac Clallan Muir must withdraw his men. Rick, that may not be so long, unless you have gold and grain to send. If they are to feed their children, the dunnhie wassails must go and work their lands. My father cannot forever keep them as Guardsmen, and he cannot send other clans whose chiefs have no love for this place where crofters are taught to defeat warriors."

"I know. I suppose the first thing is to send some Drantos troops to help keep watch. Only I'd want to send Chelm soldiers, and we'll need them all against the Westmen. I'll need Caradoc and his archers in the west, too."

"Strip away Caradoc's archers, and your University will no last the season," Tylara said. "Your starmen will needs be alert all the time, and even so there are few enough of them to face a thousand hillmen."

"The University must survive, Tylara."

She had been ready to reply, but something in his voice stopped her. "At the expense of our lands?"

"At all expense. Tylara, every six hundred years this planet, all of it, all its peoples, are knocked back into a dark age. That has to stop. Has to, and the University is the only way."

"Then we must find ways to protect our University," she said. "It too will be part of our children's rightful inheritance. We must preserve Chelm as well—and I doubt not that I have for a husband the only man alive who can do all that."

The rooms were perfect duplicates of Rick's office suite in Castle Dravan: small office with writing desk, larger conference room with slab table and side boards with wine cruets. The walls either had maps painted on them, or were smooth-surfaced and whitewashed for writing. A charcoal brazier stood in one corner, and a rack for cloaks and weapons in another. Apelles had even duplicated the carvings on the chairs . . .

"Within a ten-day we meet with the Grand Council," Rick said. "And before that, we'll meet with Lucius and Octavia and Drumold. But you're *my* council."

Tylara nodded agreement from her place at the other end of the table. Between them sat Elliot, Gwen, Warner, and Art Mason. "This is not the Council of Chelm," Tylara said. "Nor any lawful group. Yet—"

She didn't finish the sentence. She didn't have to. This was a meeting of the starmen who held the power of gods. For a moment she seemed very vulnerable.

"I think you'll like Octavia," Gwen said. "That is, if you can get Ganton to spare her for a couple of hours." They all grinned at that; they'd hardly seen her since she arrived with Gwen and Warner.

First came reports. University research projects. The quest for movable type—

"—but I wouldn't print any books yet," Gwen concluded.

"Why not?" Rick asked.

"Because the *Shalnuksis* can't possibly misunderstand their significance," Gwen said. "They'd *know* they were faced with a major outbreak of technology. God knows what they'd do."

"They may anyway," Rick said.

"Also, do you want to just throw all these changes at Tran?" Gwen asked. "You're going to lose control of the situation anyway—"

Rick saw Tylara's frown.

"—and some changes are more unsettling than others."

"I'll think about it. Meanwhile, keep working on it," Rick said. He sighed heavily. "We haven't a lot of time. Next order of business. Elliot, you were with Parsons. He tried to run things by force. I've used a different policy. What do the men think of my way, now that Parsons is dead?"

"Cap'n, I was dead wrong about you, and I've said so," Elliot said.

"I'm not after an apology, Sergeant Major. I want an assessment of the situation."

"Sir." He looked at the ceiling for a moment. "Colonel Parsons had not yet attempted to plant *surinomaz*, but it's reasonable to suppose he'd have done no better at that than he did in holding the land," Elliot said. "While he was in command, we lost Corporal Hartford to guerrilla activity. Five more troopers were severely wounded. A total of twenty-three successfully deserted.

"Since you took command, Private Reznick has been killed in action, and three others have been severely wounded, all in battles. There have been no losses to guerrillas. Ten former deserters, eleven counting Mr. Mason, have returned to duty, and nobody has run off. Troop morale is high. We have over six hundred acres in *surinomaz*, and I guess there's no revolt brewing out there even if the peasants aren't too happy about growing the stuff." He shrugged. "On the evidence, your way works."

"And the men realize that?"

"Most," Elliot said. "All that count."

Meaning there are things you aren't telling me, Rick thought. But no point to that now. "The key to 'my method' has been to cooperate with the legitimate rulers here."

"You have done more than this. You have become one of us," Tylara said.

"The point is, I've tried to regularize our positions. One key to that is Wanax Ganton. Another has been the triple alliance of Drantos, Tamaerthon, and Rome."

"I would place your friendship with Yanulf and the Priesthood of Yatar at equal importance," Tylara said. "Especially as The Time approaches. Husband, no one has more admiration for you than I. I also know that you do not recite your accomplishments to gather praise from us. What is it you wish to say?"

"I have a policy question," Rick said. "But I wanted everybody to look at it from the right direction. The question is— what do we do about Ganton?"

"What should we do?" Gwen asked. "I mean, what are the choices?"

"You've watched him with Octavia. That's the first question, do we encourage this match? Beyond that. Do we want him to be Caesar?"

"Does he want to be?" Gwen asked. "Not that it would be automatic. The position isn't really hereditary."

"True," Rick said. "Look, here's the situation. The Westmen are coming down off their plains. Lots of them. They're pretty good troops. Probably can't take castles—" he looked to Mason for confirmation.

"Not by storm," Mason said. "Not stone ones, anyway. But they can wipe up anything else. Murphy had the best ditch, logs, and earth system I've seen on this planet, and he wouldn't have been able to hold much longer—would have lost already if it hadn't been for the battle rifles."

"So what'd you do with him?" Warner asked.

"He's set up in that castle Harkon used to have," Mason said. "With a lot of peasants to guard. He'll be okay until the food runs out."

"So we can hold castles, but not the land," Warner said. "So how do we feed those people?"

"Going to be worse than that," Mason said. "Below the Littlescarp things are too wet. Up on the high plains, that hot wind that comes down from the desert is drying things out."

"Probably the source of some of our rain," Warner mused.

"Could be," Mason said. "But for sure it won't do the crops much good. I don't know what the climate's going to be like, but up in the high plains it's been the driest spring anyone can remember."

Gwen was studying the map on the far wall. "Could we abandon the high plains?"

"It is my land," Tylara said. "Mine and Rick's."

"It's nobody's land if there's nothing to eat," Rick said.

"Captain, you have to hold it anyway," Mason said. "Otherwise the Westmen will ride right across to the Littlescarp and come down into Drantos proper. I'd rather fight them up there where they don't have so much room to spread out."

"The legends are relatively clear," Gwen said. "The Westmen swept all the way to the gates of Rome during one of the times of turmoil. Possibly the last one."

"So we'll have to stop them. Only who commands?" Rick asked. "Me?"

"You can't," Elliot said. "The *Shalnuksis* are coming, and you've got to deal with them. And somebody's got to keep the *surinomaz* crop growing—"

"There's the University situation, too," Gwen said. "It really is getting serious."

"Tylara told me," Rick said.

"Yes, the minor clans see much booty and little danger," Tylara said.

"Which makes for sticky diplomacy with Mac Clallan Muir, and you'll be personally needed," Gwen said.

"More than that, Captain," Elliot said. "If you send a sizable army up into drought country, the logistics are going to get sticky. With Apelles and his clerks to help I can probably handle most of the administration, but somebody's got to enforce our decrees. There's nobody except you to stand up to the barons."

"Can Caradoc command?" Warner asked.

"I suppose he must go," Gwen said.

"Yes, he'll be needed out there, but he can't be commander," Rick said. "He hasn't enough rank yet. We can groom him for promotion after this. But it'll be a long campaign."

"Then you certainly cannot go," Gwen said.

"Yeah," Rick said. "But more than one empire has come apart because it couldn't solve the problem of nomad light cavalry. We've got better armor and equipment, but Murphy says there'll be a *lot* of Westmen. It'll take discipline to beat them."

"For a long war that requires discipline, count not on Drantos warriors," Tylara said. "Even those of Chelm."

"That's the problem. The Westmen won't fight until they've got an advantage. We can win every ten-day and get nowhere, but any defeat can be disaster," Rick said. At Manzikert the Byzantines won the day but at dusk became scattered. They were cut up in detail. After that Alp Arslan's Turks ravaged Asia Minor so thoroughly that when the Crusaders went through a generation later they found brambles growing in what had once been thriving cities.

"If you want disciplined troops, you need Romans," Gwen said. "You could ask Caesar for a legion or two. Oh—of course! There are only two men in Drantos who could command Romans. You and young Ganton. And if he leads Roman soldiers in a successful battle, then he really is eligible to become Caesar."

Tylara looked at Gwen in surprise, then nodded agreement. "So this is what you meant when you began. When you asked what we are to do with Wanax Ganton." She shook her head slowly. "To ask such a question is high treason—my lord, you have been with Ganton these past four ten-days. You must know better than we what we must do. As you always do."

"I don't *know*," Rick said. "But I don't see we've much choice. Can we put together a disciplined force without Romans?"

"Only if you lead it," Tylara said. The others nodded agreement.

"So we need Romans. Can anyone command except the Wanax?"

"Only Publius," Tylara said. "He might command both Romans and our bheromen." Rick winced, and Tylara nodded agreement. "Aye, he is quarrelsome and likes not 'barbarians.' And I think he will like even less this conceit of Ganton as Caesar."

"There's an understatement," Gwen said. "But you won't get Publius to come west anyway. He's got all he can do as Marselius's proconsul."

"I agree," Tylara said. "But though Romans will obey their officers, the bheromen will not follow Roman legates. And we cannot trust the defense of our western lands to Romans alone."

"What's the rest of it, Captain?" Warner asked. "You obviously thought this far already." Elliot gave Larry Warner a sour look, but still nodded agreement.

"First thing, if we've got Roman armies in the west, we want Dravan held by somebody trustworthy, which means Tylara."

There were murmurs of agreement.

They all agree. Why not? They won't be separated from their families. Well, Caradoc will. And Reznick's kids won't ever see him again. We didn't even ask them. Rick lifted a small bag onto the table. "These are Reznick's personal effects," he said. "Some of the stuff goes to his wives."

"What'll happen to them?" Warner asked.

"Dirdre wants to take the kids and go stay with Murphy," Rick said. He shrugged. "She thinks the kids will do better with their father's partner. There's nothing left for her back south, and she's not happy here."

"That's Honeypie," Warner said. "What about Marva?"

"She has no plans."

"They don't have any status here in Drantos," Gwen said. "Both would be welcome at the University, where it's not so important—"

"We'll ask Marva. Dirdre's pretty well decided," Rick said. He opened the bag. "The point is, most of his personal gear goes to Dirdre and Marva, but *we* decide who gets star weapons." He took out a .45 Colt automatic and opened the action. "Unless somebody objects, this goes to Tylara. She'll need it."

Rick hadn't expected any objections, and there weren't any. He slid it down the table. Mason caught it and handed it on to Tylara. She let it rest on the table in front of her.

"Lafe had another personal weapon," Rick said. "This Browning automatic. I think we ought to give it to Ganton." He worked the action a couple of times. "Nice piece. Elliot, do you think the troops will object?"

"I was just wondering about that, Captain," Elliot said. "No,

I don't think so. It makes sense, the way you've got things set up. We can probably outdraw him anyway . . ."

"There is perhaps a better way," Tylara said. "Have the Ladies Dirdre and Marva give it to Wanax Ganton in the name of Lord Murphy. If he accepts it before the Council it will settle the question of their nobility—and by inference, that of all the consorts of starmen."

"He's sure not going to refuse," Rick said. "You don't mind this wholesale elevation of commoners?"

Tylara laughed. "What was I, except the daughter of Mac Clallan Muir, until I married the Eqeta of Chelm? Of all on Tran, I am least likely to object to giving widows their rights."

"All right. That's two problems done. One more. The University. I'll send some Drantos troops up—maybe their officers can become students. But I'm also going to ask Marselius for a cohort of Romans."

Everyone looked at Tylara. She spread her hands. "I like not legions coming west, and I like this no more. Romans in Tamaerthon! But I see the need, and I believe my father and my brother will also. But there may be trouble with the other clans."

"Maybe some of them would like to volunteer for the war," Mason said. "Come west with Caradoc."

"Why would they go?" Warner asked.

"Loot." Mason reached into his pocket and came out with a length of intricately plaited golden wire. "The Westmen carry everything they own, and most have some gold."

"That is well conceived," Tylara said. "It may be that no small number of landless ones will come." She laughed. "I think they will cause no problems in Chelm!"

They'd sure as hell better not, Rick thought.

"Might even settle some of them up there," Mason said. "There's lots of good land gone to ruin. Be more by the time the Westmen get done. Not much rain this year, but it's good land even so. Parts are a lot like Tamaerthon."

"That takes care of some of the hotheads," Warner said. "But what we really need is to unify Tamaerthon under Mac Clallan Muir."

"It will not be," Tylara said. "There is too much jealousy. Lord Rick has brought a crown to the clans, but he cannot give it to my father. Nor can he take it himself."

"Not and work with Ganton," Elliot agreed.

Another problem, Rick thought. Like a ticking time bomb. Cross that one when we come to it. "We are agreed, then?" he asked. "Then I'll send for the others." One meeting done, two to go.

25

The field stank, and from within it came strange sounds: snarls, wild birdsongs unlike any Rick had heard elsewhere; mysterious rustlings of leaves.

"I would go no closer, lord," Apelles said. The blue-robed priest gestured expansively. "This hill is safe, but closer the wild things might reach us. Lamils, grickirrer, even the birds. When they have been long within the madweed, they fear nothing, and even a scratch can be death."

"Necrotic products," Rick said. He took out his binoculars and examined the field of madweed. It seemed ringed with small rotting corpses; the lamils, which ate madweed pods and died in frenetic convulsions. O.D.'d on joy, one of the mercs said. The stench was overpowering even here, fifty meters from the field.

In front of him were hundreds of acres of madweed, the

largest patch anyone in living memory had ever seen. Keeping that patch growing took work; left to itself, madweed grew until choked out by a tough, thorny vine that acted much like a predator, living on the decay of madweed and lamil alike until it produced a tangle of poisonous madweed and thorny vines impenetrable to anything larger than a rabbit. One of the major tasks of Tran farmers was to root out the madweed and destroy it with fire while being careful not to breathe the smoke.

Here they were required to grow it, and they didn't like the job. That was obvious: from Rick's hill he could see a dozen mounted men-at-arms watching the field, and he knew there were more nearby.

Rick scanned the field. Peasants wearing leather leggings and aprons and thick leather gloves moved carefully with machetes. They trimmed pathways through the plants. Behind the machete wielders came women and children with hoes to chop out the vines and other weeds. Behind each group of women and children were adolescents armed with spears. Despite the thick leather armor they moved carefully and alertly.

Rick dismounted and moved toward the field. Apelles reluctantly followed.

"Must we get so close?"

"Yes." The whole damned country is in an uproar over this stuff. I can at least see it up close. Rick contemplated the nearest plant. Three stems formed a triangle nearly ten feet on a side, and rose over six feet high. The ground inside and around the triangle was thickly overgrown with spotted, scaly creeper. There were two dead lamils inside the triangular mass. Another animal, about the size of an Earth rabbit and very much alive, peered at them from the tangled edge of the madweed plant. Its face wore an expression of complete stupidity, almost a cartoon of idiocy. One of Rick's troops had dubbed it "dumbbunny"; it wasn't hard to see why.

"Careful," Apelles whispered. He held his staff like a spear pointed toward the animal. "Back away, slowly."

The young priest was very serious. Rick slowly drew his pistol and slipped off the safety as he followed instructions. After a moment the dumbbunny wriggled out of sight into the creeper.

"The leaves are not yet strong and the seed pods not yet developed," Apelles said. "I doubt that the grickirrer would

have attacked us. But one does not know, and when they are mad from chewing the pods, they fear nothing. Of those bitten by them, one of three dies in agony."

Rabies? Rick wondered. No Pasteur treatment here, and McCleve didn't know how to develop it. "Pretty hard on the harvest workers," Rick said.

Apelles nodded.

"Who are they?" Rick asked.

"Some are convicts promised a full pardon after two seasons," the priest said. "Others are landless, who have been promised fields of their own. And slaves purchasing their freedom."

"It can't be much fun."

"No, Lord. And even with leather greaves and leather aprons, we will lose some. That is why we need cavalry, to prevent them from running away."

"Be certain they know they'll be rewarded," Rick said. They reached their horses, and Rick mounted. "Give them plenty to eat. Tell them their families will be cared for if they are killed. And see that our promises are kept."

"Aye, lord," Apelles said. "We do this already."

"Yeah." Rick reined in and looked back over the fields. We reward them, but it still takes cavalry to keep them working, and I damned well don't blame them.

He rode back to the castle at a gallop.

Mad Bear of the Silver Wolf clan kept the old custom this morning. He rose well before dawn, when the Child of Fire and the Death Wind Bringer were still in the sky. They gave more than enough light to let him find the highest place near the camp. He climbed to the top of the rise, and there raised his lance to the east, west, south, and finally north from whence came cooling winds and gentle rains. Then he kept watch until dawn.

He had not done this since before the Warriors' Meeting of the Silver Wolves judged that the clan should move east, into the Green Lands. If human enemies came, the four warriors who watched by night would be enough to give warning. If other enemies came, no warning or battle would save his people.

And perhaps there would be no demons. Certainly there could be none from the west, where the Death Wind already blew. Not even a demon could live in a land where no man could travel longer than his waterskins would last.

Now the families who had chosen him leader were camped farther east. They had not yet gone down through the Mouth of Rocks and into the Green Lands themselves, but the grass was no longer a brittle brown stubble underfoot. The horses could carry their riders when needed, and the babies no longer wailed all day at their mother's dry breasts until they died. It might even be possible to take old Timusha along some days' journey farther instead of leaving her to die. She had great wisdom. Something she knew might save all of Mad Bear's people until they reached the Green Lands.

So Mad Bear walked out under the night sky and kept vigil. He hoped it would prove a wise use of the strength he would need for the fighting that awaited them in the Green Lands.

He was thirsty by the time the sun rose. He'd been much thirstier in days past, and compared to the ordeal of his initiation, this thirst was nothing. He watched as the Father Sun gave color back to the plains and drove away the Child and the Bringer and all the lesser stars. A light breeze puffed against his bare chest, bringing the scent of horses and dung fires and the sounds of the camp waking to the day. For a band which numbered no more than three hands of tents and thrice as many mounts, they made much noise. They would have to make less in the Green Lands, where they would have enemies again.

After the horses were led out to graze, Mad Bear saw Hinuta climbing up to him. He would not have admitted it to anyone save the Father Sun, but he was glad to see that Hinuta carried a waterskin.

"What news?" he asked, after drinking.

"A rider has come from the camp of the Two Waters, a half day north of us. He bears a message from their High Chief. Will we ride with him as far as the Mouth of Rocks? If we ride well together that far, he will let us go on with him until we reach the other Silver Wolves."

"He is generous. Or has he too few warriors of his own?"

"I think it is not weakness. If he lacks men to defend his women and horses, why let those not his clansmen in among them? That is turning the wolf among the newborn colts."

"True." The people who followed Mad Bear had been chosen to be the last of the Silver Wolves to leave the clan's ancient grounds. Someone had to do this, to perform the last sacrifices to the Sky Father and the Warrior, and see that the shrines were left clean and safe from defilement. The lot fell on Mad Bear and his people, and they called themselves honored, until they finished their work and learned that the rest of their clansmen were ten days' march ahead of them. Try as they might, they hadn't closed the gap.

"It would also be admitting our weakness, to shelter under the wing of another clan," said Mad Bear.

"If they do not know of our weakness, they are more stupid than the ranwang." Hinuta drew his sword and sat down to work on the leather wrappings of the hilt. It was one of only five swords among the warriors who followed Mad Bear, won by Hinuta's father from a Green Lands warrior many years ago. Hinuta took good care of it, although he could not use it with much skill. It would have been dishonorable to question his right to his father's gift. Also, he was a good-natured, generous man, who would share his last mouthful of water or sack of grain with those in need.

Mad Bear thrust his lance point-first into the ground and prayed for the Earth to strengthen it. Then he walked slow circles around it. It was certain that they would not overtake their own clan before they reached the Green Lands. They might even have to travel for some days in the Green Lands themselves before they saw another Silver Wolf. And they were only a hand of hands of warriors.

In the Green Lands, it was said, the warriors lived in stone houses, hard to set on fire. When they rode out to battle, all of them carried swords or long lances, and wore iron shirts to cover their bodies. They were not cunning in war, so it was not hard to force them to fight against odds. Unless you could do that, however, they were very hard to kill. And each stone house might hold several hands of warriors, and there were many stone houses in the Green Land.

It was still possible that the chief of Two Waters meant treachery. But it did not seem likely, as long as the rest of the Silver Wolves were far out of his reach, ready to take vengeance. It was very certain that the Green Lands did not seem a good place for a small band to wander alone. At least they should have a strong friend close at their backs.

"We will ride with the Two Waters," Mad Bear said finally.

"Or at least we will, as long as no warrior of ours has an unjudged blood-feud with any warrior of theirs."

"The Two Waters people have long memories," said Hinuta. "You should ask old Timusha. She will know."

That seemed good advice, but when they got back to camp they found the women keening around the tent where Timusha lay dead; she had never awakened. Mad Bear felt uneasy. To have her die as he was coming to ask her advice and wisdom seemed an evil omen.

He would keep watch all tonight, with the point of his lance propped under his chin to prick his flesh if he so much as nodded. Perhaps Timusha's death was a punishment for his not watching according to custom. He would also give her a horse sacrifice beside her grave, although she was a woman and not a warrior. He had been ready to listen to her as though she were a warrior, so perhaps it could be said that made her one.

The head of the column had vanished over the hills to the west before the rear guard left Castle Armagh. Within an hour the road was obscured by dust, and from the castle tower Rick and Gwen saw only occasional glints of sunlight on a helmet or pike—or caliver barrel. As the last troops left the castle, the semaphore towers linking Armagh with Dravan came alive, warning the garrisons ahead to be ready for the main army.

For a while they were able to see the flash of red at the column's fore: Caradoc's Roman cloak, a gift from Publius Caesar. With it had come other gifts for Caradoc: a new back-and-breastplate from Drumold, and Tylara's gift, a magnificent black gelding fit for a knight or greater. Mounted on his new charger and dressed in his finest, he looked every bit the warrior commander, and his troops liked that. Rick anticipated no problems promoting him after this campaign, and he looked forward to it. He could use another trustworthy general.

Rick watched the Mounted Archers until they rounded the flank of a hill and vanished. Below in the castle courtyard, sergeants' voices rasped. "Line up and keep your eyes front, you lamils! Now it's back to work!"

The newly raised Second Company of the Guards was about to march out for archery practice. So far they seemed to be shaping up fairly well. Certainly the cadre sent from Mason's First Company was working hard enough! They had incentive, of course—the better they did, the more secure their promotions. When rank meant not only honor but a better chance for yourself and your family to live through The Time, you worked hard to hold on to it.

It had been hard to persuade some of the veterans that there was honor in staying behind to train new troopers. They all wanted to go out with the column. Rick shook his head and turned back to watching the road.

After Caradoc and his personal guard came more troops, mostly Romans under their legate Titus Frugi. Tylara had been surprised at Caesar's choice of commanders, but Rick thought it made excellent sense. Frugi was a good general; and he couldn't possibly be tempted to revolt when at the head of a single legion stationed deep within the territory of Marselius's most powerful friends.

Finally, nearly a mile behind the column's point riders, rode Wanax Ganton with Camithon, Tylara and her children, and Lady Octavia. Perhaps because the ladies were traveling with him, it had not been difficult to persuade Ganton to take a safe place in the middle of the column rather than be at its front. "Roman generals do not risk their troops by acts of foolish bravado," Rick had said, and perhaps that had also stung the young king.

"He'll do," Rick said aloud.

Gwen had put down the binoculars now that Caradoc was out of sight. She looked very attractive in her skirt cut off just below the tops of her boots. It would have been thought scandalously short, except that she'd started a new fashion; now half the young women of Drantos had whacked off their skirts. "Who'll do?" she asked.

"Ganton."

"I think you're right," Gwen said. "He seems sensible enough." She giggled. "Handsome, too, but I feel sorry for his lady friend just now. I hope he doesn't get over-amorous for a few weeks—not until he's willing to take that pistol off! I'm sure he'd wear it to bed."

"I can't imagine that Octavia is sleeping with him," Rick said.

"Not yet," Gwen agreed. "But don't make book for the summer. She likes him. Sure, he's a good catch, and the throne of Drantos is probably safer than anything Caesar's relatives can expect just now. But Rick, she really likes him."

"Interesting. He's pretty thoroughly smitten too. Can it be we jaded old dynastic manipulators have made a love match?"

"I hope so," Gwen said seriously. She sighed. "Or do we believe in love matches any more?"

"What's that supposed to mean?"

"Nothing. You've got Tylara—would you stay with her if she were a peasant's daughter?"

"Gwen, I hated seeing her ride off today!" And my children—

"That's not what I asked. You know damned well you wouldn't have married her if she hadn't been important," Gwen said. "Love and marriage. Or marriage and then love. Or just marriage. Any of those seems to work, doesn't it?"

The middle of the column vanished over the crown of a far hill. Just as they disappeared, Rick thought he made out long dark hair tossing in the wind, and a wave of her hand. He closed up the binoculars. "I thought you were in love with Caradoc."

"What's love?" she asked. "I respect him. I care for him, and he protects me. Sometimes from myself."

The shadows were getting long. Rick led the way down from the tower. It stood above his apartments. An oil lamp had been lighted at his table, and a large pitcher of wine stood next to it. "Dinner in an hour or so," Rick said. "Glass of wine first?"

"Sure."

He poured and handed her a goblet. "I really thought you were in love with Caradoc."

"Oh, let it alone, Rick. I am, I guess. But—well it's not really the same. I wouldn't—I wouldn't get on a flying saucer for Caradoc. But he isn't going to ask me, either. And what about you? Don't you sometimes get enough of your raven-haired contessa's dynastic ambitions?"

"Come on, she's wonderful! Who else could I trust to hold the strongest castle on Tran?"

"So do you keep her for love or advantage? You needn't answer. Just as I don't have to answer you." She sipped the wine. "This is quite good."

"Yeah, it turns out Sergeant Lewin used to live in the California wine country. He's been giving them tips."

She sipped again. "Rick, when will they come?"

"Who?"

"The *Shalnuksis*."

"I've got skywatchers looking for satellites from Tamaerthon to Dravan—you've got as good an idea as I have, Gwen."

"Mostly I'm reminding you of something. Distilling. Hammer mills. Printing presses. If they see real changes on Tran, they'll do a *lot* to wipe them out."

Rick sat heavily. "Yeah, I know. But we have to do *something* for these people! Gwen, I was out there in the *surinomaz* fields last week. Week. Hah. We don't even have weeks. But I was out there, listening politely while Apelles told me about the cavalry patrols that herd the peasants back to work—have you seen *surinomaz*? I'd imagine working in that stuff is as close to hell as you can get. And I'm making people do it!"

"Rick, you've no choice—"

"Like hell I don't. I could run. Vanish somewhere."

"That wouldn't be very smart," Gwen said. "In the first place, you wouldn't like it much, hiding out. But suppose you did. Are you mad enough to suppose that one of your men wouldn't try growing *surinomaz*? Or that any of them would be gentler than you? Do you really think anyone *cares* what happens to peasants?"

"You do."

"Maybe a little," she said.

"I think that's the worst of it," Rick said. "Nobody really gives a damn. Even Tylara thinks I'm crazy, worrying about people who aren't clansmen—"

"It's going to get worse, too," Gwen said. "And you're avoiding the subject, which is how far can you go in making changes before the *Shalnuksis* bomb you out?"

"Yeah, but look, if we disperse knowledge far enough, the *Shalnuksis* won't dare try to destroy everything. They'd have to drop enough bombs to make the planet uninhabitable, and that would ruin their little drug racket. They can't risk that . . ."

"Can't they?" She shrugged. "Rick, I don't know. Les may have known, but he didn't tell me that much. I do know the *Shalnuksis* are afraid of wild humans. Another thing, suppose what we do—"

Her look of fear was contagious. Rick automatically lowered his voice. "Suppose what?"

"That what we do gets back to the Confederacy. That they

find out Tran exists. Then it wouldn't be *Shalnuksi* businessmen we'd have to deal with. It might be somebody who thinks this whole planet is a cancer!"

"Christ almighty! But how would they know?"

She laughed. "A hundred ways. The *Shalnuksis* tell them. They send a human pilot and *he* tells them. Inspector Agzaral decides to make a new deal. Rick, I don't *know*, I can only make guesses from what Les told me."

"Yeah. But—Gwen, I don't know either, but I do know I've got to do *something!*"

"To assuage your conscience," she said. "You're forcing the peasants to work the fields, so you need a higher cause to justify it."

"I—yeah, I guess that is it," Rick said.

"So why are you ashamed of being ethical?" Gwen asked. "For that matter, you *have* a higher cause. The University, for example. Rick, did you ever read a book called *Connections?*"

"I saw several of the TV episodes."

"Well, I wish we had that book," Gwen said. "But I can remember some of it. How glass-making led to a shortage of wood, and that made coal valuable, and coal mining needed pumps, and that resulted in the steam engine. And acetylene, and illuminating gas, and coal tar—Rick, we've already changed life on Tran, it's just that you can't see the changes from orbit. Unless you've studied Earth history, you wouldn't see them no matter how closely you looked. There are a hundred students who *think* now. Maybe not well, but they ask questions, they wonder *why* things happen, and they know the difference between chemistry and alchemy. We'll send them all over the planet."

"That's your work."

"No, it's yours," Gwen said. "I know who keeps the University going. If it survives—"

"Your University has to survive," Rick said.

"Ours. And I want it to, but we can't be sure."

"How will they know?"

"They're not above capturing and interrogating you," Gwen said. "Not at all."

"I know. But I'm not going near them without minigrenades. Their detectors don't seem to find them—didn't on the Moon, anyway. Pull the pin on one of those and they'll have to scrape the walls."

She looked at him thoughtfully. "You'd do it, too. Will the others?"

"Elliot will, I think."

"What if they take a local?"

"They might do that. But most of the *Shalnuksis* are *lazy*, Gwen. You didn't know the local languages when you landed. How much time will they put in learning? And most locals don't know about the University, and the ones that do don't know where it is—how many can even read a map?"

"I hope you're right," she said. She got up and paced around the room. "You—don't even mind," she said. "You *like* for me to know things you don't."

"Sure—"

"It's not sure at all," Gwen said. "All my life men said they wanted me to be smart, but when I showed I could do something better than they could, they left me." She stood at the window and watched the darkening sky. "You're not like that. Why?"

"Too much to do, I guess." He got up and joined her at the window, knowing what would happen next, not wanting it to happen but unable to stop himself.

She turned toward him. "It wasn't fair, you know."

"What wasn't?" he asked.

"Meeting Tylara just after we were put on this planet. Les—expected us to stay together. I think we would have, if we'd had a chance. If we hadn't met her so soon."

"And?" He put his hands on her shoulders.

"I have to go back to the University tomorrow."

She moved closer to him, and after that they didn't talk at all.

He woke startled and sat bolt upright. Gwen was on the other side of the room, fully dressed. "Hello," she said.

"Where are you going?"

"To dinner, of course." She came over to sit on the edge of the bed. "We're both crazy, you know that? Caradoc would kill you. He'd *have* to try. And Tylara would have me boiled over a slow fire."

Rick shuddered. "Sorry. That image is just a bit too graphic. She might do it."

"Adds a bit of spice, doesn't it? Stolen fruit's the sweetest and all that."

"Gwen—"

"No," she said. "I do *not* want to talk about it. Rick, we're not in love, but we'll always be a bit special to each other, and in this crazy place maybe that's all we can ask for. And now I'm going down to supper, and after a decent interval you'll come join me, and we'll just plain forget this happened."

"Do you want to forget?"

"No," she said. "No, my very dear."

"Would you get aboard a flying saucer for me?"

"I don't have to say." She jumped away from him before he could catch her. "See you at supper."

PART SIX

Wanax
and
Warlord

26

Tylara do Tamaerthon, Eqetassa of Chelm and Justiciar of Drantos, looked about the great hall of Castle Dravan with feelings of satisfaction. This was home as it should be, lacking only her husband. Her guards stood like statues along the far wall. The floors were newly scrubbed, the tapestries newly cleaned. Her well-trained servants were carrying away the remains of an excellent meal and had brought in flagons of the new wine. There was nothing to apologize for.

Not that Wanax Ganton noticed. He had eyes only for the Lady Octavia, and might have eaten straw from filthy plates for all he knew. Soon enough he would leave the table, to find some excuse to be alone with the Roman girl. Tylara smiled faintly. Octavia knew what she was doing. Or she'd better. She seemed genuinely to care for the young Wanax.

And he for her. Tylara fingered the Colt at her waist. I

273

believe he would give his *binoculars* for her, though possibly not the *Browning* pistol, she thought. Rick wished me to encourage this match, but in truth I have little enough to do.

Caradoc, with the young Roman officer Geminius, sat across from Wanax Ganton. The archer seemed nervous. Was it because he was at table with his superiors? Tylara didn't think so. There was too much of Tamaerthon in Caradoc son of Cadaric; he wouldn't be awed by royalty—especially royalty not officially present. Someone had told Ganton of a strange custom, *incognito* Rick had called it, whereby a Wanax might travel as an eqeta, or even a bheroman, and be treated as such, even though everyone knew he was *really* the Wanax. It seemed strange, but Ganton had insisted, and it seemed to work. Tylara doubted that Caradoc was much agitated by the Count of the North.

And Caradoc certainly isn't afraid of *me*, she thought. We grew up together. If my first husband hadn't been shipwrecked in the Garioch, our friendship might have become something more than that. How little I knew, how few my ambitions as daughter of Mac Clallan Muir! I might easily have wed the son of my father's henchman...

A sudden thought struck her. Caradoc was one of two living men who had seen her naked. No, five if she counted the priests of Yatar who delivered her children, but why should she? They'd not looked upon her as men do at women. Nor had Caradoc, when he'd rescued her from Sarakos's bedchamber. Involuntarily she shuddered at the memory of Sarakos and his crone torturer.

My first time to lie with a man. She shuddered again. And to this day I must drink wine before I bed my husband, and that is shameful, for I love him as few women can ever have loved a man. Yet he knows, and he feels the loss. What can I do? Yatar has given us so much, we cannot complain that he holds back the final drops from the cup.

But if Caradoc had not come when he did! Involuntarily she nodded in satisfaction as she remembered the dead guards outside her room. Caradoc had killed four soldiers and taken her away through secret passages, out of this very castle.

"*Coronel* Caradoc," she called, using the new title of rank that Rick had conferred on him. "You have won a great victory. Tell us of it. As hostess I command it." And that's why he was nervous! He doesn't like to talk about himself, and of course he has to. "Footman! Fill *Coronel* Caradoc's cup, that he will not thirst as he tells us of his victory."

He tells the story well, Tylara thought. *But he tells more than he thinks.*

The situation didn't sound good at all. The Westmen rode where they wanted to go, and their horses were so much faster than Drantos horses that they could seldom be brought to battle against their will—and they would not fight willingly unless they held an advantage.

"And so the Lord Mason conceived a plan," Caradoc said. "I regret that he is not here to tell of it."

Mason and Camithon stayed at the new army camp on the high plains, while Caradoc and Geminius and a number of Roman supply officers came down to Dravan for supplies. There'd been no need for Wanax Ganton to come with Caradoc, but Octavia's presence had been an irresistible attraction.

"A wagon train," Caradoc said. "With a cavalry escort, to travel north and west, riding quickly as if hoping to avoid the Westmen. And certainly it was a clever ruse, for within two days the Westmen saw us and began to stalk us."

And that must have been unnerving, Tylara thought. *To be followed by enemies you could not strike . . .*

"At first they sought to draw the escort away from the wagons, to induce us to fight at a time and place of their choosing. Fortunately they did not succeed."

Not fortune, Tylara thought. *Not fortune, but good planning. Most of the cavalrymen were either Romans or Guardsmen; there would be few of the armored nobility of Drantos in* that *group, not if Mason had planned it. Yes, and Ganton knows that. Does he understand why?*

"Arekor, the priest of Vothan who lived so long among them, said they do not like to fight at night. It is a matter of their gods and demons. Yet we did not know how much of this to believe, and we made camp more in the Roman manner than our own. But perhaps Arekor spoke truth, for although we heard their cries and saw their camp fires, we saw none of them at night."

He took another sip of wine. "Of course we had no real hopes they would attack a strong camp, and they did not. They waited until we had loaded the wagons and were well away from the camp, then struck at us to cut us off from it." He paused to let a steward refill his cup.

"Hundreds of them," Geminius said. He was a young man, and his speech was careful and precise in the Roman manner. A young lordling, higher in rank than his years deserved, Tylara thought. Yet the other soldiers thought him competent enough. "I confess I was near unnerved," Geminius continued. "By Lucifer's hooves! They came swiftly toward us, a veritable flood, and there stood Caradoc, the only calm man in the column! On they came, and still Caradoc did nothing! I had thought we waited too long."

"The Lord Mason had said 'Wait until you see the whites of their eyes,' and in truth we came near that," Caradoc said. "Then we threw off the covers from the wagons, and the archers and musketmen hidden inside them fired as if they were one man. The Lord Mason had said that first firing would have the greatest effect—"

"By the Lord he was right," Geminius said. "The slaughter among the horses was great. As great as when the Lord Mason used his star weapons at Pirion."

"You were at Pirion?" Wanax Ganton demanded. "With Publius?"

Octavia laughed, then busied herself with a napkin.

"Nay, lord, with Legate Valerius and the Eighth Legion," Geminius said.

"Hah!" Ganton banged his flagon against the table. "I led the chivalry of Drantos that day!"

"Lord, I remember it. Was not your helm golden? Attended by a black-clad Guardsman carrying a banner of the Fighting Man?"

"Aye!"

"And you rode next to a gold-bedecked barbarian riding a great black stallion and swinging the largest sword of my memory," the Roman said. "He was attended by the Great Banner of Tamaerthon."

"Aye," Ganton said. "I carried the banner of my house, not that of Drantos, for the Lord Rick was supreme that day. Ho, you do recall!"

Unlikely, Tylara thought. But the story has been told often enough, and what detail would he not have heard by now? My father is easily enough described—

Ganton's face fell. "My only battle," he said. "And I interrupt Caradoc telling of his victory. Forgive me, *Coronel.*"

Caradoc looked embarrassed.

They have had too much to drink, Tylara thought. *I should end this night before one says too much.*

"Come, finish your tale," Ganton said.

"There is little more to tell," Caradoc said. "As instructed, we fired at the horses. Westmen on foot are no match for Tamaerthan archers."

"Nor for Drantos warriors," Geminius added.

"Aye," Caradoc said. "And then we brought forward the wagon with the Great Gun. Pinir the son of the smith fired it with his own hand, and lo! it did not burst. It made great slaughter among the horses of the Westmen, for it was loaded with all manner of small stones, aye and lengths of chain."

What Caradoc called the Great Gun was what Rick called a "four-pounder." Tylara had three in the arsenal of Castle Dravan. More importantly, she had five larger guns capable of destroying siege towers. Dravan well defended had never been taken; held by a handful, it had stood against Sarakos until he brought up great siege engines. With the new guns even those would fail . . .

"And thus we defeated them," Caradoc said. "I fear it does not make a great tale."

"But a great victory," Ganton said. "Would I had been there."

"You will see more of battles than ever you want," Octavia said quietly. "And soon enough, I think."

"Lord, a great victory indeed," Geminius said. "And by Our Lord's death, more of a tale than Caradoc would have you know! The sound of the guns frightened our horses, and when the Great Gun was fired, many were in panic. Our victory was nearly defeat, for the Westmen began to circle and dart toward us, and there was naught to hold them save the Tamaerthan archers, for the *guns* are not quickly readied for another volley, and our own cavalry was useless! Aye, even Romans! My own units, I confess, veterans all, were in disarray.

"Then suddenly, through the noise of battle, all could hear Caradoc. He vaulted into the saddle and rode round, rallying Roman and Drantos horse alike. 'Follow me!' he shouted in a voice like thunder, and he led us through and behind the Westmen, thus holding them in play until the archers and pikemen and musketeers could finish their death work. In truth it is Caradoc's victory we celebrate here."

"Hah," Ganton said. "And what have you to say of this, *Coronel?*"

"Lord—"

"Come now, my lords," Tylara said. "In Tamaerthon it is the custom to boast of one's deeds. It is not so in Drantos. Which customs would you have him honor, my Lord of the North?"

Ganton took another deep drink of wine. "I will find bards to tell of his action, then," he said. "He should be rewarded. Are there no bards to sing of this?"

Octavia moved closer to Ganton. Tylara couldn't hear what she said. Suddenly Ganton shouted. "Aye! My lady, my lords, it has been greatly convenient to be here as a bheroman. I see, though, there are times when it is well to be Wanax." He stood. "Morrone! Morrone, where are you? Ho, Guards! The Wanax of Drantos requires his Companion! Find Lord Morrone!"

"Here, sire!" Morrone rushed into the hall. "Forgive me, I was napping in the corner—"

"Cease prattling and fetch me my sword!" Ganton shouted. "Quickly, quickly!"

"Aye, sire." Morrone ran to the far end of the hall and returned with a broadsword.

Ganton took it. *"Coronel* Caradoc, come forth! Kneel!"

"Aye, sire—"

"My lady, have I your consent?" Ganton shouted to Tylara.

"Aye, sire!"

"Then I, Ganton, Son of Loron, Wanax of Drantos, declare and proclaim Caradoc son of Cadaric worthy of the honors of chivalry." He struck Caradoc on each shoulder with the flat of the sword. "Arise, my lord. You shall have suitable income as befits your new station; and henceforth you shall be known as Lord Caradoc do Tamaerthon."

The pen wrote well. A *space pen,* Rick had called it when he gave it to her, but he had not explained what that meant. But it was certainly easier to use than a gull quill.

And so it was done. And I think well done, my husband. Caradoc has ever been a friend to this house, and I cannot believe that if Ganton gave him every honor within his gift he would change his loyalty. More, his interest runs with ours, as he is married to Gwen.

And a good thing, Tylara thought. Gwen must always be a temptation to Rick. She speaks his languages, and with her he can say what he will. Tylara looked to the mirror on the table. I think I am prettier than she. But— She looked to the bed and set her lips in a grim line. It is likely she is more skilled in the ways women attract men. Especially starmen. Yet men hold honor high. Surely Rick will not betray his friend and companion, his trusted henchman?

He has known other women since we were married. It must be. But he has been careful. There have been no stories, nothing whispered through the halls. Two women have claimed to carry Rick's bastards, but they have been proved to be liars. One could not have been in the same city with Rick when her child was conceived! And the other did not know of the strange surgery that prevails in his homeland.

She thought of Rick with another woman, and writhed. No matter how hard she tried, when she imagined Rick straining and groaning with another, the face beneath him was Gwen's. Enough! She lifted the pen again.

But though Caradoc has won a victory, I think the war goes not well. The Westmen ride where they will, and we hold only castles and walled towns. There will be no crops throughout much of the high plains. The Roman scribes will tell you what now is required to feed the army and its horses. I cannot think those numbers will please you, nor will they please the peers of Drantos. The taxes of this war, added to what you require to keep your fields of madweed, would have ruined us if we had not the new plows. They may ruin us yet, though the first harvest in the Cumac has yielded more than we previously took in two. And the new forges and foundries produce wagons to carry the grain, so that we are able to send it to the high plains for the army. Yet I fear there will come a time when we have not wagons, horses, and grain in the same place at the same time.

The Westmen are the death of the earth. Arekor, the priest of Vothan who lived among them, has told Caradoc— Lord Caradoc!—that they do this from policy. They burn and destroy, and pull down not only buildings and walls, but the very terraces, and stop up wells; for they live on so

little that they can live in devastated lands when none of
their enemies can. Thus do they keep the lands above the
Westscarp in desert, and thus will they make desert of our
lands above the Littlescarp if we cannot expel them or kill
them.

She set the pen down and got up from the table. The next
part would be very hard to write. A flagon of wine stood on
a side table near her bed, and she filled a goblet.

I seldom drink wine, she thought. She looked at the empty
bed. Except at night, before I go to my husband. Even now,
even now, though he is gentle and kind and loves me. And
though I love him with all my heart, I know I pleasure him
little that way, though he says this is not so.

My husband, as you desired, we held a Council of Chelm
to consider defenses against the Westmen. Hilon the blacksmith of Clavton, who sits in my council—

She frowned and crossed through the last two words.

—in our Council of Chelm, proposed that instead of
supporting the army in the high plains, his town will buy
the knowledge of how to make Guns, and pay to have the
burghers taught in their use, and will buy firepowder.

He spoke thus: "If we put Guns on the town wall, let
the Westmen come to us. We will break their teeth. Much
of that and they will cease to chew on us." You may imagine
this was not greeted with joy by bheroman Traskon son of
Trakon in whose lands Clavton lies.

For it cannot be long before the towns find ways to buy
these Guns, and then they will be as safe as Dravan, and
how will their lords rule then? And now I think, nor town,
nor Dravan is safe! For I had believed that with the Guns
Dravan would be safe from siege towers, yet how are we
safe from Guns which can batter down our very walls?

My husband, great and momentous changes are upon
us, and I no longer know what I must do to protect our
children. I have often thought you know not enough of
Drantos and Tamaerthon and this world of Tran to rule it.
Yet if you do not, no one does, for only you know what
has been unleashed upon us and what I will live to see.

She tapped the table with impatience, searching for the

words to tell him of her fear without sounding afraid. Finally she wrote again.

> For now you are my life as never before. Always I have loved you. Now I must needs obey you, for I know not what else I can do to preserve what is ours. And though I have not always understood, yet I have tried to make your work my work, and your cause my cause; and now that must be so no matter how little I understand.
>
> My fear is that I shall be asked to do that which I cannot do. But I am comforted, for you will never ask of me more than I can bear.
>
> My lord, my life, my love, I am,
>> Tylara.

27

Rick cursed as he drank the bitter caffeine drink that for want of a better word he called tea.

His orderly watched the footman carry out the soiled breakfast dishes, then turned back as Rick cursed again. "My lord?" Jamiy asked.

"Nothing," Rick growled. "Leave me."

"Aye, lord." The orderly hesitated. "You are to see Chancellor Yanulf this morning."

"And then Sergeant Major Elliot, and after that I have letters to dictate," Rick said. "Yeah, I know. Give me this much time." He held his fingers half an inch apart, indicating about ten minutes: the time it would take for a standard beeswax candle to burn down that far. Time measurement was not very accurate on Tran...

What the hell does Yanulf want, coming here from Edron

without notice? I'll find out soon enough. Another goddam day of work and another night alone. Why didn't I figure a reason for Gwen to stay—

Because, you damned fool, your wife would kill you. More likely kill Gwen, and it isn't just a figure of speech. Besides, it isn't Gwen you want, it's Tylara. Remember?

Yeah, and it really is. Only—

Only nothing, buster. Forget it! What's next? Your wife doesn't understand you? Tell that one often enough, and it'll be true. Or maybe that's what you want? You could do it. You have the guns. Leave Tylara, go to the University and shack up with Gwen. You could change the whole history of the planet that way. Of course, all this stuff you've worked for goes down the tubes, but what the hell, a good lay is worth a lot, right?

Sure, with Isobel and Makail growing up to hate me. There'd also be the Caradoc problem.

"Hell," he said aloud. "It's not even tempting." He drained the cup of lukewarm bitter tea.

Yanulf was attended by Apelles and two acolytes. The acolytes were dismissed at Rick's study door, but Apelles came in with the Chancellor. Yanulf looked older, as if he'd aged a year in the past few months, but his voice was as hearty as ever. He greeted Rick warmly, and Rick stood to clasp the priest's forearm before they sat at the conference table.

"And what brings you from the capital?" Rick asked.

"Not good news, I fear," Yanulf said.

"I didn't think it would be."

"This could be a matter for the Eqeta's Court," Yanulf said. "It would have been, had not Apelles sent the matter to me."

Rick frowned. "I'm not sure I understand."

"Technically, he has interfered with your justice," Yanulf said. "Yet I see not what else he could have done."

Rick warily eyed the two priests. "Why not tell me?" he demanded.

Apelles looked to Yanulf, then back at Rick. "It is a matter that I cannot resolve, lord." He looked down at the table, then across at the maps, finally back to Rick. "A petition of right, on behalf of Nictoros, Priest of Yatar, was brought to me three ten-days ago. As is my duty, I sent forth writs inquiring into the matter, intending to lay it before you in open court." He paused again.

"And instead you wrote the Chancellor."

"No, lord."

"You just said you wrote to Yanulf!"

"Aye, lord, but I did not write to the Chancellor. I referred the matter to Yanulf, Archpriest of Yatar, for it is a matter which touches the very honor of our god!"

O Lord, Rick thought. What are we in for? The classic confrontation between Church and State? Becket and Henry II, played out here? "Suppose you tell me about it."

Again Apelles looked to Yanulf, who nodded slightly. "Nictoros was born villein," Apelles said. "Within the lands of Bheroman Enipses. During the rebellion against Wanax Loron, Nictoros fled the land and took refuge with Galdaf, Priest of Yatar."

"Many fled in those times," Rick said. "And I think I see the problem. Enipses is a loyalist. Supported Ganton during the civil wars, supports Tylara and me now. The baron wants his villein back, and the church won't turn loose their priest. That's an easy one—"

"He was found to have both intelligence and a desire to serve Yatar," Apelles said, "and was made an acolyte, and in due time consecrated as Priest of Yatar. He later found favor with Bheroman Enipses, who appointed him to be priest in his own household."

Maybe it's not so simple, Rick thought.

"The war continued. Wanax Sarakos, aided by the starmen serving Colonel Parsons, invaded the land and drove Bheroman Enipses from his castle. Nictoros remained, as was his duty, and tended the caves beneath the castle. He fled only when the usurper placed there by Sarakos dismissed him."

"He fled to Dravan," Yanulf said. "And assisted me there. And learned from me. He learned much about The Time, and what must be done, and showed quick wit and understanding."

And you liked him, Rick thought. "I see." He tried to keep his voice noncommittal.

Apelles continued the story. "Then you, Lord, defeated Sarakos and brought the starmen to your obedience. When Bheroman Enipses returned, he dismissed Nictoros as priest of his household, saying that Nictoros should have accompanied him to exile rather than remaining within the castle. Nictoros departed, but you, lord, were pleased to appoint him priest in the Eqeta's free town of Yirik, where there are also extensive caves and a large temple of Yatar."

Rick looked to Yanulf. "I don't recall the appointment. On your advice?"

"Yes. The order was signed by the Eqetessa. I did not agree with Bheroman Enipses, but certainly there was no need for dispute. Yirik was without a priest, and I had high regard for Nictoros's abilities." Yanulf fingered the medallion hanging from his golden chain. "It was a mistake," he said finally. "I should have sent Nictoros to a village beyond Enipses's domains. Perhaps even outside Chelm. But I did not. Continue, Apelles."

"Then, lord, came your decree, requiring each bheroman to send laborers for the madweed. And other decrees, requiring grain to feed the madweed workers. These taxes fell heavily on Enipses, for he had lost many of his villeins during the wars, and thus last autumn much of his grain rotted unharvested before the rains destroyed it.

"Then came the Westmen, and still more taxes; but meantime The Time approaches, and Nictoros attempted to prepare as commanded by Yanulf."

Uh-oh. I see it now, Rick thought. And—

"Bheroman Enipses accused Nictoros of interfering with the collection of taxes; of taking grain belonging to the Wanax, which is a treason. But instead of applying to you for a writ to allow his constables inside Yirik, he waited with patience. This was rewarded, for Nictoros foolishly travelled beyond the town walls, and Enipses had men waiting, who brought Nictoros before the bheroman's court. He was found guilty; and sentence of death was passed. But, because the grain taken was placed in the caves of Yatar, and because Nictoros was a priest, the sentence was remitted to enslavement." Apelles shrugged. "He was sent here to labor in the fields of madweed. You may imagine my amazement when as I inspected the fields I was greeted in ways known only to the priesthood, and I was given a properly drafted petition of right."

That would be a surprise. The petition of right was a monopoly of the Yatar priesthood. It implored a ruler—bheroman, eqeta, even Wanax—to obey his own laws. It didn't have to be granted, but once it was, the matter was for the courts.

"I still don't understand. If you present me that petition, I'll certainly grant it. Let right be done. Then it's a matter for judges. Bheroman Enipses may not like it, but—" He stopped, because Yanulf was shaking his head. "What now?"

"If your judges examine the matter, they will find for Bheroman Enipses," Yanulf said. "Nictoros does not deny taking grain gathered for taxes and placing it in the caves. Nor would he return it when Enipses demanded it. Nor did the bheroman enter the caves, nay nor threaten to, but with great respect pronounced that what was done was done, and new grain must be gathered for the Wanax."

"But he arrested the priest," Rick said. "I see. But—if he's guilty, whatever possessed him to send in a petition of right?"

"Perhaps he believes he was right," Yanulf said. "Perhaps I believe he was right. But it is not law."

"Tear up the petition," Rick said. "I'll issue a pardon. Or you can draft one for the Wanax to sign."

"Would it were so simple," Yanulf said. "But it is not. The priests of Vothan know of this. They are asking Bheroman Enipses to dismiss all the priests of Yatar within his lands."

"In whose favor?" Rick asked.

"Perhaps they will not be replaced at all," Yanulf said. "Or perhaps by those who mouth the words of service to Yatar, but own allegiance to Bacreugh."

"Who the devil is Bacreugh?"

"Bacreugh is a priest of Yatar, from an order formerly known mainly in Tamaerthon. He is allied with Mac Bratach Bhreu. A kinsman, in fact."

"I see. Drumold's only real rival. But why is he followed in Drantos?"

"He preaches words comfortable to the nobility," Apelles said. "And he has made strong alliance with the priesthood of Vothan."

"More," Yanulf said. "You have been told of the vision of the Roman Bishop Polycarp?"

"Yes. Yatar and Jehovah are one. I wonder how the Jews will feel about that . . ."

"What are Jews?" Yanulf asked.

"Followers of Jehovah, but who believe the Christ has not yet come. They have strong dietary laws, and passionately believe there is only one God."

"There are no such in Drantos," Yanulf said.

"And now that I think of it, it's not likely there are any on Tran." Until now. How many of the mercs are Jewish? Bilofsky, I suppose. Lewin. Goodman. Schultz, only he's still down south. None of them seemed particularly devout, but you never know.

"The priesthood of Vothan laughs at Polycarp," Yanulf said. "And they do not favor the Roman alliance. Now through the followers of Bacreugh they seek control of the caves of Yatar. Bheroman Enipses may well yield those under his castle."

"Bacreugh and his order should be suppressed. And the priests of Vothan made humble," Apelles said.

Oh, no, you don't. You won't get me involved in religious persecutions. "I do not agree. But were it desirable, it would not be possible. Vothan has powerful friends." Including some of my mercs. They may not be believers, but they're superstitious enough. And a lot of the army is devoted to Vothan, or at least scared of him.

"You see now why this should not be seen in open court," Yanulf said. "And why young Apelles referred the matter to me."

"Sure. You're trying to undermine civil authority," Rick said.

"Nay, lord!" Apelles said. "We are loyal."

I'm sure you think so. But if nothing else, you're inventing benefit of clergy, which apparently they don't have here. Still, the priesthood of Yatar, as organized by Yanulf, is the nearest thing to a literate civil service I have. They also have a monopoly on paper. I can't do without them.

"First," Rick said, "I hadn't known how serious Enipses's labor problem is. We'll have to do something about that."

"At harvest time there will be labor shortages everywhere," Yanulf said. "It has always been so."

Rick scribbled a note: "Get Campbell working on a reaper."

"There is a machine," Rick said. "A way to harvest grain — grain! Where is the place for Hestia in this vision of Polycarp's?"

"As the mother of Christ," Yanulf said. "For as you know, the Christ was born of a virgin. Polycarp preaches a doctrine which he calls 'Immaculate Conception,' under which Hestia took on the flesh of a mortal in order to bear a son to Yatar."

"And you believe this?"

Yanulf frowned. "I know not what to believe. One thing is

certain, the prophecies of The Time are true. And they were revealed by Yatar himself. The Romans know much of The Time, and thus must once have known Yatar." He shrugged. "Perhaps Polycarp is correct, their Jehovah is Yatar. The names are not unlike."

"Fortunately we need not decide the matter today," Rick said. "For the problem at hand, I will remit some of Enipses's taxes. You will send a persuasive emissary to bear that pleasant news. Someone who will persuade Enipses that it would not be wise to make great changes in the governing of Yatar's caves. Someone to point out that neither Wanax Ganton nor I nor Eqetassa Tylara would favor Bacreugh's cause."

"That may be sufficient," Yanulf said.

"As to Nictoros, I will issue a pardon."

"Who will make up what you remit to Enipses, lord?" Apelles asked.

"We'll have to work that out," Rick said. "Maybe you could see to it?"

"We will do that," Yanulf said.

Sure you will, Rick thought. And that'll fall on some poor schmuck who's irritated his local priest. But what the hell can I do?

I can get Campbell working on that reaper.

When dusk came, Jamiy brought in lamps. Rick sighed. They still hadn't managed good lamps. These burned a mixture of oil and naptha, and gave better light than the older tapers, but the light was still too dim, and gave him a headache. One day, he thought, I'll need spectacles, and I won't have them. And then what? But this has got to be done.

Ganton had summoned the chivalry of Drantos to the high plains. Rick was horrified. He could see no use for that many undisciplined heavy cavalrymen. Useful or not, though, they had to be fed. Wagons, horses, grain, all had to be found and sent in a steady stream, and since the bheromen had contributed their share and more, a lot had to come from the free towns— who weren't anxious to provide it. Writs had to be prepared, spies sent to find new sources of wealth to tax, constables sent to harass the obstinate . . . He worked for two more hours.

"It is time, lord."

Rick looked up from his paperwork to see Padraic.

"The night meal is prepared. You wished to be called," Padraic said. "The guards wait outside."

"Thanks. Come in, Padraic. There's wine over there. Pour some for both of us, and sit down." Rick carefully stacked the papers and parchments and leaned back in his chair. Far out to the west he saw moving lights in the semaphore tower, and wondered what message was coming in.

When Padraic brought the wine, he lifted his glass. "Cheers," he said, and laughed when his archer captain looked puzzled.

"An expression from my home world," Rick explained. "Tell me, how have the men taken the news of Lord Caradoc's promotion?"

"Well, lord. It gives hope to all, that one may rise high if one has talent and is willing."

And loyal. Let's not forget that one. "Yes. Well, here's to Lord Caradoc!" They touched glasses and Rick drained his, then held it out for a refill. "Tell me, Padraic, you were raised in Tamaerthon—what do you know of Bacreugh?"

There was a crash as Padraic dropped the pewter goblet. He bent quickly to pick it up and refill it.

Rick drew his Colt and clicked off the safety. He held the pistol concealed below the table. "Sit down," he said. "I think we'd better talk."

"Aye, lord. How did you find out?"

"I have ways." What the hell have I found out? "Now tell me about it."

"Lord, there is little to tell. My grandmother is sister to the mother of Mac Bratach Bhreu, and thus I am kin to Bacreugh. It was a kinsman who approached me."

"What did he offer?"

"He said that a friend to Bacreugh wished to speak with me, and that he would offer me honor and gold," Padraic said. "I told him that I have honor enough, and it may not be had for gold. Lord, what should I have done? For I cannot betray my kinsman, and indeed he *said* nothing of importance."

"What did he say?"

"Only that. Only that Bacreugh—he said a friend to Bacreugh, but I surmised that the friend would be Bacreugh himself—wished to speak with me, and it would be much to my interest to do so; that he would offer me honor and gold, and

I need do little—but what I would be required to do he did not say."

Rick thumbed the Colt's safety on. "But you guessed?"

"No, lord."

"Then why did you drop the goblet?"

"I had heard you can hear thoughts, Lord. I had not known it was true until now. For I was at that very moment wishing I knew what Bacreugh wished of me."

"You can do better," Rick said. "You must know they intended for you to kill me. Or to let one of them get past you and do it."

"Nay, lord, I do *not* know it. I know only that Bacreugh wished to make an offer—and that he is a kinsman, as was the man he sent to approach me."

"What other kinsmen have you within the Mounted Archers?"

"Only Caradoc, lord."

"That's right, Caradoc is your kinsman—he is kin to Bacreugh, then."

"Aye, lord. He is related much as I am."

"Did you tell him about this?"

Padraic laughed. "No, lord. Lord Caradoc is—quick to defend his honor. I was his chosen under-captain. He might have seen an offer to me as an insult to him, a matter for blood. And I cannot think he would wish blood-feud with his own kin."

There was a furious knocking on the door. "Captain!" someone shouted. Rick recognized Elliot's voice.

"Come in, Sergeant Major."

Elliot was breathless. He held a paper in his hand. "Just decoded this from the semaphore, Captain. They've spotted a satellite over Castle Dravan!"

28

Elliot put the decoded message on Rick's desk. "Just as you told 'em, Cap'n. Right after the True Sun set and while the 'Stealer was low on the horizon, they saw a bright light moving across the sky."

"Direction?"

"Southwest to northeast."

"Has to be a satellite," Rick agreed.

"I checked the shrine," Elliot said. "Nothing on the radio, and there's been somebody there all the time."

"Hmm. They don't want to talk with us."

"Not yet, anyway."

"So the next question is, who is it? *Shalnuksis* or a human? They're a little early for *surinomaz*, and I'd think they'd know that. They're making observations they don't care to have us know about. Any ideas on that?"

"None I like."

"Me either," Rick said. He took a blank sheet of paper and began to write. "REWARD THE OBSERVER. THEN COME AT ONCE. BRING CHILDREN. IMPERATIVE ARMAGH THOUGHT MAJOR AREA OF INTEREST."

He handed it to Elliot. "Get this coded and see that it goes off to Tylara."

Elliot glanced at the paper. "Maybe it'd be best for the kids to stay at Dravan."

"I thought of that, but— If they're here to drop bombs, I'd rather Tylara stayed at Dravan too. In the caves."

"Think she'd do it?"

"No." Rick took the message and crossed through the words "BRING CHILDREN."

Elliot nodded agreement. "Not likely anything'll happen."

"Not this time," Rick said. "Not this time."

The field stank of too many men and too many horses. Even in the headquarters tent which was carefully placed upwind of the main encampment, the smell was there, despite the moaning hot wind that blew down the Westscarp. Lordy, I want to go home, Art Mason thought.

The adjutant brought in a paper and handed it to Mason. Art examined it and whistled. "If we don't do something pretty soon," he said, "we're not going to have any army left."

"Surely you exaggerate," Ganton said.

"Hardly, sire," Camithon said. "One always loses more men to sickness than the enemy. We have been very fortunate— no. I will not say fortunate, for it is not fortune. Thanks to Major Mason, we have had fewer losses than any army in my memory."

"Morning report's pretty bad even so," Mason said. "Still too many down. Too many flies in camp. The Romans are all right, but I can't make the others dig the latrines deep enough. And this hot wind gets to them. We're losing troops to pure funk. Last night a trooper got up at midnight and ran out and started hacking down a tree, shoutin' that he hated it. Beat it up pretty good, too. Nobody in his company did a damned thing, except one guy yelled out 'Give it a whack for me, I hate it too.' That sounds funny, but it's not, not really. Yesterday we lost two archers to a knife fight."

"Many of the knights will depart also," Camithon said. "Their time of service will expire, unless we find ways to pay them."

"You mean that I summoned them against your advice," Ganton said. "Do not bother to deny it. You may even be right. Yet my father lost his throne through failure to keep peace with the great lords of Drantos. It is an error I shall not make."

"Reckon it can't hurt to have 'em here to keep an eye on 'em," Mason said. "And even with 'em here, we're spread pretty thin, keepin' patrols going everywhere. Reminds me of Viet Nam, some."

"I know not that place," Camithon said.

"No sir, I don't reckon you would," Mason said. "Thing is, we won every damn battle in Viet Nam. Troop for troop we had the enemy out-matched every which way. Only one problem. We lost the flipping war."

"Some day you must tell me that story," Ganton said. "Meanwhile, we have the chivalry here, and some will remain even after their time is expired. Not all are more concerned for rights than for the safety of the realm."

"Been more like that we wouldn't have lost 'Nam," Mason said. "And I reckon we need your heavies. Light horse can't beat the Westmen. Knights can, if they'll stay together and fight together."

"And yet we plow sand," Ganton said. "The Westmen avoid us. They burn and destroy, and run away when we ride after them. Are they so much better than we, that they lose no men to sickness?"

Mason made an ugly sound, then shrugged. "They're used to living on short rations."

Ganton turned to the maps on the table. He used his dirk to trace westward along a river bed. "I would employ the bheromen and knights in some useful endeavor." He bent over the map. "The Westmen are said to have a great encampment here," he said. "Will they defend it if we attack?"

"We could ask that Arekor chap that lived with 'em," Mason said. "But it probably depends on what we attack with."

Camithon fingered the scar on his cheek and nodded. "Aye, though I do not like to say it. They fear Romans more than us. Romans and Tamaerthan archers."

"Perhaps we could make them fight us," Ganthon said. "On terms we like."

"Wouldn't mind seeing how," Mason said.

"Star weapons," Ganton said. "Used against their horses in camp. They will come forth to fight if their horses die."

"Probably true," Mason said.

"You do not sound joyful," Camithon said.

"I keep remembering Viet Nam," Mason said. "The French were there before us. They kept saying that if they could just make the enemy stand up and fight, they'd have it made. Eventually they did just that. At a place called Dien Bien Phu . . ."

Camithon and Ganton listened as Mason told the story. Later, Ganton summoned a servant to bring wine, and they drank a toast to the brave Legionaries and paras who died in the strongpoints with the strange names of Gabrielle and Isabelle and Beatrice.

"Did Lord Rick then name his daughter for that place?" Ganton asked.

Mason shrugged. "Don't know."

"There is more to this matter of forcing the enemy to fight than one may think," Camithon said. "Majesty, it is my counsel that we withdraw. The Westmen will follow, and when they have come far enough we can bring all our strength against a part of theirs. With the aid of the *balloon* we can find their weak points."

"The *balloon* is worth much, truly," Ganton said. "Yet consider. It cannot move across the land like the—the *helicopters* Lord Rick had on his world. And any land the Westmen take they render worthless. If we abandon Lord Rick's lands, perhaps he will understand—but will Eqetassa Tylara? Tell me, Lord General, do *you* wish to explain this strategy to her?"

Camithon threw up his hands. "Shall we then risk all to avoid the wrath of one Tamaerthan—lady?"

"They are my people," Ganton said. "I am as sworn to defend them as they to serve me. Is this not true?"

"Aye—"

"Then let us hear no more of withdrawal."

Camithon gently stroked his scar. "Then it is Your Majesty's wish that we attack the camp of the Westmen?"

"It is."

"I can but obey." Camithon looked to the map. Mason had put small parchment squares on it, each representing a unit of the Royal and Allied forces. Camithon had never seen such a thing before, but it made planning much easier. "If we are to move westward and attack, it were well to take all our forces," Camithon said. "All we can feed. And all the star weapons."

"Need some reserves to guard the supply route," Mason said. And the ammunition, for that matter. "But we'll want all the weapons."

"Let Westrook become the new supply center," Ganton said. "It is a strong place, and I doubt that Lord Murphy would leave it to his companion's widow if he were not certain of her abilities."

Mason nodded sourly. Her abilities my eye, he thought. I had a hell of a job gettin' Murphy out of there, and even then he wanted to leave the flippin' 106. Horse tradin', with *me*, over what weapons to leave in that castle, just like it was his home. Hell, I guess it is. Murph's found a home, and I doubt we'll see much of him if he lives to see the end of the Westmen.

"If Westrook is to be the supply center," Ganton continued, "then we must advance through *here*." He pointed on the map. "We will not want the Westmen to know what we are doing, yet we will wish to be certain that our wagons are not delayed at the river crossing." He looked thoughtful, then nodded. "The Romans are good engineers. Let the *cohortes equitates* carry timbers and all other things needful for quick construction of bridges here, and here. Our forces can come by many routes. The Westmen will not divine our intent, and we need not be so concerned for supply."

"An excellent thought," Camithon said. He looked at the young king with new respect.

"And I think we will not raise the *balloon* until after the attack on the camp," Ganton continued.

"Sure help the artillery to have it up," Mason said. "For target spotting—"

"Yes," Ganton agreed. "And we shall do so. But think, it is too valuable to use as a lure, and when it is raised it will draw all the Westmen toward our main strength. Would it not be better to let them seek us as the star weapons fall among them?"

Camithon frowned. "If the *balloon* is needed, we can guard it with a small band—"

"No," Ganton said. "Think, my lord. A small band will fall prey to roving Westmen, and there are sure to be such. If we leave enough men to guard it, we should leave them all—else we divide our strength. That is what the French did at this place, Dien Bien Phu, and we have learned the cost to them."

Christ on a crutch, Mason thought. Maybe the kid understands this stuff better'n me. Hell, I'm no officer. I'm an NCO who got lucky.

Unconsciously Mason straightened as he turned to speak to the Wanax of Drantos.

29

The office was a penthouse on top of a two-story building, a veritable tower here. It was richly furnished, with thick carpets, elaborately carved furniture, and brilliant tapestries. Leaded glass windows looked out on green Tamaerthan hills to her left and a quiet quadrangle on her right. Gwen Tremaine had once seen *National Geographic* photographs of a European university Rector's office, and she'd had her staff make as near a duplicate as they could.

The high-backed chair was large enough to swallow her completely, and since it faced the desk rather than a window, when she curled up in it she was utterly invisible from the outside. She tucked her feet up closer—

And if you regress any further, you'll be sucking your thumb, you twit! she told herself; but she didn't move from the chair.

Regression feels fine. Safe, even.

Hah. You can't run away from yourself, no matter how far you go.

Thanks a lot. But it isn't myself I'm running from. At least I can't see the sky. She reached forward to the desk and lifted the note from Larry Warner. Her hand hardly shook as she read it.

> Gwen: a couple of the lookouts on Ben Harkon report seeing a "walking star" not long after dusk last night. From the path it's got to be a satellite. I'm going into town about the reaper. Good luck.

We'll need luck, she thought. They're up there looking for progress, and they'll find it. Then the bombs fall. Glory, why shouldn't I be afraid of the sky?

It's not the sky, it's who might be in that ship—

I'm not afraid of Les.

No? Then who stuffed the transceiver into a bale of *garta* cloth, and what do you expect will happen when he calls and you don't answer?

I don't know. Maybe he'll go away and leave us alone.

Oh, that's what you want? I thought you wanted Les!

Sometimes.

Often.

Often, she admitted. But mostly I don't want to hurt the University. Or Caradoc—

Or Rick?

Or Rick.

Because he's saving the world? Or because there's a chance, just a chance, that he might tell Tylara to go to hell and come shack up with you? Who do you want? Rick, Les, Caradoc— or all of them? At once or one at a time?

"Shut up!" Her hands found a Roman crystal pitcher. She hurled it against the desk. It caromed off a stack of papers and shattered against the wall. Then she sat still for what seemed a long time despite the work she had to do.

"My lady?"

Gwen looked up to see Marva. "Yes?"

"The Lord Campbell is here to speak with you." Marva eyed the wine spilled on the desk and the broken glass on the floor. "Shall I have that cleaned?"

"Yes, please."

Marva took a small bell from her sleeve. Two servant girls came in to mop up the floor as Marva tidied the desk and blotted wine from the papers.

"Do you like it here?" Gwen asked in English.

Marva hesitated. "Yes, my lady. It is"—she groped for the word—"useless to wish for what can not be."

Whatever that is, Gwen thought. What might you wish for? Your husband again? Ben Murphy? Fortunately for me, you can't have either one.

Lafe Reznick's second widow had become nearly indispensable, a combination of housekeeper, lady in waiting, secretary, and den mother. The students saw her as nobility, the widow of a star lord, yet someone they could speak with. Much information came to Marva, but she gave little in return, except to Gwen.

"You may bring Lord Campbell now, if you please, my lady," Gwen said.

"Yes, my lady." Marva ushered the servants out.

Gwen patted her hair into place and tried to look calm as the red-haired engineering professor came into her office. "Yes, Bill? What can I do for you?"

"Steel," Campbell said. "I need a lot more, and I don't have it."

"For the reaper?"

"Yeah."

"Larry's gone into town about that—"

"He won't get anywhere. All the locals claim they've paid their taxes. They have, too. But Lord Rick wants a goddam progress report every goddam night! Now what am I going to do?"

"You're going to stop shouting at me and have some wine, to begin with."

Campbell started to say something, but caught himself. Then he grinned. "Yes, ma'am. What wine?"

"Oh—" She pulled the bell cord. Marva came in almost instantly. She was followed by one of the girls with a new pitcher and goblets.

"Good service," Campbell said. "Thanks, Marva, I can handle things now."

"Yes, my lord—" Marva indicated a place for the tray, waited until the girl had put it down, and waved her out. "Will there be anything more, my lady?"

"Thank you, no—"

"I will wait outside."

"Cold one, that," Campbell said when Marva had gone.

"You're not polite to her."

"The hell I'm not—"

"You're not," Gwen said. "You call her by her first name—"

"Just to be friendly. She speaks English—"

"But she is *not* an American, Bill. You and I can talk informally, and you think because you say it in English you can talk that way to Marva, but you *can't*. Bill, Caradoc calls *me* 'my lady' most of the time. And have you noticed the way Rick speaks to Tylara?"

"Well, sure, but Tylara's one of the great ones—"

"Marva is *noble*," Gwen said. "To you it may seem a little silly that she's something special because your friend Lafe Reznick married her, but to her it's not." She threw up her hands. "Anyway, that's why she seems cold toward you. Call her 'my lady' once in a while. She'll warm up fast. Now what about your iron?"

"The Romans have iron."

"I'm aware of it."

"Can you get me some?"

"I'm also aware of what they'll want. Guns and gunpowder, and we don't have any to spare. But something just came in that may change things." Gwen flipped through soggy papers on her desk until she found the one she wanted. "Intelligence reports. The Romans will have a *big* harvest this year, and they're very low on slaves to bring it in. If you could have your reaper—"

"If I can produce something that works, the Captain will send it west. No matter how good I am, there won't be enough equipment to send to the Romans. Not this year."

Gwen shuddered.

"What's the matter?"

"I can't trade them guns, and I can't promise them a reaper. There's only one thing I can send."

"Yeah." Bill Campbell went over to the window and looked out onto the University quadrangle. He spoke without turning back toward her. "They tell me the life of a Roman slave isn't so bad. No worse than peasants in Drantos."

"I'll keep telling myself that," Gwen said. "Maybe if I tell myself often enough, I'll believe it. Meanwhile—"

"Meanwhile I'll send some troopers out into the Pirate Lands," Campbell said. "Those people will drown or starve within the year anyway. Best to do it quick, before the so-called roads are too muddy. It's starting to rain again."

"That should help the crops," Gwen said. She smiled grimly to herself. Also, the clouds will hide the sky . . .

Mad Bear woke to the sound of screaming horses, but he could not comprehend. Walking Eagle, chief of the Two Waters, had been generous when Mad Bear's band left him to return to their own Silver Wolves. His farewell gifts had included a barrel of the strong water the Green Lands folk made from grapes. It made men sleep sounder than beer or fermented mare's milk ever could, and Mad Bear had sat late drinking with Hinuta.

Another horse screamed in agony. Mad Bear leaped from his pallet. Then the *sky itself* screamed, and then there was a great sound, much like the sound the wizard-weapons made, and there was enough light to brighten the inside of the tent although the flaps were closed against the death bird. The captured slave woman squealed like a ranwang and burrowed under the hides.

Mad Bear ignored her and grasped his weapons. He saw clearly now. The wizards were attacking the camp. Attacking at *night*. Walking Eagle had said the wizards controlled demons. Did they then own the demons which made the night dangerous for the Horse People? They seemed to have no fear of them.

Well, the night will not be long. Suns climb the sky, and then we will have vengeance. He untied the tent flaps and went outside. Tents were burning, but the camp was lit brighter than burning tents could have made it. The sky screamed again, and there were more of the thunder sounds.

"UP! UP!" Mad Bear ran among his people. "To arms! Or will you allow the wizards to slaughter you like wolves bringing down a sick horse? Up, up!"

He was nearly trampled by a pain-maddened horse. It galloped past in panic, its mane on fire. Mad Bear leaped aside and fell, and again he heard the sky screaming. This time he saw it, a trail of fire across the night skies. It fell into the camp and there was more wizard-thunder, with flame and smoke.

The shaman Tangra'al rushed from his tent and raved at the skies. He screamed the old legends, of *skyfire* and folk who rode across the sky in iron chariots. They were stories from Mad Bear's childhood, and he felt a tingle at his spine as he remembered; but he dashed at the shaman and struck him so that Tangra'al fell to the ground.

"They are only men!" Mad Bear screamed to his clan. "Those who fought at the Wagon Battle heard the wizard-thunder and felt their flame, but the wizards died as easily as any of the Green Lands folk! Arm yourselves!" He ran through the camp shouting; but inwardly he was afraid. The sky gods had made themselves enemies of the Horse People and had sent the wizards against them. Why? First the lands turned brown and the Horse People had to flee to the east. Now they faced enemies who held the thunder. Why?

But there was worse yet to come. Half a score of horses stampeded in panic and trampled his tent. Mad Bear knew that not all his warriors and few of his women had got out safely, and he cursed these foul enemies, wizards so evil they would turn the Horse People's mounts against them!

In time the wizard-thunder died away, and the Horse People were left to count their losses. From one trampled tent alone Mad Bear's band pulled out a warrior and three women, two of them slaves, who would not see dawn. Another warrior had been thrown from a horse and struck his head. He lay mewling like a baby, and he fouled himself. All across the great camp it was much the same, and the toll among the horses was worse.

But the sky brightened as the Father Sun approached. Soon the night watchers came in.

There would be a battle. Riders who had followed the retreat of the wizards brought words that made that certain. There were many who followed the wizards. Grey Archers, devils in women's skirts who could shoot as far and as straight as the Horse People. There were also many Riders of the Red-Cloak Chiefs, who fought as though one man's thoughts guided all the horses and men of their war band. It was no shame to the riders that they had not dared follow closely. Yet they had followed.

The wizards and their friends had all gathered in one place, less than half the morning's ride from the camp. It was a place the Horse People knew well, a valley of rolling hills. At its bottom snaked a wide stream no deeper than a stallion's knees, and there were no hydras in the muddy waters. And there the wizards had halted—

Do they challenge the Horse People? Mad Bear's heart rose within him, and he leaped upon his greatest stallion. "My people! Have we not said that those the gods will destroy are first driven from their senses? The sky gods are no friends to these wizards! The wizards await us, in a place we know well, in a place where we will triumph! We shall have the battle the Warrior desires, and this day we shall send many of the wizard-people to the Warrior's Lodge!

"For what do we face? Men of the Iron Houses, and this in a place we would have chosen! Have they not always been easy enough to kill?

"To arms! Fill the waterskins, and send for all the Horse People who camp through the plains and hills! Summon all the clans! All the clans shall fight as one this day, all the Horse People as brothers, for is this not the will of the Warrior? Come, come, we shall fill the Warrior's Lodge!"

30

Private Hal Roscoe shaded his eyes and stared down the valley in wonder. "Jesus Christ, Major, where'd they all come from?"

Mason waved him back into action without answering. Damn good question, Art thought. There must have been fifty thousand of the mothers, two or three times as many as Mason had expected, and they swarmed all across the valley of the Hooey River, on both sides and in the river itself, shooting as fast as they could, then closing in with lances and lariats and those goofy bronze swords. Anyone with a dead or hurt horse was a goner. Not even the mercs could cover him.

The whole operation had gone sour. "No battle plan survives contact with the enemy," Captain Galloway had told Mason; and Lord God was that true! Westmen had come boiling in from all directions, and despite everything the pieces of the Alliance army had got separated.

Now Mason's troops held the top of a hill only a little higher than the rest of the knolls that sprinkled the Hooey Valley. The visibility was lousy. Too much dust, and too many of those damned little hills. Mason cursed again as he scanned the valley with his binoculars. The Drantos ironhats were across the river on another hill, facing their own share of Westman. And everything *flowed!* Caradoc's Mounted Archers had stayed with the mercs. Now they were out in front of Mason's troops, and the mercs didn't dare fire because the archers and the Westmen were all mixed together.

Vothan alone knew where the Romans had got off to. Mason looked down the valley toward the balloon. They'd set it up in a strong place, where the Hooey Valley narrowed and flowed between much higher hills. He'd left Beazeley and a hundred guards to babysit it. The whole army of Drantos was between it and the Westmen. It ought to have been safe enough.

Ought to have been. The balloon was aloft, but the observers weren't paying any attention to Art Mason. Why hadn't they seen just how many Westmen there were? Every goddam war, on every goddam planet, the skyboys fight their own battle and let the grunts carry the can! Too damn late now. Art swept his binoculars along the limits of his vision. He couldn't see too far because of the damned low hills—but there was more dust rising in the west, which meant more Westmen.

Mason cursed. This could get sticky.

Across the river the mass of Westmen facing the Drantos knights thickened, churned, and split off a detachment. They cantered into the river, throwing up a cloud of spray and gravel.

"Murph!" Hell, I'm screaming, Mason thought. Scared spitless. Well, maybe I got a right to be. Wonder, if we buy it, will we go to Vothan's Hall? Or Heaven? Or someplace else, and would someplace else be better'n nowhere at all? "Murph! Put a couple rounds in the river!"

"Roger!"

The recoilless spewed flame. The first round was white phosphorus. Steam puffed up where the burning bits hit the water. Then a high explosive round took out nearly a score of Westmen. That slowed them enough to let some of the calivermen reload, and when the Westmen came on they were hit by a rolling volley, each man firing as soon as he heard the gun of the man next to him, fire rippling down the line with the one remaining four-pounder to punctuate the end of the volley.

It wasn't enough. There were too many Westmen trying to cross that river, and they could shoot even with the water up to the bellies of their horses. The arrow-hail came down again, and suddenly there weren't enough Mounted Archers to stop them. For the tenth time that morning Art wished the other four-pounder hadn't been abandoned with a broken carriage axle.

"Hey, Art!" Murphy called.

"Yeah?"

"Hell, I know we were supposed to make 'em mad enough to fight, but goddam, this is *ridiculous!*"

Three of the troopers laughed, but it sounded a little hollow. Down below, the Westmen came on. A lot of the calivermen were down, and the rest were shaky. One platoon broke and ran. Caradoc, his red Roman cloak streaming out behind him, rode in to rally them. Some of his personal guards leaned from their saddles to collect guns. Then the whole crowd began to pull back, with the Westmen's arrows following them. Three men and a horse went down around the four-pounder, and the remaining gunners abandoned it to scramble higher up the hill.

By now the Mounted Archers had retreated far enough that the Guards and mercs would pretty soon have a clear field of fire. Mason sidestepped his horse and unlimbered his own H&K before he thought better and slung it again. Thinking like a corporal again, Art, he told himself, he rode around to check the position of the other mercs.

They were set up about as well as they could be. On the left flank, Walbrook had the mortar, with Bilofsky nearby with the light machine gun. "Take care of that thing," Mason shouted. "That LMG may be all that's 'tween us and Vothan's Hall!"

"Right-o!" Bilofsky answered. He grinned cheerfully. "Don't worry about a thing, Major."

Murphy and the 106 were in the center of the line. There was a problem about the mortar and the 106. They'd used most of the ammo in the bombardment of the camp. Now there wasn't enough left to defend themselves. Maybe that's justice, Mason thought. Frig that. He used his binoculars to watch the situation develop. Now they had a clear shot.

"First Guards. On my command, IN VOLLEY—FIRE! Fire at will!" The platoon of Guards let fly with their calivers. Meanwhile the other mercs blazed away with rifles. Most fired single shot. Somewhere a trooper had switched to rock and roll. He'd be out of ammo pretty soon.

They all fired low, as they'd been taught, and the volley emptied few saddles, but it did dismount a lot of Westmen. They leaped from their falling horses—and kept coming. Soon they were in among the dismounted archers, using spears and knives and a few swords, and small axes like tomahawks.

"God Almighty!" Pfc. Roscoe yelled. "Those are *mean* little mothers!"

"Kinda my sentiments too," Murphy said. "Art, we going to get out of this?"

"We can sure as hell try."

The LMG got in the act, bringing down nearly a hundred Westmen, and Art began to breathe a little easier. The mortar chugged away, lobbing WP and HE into the advance, and suddenly the Westmen didn't look so confident—but they were still coming. It wasn't going to be enough.

"Stand by to pull out!" Mason shouted in English, then switched to Tran dialect. "The First Guards will withdraw! Trumpeter, sound 'Boots and Saddles.' Rendezvous at Point Blue One." That was the mouth of the valley where Beazeley's squad was guarding the balloon and the reserve ammo. A strong place. Maybe not so easy to get out of, but easy to hold. Mason shook his head. Wish the captain was here. What would he do? Don't matter. What I'm going to do is get my shit together. Then we can make a stand or run like hell, depending. That's what the Drantos troops have done. Got a strong place across the valley where they can think things over. Wonder what they intend doing?

There were more arrows, and suddenly Bilofsky rolled over, staring at an arrow sticking out of his chest. The damned fool wasn't wearing armor! His number two, Pfc. Arkos Passavopolous, took over, but the belt ran out a long time before the Westmen did. Mason rode over. "Hey Ark! Get Bilofsky onto a horse!"

"No hurry about that, Major. Best I save the gun first."

"Shitfire. Okay, do it, fast!" Then his horse spooked, and while it was bucking another flight of arrows came in. The horse screamed and reared, and Art threw himself out of the saddle before it could fall on him. He went one way and the H&K went another, and now there was nothing left but the Colt. Mason held it in both hands and squeezed off rounds. One Westman down. Another, and another, but more were coming up, trampling over the dead and dying, lots more than he had rounds for the Colt, and Mason decided he hadn't really wanted to live forever. . . .

A great black horse loomed up behind the advancing Westmen, and a sword whirled and came down. A Westman tried to keep going with one arm off, and didn't make it. Another fell headless. The horse trampled two more, and then calivermen and Tamaerthan troopers were among the Westmen. The calivermen used bayonets with effect, and a few had reloaded and were able to fire. More of the Tamaerthans charged in, and the Westmen began to thin out. Then there weren't any at all.

Mason stood up as Caradoc rode up the hill. "Thanks."

Caradoc grinned and pointed with his bloody saber. Squads of troops moved off to deal with dismounted Westmen. The archer captain waved again, and another trooper brought Mason a fresh mount, and now they had a few minutes breathing spell, but it was still going to be close.

Then he looked up and saw a new army of Westmen come over the ridge, and Art Mason wondered how many would make it to Point Blue One.

There was no water on the hill where the fighting men of Drantos were gathered. Wanax Ganton had been about to drink when a young staff officer brought the news from Camithon. "The spring was filled with dirt and dung, Majesty. It will be long before it flows again."

Ganton thrust the plug into the mouth of the waterskin and handed it back to Morrone. So be it. "From this moment, the water is for the horses," he said. "Tell the captains."

"Aye, Majesty." The young officer hesitated, then set his lips. "Lord Camithon bids me say we have lost above two hundred men at arms killed, and another five hundred have been given to the care of the priests of Yatar."

"That many," Ganton mused. He straightened. "Tell Lord Camithon I will join him soon, and meantime he is to do as he thinks best. And tell all about the water."

"Aye, Majesty."

When the messenger had gone, Morrone whistled through

pursed lips. "An eighth, more than an eighth of our strength lost, and now we are at bay, trapped upon a hill without water. What will we do?"

"I do not yet know," Ganton said. "First we will show ourselves to the soldiers. As we do, we will discover how it fares with them, and whether they will fight. And then we will take counsel of Lord Camithon. He has seen more battles than I have of years. Doubtless his advice will be good." And if not, I must yet listen. The Lord Rick has often told me that battles wander far from what we plan, and by Yatar this one has done so! Now we need harmony among the captains, and they must not believe I quarrel with Camithon.

He rode along the ridge with only his banner bearer and Morrone. Sometimes he stopped to hear a wounded man's message, or to praise a deed he had seen or been told of; and always he listened as he rode past. They cheered him yet, and he felt glad. They would follow him.

Across the valley the thunder of star weapons grew, then died. He climbed higher on the ridge and used the binoculars. There was no doubt of it. The Lord Mason was retreating, taking with him all the mounted archers and other Tamaerthan warriors as well as the starmen. Ganton was shocked at how few Tamaerthans remained.

Yet there were no instructions from the balloon. It floated high above the battle, but Ganton could not see the men within it. Had they been killed? Despite all his warnings, the forces of the Alliance had become separated, and the balloon left guarded only by a few. No one had desired it, but the Westmen had poured from behind every hill, across every ridge and through every valley, more Westmen than anyone believed possible, and bands of them had got between the host and the balloon.

Perhaps there would be no messages from the balloon.

He recognized Caradoc's scarlet Roman cloak, and saw figures in starman uniforms. Some lay still, lashed across saddles. The towering soldier they called "the Great Ark" rode a captured pony so small that his legs nearly touched the ground. Others had rigged poles out behind their horses and had lashed equipment onto them. They retreated in good order, fighting their way toward the balloon.

The valley below was a cauldron. Ganton swept his binoculars across the land again. The Westmen seemed divided in counsel. Some rode after Mason. Others milled about, shouting at each other.

And meantime there was nothing to do but wait, while the day grew warmer. Ganton cursed softly and once again looked toward the futile balloon. Where were the Romans? Were they gone as well?

Mad Bear was trying to keep his horse from drinking the foul waters of the river when Hinuta rode up. He had a score of Silver Wolves—and as well a hundred Two Rivers, and dozens more from other clans.

"Rejoice, Mad Bear, your deeds have been told throughout the Horse People, and many clans would follow you."

"Ah." Mad Bear looked again. There was one missing. "Where is Tenado, my son?"

"He turned his back on a dead Ironshirt," Hinuta said simply.

"Aiiiy." But this was no time for lament.

"I have brought the Ironshirt's hair. You may offer it to the gods," Hinuta said. He handed over a bloody bundle.

"You have my thanks," Mad Bear said. He looked around the valley. "The Ironshirts are worthy fighters. They die well."

"Many of them have not died at all," Hinuta said. "And many of the Red Cloaks have gone off down the river, where they hold the small hills near the trees."

"Ah."

"Let us gather our people and go join the battle against them. Tens of tens of tens would follow Mad Bear—"

"Nay." Mad Bear shook his head and pointed to the southern ridge covered with the horses and banners of Ironshirts. They had dismounted, and hid their horses behind their great shields. There were many of their archers as well. Ironshirt archers from the stone houses used a strange bow with metal parts to do the work of a man's strength. The bows would not shoot so often, but they ranged nearly as far as those of the Horse People below them.

"Those have not died either, and their chief of the golden hat rides among them. Kill him and the others will flee," Mad Bear said. He rode over to be near Hinuta. The loss of Tenado ate at his heart, but he could never show that. Instead he clapped

Hinuta on the shoulder. "It is a great day!"

"A great day for the Warrior," Hinuta agreed. He eyed the encamped Ironshirts and grinned. "It was well that we stopped the spring on that hill. And if the Ironshirts will stay long—"

"Their horses will go mad. If the Horse People can fight as one, then we will send them all to the Warrior," Mad Bear completed. "Despite their wizard-fire." They both had seen the Mountain Walkers struck down by the wizards' thunder. "Go among the Horse People, and say that Mad Bear will lead them against the Ironshirts, as many as will follow."

Only the oath-bound warriors of his band *had* to obey; but many had heard of the deeds of Mad Bear, and many would come, would follow him. Soon there would be tens of tens of tens. Mad Bear would lead them toward the Ironshirts, then pretend to retreat. The Ironshirts would charge as they always did, and this battle would end.

And that would be well.

They had to fight their way into Point Blue One. It took four rounds from the 106 and a full belt from the LMG before the last of the Westmen were driven out. Mason shouted orders and the troops began setting up a perimeter, leaving Art to deal with what had been the headquarters area.

The balloon crew was dead. Flyboys and ground crew, all bristled with arrows, the airmen lying huddled in the bottom of their wicker basket. Near the wagon was Ski, big scar and all, with a dozen arrows just for him, and his scalp and ears cut away as well. The Tamaerthan and Drantos riggers had been hacked with swords, and the acolytes of Yatar literally dismembered. Art looked at the bloody scene and grimaced.

Just like the king said, Mason thought. A roving band. Something. Christ, who'd have thought they could get past all of us? Or that there'd be so many of the little mothers—

One of the piles of dead began to move. Mason had the safety off the .45 when Beazeley's bloody face popped out of the heap of bodies.

"I'll be dipped in shit! Welcome back, buddy," Mason said.

"Feel more welcome if you'd point a different way," Beazeley said.

"Guess you would." Mason didn't holster the weapon. "Know where the Romans went?"

"Last report they were over that way." He pointed off to the north. "But about then we had other things to worry about."

"When'd you duck?"

"I was about the last one," Beazeley said. "Figured there was no point in standing up, so I dove in, with my friend here in my mouth just in case . . ." He showed his pistol, then looked at the hacked and mutilated bodies of Ski and the priests and shuddered.

"Okay," Mason said. "Back to the line. Wait." He took out a flask. "Have a belt."

"Thanks. Ah, McCleve's finest. Must be a month old. Good stuff." He drank again.

Mason scanned the area with his binoculars. Over to his far right there was a lot of dust, and a sound that might have been Roman trumpets. Between them and the Drantos ironhats a band of Westmen was crossing the low ridge, headed north and east. It looked as if they were trying to get behind the Romans.

"Holy shit!" Beazeley yelled.

Mason looked around. Another band of Westmen were coming across the ridge to his left.

Dien Bien Phu, hell, Mason thought. It looks more like Little Big Horn.

31

Ganton felt reassured when he had completed his inspection of the army. Camithon had arrayed the host well. The men were dismounted to rest the horses. Above every approach to the hill stood a band of crossbowmen protected by the shields of men at arms. Behind them were walking wounded to reload, and dismounted knights taking their ease. From this height a bolt could slay a Westman's horse before his own arrow could pierce armor, and a Westman on foot was no fair match for a Drantos warrior.

Ganton wasn't worried about a fair match. He wanted the Westmen dead, or at least driven from his land. If he could have slain them all with his Browning, he would have done so.

"Hah. And what of your love of battle?" Morrone said. "Glory for your bheromen. What of that?"

"I had not realized I was speaking aloud," Ganton said. "And there is precious little glory here . . ." He used his binoculars to look across the valley. Mason had retreated to where the balloon had been tethered and hauled it down. There was still no sign of the Romans. Had they taken a defensive position somewhere out of sight, or had they left the battle entirely? If they had run away, then Ganton's army would never leave this valley.

He moved on toward the end of the ridge, and now arrows fell more thickly around him. As he drew near to Camithon's banner, he saw why. The end of the ridge rose higher than any other part, but also jutted out toward the river like the prow of a ship. It was too steep to allow crossbowmen to perch on it, and the Westmen could ride in close enough to fire their arrows and receive only a few crossbow bolts in return.

Ganton dismounted. He had to scramble along the ridge to reach Camithon, who stood partially protected by guardsmen's shields.

"Majesty, this is no safe place for you!"

"It is no more dangerous for me than for you, my lord general. Now—what is your counsel?" When the Westmen first struck and the Drantos horses began to tire, Ganton had not objected when Camithon brought the troops to this hill and set them in a defensive perimeter. Doubtless the general had a plan in mind. Now, though, it was time to learn it. "We are safe and in good order for the moment, but we are not eagles to make our homes here."

Camithon grinned and waved the ancient battle-ax he had carried into every battle since his youth. "First, Majesty, let us get off this knife-edge." He led the way back along the ridge. "As to counsel, I would know better if I could see what you see."

"Ah." Ganton lifted his binoculars to hand them to Camithon. "First, though—" he said. He swept them along the river bank, then up to where Mason's banner stood with Caradoc's. A waving orange flag, invisible without the binoculars, caught his eye. "Ho! A signal! Fetch the scribes!"

A runner dashed down the ridge and returned with three young acolytes.

"I am Panilos, senior acolyte, Majesty," one said. He couldn't have been more than fourteen years old; the others were even younger.

"Take these, lad," Ganton said. He handed over his binoculars, noting that Panilos had no difficulty in using them. "Read me that signal from the Lord Mason."

"Aye, Majesty," the boy said. "Laran, make the signals. Wannilos, are you ready?"

One of the scribes held wax board and stylus. "Aye," he said. The other waved his flags while Panilos peered through the dust.

"R-O-M-A-N-S D-U-E N-O-R-T-H O-F H-E-R-E STOP," he called.

Panilos called off the message and Wannilos wrote it on the board, while the third acolyte acknowledged each word. They worked quickly, too fast for Ganton to follow. When they were done, Wannilos read it off.

"ROMANS DUE NORTH OF HERE. THE ROMANS HAVE TAKEN HEAVY LOSSES BUT ARE IN GOOD ORDER. WE HAVE LOST MORE THAN HALF THE ARCHERS. BALLOON DISABLED. STAR WEAPONS LOW ON MISSILES. SUGGEST WE WITHDRAW."

"If the Romans are due north of Lord Mason, they must be there," Ganton said. "Beyond those hills. There is enough dust there." He handed the binoculars to Camithon.

The old general held them gingerly. "Majesty, the Romans are not where I expected them to be. Now the Westmen will move to cut us off from the Romans. We must hasten to decide what to do. First, I will examine the battlefield. I wish to see the Romans."

The Roman position was north and east. Sight of them was cut off by trees as well as dust. From further south on the prow of the ridge they might be visible. Camithon took the binoculars and moved gingerly out along the knife-edge. Ganton wanted to call him back, but that would not be seemly. Instead he followed.

They had gone half the way when Camithon straightened and cried out. Ganton ran forward. Camithon was falling when Ganton reached him, and only then did he see the arrow sticking out of the general's left eye. Blood poured down over his scar. Ganton leaped to hold him, but the old man's dead weight was too much. They fell off the ridge and rolled down the hill.

"Rally!" Morrone screamed. He leaped down the hill to get below his king. "Guards! Shieldsmen!"

Other knights jumped down from the ridgetop to form a shieldwall. Behind them king and captain lay together on the ground.

Ganton heard none of this. With his ear practically against Camithon's lips, he strained to listen to the man who had been more to him than his father ever had.

"Make them stay together, lad. Use them well. And not too early—" The voice faded out.

"My Lord Protector. My friend," Ganton whispered.

The voice came from lips flecked with blood. "Lad—" Then only a final rattle.

Ganton raised the dead form and laid his general's head in his lap. He bent to kiss the bloody lips. Then he stood. A shower of arrows fell around them, and he realized it was his golden helm that drew the Westmen. Had his vanity killed his oldest friend? "Bear him upslope with honor," Ganton said quietly.

Then he saw Camithon's fallen battle-ax. He pointed to it. "I will carry that," he said quietly. A knight handed it to him. Ganton slipped the thong about his wrist and whirled it until it blurred, remembering the hours Camithon had made him spend in the courtyard attacking wooden stakes.

There were shouts from above. Shouts and moving banners, with panic in some of the voices. "The Wanax has fallen," someone shouted.

Ganton scrambled furiously up the crumbling sides of the slope. It was steep, and his armor was heavy. The battle-ax hampered him, but he held it grimly. No one else would carry *that* ax, not today and not ever. Camithon had no son . . . no son of his body, Ganton corrected himself. He has son enough today.

They had rolled farther down the slope than he had thought, and the climb was exhausting. His chest heaved with the effort. Then two Guards leaped down from the ridgetop. One extended his hand and pulled Ganton up. It wasn't dignified, but it helped him get up the slope.

"My horse!" he called to his orderly. "Bannerman! With me!" He spurred the horse to ride back along the ridge, hearing the cheers of his bheromen and knights as they saw the golden helm. "I am unhurt," he shouted. When he was certain there would be no panic, he returned to the southern tip of the ridge.

"Majesty, dismount," Morrone pleaded. "If you are hurt—" He didn't finish the sentence. He didn't have to. With Camithon dead, there was only one person the knights would follow.

Will they follow me? Ganton wondered. An untried youth, who has fought in one battle, one part of another; who has led them onto this hill of dusty death . . . what did Camithon intend? He had a plan, but I know it not.

And it matters not. It is my battle now, mine alone, and that is all I may consider now.

Some of the knights were standing by their horses. A few had mounted. Ganton rode toward them. "What means this, my lords? I have heard no trumpet!"

"We need no trumpet to tell us what to do."

It was difficult to know who spoke, but from the shield markings and scarf Ganton thought it must be Bheroman Hilaskos, an important lord who led many lances to battle.

"And what would you do, my lord?"

"Cut through the enemy!" Hilaskos said.

"And then?"

"And return to our homes."

"You would run away, then?" Ganton kept his voice low and calm, though it took a great effort to do that.

"No man calls me coward. But what honor is there to perch on a ridgetop until we die of thirst? The battle is lost, sire. It will not save my lands nor yet the realm for my lances to be lost with it."

"Your lances will not be lost, nor yet will you," Ganton said. "It is your Wanax who commands here. Dismount."

Hilaskos hesitated. "Dismount," Ganton said. "Or by Vothan I will take your head in sight of your knights. Dismount and kneel!"

One of Hilaskos's squires came forward to hold his master's bridle. The baron hesitated a moment more, then got down from his horse. "Aye, sire," he said. He knelt. "I see we have gained a true Wanax this day."

The others dismounted, and Ganton rode again along the ridge. This time there were more cheers, and no dissenters.

"And what will we do now, sire?" Morrone asked when they were out of the others' earshot.

Ganton continued to scan the battlefield. "I do not know," he said.

Art Mason watched the priest of Yatar place the Guardsman's beret over his face and signal to the acolytes who were acting as stretcher-bearers. They picked up the dead man and carried him to the line of bodies already laid out just below the crest of the hill. A long line, too damned long, Art thought, and not all the Guards' dead were in it.

And the priests had armed themselves with fallen Guardsmen's daggers. For Westmen? Or for the wounded if they had to retreat? For the hundredth time Art wondered what Captain Galloway would do.

The situation looked sticky. There were only two qualified signalmen, and it would be a waste to send them up in the balloon even if they could get it repaired. The damned low hills would let the Westmen get close enough to shoot the balloon observers before the basket could rise out of range. Because of the hills there were thousands, tens of thousands of Westmen out there in a killing ground, but no way to kill them. Not enough ammunition, no clear fields of fire; they were down to four bombs for the mortar and no more than a dozen rounds for the 106.

Running low on ammunition, but not low on Westmen. Not at all.

He looked across at the Drantos forces again. They seemed intact, almost no losses, but they sat there on top of their damned hill. They'd acknowledged his message suggesting withdrawal, but they weren't doing anything about it. The Romans weren't acknowledging signals at all, which wasn't surprising; they were only visible for short intervals when the dust cleared. They'd only had one semaphore expert with them, and he was probably lost.

"So what do we do, Art?" Murphy asked quietly.

"Wait."

"For what?"

"I don't know, but you got a better idea? If we pull out—" He pointed to the low sunshade awnings the priests had erected to give shelter to the wounded.

"Yeah, I got that picture," Murphy said.

"Besides—"

"Yeah?"

"Hell, Ben, I don't think we *can* pull out." He pointed to the north. "A mess of 'em disappeared in that direction. More went east. Not enough to worry about, if that was all of 'em, but enough to ambush us good while we're trying to hold off pursuit."

"Well, we gotta do *something*."

"Yeah, maybe I'll think of it," Mason said. "Crap, Ben, you know I'm no mucking officer."

"Maybe not, buddy, but you're all we got now," Murphy said. He took a flask from his pocket. "Shot?"

"Yeah—no. Not just now." He lifted the binoculars again.

Arrows fell around Ganton, but none got through his armor. Three knights held shields around him as he stood at the very tip of the ridge. From here he could see almost all of the battlefield.

The three groups of the Alliance formed a right isosceles triangle with the Romans at its apex. Across the valley, on the other side of the river, stood the Captain-General's banner with Lord Mason's. Caradoc's stood close by them. Due east of Ganton and almost due north of Mason, the Romans held two more hilltops. He was separated from the Romans by a south-ward-jutting finger of the woody ridge that formed the north bound of the Hooey Valley.

I am the only one who sees all this, now that the balloon is gone, he thought. Knowledge is power, Lord Rick says. To know what the enemy does not know—what is it I know that they do not?

I know where all the Westmen are, and none of them can know this, for they are separated from each other by the low hills in the river valley. Even those on the tops of the knolls see only to the next hill.

And they are divided. The two largest groups face Lord Mason and the Romans, and those two groups are separated by the river. While below facing us—

Below were perhaps five thousand Westmen. A formidable number, but nothing for the host of Drantos to fear. Small

groups of Westmen rode up and down their line, shouting to their comrades, and from time to time riders went toward the enormous bands facing the Romans.

If the Alliance forces were out of—*supporting distance,* as the starmen called it—so were the Westmen. And the Westmen had no wanax, no single commander.

"Stay here. They must believe that I will return," Ganton ordered the shieldmen. He moved back along the ridge to Morrone. "Send messengers," he said. "Water the horses. The host is to make ready to mount. I want no trumpets to sound until we are ready to ride. The squires and walking wounded will stay to protect the wounded and priests. The rest will prepare to charge. Go quickly now."

Morrone grinned like a wolf. "Aye, sire."

Ganton looked up at the vault of the sky. Father Yatar, give me clear sight. Is this right action?

There was no answer. Or was there? Far away he thought he saw an eagle circling above the valley. Almost he raised the binoculars, but then he let them dangle.

It is an eagle. It is an answer, he told himself. It is enough.

Morrone came up. "All is done as you ordered. Now let me aid you with your armor."

"Aye. Stay with my banner," Ganton said. "And if I fall, lead the host."

"Where, Majesty?"

"There." Ganton pointed southeast. "Through yonder band of Westmen. Ignore all the others. You and I will be at the left of the host. The others will form to our right. We break through that line, and ride eastward along the valley to there." He pointed again to where the finger of ridge and trees separating them from the Romans jutted down into the valley. "As soon as we have rounded that small hill, then charge northeast."

Morrone frowned. "Away from the Lord Mason?"

"Yes." He raised his voice to a shout. "Is all in readiness?"

A shout rippled down the line. "LONG LIVE WANAX GANTON!"

"MOUNT!" he ordered. He swung onto his charger. "Morrone, stay with me. I want nothing save my armor closer to my back than you!"

"With my life, Majesty!"

"Sound the trumpets!"

The wild notes of the cornets blared up the line. Kettledrums added to the din. The Westmen down below looked up, startled. Ganton whirled the ax above his head. "FOR DRANTOS. FOR CAMITHON AND DRANTOS!"

The line of heavy cavalry moved ponderously forward, until there was no sound but the thunder of hooves and the call of trumpets.

32

Mad Bear had once seen the side of a hill fall when the earth shook. Boulders the size of men had rolled toward him faster than a horse could trot, and dust went up until it seemed it must reach the Father's feet.

He remembered that now. There was dust in plenty, and it was as if the hill had fallen upon him—but now, each boulder was a man dressed all in iron, mounted on a horse so tall it seemed that a Horse People's stallion could pass under its belly, and those great horses wore iron!

The hill was alive with banners, and the earth shook to the thunder of hooves. Trumpet calls rent the air, trumpets and kettledrums and the triumphant shouts of the Ironshirts as their great lances came down.

Mad Bear had fought Ironshirts before, but always on an open plain. He had never imagined such a host of them coming directly toward him. He knew that he saw his death, his and all the Horse People who had stood with him. Somewhere downriver were more of the Horse People, but not enough had come, and now—

Now there was nothing save honor. The Warrior would see that Mad Bear could die as a man, and that was all he could hope for.

He wasted no time with words. The thunder of the charging Ironshirts was too much. No one would have heard him. Instead, he counted his arrows. A hand and one more. Not enough, not nearly enough. Well, that would have to do also. He would shoot his arrows and ride away. Perhaps the Ironshirts would scatter as they followed. He nocked an arrow to his bow and tried to aim at flesh, not iron.

"For this was I born!" Ganton spurred his charger ahead. The line of Westmen had turned to face him, and they shot arrows as swiftly as they could. Here and there they struck home and a horse went down, causing others in the lines behind to swerve and stumble; but the host swept on inexorably.

"For this was I born!" he shouted again.

His lance took the first Westman in the throat, spitting him like a boar. Ganton let the lance dip and sweep behind so that his motion pulled it from the fallen enemy. He barely had time to raise it again before it struck home in a Westman pony. Ganton let it go and took the axe which hung by its thong from the saddle horn. As he swept past another enemy the ax swung to crash through a bear-tooth and leather helmet and split the skull below it.

"Sire, let us pass!" Two Guards rode alongside. "We have lances. Let us lead."

Almost he cursed them; then he thought again. If I fall, the day is lost. Morrone cannot do what must be done. And that is not right, battles and kingdoms should not stand and fall by one life, but today it is so. "You have my thanks," he shouted, and waved the Guards past. More drew alongside, and soon he was surrounded. Not by Guardsmen alone, he saw. Bheromen and knights, all eager to ride between him and danger.

If my father could have lived to see, he thought. And I live through this day, the throne is safe. Throne? Dynasty! Our children, mine and Octavia's, will hold this land forever!

Wanax and followers rode on until they were through the lines of Westmen.

"Trumpets," Ganton called. "Sound the rally. Bring the host toward me."

The trumpets sang as his bannermen raised high the Royal Banner of Drantos and the Fighting Man. Then a dozen Westmen galloped past. They lay flat to their horse's necks, their quivers empty. They were pursued by a score of Drantos horsemen thundering along behind the banner of Lord Epimenes. "Hold!" Ganton shouted. "HOLD!"

"The cowards flee!" the bheroman shouted.

They must hold, Ganton thought. He drew the Browning and fired toward Lord Epimenes's banner. There was no knowing where the bullet went, but the sound was heard even in the din of battle. "HOLD!" Ganton shouted again. "Lord Epimenes, stay with me! We have better work than tiring our horses in pursuit of empty quivers! Leave them for the esquires, for we have work worthy of bheromen and knights!"

Epimenes reined in. It wasn't clear whether he had been won over by Ganton's words or by the ax and pistol the Wanax carried, but the futile pursuit was stopped.

"Trumpets, sound the walk," Ganton shouted. In a more normal voice he spoke to the group around him. "We have broken through the first line. When we reach the top of yonder rise, we charge again. Morrone!"

"Sire!"

"Ride to the right flank, where Lord Enipses commands, and be certain that he follows where we lead." He pointed up the valley. "Lord Epimenes will remain to guard me. And return safely—"

"Aye, Majesty."

Ganton rose in his stirrups and grinned as he saw the heaps of dead Westmen behind them. A few Drantos knights lay among them, and more stood dismounted; but the host was an intact fighting force. He used the ax to point up the hill, and felt a lump in his breast as he thought how often Camithon had gestured with that ax. "Forward," he said.

The host swept north and east.

"Major!" Hal Roscoe ran up shouting. "Here they come again!"

"Yeah, I see 'em," Mason said. He looked up and down his line and prepared to hold off yet another charge from the enemy.

If there'd been more ammo for the mortar—

It's no friggin' good. Mentally he counted magazines. Enough to get out of here, he thought. Hold 'em off until dark and go for it. We'll lose the wounded, and a lot of the equipment, but I don't see what else to do. We can't go after 'em, and these damn little hills give us too little clear field of fire for the rifles.

"Make ready to shoot!" he shouted. "Rolling volley from the left. Take aim! Fire!"

The calivermen fired and reloaded as fast as they could, and Mason used his own H&K to good effect. No point in acting like an officer now, he thought. I'm not all that good a one anyway, and there ain't that many orders to give—

"Cross the valley, Art!" Murphy yelled. "For God's sake, look!"

Mason stared across the river. "Holy crap! Look alive, troops! Looks like our little king's remembered us."

The Drantos heavies were coming down the hill. *All* of them. At least all that had horses. A few had drawn right up to the top of the ridge and set up a shield wall, but damn near the whole army of Drantos was riding down that hill.

The wild charge came down the mountain like a wall. From Mason's distance it looked like a huge wave that washed across the line of Westmen, leaving a wake of dead and dying behind it as the armored men simply rode the lighter horsemen down.

The front ranks were damned near solid with banners, and right out front on the left wing was the biggest banner of all, the Royal Standard of Drantos, and yeah, that was the golden helm that crazy kid fancied. They were coming straight toward Art Mason.

Then they swerved left, pivoting around the golden helmet.

"What now?" Murphy asked.

Mason frowned. "Don't know. But I'll bet you anything you like that kid knows what he's doing."

Murphy shaded his eyes and watched the last of the Drantos heavies vanish into the dust, then turned back to picking off advancing Westmen. "I sure hope you're right," he said.

Julius Sulpicius, *primus pilus* of the Fourth Legion, rode up to Titus Frugi and saluted. "Those scouts we sent forward are late coming back," he said. He could have said that it was unlikely that they would return at all; but there was no need for that. One didn't work up to First Centurion of a legion by chattering at generals of Titus Frugi's years and experience.

Frugi cursed under his breath. That was the fourth scouting party he'd sent upriver. One had returned, unable to pierce the combination of Westmen and dust. The other three had not come back at all.

From time to time Titus Frugi had made out a gleam on the tip of a ridge far up the valley; a gleam and what seemed to be a banner. The sketch maps the *frumentarii* had made of the Hooey Valley showed that point as part of a defensible ridge, and Frugi wondered if the army of Drantos had taken refuge there.

Certainly the starmen and their Tamaerthan allies were holding another hilltop across the river.

"Third Cohort says the barbarians are thickening up toward the rear," Sulpicius added. His fifteen years of following the eagles gave him the right to say more, but with Titus Frugi that wasn't needed. His tone made the implied question clear enough: isn't it about time we get the hell out of here?

It was, but that didn't much appeal to Frugi. Withdrawing without orders would endanger an alliance that was all that stood between the Westmen and the Roman borders—if the legends were right, these Westmen had once come all the way to the gates of sacred Rome herself! No. Better to stand here, even if it cost the legion.

But—are we doing well? he wondered. We have taken positions here, and none will come past us, but what good do we do? From time to time the Westmen would try the Romans' mettle, but when they found they could not induce the Romans into futile wild charges they soon abandoned the sport. Now there were thousands—perhaps tens of thousands—of Westmen somewhere out in front of the legion, but they would not stay to receive a charge. Titus Frugi had fought many enemies in his service to Rome, but never one that he could not *find!* Yet between the dust and the hills that was precisely the difficulty; and if he thrashed about in that dust searching for the enemy, the horses would tire, and then he would indeed be lost.

Trumpets sounded at the forward outposts, and now the decurion and men he'd stationed out there as a screen were galloping back toward the main lines. More trumpets. "TO HORSE!" they sang, and if the centurions ordered that without asking Frugi's permission, the enemy was in sight! As he rode forward, the first of the Westmen came over the brow of the small hillock in front of the Roman lines.

The centurions knew their business. The *cohortes equitates* came forward with their shields and spears to protect the horse archers, while the cataphracti shot the Westmen down—

Shot them down, and the Westmen hardly resisted!

"This is no charge!" Titus Frugi shouted.

"Legate, you are right!" Sulpicius shouted. "They flee! But— what?"

Could it be a trick? No. The Westmen were clever, even devilishly clever, but they had not the discipline to sacrifice so many as a ruse. No, they fled an enemy behind them, fled in terror—

"Trumpet to arms!" Titus Frugi called. "Sound the 'Make ready.' The legion will advance! Fifth and Sixth Cohorts to the wings to cut off enemy escape."

A cheer rang down the lines. Even the iron disciplined Romans hated standing in place to be shot at.

"At the walk!"

The Roman line moved forward, down the slope and up the next, into the dust beyond. As they did, more Westmen poured out. The centurions hastily put men with shields and lances in the front ranks, spacing them so that the archers in the next rank could shoot between them. The *cohortes equitates* clung to the saddles of their mounted comrades; when the Westmen charged they moved expertly forward with spear and shield to catch the Westmen from below while the cataphracti threatened them from horseback. More Westmen died.

Then they were over the brow of the hill. The narrow valley below was a cauldron of dust and noise, trumpets of Drantos mingled with the screams of the Westmen and their horses. The Westmen were bunched together, trapped in the small valley so that they could not use their weapons, and with the Drantos force between them and the river, and the Romans coming in from behind, they could not run away.

The legion moved forward to crush Caesar's enemies.

Ganton whirled the ax around his head, for now it was work for axes and swords. There was not room enough for a charge. None was really needed. The Westmen tried to flee, only to pile upon their fellows; then they turned to face the host of Drantos, but when an unarmored man with a bronze sword faced a steel-clad knight with longsword or ax, there could be only one outcome.

"They do not flee!" Morrone shouted. He hewed down another enemy.

Ganton was as blood-spattered as Morrone. His Browning was long since emptied, and he had no time to reload. Also, sometime during the charge he had lost his hatred of Westmen. Now he wanted only for the battle to end. I know what Lord Rick must feel, he thought. There can be enough killing, enough and more than enough. Yet we do what we must do. "It is the Romans," Ganton answered.

A Westman warrior broke through the leading ranks and dashed at Ganton, thrusting with a captured Drantos lance. The lance crashed against his upraised shield. The wooden shield cracked through the middle, but as it did it caught the Westman's lance. Ganton swung the ax to cut through the shaft, raised the ax and swung it again. His wrist had long ago tired, and the ax twisted as he struck so that only the flat smashed against the steel cap the warrior wore, but that was enough. The man went down, but there was another behind him, and Ganton's shield was gone. Desperately he tried to avoid the stroke—

Morrone charged forward and spitted the man with his sword.

Ganton waved acknowledgment. By now they had saved each other more times than either could remember.

"The Romans?" Morrone asked.

Ganton frowned. What was this question, and why should

he answer questions at all? His head pounded with the sound of horns and drums, and he was exhausted. A council chamber with too many offering advice seemed an ideal place; but he knew he must keep his head.

What of the Romans? Ah. He remembered what he had said before the Westmen had attacked him. "They are ahead there," Ganton said. "I had hoped they would have sense enough to charge when we drove the Westmen toward them, and it seems they have. And could I but get to them—"

What would I do? I had a thought, and now it is gone, yet I think it was important. Could I get to the Romans—?

Ah. He stood in his stirrups. "Morrone!"

"Sire!"

"You command until I return. The Great Banner remains with you, and you speak with my voice. I must go to the Roman commander. Lord Epimenes!"

"Sire!"

"I give you command of my household. Join your men with mine and let us be off, for there are yet great things we may do if I can but speak with the Romans."

"Majesty! Command me!"

He must know how many will fall if we batter our way through that mass, Ganton thought. Yet he is eager to come. That is more brave than sensible. Aye, many of my bheromen are that way. Armored from head to foot and from ear to ear. But loyal, and today I need loyal men. Today they obey me as they would Lord Rick! For today I have given them the kind of battle they pray for through long winters, the battle they have dreamed of since first they couched a lance. Yatar—aye, Yatar and Christ!—grant that their loyalty continues.

He let himself be surrounded by Guards and the knights who followed Epimenes. Then they lowered their lances and charged toward the Westmen. "For Drantos and Camithon!"

The tribune Geminius rode up to Titus Frugi and saluted. "A party of Drantos nobility approaches, Legate. They have cut their way through the Westmen."

"Aid them."

"That is done, Legate."

Frugi nodded acknowledgment. Drantos warriors were not noted for their cooperation with others, but whoever was coming had risked much.

A headquarters optio rode in at the gallop. "Centurion says it's the banner of the Fighting Man!" he shouted.

"That's the Wanax himself!" Geminius exclaimed. "But why has he come? He has come without his royal banner!"

"I am aware of that," Frugi said impatiently. "Prepare to give him the proper honors and spare me your chatter. We will know soon enough why he has come."

That didn't stop the junior officers from making guesses, but at least it kept them from distracting him with them. Meanwhile, Sulpicius had reports from the cohort commanders.

Then the Drantos party rode in.

"Hail, Majesty!" Frugi called.

"Hail, Legate. We must speak, and quickly." The young Wanax gestured, and one of his squires leaped down to hold his horse as he dismounted.

Frugi noted the others in the royal party. Knights and bheromen, seasoned veterans all, carrying bloody weapons. They had come through much to get here—it was significant that veteran warriors would follow this boy king. Frugi wearily dismounted.

Ganton drew his dagger, knelt, and in the hard ground began to *draw a map* of the battle. It was not the best map Frugi had ever seen, but it would do. Aye, Titus Frugi thought. A map drawn by a lad who had never thought of maps as a weapon until the starmen came; it will do well enough indeed.

"We have nearly half the Westmen trapped between us," Ganton said. "As their ranks thin they will begin to escape; but we will kill enough, I think." He used his dagger to draw a circle around that combat area.

"The rest of the Westmen are here, across the river from us, encircling the Lord Mason. They face only star weapons, but so long as they do not attack the Lord Mason, they have little to fear because of the hills. There are not enough starmen to go seeking them."

Frugi nodded. "What know you of the *balloon?*"

"It does not rise," Ganton said. "I do not know why. But because it does not rise, the Lord Mason knows little of where the Westmen are. Yet they are here, and here, and—"

"I see," Titus Frugi said.

"The Lord Rick has taught me not to send all my forces into battle at once," Ganton said. "To hold what he calls *reserves*. I believe it is also the Roman way."

"Yes," Frugi said. He looked thoughtfully at the young Wanax. There were many more years behind the boy's eyes than there had been when they planned this battle.

"If you will divide your *reserves* into two parts, and send them here and here, then much can be accomplished," Ganton said. He drew lines on the map to indicate positions flanking the mass of Westmen facing Mason and Caradoc. "For in no more than a Roman *hour* the slaughter here will be finished, and the army of Drantos will be able to charge again. If we charge across the river, we will take the remaining Westmen from behind, driving them into sight of the starmen. Your *reserve* force will prevent them from escaping to the sides, and the star weapons will finish the task, I think."

"Unless the Westmen dislodge the starmen."

"No," Ganton said. "True, I have not spoken with the Lord Mason—but I do not need to do so. I know the Lord Mason and the Lord Caradoc. They will have a strong position. They will not be driven out by Westmen fleeing in panic."

"Umm," Frugi said. "Will your horses be able to make a second charge?"

"Aye. I have sent the—*support troops*—to the river for water. Our horses are well fed, thanks to Lord Rick and the Roman scribes who aid him."

He has indeed grown, Titus Frugi thought. And would be a formidable enemy to Caesar—

"For I have learned," Ganton said with a rush. "Neither I nor my knights, nor Lord Camithon himself, ever before dreamed how important it would be that a bushel of oats travel from a farmer's field to the belly of a war horse on the high plains. But I have learned. Aye, Legate, our horses are strong, and soon they will have water. They will charge truly."

Titus Frugi shaded his eyes and stared into the dusty valley below. The Wanax is right, he thought. An hour should see the end of that slaughter. Barbarians not fighting under one chief are not known for their readiness to come to the aid of doomed comrades. The reserve will not be needed to meet a rescue attempt. One cohort can hold the rear, and if this lad truly knows the position of the enemy we can yet have a decision this day.

"I suggest further that Drantos take the center," Ganton said. "The chivalry of Drantos is best employed in a single striking mass; your legionaries are better at maneuver. And we will strike directly here—" He used the dagger to draw a thick arrow.

"You have tested the depth of the river, then?" Frugi asked.

"I have seen the Westmen crossing it," Ganton said. He held up his binoculars. "With these. At the crucial places the water comes to the bellies of the Westman ponies."

"Ah." Titus Frugi straightened from where he had bent over the map. The headquarters officers leaned forward eagerly. Frugi hesitated another moment, then asked, "What think you, Primus Pilus?"

"I think well of it, Legate," Julius Sulpicius answered.

"And there is no need to ask you, Tribune Geminius. Either you approve or you have adders under your breastplate. Very well. Tribunes, go and ready the cohorts. Wanax, how will you alert your own forces?"

"I will ride with you until we reach them," Ganton said. "If that is acceptable to you."

"More than acceptable." And I am glad enough to have you as Caesar's friend, for you would be a formidable enemy. Our military handbooks will need revision after this day, for they say that Drantos is a barbarian kingdom—and that is true no more.

33

Pfc. Passovopolous had just finished reporting the LMG back in action when Mason heard war-horns. They grew louder. A hundred Westmen rode at a gallop out of the dust across the river. Then, suddenly, the Royal Banner of Drantos burst from the dust-cloud behind the Westmen. In another moment, the opposite bank of the Hooey was alive with banners.

"Murph!" Art shouted. "Use that one-oh-six! Targets of opportunity—"

"Rog!"

"Ark! Get ready with the LMG. Looks like they'll drive the bastards right out in front of us."

"Right," Passovopolous said.

"Reckon you were right," Murphy said. "Fire in the hole!" The 106 roared, and a white phosphorus shell burst among a cluster of Westmen trying to organize at the river bank.

"Right about what?"

"Kid knew what he was doing."

"Yeah," Mason said. He sure did.

The LMG chattered, joined by the crackle of fire from H&K rifles; the Westmen's abortive attempt to rally at the river bank dissolved before it was fairly begun.

Then everything happened at once. The dust-cloud erupted warriors, Drantos knights and Roman cataphracts. They charged down the river bank and straight on into the shallow river, slowing for a moment there but building momentum again. By the time they had crossed the river, the Roman and Drantos forces had mixed, clumps of Romans intermingled with the Drantos knights, both groups led by the mixed headquarters troops of both armies. It was hard to tell which crossed the river first: the golden helm of Wanax Ganton, or the scarlet cloak of Titus Frugi.

The Westmen made another attempt to rally, this time at the top of the knoll above the river bank, but a fresh group of Romans, both horsemen and *cohortes equitates* clinging to their bridles, appeared on their flank. The Roman infantry locked shields and advanced slowly while the cavalry sat their horses and shot down the Westmen. Meanwhile the combined force of Drantos knights and Roman lancers completed their river crossing. They dressed lines, and their officers rode up and down the line shouting. Then the wild war horns sounded, and Romans and knights alike spurred to a canter.

The Westmen couldn't stand the combination of arrows from the flanks and lances from the front. Their line buckled, then dissolved. The Allied forces charged on, and the whole battle swept out of Mason's sight into a fold in the hills.

"They'll be coming over that hill pretty quick," Mason said. "No shooting at 'em on the ridge. Wait until they're just below us. That way we're sure of what we're shooting at." He sent a runner with the same message for Caradoc.

And now we wait, he thought. But this time we know what we're waiting for. It's all over but the mopping up.

Mad Bear's surprise at getting across the river after the first charge of Ironshirts was beginning to wear off when the Ironshirts charged again. Even then he was not afraid. The Horse People could win against the Ironshirts, even Ironshirts with wizard allies.

"Stay with me!" he shouted. "We can yet win. The Ironshirts

can be led into charge after charge until their horses tire, and then they are easy to kill. Stay with me!"

He was still shouting this when he saw Red Cloaks on both flanks of the Ironshirts, and more Red Cloaks at the mouth of the valley. Then he knew. The Father and the Warrior had indeed turned their backs on the Horse People.

The Red Cloaks came out of the dust behind their arrows and their terrible war horns, and Mad Bear knew that all the history of the Horse People would henceforth be divided by this day.

"To me!" he called. "If we cannot win, we can yet die as the Warrior expects! Let us all go up hill and kill the servants of the wizards!"

But few listened. The never-ending storm of Red Cloak arrows fell among the Horse People, and the Ironshirts hewed their way uphill. Their lances spitted the warriors, their great horses trampled the Horse People's mounts beneath their hooves, and their terrible iron swords and axes cut down even those who had found armor.

An arrow struck his horse in the neck, and as it reared two more took it in the chest. Two Ironshirts and three Red Cloaks cantered up the hill. They pointed at Mad Bear and spurred toward him. As they came they shouted something to him.

Mad Bear leaped upon a rock, bow in one hand and captured sword in another. He answered the shouts of his enemies with his own war cries. Then he nocked his last arrow and took careful aim at a Red Cloak. The man ducked behind a shield, and Mad Bear hastily changed his aim point to the chest of the nearest Ironshirt. At that range it went through the man's armor, and Mad Bear shouted in triumph, but then it was too late. His enemies came on. Something struck his head. He was vaguely aware that he had dropped his sword and was falling.

Titus Frugi rode up to the spot he'd chosen for a command post, to find the starman Lord Walbrook already there. Then the Lord Mason came down the hill after the *cohortes equitates* relieved his Guards.

The battle was over. There were still Westmen trapped in the valley or hiding among these low hills, but organized resistance had ended. Now it was enough to send out detach-

ments, preferably with officers sensible enough to try capturing
Westmen chiefs alive.

Westmen fought hard. At first very few surrendered, but
now that they were cut off from the river, the need to water
their horses would drive them to seek quarter. When they did
surrender, it was always to warriors; they would commit suicide
rather than be guarded by wizards or women.

"A good day's work," the Lord Mason said.

Titus Frugi nodded judiciously. "It has been done well," he
said. "And proves the alliance has value to all."

Down below, the Tamaerthan archers were wading into the
river to drag dead Westmen out to the bank. "That is well
done," Titus Frugi said. "But it would be well to get the dead
horses out also. Else the river will be too foul for drinking—"

Mason chuckled. "I'm afraid they're not thinking of sanitation, Legate. They're after Westman gold. Most of the Tamaerthan lads came on this campaign for loot."

"Ah. There is much to share," Titus Frugi said. "The legion
has collected much gold, as have the Drantos warriors. How
shall this be divided? We must speak of this with the Wanax."

"Yes, sir," Mason said.

"Meantime, your pardon—" Titus Frugi turned to greet
Tribune Geminius.

"Hail, Legate," the tribune called. "There are still a few
bands of Westmen on the ridge across the river. They left the
dismounted ones behind to cover while the rest try to escape.
Should we pursue?"

"No." He lowered his voice so that no one but Geminius
could hear. "The legion is scattered. Many of our troops have
left ranks to loot. Our horses are exhausted, and we would not
pursue as an organized force. The cohorts I could send must
remain to guard against a fresh attack. I tell you this because
there is a chance—a small chance, but a chance—that you
may yet be fit to command a legion."

"My thanks—"

Titus Frugi cut him off. "Meantime, stay here. The centurions know what must be done. It is the task of the officers
to see that we face no fresh enemies until the legion is whole
again. It is also our task to know what *not* to see."

"Yes, sir—should I then see to getting your tent erected?"

"How? By shouting orders to the headquarters troops? They

would ignore you, Tribune, and quite rightly—what could you tell a ten-year veteran optio about caring for his commander?" Frugi chuckled again. "Dismount and relax, Tribune. And invite the star lords to come sit with us, for I see that Junio has found the wine, and the Wanax Ganton approaches."

A young man who has learned much, Titus Frugi thought as the Wanax rode up with a dozen of his companions. Riders and horses alike showed the fatigue of a day's battle and two charges.

"Hail, Titus Frugi," Ganton called.

"Hail, Majesty. The day has gone well."

"Aye." Ganton dismounted and gestured to Morrone. For the first time since dawn, the golden helmet was removed.

Morrone took it from his Wanax with a gesture so graceful that the finest actors in Rome could not have bettered it. The young Wanax shook his head and tried to comb the snarls out of his dark hair with his fingers.

If there were a sculptor worthy of it, I would give him this as his subject, Frugi thought. He has won over his followers, aye and more than his followers—

Julius Sulpicius came up with a dozen other centurions. He saluted Titus Frugi, then turned to Ganton. The First Centurion looked to his fellows. All grinned.

I should halt this, Titus Frugi thought. But he saw the look that his *primus pilus* gave the foreign king, and knew it was already too late.

Sulpicius raised his arm in salute. *"Ave! Ave Ganton, Imperator!"* he shouted. "Hail Imperator!"

The other centurions echoed the cry. After a moment the headquarters troops joined, then the other legionaries within earshot. In moments the cry rang through the Hooey Valley. "Hail, Ganton Imperator!"

I see, Titus Frugi thought. He remembered the first time Roman troops had saluted him thus. Imperator. Worthy to command Romans. It was not a title lightly given, even to Romans. He could not recall when a foreign chief was so honored.

If I join this cry, nothing will convince Publius Caesar that I did not order it. But if I do not—I will lose the trust of my legion.

I was prepared to sacrifice the legion to save the alliance.

Now I can save both with words that cost no more than the good will of Publius Caesar—which I probably do not have anyway. And Ganton is worthy of all this day may bring.

Titus Frugi lifted his hand in salute. *"Ave!* Hail, Ganton Imperator!"

The cry was redoubled now. Drantos and Tamaerthan troops repeated it, not knowing what the ancient words meant, but understanding that this was honor to Wanax Ganton.

All joined in the cry. All but the Lord Mason.

"What's happening?" Mason demanded urgently. "What *is* this?"

Titus Frugi stared uncomprehendingly for a moment, then understood. "Ah. *Imperator* is a title, Lord Mason. It can only be given by Roman soldiers to one who has led them in battle. Those hailed as Imperator are recognized as worthy to lead a Roman army."

"It doesn't mean, uh, like Wanax?"

"No. They do not hail him as Caesar. Only as *Imperator.*"

"Yeah? And that's all this means?"

Titus Frugi sighed. "Certainly no one could be offered the purple who had not been hailed as Imperator."

"And if he marries Octavia . . ."

"When, my friend," Titus Frugi said. "As you well know. Nor can I think your Captain General Rick will be much surprised by this event—"

Mason shrugged.

It is hard to tell what the star lord thinks. But since I have no more of Publius's good will to lose this day—and I do know that Marselius Caesar thinks highly of his grand-daughter— He turned to his tribunes. "Geminius."

"Sir?"

"When the messengers return to camp to bring up the supplies and the surgeons, you will go with them. Bring back a *corona aurea* for the Wanax Ganton. We will also need three *coronae civicae,* one each for the Lords Mason and Caradoc, and one for the Lord Camithon's bier."

"Sir!"

"You are pleased, Tribune?"

"Aye, sir."

And so are Sulpicius and the centurions, Titus Frugi thought. Yet I wonder what will be the end of what we have begun this day . . .

Mad Bear woke in near-darkness. His head throbbed, and when he tried to lift his hands he found they were bound with cloth strips.

I am a prisoner. This is not the Lodge of the Warrior, nor is there so much pain that I have fallen into the hands of the demons. He sat up, and saw that he was in a dimly lit tent. A tent of the Horse People, not an Ironshirt tent.

At the door sat Arekor, the priest of the Warrior who had been a slave among the Red Rocks until he vanished in a raid on the Green Lands. Now Mad Bear was certain he had not died, for Arekor could never have earned so much honor as to guest with the Warrior— "So, Centaur-lover. You have come to take revenge by taunting me?"

Arekor poured water into a cup and held it to Mad Bear's lips.

At first Mad Bear refused; but his thirst betrayed him. He took a sip, then drained the cup. Three times more Arekor held the full cup out. When he had drunk the last, Mad Bear said again, "Why do you taunt me?"

"No, Mad Bear. I have not come to taunt you. I have come from the chief of the Ironshirts, and what I speak you may hear without dishonor."

"I do not believe you."

"You will," Arekor said. "For I will cut you free and give you a warrior's knife, which you may turn on yourself if you believe you have been dishonored. It may even be that an Ironshirt warrior will fight you in a single combat, risking his life to let you end yours with honor. But first you must promise to hear me out, and not to attack me."

"Swear this is true!"

The priest swore such oaths that even Mad Bear was impressed. Not even a Green Lands priest who had submitted himself to slavery among the Red Rocks would use such oaths to strengthen a lie to a warrior of the Horse People—or if he could, then nothing among gods or men was as it had been, and Mad Bear could do what pleased him.

"What I will say can bring good to the Horse People," Arekor said.

"If this could be so— Give me the knife."

"Swear first."

Mad Bear swore by the Father and the Warrior. Arekor drew a short blade of Ironshirt make, and cut Mad Bear's bonds. Then he gave him the knife.

Mad Bear turned it over and over in his hands. The priest had spoken the truth— "Are there women or wizards within hearing of us?"

"I swear there are neither," Arekor said. "Only warriors."

Mad Bear tested the blade with his thumb. It was sharp, of good workmanship, quite good enough. No one would ever take that blade while he lived. "Now I will listen to your dream of bringing good to the Horse People."

The priest began to speak.

Ganton reached for another sausage and felt the *corona aurea* begin to slip. He pushed it back into place with one hand and grabbed a sausage with the other. He could not remember ever having been so hungry.

The food was simple, but there was plenty of it. Once again he could admire Roman organization. The battle was done, and there were a myriad of details to attend to; but Roman optios saw to all that. For once the commanders could rest, with only the most important decisions brought to the command post.

The headquarters staff had set out a table overflowing with sausage and bread and jerked meat, and nearby a kettle of hot soup was just coming to the boil. There were also flagons of wine, well-watered but of good flavor. The Romans hadn't asked if he wanted his wine watered; they had simply assumed that no commander on a battlefield would drink anything else. It was something to remember . . .

And not far away was the luxury of all luxuries: an optio supervised as Titus Frugi's servants erected a tent that would contain a canvas bath! Soon there would be hot water—

Perhaps, he thought, perhaps I will be able to clean my head without shaving it. He grinned to himself at the thought, trying to imagine what Octavia would say if he came to their wedding night as crop-haired as a slave.

That wedding would not be long coming. Then, married to Caesar's granddaughter, and proclaimed a leader of Romans— He could still feel the thrill of that moment. *Imperator!* The Romans had hailed him, soldiers and officers alike, and he could now appear before a Roman army wearing the *corona aurea*. And the army of Drantos was now loyal, the strength of the throne— With Octavia as his wife—what might not be accomplished?

PART SEVEN

Sky God

34

The moving light circled.

"That is it?" Tylara raised one hand and pointed. With the other she tightly held Rick's arm.

Rick nodded as he watched the ship hover above the bare hilltop. It was all too easy to remember the first time he'd seen one of the alien craft. That had been ten light years away, in Africa, and he hadn't believed in flying saucers.

This time, I *know* what it is, he thought. Does that make it easier? There are no Cubans coming to kill me. But I don't know who—or what—will be aboard, no more than I did then.

The instructions had been clear. Bring a work crew, all the *surinomaz* harvested so far, and no heavy weapons. The voice on the transceiver had been cold and mechanical, and had not encouraged conversation.

The moving lights came down with a rush. From the foot of the hill came a wail of terror and shouts that might have been prayers, then Elliot's curses. The ship settled to the hilltop. There was a long silence, broken only by a whine from somewhere within the craft.

"Can they see us without light?" Tylara asked in a whisper.

"Yes. And hear us as well."

She tightened her grip on his arm. "Will we see them?"

She's bearing up better than I did, Rick thought. "I don't know," Rick answered. "Nor do I know if this group will be human or *Shalnuksi*."

He hadn't wanted to bring her, but she'd been persuasive. If the purpose was to convince the *Shalnuksis* that Armagh was the principal seat of Rick's holdings, they would expect his wife to be there; and if at the castle, then why not to meet the ship when it landed? "Would they think me afraid?" she asked. "Or that you would marry one who feared them?"

He'd had no answer to that. Perhaps it would help if she came. Perhaps not. He had no way of knowing how much they could find out from orbit. Certainly Armagh *appeared* to be an important place. At the moment the castle was crammed from rafters to cellars with household goods, supplies, animals, and people. There were courtiers and cooks, administrators and acolytes, scribes and scullerymaids, judges, journeymen, apprentices, and masters of nearly every trade; even two dozen of the Children of Vothan in training for domestic service, and several of their teachers.

There was nothing better than oil lamps and bonfires for light, but even so, Armagh ought to be visible from orbit. Every room and courtyard blazed as they celebrated the news of the great victory. The Westmen were driven from the land, and even now the Alliance army was escorting them northwards, out of Drantos, into the wild lands to the northwest, lands nominally part of Drantos but long ago claimed by Margilos on the one hand and the Five Kingdoms on the other. Let the High Rexja have both the disputed lands and the Westmen. Perhaps it would keep him too busy to annoy Drantos.

One problem down, another to go. The flying saucer didn't look like doing anything. Gingerly Rick detached Tylara's hand from his arm and walked toward the craft. "Hi!" he called. "Hello, the ship."

It could have been the ship that brought him to Tran. Certainly it was more like that than like the sleek craft that had rescued the mercenaries from their African hilltop. Even in the dim light of the Demon Star he could see that the hull showed stains, patches, and dents. There were bulges and flutings in random places on its surface. Les had once told them the ship that brought them to Tran was chartered; perhaps this one was also, or it might have been the same ship.

The whine muted and died, and the ship settled more heavily on its large circular landing feet. There were small crackling noises as it crushed the fragrant Tran shrubbery. A small square opened near the saucer's top, and the hillside was bathed in yellow light. Rick moved closer, carefully keeping his hands away from the .45 in its shoulder holster.

A rectangular hatchway opened into a gangway. The inside of the ship was bright with the yellow light the *Shalnuksis* seemed to favor. Rick could see crates and packages, a lot of them, many painted olive drab.

"Good evening, Captain Galloway." The voice boomed out unexpectedly, startling Rick. It was the same cold, impersonal voice he'd heard on the transceiver. It sounded like a recording, or perhaps like something synthesized on a computer. Its tones told him nothing about the person—or being—who spoke.

"Good evening," he said. He was surprised at how dry his mouth had gotten.

"You see we have brought your—supplies. Have you brought the—work crew—as instructed?"

"Yes."

"Excellent. Have them bring the *surinomaz*." The hatchway Rick was watching closed, and another, smaller doorway, leading into a much smaller compartment, opened about 45 degrees around the base of the ship. "Captain, you will oblige us by remaining where you are, while others bring the *surinomaz*."

He felt rather than heard Tylara come up behind him. Then she took his arm. "We will stand here together," she said softly.

"A—noble sentiment," the impersonal voice said. "Very well. Instruct your crew to hurry. They are to carry no metal into the ship. Is that understood?"

"Right." He turned to face down the hill. "Elliot, get the stuff loaded in that open compartment. Make sure the troops leave all their metal behind. Daggers, armor, everything. Make it sharp."

"Sir! All right, you sons, move it." There was a cacophony of sounds from lower down the hill, then Elliot's voice rose above the chatter. "Move it *now*, or by Vothan you'll be in the madweed fields before the True Sun is high! Move!"

The clerks and apprentices scurried up the hill. They were led by Apelles, who looked like a man not entirely successful at trying to be brave. None of them had been armed, so it didn't take them long to shed all of their metal. Then they carried the semi-refined madweed into the small cargo compartment.

"It is not a large amount," Rick shouted. "The rogue star isn't close enough yet. Next year is supposed to be a better crop."

"We know," the ship answered.

Rick and Tylara watched as the cargo was loaded. Finally Apelles came out and signalled they were done.

"Now stand clear," the voice called. The compartment door closed. The whining noise rose in pitch.

"I had thought they had goods for us," Tylara said. "Will it rise now?"

"I don't know," Rick said. He turned away from the ship.

"Remain there, Captain. If you please." This time the voice sounded different.

Rick stood with Tylara for what seemed a long time. Then the first compartment door opened again. "Your men may now begin to unload. They will stay on this side of the ship, and they will not carry weapons. You will remain where you are."

"All right. Elliot, move 'em."

This time there was no argument from the work crew. The clerks and apprentices sweated and strained to get the boxes outside the ship. Others brought up mules and began to lash gear on their pack saddles.

Rick could see most of the cargo as it came out. A lot of it was ammunition. One crate was labelled "Armor, Body, Ballistic Nylon, Personal Protective." Another was unmistakably Johnny Walker Black, and two more bore Meyers Jamaica Rum labels. There was a case of Camel cigarettes.

Elliot came out grinning. He was holding a portable typewriter. "Carbon paper, too!" he shouted in triumph. "And a Carl Gustav recoilless."

"Just like Christmas," Rick answered with a grin. He didn't move from his place in the circle of light. "Tylara—they didn't say you have to stay here," he said softly.

"*They* did not," she answered.

"Hey, I love you."

"I think perhaps you do," she said. She squeezed his arm.

"Talisker Scotch!" Elliot shouted. "And Rennault fifty-year-old cognac! Can't say they don't pay for what they get!"

Oh, they pay, Rick thought. They understand about not binding the mouths of the kine that tread the grain. But they won't take us home, and they gave us damned little choice about coming here.

The ship was unloaded, and most of the gear sent down the mountain on mules. The hatch closed, but the bright light from near the top of the ship continued to flood the hill with yellow light. Then the whine rose in pitch and became louder and louder. The ship seemed to lift slightly. It hung for a second, then rose swiftly and almost vertically into the dark sky.

"It is gone," Tylara whispered. "I had—you had told me. But until I saw—"

Rick laughed. "I know," he said. "Back on Earth *I* wouldn't have believed it." And I knew about airplanes, and radio, and—

"Rick." Tylara spoke quietly, but there was an urgent note in her voice. She tilted her head. "Look."

His eyes had not yet adjusted to the dark, and at first he couldn't see what had alarmed her. Then it became clear. There was a man standing beyond where the ship had been. He wore a Burberry raincoat and Irish tweed hat, and beside him stood a plain Samsonite suitcase. An instrument about the size of a small briefcase hung from a strap over his left shoulder. It glowed with faint lights from dials on its face.

The man waved. "Hello, Captain," he said.

It was Les.

"He is but a man," Tylara whispered.

"Yes. He is the human pilot who brought us to Tran."

"You know him—then he is—"

"Yes. The father of Gwen's child. Tylara, do nothing. Say nothing, except to be polite. I don't know why he's here—but that box he's carrying can talk to the ship, and that ship could destroy this whole world."

"But if the box were destroyed?"

"Then those in the ship would do whatever they wish."

"I see." She released her grip on his arm and fell silent.

"Sergeant Elliot!" Rick shouted.

"Sir!"

"Clear the hill. Move everyone out, then come back for me."

"Sir."

"Sorry about the housekeeping," Rick said. He moved toward Les. "Welcome to Tran."

The pilot nodded. "It appears that you have come up in this world since last we met."

Cold, Rick thought. Cold and haughty, as if he is master here. I suppose he is. "Let me introduce you to my wife. Tylara do Tamaerthon. Countess of Chelm and Justiciar of Drantos." He used English and spoke rapidly despite Tylara's frowns.

"Making you what?" Les demanded.

"Eqeta—that's count—"

"I know the title."

"Eqeta of Chelm, and Captain-General of Drantos." No need to tell him about Tamaerthon at all. Or the Roman alliance. Let him find out for himself—or not find out, which would be better.

"Ah. But I forget my manners." The pilot turned to Tylara and extended his hand. After a moment she gave him hers, and he bowed and kissed her fingers. "I am honored to meet you, Lady Tylara," he said. His accent was not good, but the language was recognizably Tran local.

Usually Tylara was as resistant to male charm as a suit of armor, but she smiled warmly and thanked the starman. An act, Rick wondered? Or was she really impressed? Les was certainly handsome enough, and trying to be charming, but still— "How long will you be with us?" Rick asked.

"That depends," Les said. "I've come for my wife. Gwen must have told you I would come."

"She wasn't always sure she believed you," Rick said.

"Ah. Yeah, she had a right to her doubts," Les said. "That's over now. Where is she?"

"She didn't tell you?"

Les eyed Rick thoughtfully in the dim light. "So she told you she has a transceiver," he said. "And you want me to believe she's alive and it's working."

"She's all right, and the transceiver works to the best I know," Rick said. "I take it Gwen didn't answer you, then."

"No. Now where is she?"

"That sounds very much like a demand."

Les shrugged. "Take it any way you—no. Eqeta Galloway, I would count it a very great favor if you would conduct me to my wife."

"A couple of questions, first," Rick said. "As for example—do your employers know you're here?"

Les looked startled, then laughed. "I take it you mean, did I jump ship? No. My landing is—authorized, and the time I will stay on Tran is up to me."

And I can believe as much of that as I want to, Rick thought. But there's no point in standing here on a hilltop. "Welcome to Chelm. I trust you will do us the honor of being our guest."

"Thank you. But now that I've answered your question—where is my wife?"

Persistent chap, Rick thought. And maybe not quite as cool as he wants us to think—

"The Lady Gwen is well," Tylara said. "And your son is safe and well and under our protection."

The light was too dim for Rick to be certain, but he thought the pilot's face showed joy. His voice, though, remained unchanged. "My son. What did Gwen choose to name him?"

"Les," Tylara said.

Les turned to Tylara, but before he could say anything, she said, "The Lady Gwen is married to Lord Caradoc do Tamaerthon, a knight in my service. He is one of our most trusted captains, and my husband and I are very much in his debt."

"Married," Les said.

"Last autumn," Tylara said. "She believed that you were dead or had forsaken her."

"Well, I'm not, and I didn't," Les said. "And now I'd like to see her. If you please." His voice grew more stern. "Do you think I'd have come back to this—to Tran—for any other reason?"

Tylara shrugged. "I do not know the duties of those who serve the—*Shalnuksis.*"

"So. You've told her everything," Les said.

"Shouldn't I?" Rick asked.

"I don't know." Les shrugged.

"It's walk, ride, or wait all night until I can send for a sedan chair," Rick said.

Les laughed. "I'll ride, if the horse is tame."

"It's a mule," Rick said. "More surefooted for this mountain trail. And it's certainly gentle enough. All right, Sergeant Major. Lead the way. Sergeant Frick will bring up the rear. And spread right out, gentlemen."

"Yes, sir," Elliot said. He rode on ahead, and Frick dropped back, so that Rick, Tylara, and Les rode alone.

"You have them well trained," Les said.

That didn't seem worth answering, and Rick said nothing. The trail was steep and frightening if you didn't trust the mules; the trick was to let the animals pick their own way and pace. Les seemed to be doing that.

They reached the bottom, and the trail widened. "All right," Les said. "Where is Gwen? And this—Caradoc."

"Lady Gwen is—in another part of the country," Rick said.

"And Lord Caradoc is a soldier," Tylara continued. "He is with the army in the west."

"Hah. Good battle, that," Les said.

"You watched?" Tylara asked. "But—" She fell silent.

"Saw some of it," Les said. "So. That's fortunate. Lord Caradoc is off to war, and Gwen is home alone. Good. If he stays out of my way, I won't go looking for him. No trouble at all, that way."

"He is her husband by Tran law," Rick said. And that sounds foolish.

"And I'm her husband by Earth law," Les said. "Does he have more right than me?"

You don't have any rights at all, Rick thought. You certainly didn't marry her. But it will be better to pretend.

"The case must be heard by the priests of Yatar," Tylara said. "Do you not understand? The Lord Caradoc is our captain. A knight sworn to our service—"

"And under our protection," Rick said reluctantly. Christ, this is going to be rough.

"I have no wish to shame the man," Les said. His words came slowly, as if forced. "Nor—nor do I bear him ill will."

The hell you don't, Rick thought.

"I do not wish to be disrespectful of your law," Les continued. "But I *will* see my wife."

"She is far from here," Tylara said. "The roads are poor, bandits are numerous, and our army has been sent against the

Westmen. It will be no easy journey, and we would do the Lady Gwen an ill service to send you without proper escort—"

Les laughed, a short sharp sound. "An escort won't be needed," he said. "Tell me where to go, and I can call the ship."

35

There were only the three of them at Rick's conference table. Tylara sat at his right, and Sergeant Elliot on his left, leaving the long table nearly empty.

Like to have more, Rich thought. But who? Art. Larry Warner. Maybe one of them could think of something—

"If you're going to let her know, you'd best get the message out now," Elliot said.

Rick nodded. The semaphore line to the University wasn't finished. Messages had to go part way on horseback, and even with relay stations spaced Pony Express style that took time. "I think we won't," he said. "What could I put in a message, even a coded one?"

Elliot gave him a significant look. So did Tylara.

Yeah, Rick thought: "Keep your pants on." I can just see me sending her *that* message. Hah.

"You learn anything from him?" Elliot asked.

"Not much we don't know," Rick said. "The council or whatever it is that governs the Confederation is still divided over what to do about Earth, and doesn't seem to know about Tran. Which means the *Shalnuksis* have a free hand, but we don't have to worry about the council sending the galactic navy. Not just yet, anyway."

He took Tylara's hand for a moment. She gave an answering half smile. He'd spent three hours trying to explain what he knew about the millennia-old galactic confederation and its human Janissaries, but she still didn't understand. That's all right, Rick thought. I don't either. And what the hell, Tylara has more experience unravelling plots than I do. Maybe she can understand a confederacy of a dozen or more star-faring races. According to Les, they haven't changed in five thousand years, mostly because of human slave soldiers.

It sounds nutty. It would sound nuttier if I didn't know the Turks used slave soldiers and administrators to run their empire. They called them Janissaries, and their empire stayed together for centuries.

"What about that Agzaral guy?" Elliot asked. "Is he on our side?"

"Don't know. Les won't say much about him. One thing's sure, he's playing a deep game," Rich said. "*He* knows about Tran, but his bosses don't. Yet he's a cop. Or something like a cop, anyway." Rick shrugged. "I don't even know how much Les knows. Maybe he'll tell us more."

"Yeah, if he lives long enough," Elliot said. "Christ, Cap'n, why'd it have to be *Caradoc* he's gonna put horns on? Nobody else is near that popular with the army. Even the mercs like him."

Tylara frowned. "Is it so certain that Lord Caradoc will be dishonored? Why do you think so ill of the Lady Gwen? Surely she knows what must be."

How do I answer that? Rick wondered. No way to tell her how I *know*. "Girls on Earth do not think as the women on Tran do. Les was her first love, and he will be insistent. Yet, you may be right. It may be that Lady Gwen will refuse his advances, at least until the case can be heard by a court."

"Fat bloody chance," Elliot muttered.

"You have knowledge?" Tylara asked.

"Some," Elliot said. "Look, I don't want to tell tales, but before she married Caradoc—"

"Yeah?" Rick demanded.

"Well, one night I heard shots from her room," Elliot said. "I came in to find Gwen breathing hard, Larry Warner with his hideout pistol, and Caradoc waving a bloody big knife. They straightened it all out, but—"

"But she is not a chaste woman," Tylara said.

"It's not that simple," Rick protested. "Different cultures, different—"

"I am more concerned with consequences," Tylara said coldly. "If the Lady Gwen cannot use proper judgment, then we must save her from her folly. And save the University, which is such a great part of what our children will inherit."

Damn all Tran dynasts, Rick thought. But she's right.

"My love, we both know Caradoc. He has always been quick to defend the right. Not his right alone. Ours as well. But my lord husband, my love, even now the Tamaerthan troops are returning. Caradoc will soon be here, and if he is wronged, if his wife has dishonored him, he must *act!* He will challenge Les."

"He'd probably lose," Elliot said. "I don't know what Les carries, but it's sure to be as effective as our pistols. Remember Art Mason's story? The walls of the ship shot him when he threatened one of the *Shalnuksis.*"

"And Les and the other humans are warriors," Rick finished. "Janissaries for the Galactic Confederacy." He laughed. "I don't want to believe that."

"Evidence is pretty convincing," Elliot said.

"Didn't say I *don't* believe it," Rick said.

Elliot laughed.

Tylara waited until there was silence. "It matters little whether Lord Caradoc wins or loses. He will insist upon his rights in this matter. He will insist that we come to his aid, or avenge him if he is killed."

"Army'll be on his side," Elliot said. "Hell, Cap'n, suppose Les kills Caradoc. You know damn well what you'd have to do."

"Yes." Kill Les. Or be a lord who's broken faith with his followers. My name will stink from the Westscarp to Rome. Caradoc's relatives will want my blood—Sadraic! My own bodyguard.

"Do you see difficulties I do not?" Tylara asked. "We are two. We both have pistols. Les is only one. I saw no weapon upon him, but suppose he has? He can be killed. At this moment he is guest under our roof, but that need not be forever. *We* swore no permanent oath to him."

"You don't know what you're saying! You can't know what his ship will do," Rick said.

"There is no one in it," Tylara said. "I asked him. It could be a lie, but I do not think it was."

"Nor do I," Rick said.

"Then he controls the ship with that box. When we have killed him, we will take the box and use it," Tylara said.

"Won't work," Rick said. "There are—codes. One is obvious—he will not use English to speak with the ship. And smashing the box won't work, since we don't know what orders he gave the ship before he sent it up. He had plenty of time, after all."

"But what can a ship do?" Tylara demanded. "A ship with no master?"

"A lot," Rick said. "First, it will report to the next ship that comes. God knows what it'll tell them, but it can watch everything we do. It'll sit up there in the sky and watch us, and take pictures, and when the *Shalnuksis* come it'll tell them everything."

"And then comes *skyfire*," Tylara said thoughtfully.

"Unless we can work with Les to prevent it," Rick said. "One thing's sure. We won't learn anything from anybody else. Les is the *only* chance we have to talk the *Shalnuksis* out of bombing this place back to the stone age. Why would he try, except for Gwen? Yet, with his help, what we have built, the knowledge we will leave our children, might withstand even *skyfire*. The *Shalnuksis* might be induced to bomb the wrong places. But that's only if Les helps."

"And yet, all know what a debt we owe to Caradoc," Tylara said. "His honor is ours. You speak of what we will give our children. Do you wish to give them an inheritance of dishonor?"

Yatar, Jehovah, Christ, somebody, tell me how to answer that. Please.

Tylara sighed. "You have no answer. Nor have I. It seems that now we are both called upon to do more than we can do. Lord Elliot, have you advice?"

"No, lady," Elliot said. "We need Caradoc, and we need Les. But it looks like one's going to kill the other, no matter what. Hell, it wouldn't settle anything if Gwen dropped dead!

She's the only thing Les cares about—"

"There is his child," Tylara said thoughtfully. "If the Lady Gwen were dead, there could be no quarrel—"

"Seems to me a man would be more likely to work for his wife than for a kid he's never seen," Elliot said.

"And we need Gwen if we're going to have a University," Rick said.

"You are certain?"

"Yes, I'm certain, dammit! And do you think I owe Gwen any less than we owe Caradoc?"

"I see." Tylara sighed once more, then stood. "I will not swear to lay no hand on Les forever," she said. "But I will swear to let him take us safely to the University, and stand apart from his first meeting with the Lady Gwen." She gave a shaky smile. "I think if I did not swear this much, you would guard Les night and day with your *Colt* in your hand. Even against me."

No answer to that, either. "That's a good start." And— Gwen didn't get any messages from Les. Meaning what? Maybe her transceiver's busted, but maybe she isn't listening. Maybe she's in one of her moods—"He done me wrong and then run off and left me." When she's like that, she wants his *cojones* on a spear, and if she stays that way long enough for Caradoc to come back and make her realize that she's got to be sensible . . .

Maybe. It's a slim chance.

But everything else looks like no chance at all.

This time the ship tilted slightly as it landed on a patch of softer ground. The whining sound grew louder and increased in pitch, and Les frantically manipulated dials on the box he carried. The ship righted itself.

Les inspected it critically, then seemed satisfied. "Okay, wait there," he said. Then he seemed to catch himself. He turned to Tylara. "With your permission, my lady, I'll go open a hatch."

He disappeared around the stern.

Tylara glanced at Rick, then stared at the ship. They stood together in the field, with only the Firestealer to give light.

Tylara's lips were set in a grim line.

She's scared of *skyfire*, Rick thought. Well, so am I. The interesting part is that Les is nervous. These ships must be vulnerable. Not likely I'll learn how. Not likely the troops will see anything. But they might—

He had every merc with binoculars stationed around possible landing sites, and he'd been lucky. Elliot was out there watching this one.

After about ten minutes a hatch opened just in front of Rick and Tylara. A wide gangway lowered itself.

"Welcome aboard," the ship's voice said. It didn't sound anything like Les.

Tylara took Rick's hand. "Shall we go, my husband?"

He nodded, then grabbed her to kiss her. As he broke away he whispered, "Remember. Not only Les will hear everything we say while we are in that ship. Other—"

She smiled and nodded, and Rick wondered if she believed him. After all, she'd never seen a recording device, and describing one wasn't the same as showing it—

Nothing he could do about that.

They went inside. The compartment was nearly bare. Rick looked closely. There were stains on the deck in one corner. This was the same ship that had brought them to Tran, no doubt about that.

In one corner of the compartment there were two piles of Japanese *futons*. On top of one of the piles was a package wrapped in brightly printed paper and tied with a scarlet bow. Tylara stared at it. The paper was printed with replicas of famous miniature portraits.

"It is lovely," she said. "I have not seen—"

"Ah, my lady, it is a gift for you." This time Les used his own voice, rather than the impersonal computer-generated one he'd used earlier. "Now, please be seated—"

Rick pushed the two piles of *futons* together and flopped into one of them. Tylara gingerly sat beside him. She clutched the package tightly.

"Will you not open it?" Les asked.

"I—it is so beautiful—"

"Let me, sweetheart," Rick said. He took the package and carefully worked the bow so that it came off without damaging it. Tylara took it and held it experimentally to her hair. The ends of the package were sealed with Scotch tape. Rick took out his pocket knife and slit the tape so that he could remove the printed paper without tearing it. Tylara watched nervously.

"I should have brought more wrapping paper," Les said. "I think I have some picture books. You can have those."

"Thank you," Tylara said. She sounded sincere.

The box contained a bracelet and necklace of Navajo turquoise and silver, elaborately gaudy. Tylara gasped with pleasure. "Marvelous!" she exclaimed. She put on the bracelet and admired it on her arm. "There is nothing like it in all of Tamaerthon. Or Drantos."

That's for sure, Rick thought. But of course she'd like it.

They settled onto the *futons*. "Thank you," Tylara said.

A screen in the forward part of the compartment suddenly came to life. It showed Les in his command chair on the ship's semi-darkened bridge. "There's something for you, too, Colonel," Les said. "Under your cushions there—"

Rick felt under the pile and found a wooden box, not wrapped. Inside was a bottle of Talisker Scotch and four crystal glasses packed in Styrofoam worms. There was also a bottle of Campari.

"Have a drink with me?" Les asked. "Sorry I can't invite you up to the bridge. 'Thees starship ees going to Havana, Señor,' with those minigrenades to make the point—well, the idea doesn't quite appeal to me."

"I don't suppose it would," Rick said. He tried to keep his voice calm. The grenades in his pockets suddenly seemed five times their size and weight.

"My lady might prefer Campari," Les said.

"Fat chance," Rick muttered. "She's had Scotch." He opened the Talisker and poured for himself and Tylara.

Les turned to face the screen and lifted his own glass. "Cheers, then," he said.

"Cheers," Rick said. Tylara muttered something. They both drank.

Tylara grimaced slightly at the taste. Rick frowned a question at her.

"I recall the previous time," she said. "I was pleased with your strong—*whisky*. But—"

But you'd just been raped by Sarakos, Rick thought. And this reminds you. Yeah. I should have insisted you have Campari.

"Ready?" Les asked.

"Yes," Rick said.

A moment later they were pressed into the *futons*. The screen blurred, then showed the ground falling away. Tylara gasped and moved closer to him. The ship rose, and then they were high enough to see Castle Armagh with its blaze of bonfires. She shivered slightly.

"You ain't seen nothin' yet," Rick whispered. "We're no higher than—than the highest mountains." He'd almost mentioned Larry Warner and the balloon, but there was no point in telling the ship's recorders about *that*.

The ship began to move, and Armagh slipped off the edge of the screen. The Firestealer gave enough light to recognize the major terrain features. They were going west, following the main road to Castle Dravan.

Coincidence or design? Rick wondered. After all, when they first came to Tran they'd been set down not far from Dravan, and this was the main road west . . .

Tylara pointed and looked afraid. "The children," she whispered.

Yeah. Our kids are down there— He pointed and nodded. "Yes, I think you're right, that's where we established the orphanages," he said. "Not too far from where the ship first set us down. Les, are we sightseeing?"

"Maybe a little," Les said. "Do you mind?"

"Not at all. Except if you go much farther west I'd appreciate it if the ship isn't seen. Our army's out there somewhere. They just won a big battle with Westmen—those are nomads from the high plains above the big escarpment. The Westmen already think there was too much wizardry for it to have been a fair fight."

"So if they see the ship, they might think it's impossible to make an honorable peace, so they may as well die fighting?"

"Something like that, yeah."

"No problem," Les said.

The lights below shrank rapidly, and now there were clouds below them. After a few moments the screen changed, zooming in on the plains below. They passed the Littlescarp, and the scene on the screen changed rapidly, as if the camera were searching the high plains. Then it stabilized on camp fires, and zoomed in again.

Tylara stirred. "That is the host of Drantos," she said wonderingly. There was terror in her eyes. She started to speak, but Rick pulled her to him and kissed her.

She looked startled for a moment, then nodded understanding.

I know, my darling, Rick thought. There is our army, the most powerful force you've ever seen, down there below like toy soldiers, down there where it would be like child's play to throw *skyfire* at them. But don't say it, don't even think it too loud—

"How does Yatar rule those with such power?" she asked softly. "Or—*does* Yatar rule the sky-folk?"

Rick shook his head. "I don't know," he said softly. Not even if you translate the question into modern theology. Is there a God? Is there any reason for ethics? Does the universe care one lick whether people are decent or beastly to one another?

"He rules your heart, my love," Tylara whispered. "And that is enough for me."

The screen brightened, then changed to a map of the eastern part of the settled region of Tran. At least *this* settled region, Rick told himself. He'd never learned just how far west this continent was inhabited, or whether the other continent was inhabited at all.

The map stretched from Rome to the Westscarp, and as Rick watched, a numbered grid superimposed itself. "If you wouldn't mind," Les said. "It would be well to get on with our cargo collection."

That would be for the recorders. There'd be damned little cargo at the University, but Rick thought Les must have a way to deal with that. More interesting was how he carefully didn't mention Gwen in the hearing of the ship . . .

The ship settled into the hills above the University. Les sent Rick and Tylara out, then joined them a few moments later. He was carrying his suitcase and the control box. The ship whined and rose into the dawning sky.

"Well, here we are," Les said. "What's down there?"

"My University," Rick said. "Gwen is the Rector."

Les whistled in exaggerated respect. "Oh-ho. Well, we'd best get on with it. Looks like a long walk. Should have set the ship down closer."

Tylara chuckled. "Captain," she said, "one might almost

doubt your love for the Lady Gwen. You complain of a few stadia we must walk. What of the tales of lovers who would swim boiling seas or walk ten thousand leagues to join their ladies?"

There was a pause long enough to worry Rick. Then Les laughed. "They may have had more difficult journeys," he said. "But none of them ever had a longer one."

36

The messenger from the Roman pickets brought word to Gwen Tremaine just as the True Sun rose. A skyship had been seen.

She put on a robe and covered her hair with a snood, and went to her office before she had tea.

"It was as you ordered, lady," the decurion said. "We watched the hills, and we saw it descending, not so bright as a star. I have never seen its like before."

"Few have," Gwen said.

"The cohort now searches those hills for any gifts the sky-folk may have left. If we find any, we will bring them to the University. Have you more orders, lady?"

"No. Thank you, Decurion." She opened a desk drawer and took out a bag of coins, and shook several into her hand. "Buy wine for your unit, and say they have done well."

"Thank you, lady."

As the Roman left, Marva brought tea and biscuits.

"Join me," Gwen said. She indicated a chair. Marva sat and poured the tea.

"It is good news, Lady Gwen?"

"I don't know, Lady Marva. I truly don't know."

This is my life, Gwen thought. To be in this office, to govern this University. To teach these people, and watch as their lives improve. It is my life. She twisted her fingers together. This must endure. I've got to do something. Did it really land? And who?

Suddenly she stood, gulped her tea, and ran to her apartment on the floor below. What should I wear? There's nothing here—

By mid-morning she'd turned her closets into chaos, and brought both Marva and herself to tears.

Get hold of yourself, girl! Suppose it *is* Les. Do you want him to see you like this? Send Marv for a stiff drink. Two, she deserves one for herself. And put on your regular working gown. It's the best you have except for the blue one Larry gave you, and that's too formal for daytime—

And the children! If it's Les he'll want to see his son.

And if it's a *Shalnuksi* executioner?

It can't be— "Lady Marva?"

"Yes, my lady?"

"Have Nurse take the children to the Roman fortress. She's to keep them there until I send for them. You go with them."

"Is there—do you fear the sky-folk?" Marva asked. "But will they not be like—the others we have known?"

"I don't know," Gwen said. "And I'm afraid—"

"I will see to the children," Marva said. "Then I will return."

"No! Stay at the fortress—"

"My lady, not even the fortress will prevent us from *skyfire*. My husband told me that many times. But I can ask the commandant to send the children beyond the hills—"

"No, that's silly," Gwen said. "There will be no *skyfire*. All the same—do have Nurse take the children to the fortress."

There was a knock at her office door.

"Come," she called.

Larry Warner came in. "First time ever," he said. "Nobody in your outer office. Why?"

"I sent—"

"Never mind. I know," Warner said. "The Romans sent word. They're on their way in now."

"Who?"

"Cap'n Galloway, Lady Tylara, and a starman."

"A star—*man?*"

"Yeah. All human. I described the *Shalnuksis* to the centurion, and he said it surely wasn't one of them."

"Larry, you shouldn't have described—"

"Oh, shove the secrecy up sideways! It's their planet, they have a right to know what's threatening it!" He gripped his hair with both hands.

"You'll be as bald as Telly Savalas if you go on doing that," she said. She giggled despite herself.

"Good to see you laugh," Warner said. "Now you keep your head and let me worry about mine." He drew his binoculars from beneath his professorial gown. "They ought to be just about at the town gates," he said. "Should be able to see 'em from your balcony there in a minute. Gwen—it's probably Les."

"I know."

"What'll you do?"

"That's what I don't know." She eyed him warily. "Are you about to give me advice?"

"No, ma'am." He winked at her. "You have to play this hand yourself, and I don't need to say it's important. Naw, all I was going to say is if you need somebody to watch your back, I'm available. I won't draw on the Captain for you, but short of that—"

"Larry, that's sweet of you."

He laughed. "Now that's just what a tough merc turned professor wants to be told," he said. "Sweet, for God's sake!"

She'd sent Larry away, and was alone on her balcony as the party rode in: a dozen Romans, Rick and Tylara, and a third who sat his horse like a sack of potatoes.

He can't do everything.

He can blow your University right off the map.

They dismounted and entered the building. She went back into her office and stood near the desk. *What can I say? What do I want to say? Why—*

Too late for thought. There were sounds outside, then her door opened.

He came in alone. Over his arm he was carrying—

"Oh, no!"

She'd imagined this meeting for two years. She'd thought of being haughty. Imperious. Sexy and seductive, at least as much so as she could be. Tearful. Scornful. Cool, the University Rector.

She'd never imagined that she'd collapse in laughter. She threw back her head and roared, and had to lean against the desk for support.

He held his smile until she was finished. "Well, you *did* ask if I would buy you a grass skirt," he said. "So I got you the best I could find." Then his control gave way, and he began to laugh, and she joined him, and they kept each other howling. Whenever one would slow down, the other would point to the skirt and they began again, and...

And then he was close to her. She wasn't sure what happened next. She didn't think she'd moved toward him, but there she was, and his arms went round her, and their lips met.

"Les—"

He didn't answer. He didn't need to. He held her in an iron grip, but there were tears in his eyes, and suddenly everything was the way she'd dreamed it might be, back when she had good dreams.

The grass skirt fell to the floor.

Rick's apartment was on the top floor of the University guest house, and the window looked out across the quadrangle to the town beyond.

In the traditional manner of Roman soldiers, the University cohorts spent much of their time building. The Roman camp was surrounded by coal-fired baths. A line of stone buildings was springing up next to it, while on the campus itself the Roman engineers had laid chalk lines to mark a new quadrangle.

The University was growing, but the sight could not cheer Rick. The ax would fall, and all too soon.

Meanwhile, he had a kingdom to administer. He hefted a stack of reports the Roman clerks had brought in. They had arrived by the Express Post that morning.

The most interesting was Art Mason's report.

"The Westmen are moving north as agreed. It won't be long before they're out of our territory altogether, and the only question will be whether they take on Margilos or the Five Kingdoms."

Tylara read over Rick's shoulder. She laughed haughtily. "If the Westmen attack Margilos, there will be fewer Westmen to reach the Five Kingdoms. They are as mad as the Westmen, those warriors of Margilos. And I think the Westmen know this."

"Good enough," Rick said. "So they'll go past Margilos and on into the Five. That ought to keep the High Rexja busy for long enough to get this Roman alliance firmed up. Once Ganton marries Octavia—"

"Um-hummm," Tylara said. "Did you arrange for the Romans to hail our Wanax as Imperator?"

"No, ma'am, he got that one on his own."

"You surprise me. True, I had not thought to arrange it, but when I heard, I believed you had. Perhaps Yatar does watch over us more thoroughly than we know."

Rick turned back to Mason's letter and read aloud. "Wanax Ganton proposes Ben Murphy as bheroman at Westrook. The late Bheroman Harkon left a six-year-old kid, but Honeypie has just about adopted the kid, and she and Murph will be married as soon as he gets your consent, which I'd advise you to give. I think Murph can do a good job of holding the plains here. He likes it."

Murphy's first home, Rick thought. A long way from Belfast...

"A lot of the smallholders were killed by Westmen," the letter continued. "Some of the landless Tamaerthan troops like the weather up here, and they've petitioned to take over the ownerless farms. Murphy wants to let them do it, and it looks like a good deal to me, but of course it's part of Lady Tylara's county. If she approves, we can get started fast." Rick looked up at Tylara. "Well?"

"I consent," she said. "Should I not?"

"No. It's a good plan. Here's to Bheroman Murphy." He

read the rest of Mason's report. "There is no longer a threat from the Westmen. Wanax Ganton has decided that his bheromen are able to escort them with Roman help, so we are returning to Dravan. The Tamaerthans who aren't staying up here want to get home, so Caradoc has taken them on ahead. You can use the semaphore to Dravan if you have other orders for them."

"They will not be long in Dravan," Tylara said. "Caradoc will not wait for orders. He will bring the Tamaerthan troops home—here! He will come here unless he is told not to come. And what reason could we give?"

"I don't know." Rick opened another pouch and took out still more reports. "Here's one for you," he said absently.

Tylara didn't answer. Rick looked up from his work. She was standing at the window. "He will learn soon enough," she said. She stared gloomily down at the campus and town. "He will learn, and this will all be destroyed."

"Perhaps not," Rick said. "Look, Les agreed to stay in the guest house. If Caradoc doesn't actually go looking for witnesses—"

"My husband, my love, you are not such a fool," Tylara said. "Caradoc's clansmen will learn. How could they not? Last night they visited the baths together. They were alone inside for time enough to grow three pair of antlers on Caradoc's forehead. You have sealed the town gates, and closed the semaphore, but it will do no good. He will learn."

"But what can I do?" Rick demanded.

"I do not know." Tylara sighed. "We need a miracle. Perhaps Yatar will send one." She stood a few moments longer at the window. Her hands were balled into fists. She drummed them against the window ledge. Then she came back to the desk, suddenly calm again. "Meanwhile, I must send a message to Dravan, and the semaphore office will not accept it without your approval." There was a brittle edge to her voice.

"Sweetheart, I didn't mean the restrictions to apply to *you*," Rick said.

She held her hard look for a moment, then smiled. "I know, my love. You have much to concern you. Still, I must see to our house, and quickly, so may I trouble you to put that in writing?"

"Sure." He sat at the desk and scribbled out an authorization. "I was hoping to keep anyone from telling Caradoc," he said.

"Stupid, of course. But it does put off the evil day. And maybe the horse will learn to sing."

"Horse?"

"Old story," Rick said. "Very old. A thief was about to be executed. They did that in a particularly painful way in old Persia. Before they took him away, he told the Wanax that he could teach the Wanax's favorite horse to sing hymns, if the Wanax would give him a year.

"The Wanax took him up on it, and pretty soon, there was the thief down in the stables every day, grooming the horse and singing to it. His buddies told him he was crazy.

"'That may be,' the thief said. 'But I have a year, and who knows what will happen in that time? The king might die. The horse might die. I might die. And who knows, maybe the horse will learn to sing...'"

Tylara giggled, then nodded more soberly. "Yes. Time is always valuable," she said. "But I fear that time alone will not save us."

"So do I," Rick said. "But I don't know what else to do."

"You will do what you must," Tylara said. "That I have known all my life, and learned again from you. We do as we must."

The four sat at Gwen's conference table: Rick and Tylara, Gwen and Les.

"It's just possible," Les said. He whistled, a long falling note. "Weee-ew. You're sure going for broke. Steel mills. Coke ovens. Printing presses. A full University. If the *Shalnuksis* find out—Rick, I don't know what they'll do if they find out."

"But you can help us hide all this," Gwen said.

"I can try," Les said. "And as I said, it's just possible, as long as Inspector Agzaral doesn't change sides, and he doesn't look like he's going to. Yeah, we've got a chance—"

"We," Gwen said. "You meant that, didn't you?"

"Yes, ma'am," Les said.

And that's clear enough, Rick thought. He's on our side as long as we're on his. And meanwhile Caradoc's coming back with the army.

He looked across the table to Tylara. She sat stiffly alert, cold, almost indifferent. Yet she was polite to Gwen when she spoke to her, and even encouraged Les to believe his attempts to be charming had succeeded.

Just what the hell game is she playing? Rick wondered. *And what good does it do me to worry about it . . .*

There were shouts outside, and they all rushed to the penthouse balcony. Far across town there was a pillar of black smoke. "Have the Romans organized fire departments?" Rick asked.

"Sure," Gwen said. "But they won't be needed there. That's the chimney in the coke oven. It catches fire every ten-day."

The office door opened, and Marva came in. "I do not wish to disturb you, my lady, but there is a message from the semaphore. It is marked urgent, and Lord Warner told me to bring it to Lord Rick immediately."

"Thank you," Rick said. He took the message paper. Tylara stood next to him and read as he did.

> REGRET INFORM YOU LORD CARADOC DO TA-
> MAERTHON KILLED IN STREET RIOTS ONE MARCH
> FROM DRAVAN. COURT OF INQUIRY HELD BY
> WANAX RULES ACCIDENTAL DEATH BY FALLING.
> I AGREE WITH THIS VERDICT. WANAX HAS PRO-
> CLAIMED THREE DAYS OF MOURNING AND WILL
> PERSONALLY COMMAND FUNERAL GAMES.
> WANAX HAS GRANTED LIFE PENSION AND TITLE
> TO CARADOC'S CHILD.
> AWAIT FURTHER INSTRUCTIONS.
> MASON.

Rick stared uncomprehendingly at the paper. He felt Tylara's hand on his arm.

"What is it?" Gwen asked.

"Bad news," Rick said. As he said it he felt waves of relief wash over him. He was ashamed of that. Yet— "Bad news," he said again. "Lord Caradoc is dead."

"Dead?"

"Yes," Tylara answered. "Your husband, my lady. He died in our service, and whatever honors the Wanax has not granted I will give from my purse. Husband, come, and leave the Lady Rector to her grief." She turned and marched from the room.

Gwen looked from Rick to Les. The pilot opened his arms,

an almost imperceptible gesture, and she moved toward him.

Rick carefully closed the door as he left the room. We're saved again, he thought. For a while, at least. A good man has died, but that accident has saved more than Caradoc alive ever could. We have Les, and with his help the *Shalnuksis* won't destroy everything. Knowledge will survive.

When he reached the quadrangle, they'd put out the fire in the coke oven.

Afterword

The *Janissaries* saga began with a question in Jerry Pournelle's mind. If the UFO's seen for thousands of years are really extraterrestrial spaceships, why haven't they made contact with human beings? He decided that they were kidnapping human beings for some sort of illegal business. This got Pournelle as far as the opening scenes of *Janissaries,* with the mercenaries boarding the flying saucer and Tylara's council of war at Castle Dravan.

A couple of years later Jim Baen, then sf editor at Ace Books, saw the two scenes and liked them. At about the same time Baen's boss, Tom Doherty, was starting up Ace's line of illustrated sf novels. He wanted something from Pournelle. Unfortunately, the first story they chose couldn't be expanded to the point where it could honestly be called a "novel." So they substituted the story of the mercenaries kidnapped to help aliens grow drugs on Tran.

There was no problem with expanding this story. In fact, when Pournelle hit 60,000 words, Ace was shouting, "Stop! Stop! Stop!" and the story was barely half told. *Janissaries* was destined to have at least one sequel from the moment it was finished.

Just to make everybody happier (not to mention richer), *Janissaries* sold better than anybody had expected. It sold lavishly in trade paperback, mass-market paperback, and even a hardcover edition originally intended for libraries! Foreign publishers lined up to bring it out in England and all over the British Commonwealth, in Denmark, Germany, the Netherlands, Japan, Italy, Spain, France . . .

Meanwhile, at the World Science Fiction conventions in Washington in 1974 and Kansas City in 1976, Pournelle met Roland Green, a young fantasy writer from Chicago. He'd liked Green's two fantasy novels, *Wandor's Ride* and *Wandor's Journey*. The talk flowed freely; Pournelle and Green discovered a good many interests in common (military history, good liquor, the work of H. Beam Piper). Friendship grew, a correspondence began, and eventually Pournelle proposed a collaboration on an sf military-adventure novel. Green flew out to California. When he flew back to Chicago ten days later, he took an outline of *Janissaries* II and marching orders to produce the first draft.

This meeting of minds promised well. Authors are normally as territorial as grizzly bears; any collaboration starts by having to overcome this fact. Pournelle and Green didn't have too much of this problem. There were, however, a few others.

—The logistics of a transcontinental collaboration. (Express mail and long-distance phone calls will expedite communication and empty bank accounts.)

—Technological incompatability. (Pournelle uses a word processor, Green used a rapidly-declining Smith-Corona which in fact died to produce *Clan and Crown*. R.I.P.)

—One of the worst winters in Chicago's history. (Having your bathroom drain frozen solid for three days does drive away the Muse.)

—Ace Books changing hands twice while the book was in progress. (But a good editor can help overcome even the consequences of having your publisher hawked around the public streets like a kosher dill pickle. Susan Allison and Beth Meacham are good editors.)

—Above all, the fact that like the first *Janissaries*, *Clan and Crown* kept *growing;* both old characters and new started writing their own lines, scenes, and whole chapters. (Green was heard to mutter about "The Incredible Growing Novel" or "The Mercenary Who Ate Poughkeepsie." He was not tyro enough to argue with his own characters, particularly when all of them were so well armed.)

Problems enough to keep life interesting. Still, two authors who agree on how to tell a story can usually get where they've planned to go. And of course, if you've done it once, it encourages thinking about doing it again. . . .

August, 1982

Jerry Pournelle
Studio City, California

Roland Green
Chicago, Illinois

MORE SCIENCE FICTION ADVENTURE!